Her

"This wonderfully adorable rom-com will have you giggling and kicking your feet. Griffin certainly won my heart! Sparkling with cute fun and lovely, sweet romance, *Her Knight at the Museum* is a delightful read, simply perfect for fans of *Enchanted* and *Kate & Leopold*."
—International bestselling author India Holton

"*Her Knight at the Museum* was a hilariously salacious romp full of forced-proximity goodness that had me flying through the pages faster than a jousting knight. I couldn't put it down!"
—*USA Today* bestselling author Lana Ferguson

"If readers appreciate a slight fantasy twist, they'll be rewarded with a frothy contemporary romance. . . . It will especially appeal to readers who enjoy a touch of Marvel's *Thor* in their romantic heroes."
—*Library Journal*

"Charming and steamy."
—Polygon

"A fun and juicy rom-com for connoisseurs of romantic fiction."
—*Daily Trojan*

"*Her Knight at the Museum* is as fun as it is swoony."
—Culturess

"Readers looking for a fresh and fun take on paranormal love stories will be smitten with Donovan's whimsical, witty, and wonderfully amusing romance."
—*Booklist*

"Arthurian legend meets spicy modern rom-com in this diverting contemporary."
—*Publishers Weekly*

Books by Bryn Donovan

HER KNIGHT AT THE MUSEUM

HER TIME TRAVELING DUKE

Her Time Traveling Duke

BRYN DONOVAN

BERKLEY ROMANCE

NEW YORK

BERKLEY ROMANCE
Published by Berkley
An imprint of Penguin Random House LLC
1745 Broadway, New York, NY 10019
penguinrandomhouse.com

Copyright © 2025 by Bryn Donovan
Penguin Random House values and supports copyright. Copyright fuels creativity,
encourages diverse voices, promotes free speech, and creates a vibrant culture. Thank you for
buying an authorized edition of this book and for complying with copyright laws by not
reproducing, scanning, or distributing any part of it in any form without permission. You are
supporting writers and allowing Penguin Random House to continue to publish books for
every reader. Please note that no part of this book may be used or reproduced in any manner
for the purpose of training artificial intelligence technologies or systems.

BERKLEY and the BERKLEY & B colophon are registered trademarks of
Penguin Random House LLC.

Book design by George Towne

Library of Congress Cataloging-in-Publication Data

Names: Donovan, Bryn author
Title: Her time traveling duke / Bryn Donovan.
Description: First edition. | New York : Berkley Romance, 2025.
Identifiers: LCCN 2025012894 | ISBN 9780593816615 trade paperback |
ISBN 9780593816622 ebook
Subjects: LCGFT: Fiction | Romance fiction | Fantasy fiction | Novels
Classification: LCC PS3604.O5664 H48 2025 |
DDC 813/.6—dc23/eng/20250528
LC record available at https://lccn.loc.gov/2025012894

First Edition: December 2025

Printed in the United States of America
1st Printing

The authorized representative in the EU for product safety and compliance is
Penguin Random House Ireland, Morrison Chambers, 32 Nassau Street,
Dublin D02 YH68, Ireland, https://eu-contact.penguin.ie.

For Jenifer and Jennifer

Her Time Traveling Duke

One

Oxfordshire, England
Friday, May 1, 1818

Henry Horatio Leighton-Lyons, the fifth Duke of Beresford, jerked his head to one side to avoid the man's oncoming fist—only to bring it in the direct path of the other one.

"Damnation," Henry swore, stepping back and rubbing his nose. The blow had not broken it, of course. His private boxing instructor, Quentin Dunton, pulled his punches.

Dunton grinned. He stood nearly as tall as Henry's own six-foot height and wore his black hair closely cropped, with sideburns. "Better fighters than you have put their nose in front of my left fist."

The former prizefighter never addressed Henry properly as *Your Grace*. Henry supposed one could not expect that from an American, and particularly one from Boston, the city famous for dumping hundreds of crates of perfectly good English tea into the ocean. At any rate, there was no one else to hear. The two men were sparring in the south barn of Henry's estate. He had converted it into a gymnasium, complete with Indian clubs, climbing ropes, and dumbbells.

Exercise, and especially boxing lessons, provided a distraction. Mornings were the worst: waking up to a world that no longer had his wife in it. Charlotte had been twenty-six when she died. Henry was thirty-six now, and as of today, he'd been a widower longer than he'd been a husband.

"Another round?" Dunton suggested.

"First, let me check the time." Henry had an important meeting soon. He strode to the hook where he'd hung his shirt and greatcoat, drew his gold watch out of his pocket, and clicked open the case. Then he shook his head.

"It is nearly nine. We'll have to end here."

"You are particular about time."

"It is our greatest treasure," Henry said.

A man who lost a fortune might make another one. No man, no matter how diligent or enterprising, had ever made more time to spend with his beloved . . .

But Henry was working on it. He spent long days and nights studying theories and equations, and reading rare texts he'd had translated from ancient languages, trying to work out the secret to turning back the clock.

After both men donned their shirts and greatcoats, they exited the barn and walked the short distance to the great house. With its square stone towers on either side, Everly Park had the air of a castle. Budding rosebushes lined the walkway, rising above the little white starflowers that grew everywhere on the estate.

"I think that's the first rose I've seen this spring," Dunton said, inclining his head toward the mauve bloom with tightly packed petals.

"They call those Early Cinnamons," Henry said, "due to the spicy scent." To Henry's nose, it was incense, rather than cinnamon, that mingled with the fragrance of the rose. Henry knew the name because of Charlotte. She'd had the gardener plant more of them in the center of the knot garden. From spring to fall, when the wanderer came close to the center, the lush fragrance guided him home.

Henry didn't attempt to fill the silence. He'd never acquired the easy manners that anyone might've expected of a duke. Once he'd gotten married, his wife had been the one to keep conversations with others flowing. Henry supposed he had not been the first man to discover that the easiest way to be thought of as a fine fellow was to marry a gregarious wife.

They reached the paved Great Court, where the columns of the Corinthian portico entrance loomed over the visitor.

"I'll miss my rooms here," Dunton said. "Fit for a prince." In Henry's father's time, a prince *had* stayed in that suite, with its murals and gilded ceilings. Faced with the conundrum of whether Dunton was a temporary staff member or an honored guest, Henry had decided on the latter, given the man's minor celebrity. Dunton had not been born to privilege—his father had been a common laborer, and his mother had escaped slavery—but his triumph over an English champion had earned him headlines and accolades.

"I am glad you found them comfortable," Henry said. "Good luck with the boxing saloon." Dunton had been recruited as an instructor at a new establishment on Bond Street, but its opening had been delayed, which had prompted Henry to extend an invitation to Everly Park.

Dunton flashed a smile. "Perhaps you can tell your friends to become members," he suggested, with typical American boldness.

"I am afraid my friends are mostly astronomers." *Colleagues* would've been the more accurate word. "They do like to fight, but not with fists."

Henry himself had no remarkable talent for the pugilistic arts. Nonetheless, he did have more than his share of determination.

Over the past few months, with Dunton's excellent instruction, he'd made real progress.

Dunton gave Henry a sidelong look. "Why did you want to learn to box?"

"I beg your pardon." Henry wasn't accustomed to anyone asking him why he did anything.

"Who do you want to give a beating to?" Dunton clarified, apparently mistaking Henry's affront for confusion.

Death himself, Henry supposed. "I thought it would be useful to have the skill." His father's words came to his mind. "A gentleman should be capable and competent in every circumstance."

Dunton's suite was in the West Court, and Henry's private quarters were in the center. They shook hands, and Henry wished him safe travels.

As they parted ways, Henry felt a pinprick of regret that he hadn't dined with the man instead of continuing to take his evening meal in the library. But Henry had heard that Dunton had chosen to eat with the staff rather than on his own, and no doubt they'd been more agreeable companions.

Henry passed the state dining room, designed to accommodate forty guests. White cloths protected the furniture from dust. An acquaintance had suggested that Henry should get away for a while. Go to Brighton, perhaps.

And do what? Walk alone on the beach? What could be more dismal?

Henry wasn't going anywhere.

At least his own house held whispers of Charlotte. At the breakfast table, her reading aloud the papers devoted to gossip and scandals. In the library, her telling him about her studies of mythology and folklore. In the bedroom, her clever hands, her lovely body, and her cries of pleasure. Learning how to elicit them had been his most rewarding field of study by far. Those memories were both a torment and a solace, late at night when he lay by himself in the dark.

Now Charlotte was a box full of bones in the cold churchyard, abandoned while the rest of the world ticked on with their lives. But not Henry. His soul carried memories of her like a chalice filled to the brim with wine, ever so carefully, not willing to spill a drop.

By nine thirty, he was washed, combed, clean-shaven, smelling faintly of the American cologne he favored, Caswell-Massey Number Six, and impeccably dressed, from his very white cravat to his gleaming black shoes. In his drawing room, he encountered his butler, Brady, and asked, "Is my solicitor here?"

"I'm afraid not, Your Grace," Brady answered. A wiry man in his mid-fifties, he had been with the family for decades; Henry could remember when the man had had a great deal more hair.

"Well, that is a confounding nuisance," Henry said. "A gentleman is always at the proper place at the proper time."

"Yes, Your Grace."

"Do not delay breakfast. He may join me if he deigns to arrive."

Brady retreated, and a maid soon brought a tray of hot rolls, butter, an orange, and tea to the drawing-room table. A minute after that, Brady returned and set down a much less welcome silver tray heaped with letters.

Henry cleared his throat. He rarely made personal inquiries, and felt awkward doing so now. "How is your wife, Brady? Is she well?"

Brady's eyebrows shot up in surprise. "You are very kind to ask, Your Grace. She suffered a chill last week after getting caught in the rain, but she has quite recovered."

The Duke of Cumberland had once suggested that Henry's father shouldn't have permitted the butler to marry and occupy the nearest cottage to the house. Then again, the Duke of Cumberland had recently been attacked with a poker by his own valet, so perhaps there was something to be said for indulging one's servants.

"And your daughter—Mary, is it?" Henry asked Brady. "She is also well?"

"Yes, Your Grace, Mary, though we call her Molly. She is very well indeed, thank you."

Henry nodded, having his own reasons for confirming the girl's Christian name. Charlotte had been fond of her, and had spoken once of settling an allowance on her once she came of age, the better to attract a good husband. Henry had recalled this two weeks ago when he'd overheard the butler telling the head housekeeper about his daughter's upcoming eighteenth birthday.

This was why he'd arranged a meeting with his solicitor. It rarely occurred to Henry to do something so charitable, and he found it supremely irritating to be delayed in doing so.

Henry poured a judicious measure of cream into his tea and eyed the daunting pile of letters. "I receive more invitations by the day."

"There are only a few weeks left in the London season, Your Grace," Brady said.

And apparently, society believed the time for grieving was long past. "One would think my lack of a wife was a national emergency."

Brady allowed himself a smile. "I believe that is the prevailing opinion, Your Grace."

Henry had three sisters, all much older than him, with titled husbands and healthy children, whom he'd not seen since the funeral, over two years before. His deceased parents had succeeded late at producing an heir, and his mother had died in childbirth. Henry's title and the estate would go to a male cousin who lived in Yorkshire. Each of his sisters would inherit a small fortune. And a portion would support his new foundation, the World Astronomical Society.

Barring the matter of Brady's daughter, it was all settled to his satisfaction. But he was constantly urged to attend balls and recitals, where unmarried ladies of breeding age could be paraded in front of him.

Henry picked up the card on top. It was an invitation to a ball from none other than Lady Vail, whose last letter he had not answered. He dropped it again as though it were contaminated.

"Lady Vail was one of those shrews who tittered behind their hands about Charlotte," he told Brady. Their spiteful gossip had made its way back to Henry. "Saying that her stone collecting was eccentric, and that she wasn't pretty." Charlotte had told him her own family considered her merely *handsome enough*, with her straight brown hair, deep-set hazel eyes, and square jaw.

"The duchess was a great beauty, Your Grace, if I may say so," Brady said, with his natural Irish charm. "Shall I tell Mr. Wilke you still plan to meet him in the library at ten thirty?"

Henry sighed. "Remind me, Brady. Why did I hire a painter, again?"

"Because the headquarters of the World Astronomical Society in London will have its grand opening soon, and your colleagues insist it must be graced with your portrait."

Henry hoped that the group would support astronomers, mathematicians, and physicists across the globe, particularly ones with limited personal means, for generations to come. And if the work of one of these fine minds aided his own pursuit of the mysteries of time travel, so much the better.

Brady added, "And an engraving from the portrait can be used in official publications, which will encourage more scientists to join—"

"Yes, yes," Henry groused. "Did I not ask Mr. Wilke to paint the background first?"

"He has already done so, Your Grace."

"Very well. That will be all."

Brady inclined his head and retreated.

Henry found at the bottom of the small pile a welcome letter from a colleague in Padua. He tore it open and scanned the man's new thoughts about light and motion. Neither the handwriting nor the English was good, but Henry was intrigued and tucked it in a drawer of his writing desk for further consideration. Then he composed a reply to the first invitation.

My dear Lady Vail,

I would not have you think that you were forgotten. On the contrary, I often reflect upon those vicious words with which you maligned that paragon and angel who was my wife, and I assure you that I would sooner light myself on fire than spend a moment in your company.

Please accept this expression of my sincere sentiments,
The Duke of Beresford

He folded the note, addressed it, and secured it with red wax and his family's signet seal: a lion showing its claws. He set it on the tray of mail to go out, then headed to his library, leaving the other invitations unanswered.

Any lady would love his title and his wealth, but there could be no one now, in England or abroad, with whom he could share the kind of connection he'd shared with his wife. No matter how many balls, dinners, and recitals he attended, he would never fall in love again.

Two

Rose Novak, the maid of honor, felt a pang of wistfulness as her friends Emily and Griffin kissed on the Grand Staircase of the Chicago art museum, amid cheers, raised cell phones, and applause.

What would it be like to have a man kiss you like that? A *good* man. Rose had dated plenty of the other kind.

Daniela Huerta, the short, dark-haired bridesmaid next to Rose, leaned closer. "I'm *so* glad I didn't have to wear shapewear." The bridesmaids, as well as the bride, were wearing medieval-inspired green gowns with scooped necklines and bell sleeves. Naturally, Rose loved the witchy vibe.

"Me too," Rose whispered. Being on the plump side, she probably would have, if they'd been given some kind of spaghetti-strap slip thing. "The last time I did, I had so much trouble getting out of it, I accidentally punched myself in the face."

Daniela snorted. The just-married couple finally came up for air.

Rose stepped forward to give her best friend her bouquet back, murmuring, "That was beautiful. And you look perfect."

Emily's gown had a black bodice and lavish gold embroidery. Only a few people knew that green and black had been the colors of Griffin's noble house, back when he'd been a knight in the early fifteenth century.

Emily gave her a quick hug. "You're the best maid of honor ever." Behind her, Griffin nodded, beaming.

Rose's heart warmed. It always felt good to be able to help.

A petal had fallen from Emily's floral crown onto her dark brown hair. Rose was wearing her own chaotic light brown curls in an updo, out of the way. She plucked the petal out of Emily's tresses and tossed it in the small tote bag she'd turned into a wedding emergency kit.

"Go to the reception hall," Rose told Emily. "We'll all follow you."

"Right, right," Emily said, adorably distracted.

"But I'm hungry *now*," a small boy's voice wailed behind Rose. She turned to see the five-year-old ring bearer on the verge of treating his father Marcus, the best man, to a meltdown.

Rose hustled over to the kiddo. She pulled a packet of cheese crackers out of the emergency kit, caught Marcus's eye with a questioning look, and waggled it. He nodded gratefully, and Rose crouched down to get the boy's attention.

"Here you go, buddy," she said. His face lit up as he grabbed them.

"Nice save," said a groomsman in a green doublet—the one Rose had been determinedly ignoring all day and all through the rehearsal and dinner yesterday.

She didn't exactly look at Aaron Coleman as she rose to her feet again. Of course, she hadn't been able to avoid a couple of glimpses of him. He had close-cropped brown hair and a strong nose and jaw, and he was eight years older than her age of thirty-three. Hilariously, his age and his occasional dad jokes had made her think he might be more dependable.

"You can't ignore me forever," he said.

"Apparently not."

The year before, a life-sized stone sculpture had gone missing from the museum, for the simple reason that Griffin had happened to *be* that sculpture, and had come back to life. Aaron, an FBI agent with the Art Crimes division, had gone undercover to investigate— which had included pretending to date Rose.

When she'd found out, she'd been crushed. She'd hoped that she'd finally found a great guy who liked her just for who she was. But part of her hadn't even been surprised.

Aaron sighed. "I wanted to tell you that I'm sorry I led you on. It was the job."

"I've dated liars before." She crossed her arms. "You're not better because you've turned pro."

Guests filed around them, including Jason Yun, a senior curator at the museum and Emily's boss's boss, wearing a navy tuxedo. Emily's wedding, with a bunch of museum people, was *not* the place for Rose to have it out with her fake ex.

Aaron said, "I really did like you. Okay?"

She scoffed. Easy to say, since he lived in D.C., so he couldn't date her, anyway. He just wanted her to make him feel better. And honestly? That wasn't her job. Out of the corner of her eye, she spotted the auburn hair of her younger brother, Ryan. He was chatting with Daniela.

"I . . . I have to talk to my brother about something," Rose told Aaron and walked away.

Ryan was also a groomsman, and he knew about Griffin's true identity. The two had become friends when he'd tutored Griffin through community college algebra. As she reached him and Daniela, she realized they were looking at a large painting in a fancy frame.

It was a portrait of a gentleman. His hair was dark and thick, and he had short sideburns; his intense brown eyes, under straight brows, commanded her attention. If a man had stared at her like that in real life, she wouldn't have known if she was going to get lectured or get lucky. Maybe both? It might be worth sitting through the first thing to get to the second.

"Who's this?" she asked Daniela.

"We just acquired it from a private collection. I was telling Ryan I'm going to be working on it next." Daniela worked in Paintings Conservation.

"He looks so familiar. Is he famous?" Rose glanced at the museum label. PORTRAIT OF HENRY LEIGHTON-LYONS, DUKE OF BERESFORD, ENGLAND, 1818.

Daniela shook her head. "The artist is," she said at the same time Rose read the name: Walter Wilke.

"Oh yeah," Rose said. "He did *The Sleeping Duchess.*"

In that painting, a woman in a filmy pale pink gown lay on a bed with her eyes closed and her arms flung above her head in blissful abandon. Rose knew from art history class that in its time, it had caused a scandal. The woman looked like she'd just had *very* good sex.

Rose added, "I had that poster in my dorm room."

"So did half of all college girls," Ryan teased.

"Still have that *Pulp Fiction* poster?" she teased back, and Daniela smirked.

"Yeah. I'm a man of culture."

Rose looked back to the painting in front of them. "I've definitely seen this before."

The duke, wearing a black suit and some kind of man-scarf, stood next to his desk. One of his hands gripped the handle of a walking stick; the other rested on what looked like a fancy compass on a stand, with ornamental details and a blue stone embellishment at the bottom. Behind him stood cases filled with books and other objects. A drawn velvet curtain revealed distant hills and trees.

"What do you have to fix?" Ryan asked Daniela. "It looks fine."

"At one point, it was stacked against another painting." She waved her fingers gracefully near the border. When Rose squinted, she could make out a few faint lines. "Plus it's dirty."

Rose looked again at the museum label. "It says he was an amateur astronomer who founded the World Astronomical Society." She thought a lot about the stars and planets herself, though not in a scientific way. "I thought dukes just went to parties and counted their money."

Ryan shrugged. "I guess if you're a duke, it's easy to study whatever you want."

Rose felt a little ache in her chest at that. Ryan had gone to Northwestern, planning to double major in mathematics and physics. Their parents hadn't left them a lot of money, but thanks to his good grades and near-perfect test scores, scholarships had covered most of his tuition.

But he'd struggled with addictions, and before his senior year, he'd dropped out. After breaking into his drug dealer's girlfriend's apartment, he'd gotten a three-month jail sentence—way too harsh, in Rose's opinion, since he'd been trying to steal back money the dealer had stolen from *him*.

Now Ryan worked for a furniture moving company. There was nothing wrong with that. Their parents had worked hard, honest jobs, too. But at one point, he'd hoped for so much more.

"This guy lived a good long life, especially for those days," Daniela commented. Rose looked at the label again. He'd lived from 1782 to 1864.

Ryan said, "We should get going."

He was right. The gallery had cleared out, and members of the wedding party shouldn't be MIA at the reception.

As they started walking again, Daniela said to Rose, "I meant to tell you before, I love your necklace."

"Thanks!" Rose touched the pendant she'd discovered at an antique stall at a street market. "It's a moonstone."

"I thought those were white."

"They usually are. Blue ones are rarer." Especially ones like this. A four-pointed star seemed to glow within its depths when it caught the light.

"Does it mean anything?" Ryan asked.

Rose had already told Daniela that she dabbled in magic. It hadn't been typical bachelorette party talk, maybe, but Rose had always been kind of an open book.

"Some people think moonstones help couples reunite, but that doesn't apply to me. And some people call it the traveler's stone, but I'm not planning to go anywhere soon." She shrugged. "I just bought it to wear on the full moon."

"You said the full moon was good luck for a wedding, right?" Daniela asked.

"Oh, yeah. A full moon is so powerful. And it's especially amazing that this one is on May first."

"May Day?" Daniela asked.

"Yes, Beltane." Rose couldn't resist explaining. "It's when the Green Man weds the May Queen. When he first meets her, he's been ruling over the winter by himself for months, and he's proud and kind of a jerk, and she's not impressed with him at first. To be with the May Queen, he has to give up his old ways."

"That's beautiful," Daniela said.

"Right? And this full moon is in Libra, which is perfect for partnerships. Friday night, which is sacred to Venus, the goddess of love." As they reached the reception hall, she added, "I did a marriage spell for Emily and Griffin earlier. It's probably the most magical timing for a love spell in a hundred years or something."

Daniela cast a curious sidelong look. "Do you ever do spells for yourself?"

"Um . . . yeah, sometimes." Rose couldn't remember the last time she had, though.

They walked into the huge space on the third floor of the Modern Wing. Skyscrapers twinkled beyond the floor-to-ceiling windows on either side. Several candelabras rented from a theater supply shop, each holding dozens of candles, hung from the ceiling, and custom-made banners screen-printed with Griffin's coat of arms decorated the back wall. Round tables with white cloths had been set up around the room. Griffin and Emily stood in front of the head table, and several guests waited in line to hug them.

"Wow," Daniela breathed and turned to Rose. "Are you posting about this?"

Rose, who was a social media manager at the museum, shook her head. "They didn't want me to."

"Yeah, that makes sense," Daniela admitted.

The Art Institute of Chicago website could always use more photos for their events page. And the fact that Emily worked in Objects Conservation there made her museum wedding even more romantic. But after Griffin had come to life the year before, Emily had been the prime suspect in the case of the missing statue. Rose knew that Emily was relieved that everyone had finally forgotten about her.

"I'm going to get a drink," Daniela said, pointing to the line to the bar in the corner. "You guys want anything?"

Ryan and Rose both shook their heads. Ryan had been sober for almost two years, if he was telling the truth, and Rose was 95 percent sure that he was. He'd told Rose before that he didn't mind if she had a glass of wine when she was around him, but she never did.

As Daniela retreated, Rose turned to set her bridesmaid bouquet on a nearby table. Her gaze fell on a yellow stain on Ryan's doublet.

"How did you get mustard on you?"

"Oh, shit," he said, looking down. "I stopped at the Wiener Stand."

She snatched a Shout wipe from her emergency kit and tore the packet open. "That place is such a tourist trap."

He shrugged. "I was out of groceries." He was so bad at keeping healthy food at home. Rose made a mental note to bring some over again soon.

She scrubbed at the spot. "Did they call you a motherfucker again?" The hot dog restaurant was famous for being disrespectful to their customers. Rose had gone there only once, and had been called *sweet tits.*

"No, she was like, 'Get your Ren Faire ass up here!' And then it was, 'Does the carpet match the drapes?'"

Rose snorted as she put the used wipe back in the bag.

"What was the G-Man talking to you about?" Ryan asked, darting a look in Aaron's direction.

She sighed. "I think he wanted a second chance."

Ryan raised his eyebrows. "Would that ever happen?"

"Not in this lifetime."

"We only get the one," he said.

"So why did Mom always say I was an old soul?"

"That's what you say when your kid's a weirdo." She smacked him on the shoulder, and he laughed.

Before the dinner, Emily's father welcomed everyone. The best man, Marcus, gave his speech in character; he'd been promoted from knight to master of ceremonies at Medieval Legends, the dinner theater and tournament where he and Griffin both worked. Then Rose, with slightly jangled nerves, gave her maid of honor speech. She'd kept it short so she wouldn't mess anything up, but as she concluded, she got teary and her voice wobbled.

"Shakespeare wrote, 'Doubt thou the stars are fire; doubt that the sun doth move; doubt truth to be a liar; but never doubt I love.' And I know that if Emily and Griffin can be sure of one thing in life, it's their love for each other."

Everyone applauded as she sat down, relieved. She'd loved that Shakespeare quote ever since she'd come across it in an English lit class. It was when she'd first started reading about astrology . . . and was there anything more romantic than the stars?

Late in the evening, she told Emily, "I better get home and check on your pup." Emily's beagle mix, Andy War-Howl, was staying at Rose's apartment while Emily and Griffin spent the weekend at a fancy hotel downtown. Griffin was still finishing up his spring semester at the community college, so he and Emily had a honeymoon trip to England planned for the summer.

"Thank you so much again!" Emily said. "I hope he's no trouble."

"Of course he won't be!" Rose assured her, and exchanged goodbye hugs with them both. She found Ryan and let him know she was heading home.

On weekdays, she took the Pink Line home from the museum, but since it was late on a Friday night and she was tired, she opted for an Uber. The ride felt quiet after the loud reception.

The skyscrapers gave way to shorter buildings and quieter streets, and the car turned into her neighborhood. They passed the old brick church, built by Czech immigrants. When Rose's Grandma Novak had been a girl, before the family had moved to Cicero, she'd attended services at that church every week. The area looked very different now, with its proliferation of bright murals, its Mexican restaurants and trendy coffee shops and bars, and its funky little art galleries. Her grandmother would've complained about the graffiti and the noxious metal scrapyard nearby, but she would've been thrilled that Thalia Hall, a beautiful building with a theater that had closed in the 1960s, had been renovated and housed restaurants and regular concerts.

Rose loved it here. But as the car passed the pizza place with the mural of an Aztec warrior kneeling over his dead lover, which looked all the more romantic in the shadows and streetlight, loneliness settled in her heart.

When she reached the second floor of her walk-up apartment building, she heard Emily's dog Andy War-Howl give one of his trademark baleful howls. She went inside and turned on the lights. The large beagle mix put his paws up on her thigh, his tail joyfully wagging, and she petted his velvety ears.

Rose's mother had once said that you might as well paint the walls in a rental, because landlords always found reasons not to return your deposit, anyway. Fully aware that this was iffy financial advice, Rose had painted the rooms in the soft colors of some of her favorite crystals: pale citrine yellow in the eat-in kitchen and living room, rose quartz pink in the bedroom, amethyst purple in the guest bedroom, and the aqua hue of chrysocolla in the bathroom.

She took Andy for a quick walk, and when they returned, he hopped on the sofa and wound himself up in her tie-dye blanket like a pup burrito. Since she'd abstained earlier in the evening, she poured a glass of red wine and took a sip as she headed to the bedroom. She changed into an oversize T-shirt printed with a vintage cowgirl and the message *Not My First Rodeo*, but she didn't take off the moonstone necklace. It was her new favorite. Burning a lavender candle would help her relax after a long day and night, and she remembered she had one in her little altar in the corner.

It was actually a short medical supply cabinet from maybe the

1950s: metal coated with a turquoise paint, rusting at the hinges. Because her spells frequently involved burning, the stainless steel top was ideal. She crouched in front of it and pulled open the top drawer.

She sifted through crystals and the jumble of small charm candles in various colors, but couldn't find the lavender votive. Next she searched the drawer below it, filled with herbs and roots—St. John's wort, devil's shoestring, lucky hand—as well as a mallard duck feather, a smooth piece of green beach glass she'd found at 63rd Street Beach, and a dozen other things she'd tucked away for possible magical use, like a superstitious squirrel.

No lavender votive there, either. As she closed the second drawer, she frowned at the three tarot cards on top of the cabinet. Usually, the three cards she drew in the morning gave her clues about what lay in front of her that day, but two of these had mystified her.

The Eight of Wands, with its staves flying through the air over a river, could mean great changes or a long journey. She wasn't going anywhere, and she hadn't had any big changes in a while.

The Six of Cups stood for the past: the good old days, and one's earliest memories. The card could also mean going home . . . but what did that mean, when your parents were gone?

The Lovers card, of course, referred to Emily and Griffin. Looking at it now, Rose felt a stab of immature resentment. Where was *her* soulmate?

For the most part, she was happy on her own, staying cheerful and being grateful for what she had. But lately, more than ever, she had a lingering feeling that somewhere out there was one particular man who was *meant* for her.

Daniela's question came back to her. *Do you ever do spells for yourself?*

As Rose had explained, the cosmic timing was perfect for any kind of romance spell. Why not do one to find an old-fashioned gentleman?

She took off her necklace and set it on the altar next to the cryptic tarot cards. The moonstone was supposed to reunite lovers, not find new ones, but something told her it was the right one for the occasion. A small statue of Hecate, the goddess of the crossroads and of magic itself, loomed over the cards and the stone. But for a love spell, Rose would need Venus. She found the card printed with a painting of the goddess, which she'd bought from an artist on Etsy, and propped it up against a soapstone chalice.

Then she got up, went to the satin bag hanging on the hook by the door, and delicately extracted the rose petal that had fallen from Emily's flower crown. *Perfect.* Finally, she dug a pink candle and holder out of the top drawer and lit it.

It illuminated the Six of Cups card. A castle stood in the background, with a square stone tower, and the cups held star-shaped flowers. A boy was giving one of them to a girl. She studied it for a few moments, feeling warm and fuzzy inside.

She looked up at the wall clock that had been her mom's. Two minutes to midnight. She needed to think of what to say, fast, or she'd lose the opportunity. Just a sentence, or even a phrase, would do. Concentrating, she closed her eyes.

A full incantation popped into her head. That had never happened before. As she whispered it, the tingling at the crown of her head traveled down her spine and to her fingers and toes.

> Great Venus, who was born out of the sea,
> who makes our dreams of love reality . . .

The clock on the wall started to chime midnight. An image came into her head: the portrait of the duke, Henry what's-his-name, staring at her across time and space.

> Great Hecate, the Keeper of the Keys,
> who crosses time and space so easily . . .

She hadn't expected to drag Hecate into this, but she supposed her subconscious knew what it was doing. As the clock finished chiming, she finished the incantation, still thinking of the duke.

> Please bring an old-fashioned gentleman
> to fall in love with me. So mote it be.

Three

H enry strode into the library to meet the painter, carrying his walking stick, because when he posed for the portrait, he would need something to do with his hands. The usual scents of wood wax and that curious vanilla of old printed pages had been replaced by a sharp scent that filled his nostrils.

"Good morning, Your Grace," Wilke said, from where he stood in front of an easel. He was a bear of a man, his face partially concealed by a thick brown beard. The week before, he had rolled up the colorful carpet and had spread heavy cloths under the east-facing windows.

Henry walked over and surveyed the tins, brushes, rags, and tubes on the floor. "What is that malodorous . . . odor?"

"Turpentine, Your Grace," Wilke said, pointing to an open jar. "Take care not to knock it over. It's very flammable."

Henry stiffened. "What? There are over a thousand books in here!" He'd collected many of them himself; rare volumes, and seminal works of natural philosophy. "Would you have it all go up in blazes, like the library of Alexandria?"

"I store everything in your root cellar when I'm not working," the painter said implacably. He held out a hand toward the canvas. "Would you like to see what I've done so far?"

Disgruntled, Henry stepped around to look at the canvas—and then took in a sharp breath of astonishment. In the center of it, he was depicted as a gray, vaguely man-shaped cloud, with a few thin outlines in red. But the backdrop of his study was recreated in paint in stunning detail.

The window with the velvet curtain pulled to one side, revealing the countryside under a gray sky. The many books, of course, and those curiosities that Charlotte had arranged among them. The ancient red-and-black vases from Greece. A globe of the moon, with all its known features: the Sea of Serenity, the Sea of Tranquility. Even the deck of cards on a low shelf had made it into the picture. Hopefully, no one would take that to mean he was a gambling man. Charlotte had enjoyed the solitary card game of Patience, and Henry had not touched the deck after her death.

On its stand on the table, in real life and in the canvas, sat his beloved astrolabe. Charlotte had once suggested this very place would be a fine backdrop for a portrait, and he had to admit now that she'd been right.

"You have made remarkable progress," Henry admitted. He couldn't help but feel that the unfinished painting had already revealed him . . . as a specter, haunting his own home.

"Thank you, Your Grace. What is that brass device, anyway?" Wilke asked, nodding toward the astrolabe in its stand. "It looks like a clock with its face off." He picked up a paint tube and squeezed a small cylinder of white paint onto his palette.

"I suppose it does," Henry said. The round astrolabe was the size of a dinner plate and not much thicker, its mechanisms unfamiliar to the modern eye. "Let me show you how it works." He reached for it.

"No!" the artist said.

Henry's head shot up at the man's impertinence, and Wilke grimaced. "Your pardon, Your Grace, but nothing may be moved until I am finished. If you would be so good as to stand behind the table, near that device . . . ?"

"Of course." Swallowing his annoyance, Henry took his place and stared down at the astrolabe. "I was about to say that this is several hundred years old . . . older than any clock. But instruments like these are the reason that clocks go clockwise."

Wilke frowned and shook his head. "Clocks don't go backward because time doesn't go backward."

The comment sent a pang of yearning through Henry's chest. *Not yet,* he thought.

"But how do you know that *left* is *backward*?" he asked, and was gratified to see the artist open his mouth to answer and shut it again. "This was used for many things, including identifying the stars in the sky."

"They can't have known much about the stars back then," Wilke said, swirling bits of red and ochre into the white with his palette knife.

"They did not have the vast knowledge we have now," Henry allowed. "Only a few suspected that the Earth revolves around the sun. But they knew what they could see with the naked eye. And they knew that the Earth spins on its axis."

The artist lifted his head to stare at Henry for a moment as though studying an object, then lowered his head again and added a touch of black to the mixture, graying the pale tone. Henry was aware that his complexion had grown duller over the last couple of years.

Then Wilke turned away to draw back another curtain, asking, "What do *you* use the astrolabe for, Your Grace?"

"Ah, well. Chiefly, I admire its craftsmanship. But it can also be used to deduce your longitude and latitude, or the hour and the day. Of course, for us, it's a simple matter to know where we are in time and space."

The instrument had been a gift from his late wife, and speaking of it filled him with longing. He resisted the urge to pick it up, after all.

But it couldn't hurt to touch it . . .

As soon as he did, his vision blanked.

The floor was no longer under his feet. His senses spun; his stomach lurched. Had he fainted, after all, from the turpentine?

No, he was still standing, but hunched over, leaning heavily on the walking stick still in his grip. Some beast, some hellhound, roared.

He opened his eyes and looked around him.

This was not his library.

The yellow room had an oversize, overstuffed chair and sofa as well as a dining table with four wooden chairs. A hunting dog trotted over to him and put his paws on his knee, his tongue lolling out of his open mouth.

What just happened?

Where in God's name *was* he?

A half-naked woman with sandy-brown curly hair emerged from a side doorway, a glass of red wine in her hand, singing out in a high voice, "What's the matter, buddy?"

Her generous thighs and shapely calves were on full display. A sack-like, oddly printed garment could not conceal the shape of her full, unencumbered breasts, and it barely covered her fairest flower. Henry's mouth fell open, staring at the wanton nymph.

In the next moment, her gaze fell on him. She jumped like a frightened cat and let out a deafening shriek that made him stumble back a step.

Then she threw the contents of her wineglass at him, soaking his face and white shirt.

"What are you doing here?" she screamed at him. She was plainly terrified, but Henry was enraged by her affront and the shock of it all.

He thundered back, "Where am I?"

Her fine, expressive blue eyes widened as she looked him up and down. Then her countenance brightened with—excitement? Disbelief? She covered her mouth with her hands.

"*Oh my Goddess,*" she murmured. "It's *you.*"

Four

Rose had only been hoping the spell would help her meet a nice man in Chicago.

Her spells only *nudged* things. They tipped reality into her desired direction. If she was honest, just the act of doing a spell gave her hope, and any one of her successful spells could've been explained as coincidence or good luck.

She could not, for instance, make a man from another century materialize in her apartment.

Yes, she knew for a fact that at least one similar thing had happened before. And maybe, just maybe, a stone she'd blessed and given to Emily had helped with that. But *still*.

She *had* been thinking about Duke Henry what's-his-name. And this impeccably dressed, furious, and now wine-stained man standing in her living room, cane in hand, had to be the man himself.

"Where am I?" he demanded again, and she realized she hadn't answered him the first time. He swiped a sleeve across his face and looked wildly around him.

Huh. He was *really* not happy to be here. Rose supposed she couldn't blame him. It had to be a huge shock. Did the goddesses believe he was the man for her? Or had thinking of him at the wrong moment screwed up the spell?

The latter seemed more likely. It wasn't as though she actually knew what she was doing.

His gaze landed on her again, looking her up and down, and she could only describe the expression in his eyes as *smoldering*. Was he checking her out?

Oh yeah . . . he was. Because she was wearing nothing but a big T-shirt. Sheesh. That was one way to welcome a guy to the twenty-first century.

Managing a bright smile, she said, "I'll explain everything. As soon as I put on some pants. Stay right there, okay?" She raised both her hands, palms up, then quickly lowered them again to tug down on the hem of the oversize shirt.

She turned and walked quickly to the bedroom with as much dignity as she could muster, which was almost none. After pulling on a pair of pajama shorts, she hustled back out to find him tapping his finger on the blank TV screen. He whirled around as she approached, then stared at her legs again.

"Madam," he said stiffly, "I believe you intended to get dressed."

"Oh! I did." She lifted up the hem of the long T-shirt to show him the shorts. He didn't look any less shocked.

A fresh wave of amazement rolled over her. She had a historical duke in her freaking living room.

His dark brows were drawn together. He looked even more grouchy than he had in the painting, which was saying something.

Okay. No need to panic. She'd gotten him here. If he didn't want to stay, there must be a way to get him back home again.

"Can I get you anything? Wine?" She winced. "Sorry I threw some at you."

"Who are you working with?"

She blinked. "What?"

He advanced on her, brandishing his cane practically under her nose. "You drugged me, somehow, and had me abducted to this, this place—"

"Get your big stick out of my face," Rose snapped automatically.

To her surprise, he did, though he didn't look a bit less furious. He looked wildly around the room. "You will never get away with holding me for ransom! The king's own—"

"Hold up! I didn't *kidnap* you. I . . ."

He turned and sprinted for the door.

"Where are you going?" Rose squeaked, as she and Andy rushed after him. In seconds, the stranger was out of her apartment.

Shit!

Rose dove for Andy's collar, grabbing it just in time so he couldn't rush out into the corridor. After slipping past the dog, she released his collar and shut the door in his face, then raced down the stairs after the duke.

When he reached the small foyer of her building, she was still halfway up the staircase between the first and second floor. The smell of garlic and onions from the downstairs apartment hung in the air. He flung open the door to the street.

She reached the bottom of the stairs and ran outside in her bare feet, then stopped short. She'd expected to see him running down the block. Instead, he stood on the corner, his face illuminated by the buzzing streetlight as he scanned his surroundings.

Her body felt limp with relief. He hadn't run off . . . yet, anyway. He hardly looked real, standing there in his brown jacket with the brass buttons and long tails, and the high-waisted, cream-colored trousers . . . which fit his round ass *extremely* well.

Maybe, any moment now, he'd be flashed back to his own era.

But in the meantime, she should make sure he stayed safe. Hoping she didn't step on any broken glass, she ran over and grabbed his hand.

His fingers tightened around hers as he looked down at her. A frisson of heightened awareness ran down her spine. They were close enough to kiss . . .

"Wooo!" yelled an unmistakably drunk female voice from a car zooming down the street.

"What is that!" the duke demanded, thrusting his cane in the direction of the vehicle. "A . . . some kind of steam locomotive?"

"Close," Rose said, honestly impressed. Since she was still holding his hand, she squeezed it for emphasis. "Come upstairs and have a . . . a cup of tea." He'd like that, right? "It's just me and Andy up there." A frown touched his brow. She added, "Andy's the dog. He's actually my best friend's dog, but I'm watching him. It's the first time I've had a pet. Well, except for the time I watched someone's snake, but that's a whole other story."

He was looking around them, utterly bewildered. "I suppose if you had associates, they would've aided you in the chase."

"Exactly! Come on."

He released her hand—which gave her a stupid twinge of regret—and followed her back inside. When she was halfway up the first flight of stairs, she turned around and saw he was glowering up at her.

Rose was the first to admit that she had horrible judgment in men, but even she avoided crushing on ones who were actively hostile. This guy *couldn't* be the one she'd asked for, could he?

"I think you just got delivered to the wrong place," she mused aloud. "Like one time I got a package with something called a voltage tester in it." She never had figured out how to return that package, come to think of it. Maybe she shouldn't mention that. "Which was so funny, because I don't know the first thing about electricity. Although, I might know more than *you* . . ."

"I haven't the slightest idea what you are talking about," he said crossly.

"Sorry. I should introduce myself. I'm Rose Novak. And you're Henry . . . what's your last name, again?" she asked as they reached the second-floor landing.

"How do you know my Christian name, and not my last?" he demanded.

"It's a long name. I know you're the duke of something?"

He planted the cane on the floor and thrust out his chest. "I am Henry Leighton-Lyons, the Duke of Beresford." His haughtiness seemed so extreme to her, it ventured into satire. "And I will have you know my family is close to the Crown."

"We're not into kings around here," Rose said lightly. "Nice to meet you."

"I cannot say it is a pleasure to make *your* acquaintance."

Okay, *rude.* He was definitely not the gentleman she'd ordered.

Although . . . she'd said *to fall in love with me,* not *to immediately fall in love with me.*

She went inside and gestured for him to do the same, then shut the door behind them. Andy bounded up as though they had been gone for a week, and Rose leaned over and petted him.

Then she straightened and suggested to Henry, "Why don't we sit down?" She gestured toward the couch.

As he headed in that direction, he looked around him at the computer desk in the corner. "This is a very strange room." Instead of sitting, he clasped his hands behind his back.

"I'm sure." She lowered herself into an armchair, and Andy hopped up next to her. "First of all, you're in the United States."

"You're lying," he said flatly. "I was not unconscious long enough to be transported to America . . ." His eyes narrowed. "Unless I have amnesia."

"You don't."

"I very well might," he snapped. "My head is spinning, and my stomach is unsettled."

"I guess I'm not surprised," she admitted. "Do you think you're going to throw up?"

"Throw up what?" he demanded.

Well, he probably wasn't going to get sick, if he had the energy to get so snippy with her. She suspected that if she clarified and asked if he was going to vomit, he'd get even more snippy. No doubt he thought that vomiting was beneath him.

"Nothing," she said. He was really here, standing in her living room. Every time that thought crossed her mind, she felt a little dizzy herself. "But you really are in America, in the city of Chicago."

He scoffed. "There is no such city."

Oh. "You haven't heard of it?"

"I know my geography," he said coldly. "I've heard of New York. Boston. Philadelphia. Baltimore, where we fought that unfortunate battle. Your capital, named after George Washington. And several other towns besides. But *Chicago*, Miss Novak?"

A nervous giggle escaped her. Maybe Chicago had been some little jerkwater town in his time. And even if he sounded stern, she liked the way he said *Miss Novak*.

He gave her a wary look. "Is it *Mrs.* Novak?"

She felt a flutter in her nerves. "It's Miss. What about you? You're not married, right?" The museum label next to his painting hadn't covered this.

"No, I'm not," he snapped.

"You can call me Rose," she said.

"That would hardly be appropriate. We have only just met." His jaw flexing, he straightened his wine-splattered white tie.

Right. "Well, the thing is, Mr. Lyons, uh, Leightons—"

"*Leighton-Lyons*," he corrected her. "You may address me as Your Grace."

"Yeah, that's not going to happen," Rose said, without even thinking about it.

"Americans," he muttered, pacing over to the window.

"That's right. We didn't vote for you," she quipped.

He looked back at her, an incredulous look on his face. "Nobody *voted* for me."

"Exactly," she said. "Look, I want you to listen to me very carefully, because I have something to tell you that's going to be difficult to hear."

His features settled into a stony expression. "Whatever news it is that you have to impart to me, I can guarantee you that I have already heard much worse."

His words and something in his dispassionate voice touched her heart. She wanted to ask him what terrible news he'd received in the past . . . but as he'd just pointed out, they didn't know each other well.

She took a deep breath. "You've traveled forward in time."

"*Forward?*" he demanded.

"I've got to say, I thought you'd be way more surprised at the *time travel* part than the *forward* part." He just stared at her. "But yes. Over two hundred years into the future."

He laughed, shaking his head. It was the first time she'd seen him do anything but glower, and she felt a tingle of awareness at how handsome and endearing he looked.

"Damnation," he said. "I am dreaming." Then he sketched a quick bow. Until that moment, Rose hadn't known that anyone could bow sarcastically. "Forgive me, dream lady, for my shocking language."

That confused her for a moment. "You mean 'damnation'? That's so cute."

He raised his hand as if this proved his point. "Why should a figment of my over-fertile imagination be offended?"

"I'm not a figment of your imagination," Rose explained. "And

I grew up in Cicero, so I swear in English and Spanish. And Czech, thanks to my grandma."

"Aha! See?" he asked, pointing at her. "This is a dream. 'Check' is not a real language."

"They used to call it Bohemian." She added lightly, "I'm a little bohemian in more than one way."

Henry didn't appreciate her little joke, or even seem to hear her, as he finally sat down. "I suppose it's more of a nightmare than a dream. Why would I dream of traveling to the future, when my heart yearns day after day for the past?"

Her own heart squeezed a little at this. He must've lost someone. She knew how hard that was. Well, he wouldn't have been a duke if his father had still been alive.

"I'm afraid it's my fault you're here." She squirmed. Goddess, this was going to be so embarrassing to explain. And would he even believe her? "The thing is, I'm a witch, and I did a spell."

He snorted. "That is like saying I am Oberon, the King of the Fairies."

"Well, you did appear out of nowhere. Until tonight, I thought I could only do small charms."

"Any charms you have are definitely small," Henry grumbled.

Wow. Her cheeks flooded with heat. Whoever this guy was, he was not The One.

"You don't have to be such a jagoff," she said.

"What did you call me?" Henry demanded.

"It means jerk. More or less."

"That in no way enlightens me."

"Quit being unkind," Rose said, meeting his gaze. "Is that clear enough?"

He blinked. "It was a jest."

"Jests are supposed to be funny."

"I am sorry you were distressed by it."

"And that's the classic non-apology. You want to try again?"

Henry rolled his eyes. "Miss Novak—"

"Yeah, a sincere apology always starts with an eye roll," she said. Maybe it was just as well that he didn't like her. She wasn't sure she liked him, either.

She gave a dismissive wave of her hand. "Never mind. We need to figure out—"

"Miss Novak, if I met you in reality, and in less strange and terrify—" He caught himself. "Less trying circumstances, I have no doubt that things would be different."

She peered at him. He'd almost said *terrifying*. He wasn't just grumpy; he was scared.

"I'd be scared, too," she realized aloud. "If I woke up a couple hundred years in the future, I'd be curled up in the fetal position, hoping I wouldn't get exterminated by robots." He stared at her as though she were speaking another language. "Anyway, this is reality. I mean, when have you ever had a dream this vivid?"

He frowned, seeming to give the question serious thought. "Perhaps I am unconscious. That might make it possible to have very detailed dreams, because it would be more difficult to wake."

She tilted her head. "Why would you be unconscious?"

"The turpentine. The artist said that if I breathed too much of it, it might make me faint."

Rose shivered at the weirdness of this. "The artist who painted your portrait?"

"Yes. Walter Wilke. Well, as far as I remember, he had not painted *me* yet. There was a gray shape with a few lines, where I was meant to be—"

"Is that what you were doing before you came here?" she asked. "Getting your portrait done?"

"Yes. The last I remember, I was in the library, talking to the artist."

"I saw that painting of you tonight," she told him. "I work at the big museum here in Chicago, and they just bought it."

"That's impossible. I was not even in it yet."

"You are now. I'll show it to you tomorrow." She snapped her fingers. "The painting!"

"I beg your pardon," Henry said.

"It probably wasn't just my spell that brought you here. I bet Jason acquired that painting because it's magical!"

Henry scoffed, stood up, and walked over to the window again, as if to put some distance between him and the crazy lady. "Magic does not exist."

"Says the Mr. Darcy dude in my living room," Rose quipped.

He turned to look at her as if she was an idiot. "Miss Novak, I have told you my last name is *Leighton-Lyons*."

"Not a Jane Austen fan, I take it."

"I know nothing of a Miss Austen, nor of her fan. Speak plainly."

Rose got to her feet and joined him at the window. "Look out there. What do you see?"

He shrugged. "There are those locomotive carriages or what have you, and many bright yellow lamps, and over there I see foreign words spelled out in blue and red light."

"*Libros en Español*. It's a bookstore," Rose said. "Does this look like something you'd dream?"

A shadow seemed to fall across his face. "Perhaps not," he said in a quieter voice, staring out the window again. "Perhaps I have . . . taken leave of my senses."

"*Oh*. Oh, no," Rose reassured him.

"It is certainly possible," he said, almost to himself, as though he hadn't heard her. "A man may lose his ability to perceive the world around him, substituting his own bizarre fantasies."

"I mean, that can happen," Rose allowed, "but—"

"How can I know? Where am I, truly, at this moment?" He shook his head, an agonized gleam in his eyes. "Am I standing in my library, talking to myself, while my butler and the painter and God knows who else witness my humiliation?"

That would be a horrible situation. Well, for Henry. If something like that happened to her, she could laugh it off later as a bad shrooms trip or something. Not that she'd ever done shrooms, but the truth was, nobody would be surprised if she did. He was a duke from another era. For him, losing control would be much more serious.

She got up and walked over to join him where he stood near the window. "This is really happening," she said gently, willing him to trust her, to believe her. "You never had any, um, delusions before, did you?"

He cast her a condescending look. "No, but only a fool believes himself immune to weakness and travail. I have slept so little, and worked so much, and spent so many hours in isolation." Rose felt another pang of sympathy for him. Why hadn't he gotten married? Everyone must've wanted to marry a duke, even a grouchy, workaholic one. But what had he been working on?

He went on to say, "We all know what can happen, even to a brilliant man of science."

"No impostor syndrome here," Rose couldn't help but note.

"What?" He frowned at her. "I was saying, a man may go mad when he becomes obsessed. Like Victor Frankenstein in Byron's new novel."

"Um," Rose said. "I don't think that's Byron's."

Henry looked at her in surprise. "You know of the book? There are only five hundred copies."

That made her smile. "There are more now. And it's by someone named Mary." The writer's last name escaped her.

Henry shook his head. "A female? No. It was published anonymously, but everyone knows that scoundrel Byron wrote it, for his good friend Percy Shelley wrote the preface."

"Mary Shelley!" she said, snapping her fingers. "That's the author's name."

"Hmm." He looked doubtful. "At any rate, it is a warning against trying to achieve the impossible."

She took a step closer to him, filled with curiosity. "What were you trying to do?"

He gave her a searching look. "I suppose there is no harm in telling you, as this is all no doubt a fantasy." He turned back to the window, staring at nothing. "What I want to do more than anything else. Turn back time."

A shiver went through Rose. Had *his* intentions somehow been a part of this magic? But how could they have been? He'd wanted the opposite.

"Like I said, you must be here because the painting is enchanted," she told him. "Something like this happened already. There was a stone statue, and it came to life, and my best friend got married to him tonight."

His eye roll didn't offend her this time.

"Okay, I know," she added quickly, holding up her hands. "It sounds nuts. But I should text Emily. She'll know what to do."

She went to the coat hooks by the door where she'd hung her purse and grabbed her phone. As quickly as she could, she typed out,

Sooo an old-timey duke from a

painting is in my apartment

Then her thumb hovered over the *send* button. After the FBI investigation of the sculpture last year, she should be more cautious. Henry came up from behind her, making her jump.

"What are you doing with that thing?" Henry asked, peering down at the screen.

"Oh! This is how I send a message. Like a letter. This'll go to my friend in another part of the city. Like, instantly."

He surprised her by chuckling. "Wouldn't that be convenient?"

"I can't text her, though," she said, deleting the message letter by letter. "This is her wedding night."

"Her wedding night with the statue?"

"He's not a statue *now*. I'll text Jason."

Henry was still staring at her phone. "And who might he be?"

"Jason Yun. He's the curator at the museum, and he's part of a, I don't know, secret society. They study magical art and artifacts." The key part of that was *secret*. She shouldn't be blabbing about it. Then again, who would Henry tell?

She texted Jason.

WE NEED TO TALK AS SOON AS POSSIBLE.

Then she looked at Henry and laughed. "That sounds like I'm breaking up with him." He merely looked perplexed, so she explained, "It sounds like we're, uh, romantically involved."

A line appeared between his brows. "Might I be so impertinent as to ask if you are?"

"No! I've only talked to him a few times." And only one of those times had been a long conversation. After Griffin had come back to life and the FBI had cleared Emily of stealing him in statue form, Jason had interviewed Rose about the stone she'd used in a spell for Emily.

She pondered for a moment, then added to the message,

And there's someone you need to meet.

Henry said, "Perhaps I could do with a cup of tea."

She looked up to find his intense gaze on her, setting off a burst of sparks somewhere inside her.

That was . . . dangerous, considering they didn't really like each other.

Maybe she did know a little about electricity, after all.

Five

Henry might have succeeded in convincing himself that none of this was real . . . had he not been acutely aware of Rose's physical presence, in every detail. The bronze-brown curls cascading over her shoulders. The fragrance she wore, like incense and roses.

If he were dreaming, why did he not dream of Charlotte herself, as he had done countless times? Why would he dream of a woman who was so . . . uncivilized?

And yet, her charms were *not* small. In her presence, he felt jolted back to life again, like Frankenstein's monster.

He should not be feeling that way. Even if she was real, she was certainly not Charlotte.

Seeing messages appear on the sleek tablet in her hand, though, had given him an uncanny feeling. *This is not a dream,* a voice inside him had warned. *Be careful!*

If this were really happening, he should not be alone with her in her rooms in the middle of the night, not that it had been his choice. It was hardly respectable.

"One tea coming right up," she said.

While she busied herself in the kitchen, from which he heard odd chirping noises, he idly picked up a pile of papers on the table in her sitting room. Advertisements for strange goods and services: Pizza? An oil change? She returned much more quickly than he had expected, with two large mugs instead of teacups.

"Are you reading my mail?" she asked, teasing.

"I did not know it was mail," he defended himself as she handed him one of the mugs. A little tag on a string hung on the rim.

"What is this thing?" he blurted out, tugging at it.

"What? . . . The tea bag?" She plucked an object out by the string, did the same with her own, and deposited two little wet bags on the letter.

He stared down at them, then took a cautious sip. "It is satis-factory."

She gave him a bright smile. "Wow! And here I was just going for tolerable."

"But I take it with cream," he said mildly. She would be mortified, he was sure, that she had failed to offer him either cream or sugar.

She shrugged. "Best I can do is some oat milk."

"Enough of these foolish jests," he said. "You cannot extract milk from oats."

"Sure you can. Just squeeze them really hard," she said, pressing her finger and thumb together. Then she giggled.

"I will drink it without," Henry said, slightly miffed.

"Sorry it's not high tea at the Drake," she teased. "I'm not very proper here."

That gave him, he realized, the opportunity to raise the matter much on his mind. He cleared his throat slightly.

"Speaking of propriety, perhaps I should leave after this cup of tea, before your neighbors wake."

He hadn't necessarily expected her to blush—she was cavorting about in a state of dishabille, after all—but he'd at least expected her to say something along the lines of, *Yes, you're quite right.*

Instead, she blinked at him. "Why?" While he tried to think of the delicate way to say, *So that everyone won't think you're a whore*, she added in confusion, "Where do you want to go?"

"If I met you in a public park, in the daytime hours, taking in the fresh air, that is . . ." He was rambling. "No one could suspect you of an improper association." To his chagrin, although he considered himself a man of the world, *he* was the one who was blushing.

She laughed. "Henry, how do I put this? These days, it's not a big deal to do it with someone you're not married to."

He had a strong suspicion about what it meant to *do it*. Perhaps he should've reminded her that they were not nearly well enough acquainted to address each other by first names, but what was the point, when she spoke of such shocking things?

He stood holding his mug of tea in front of him like a shield. "Surely, your family would not approve."

"My parents . . . aren't with us anymore." Sorrow shadowed her face. "It's just me and my brother."

Regret settled in the pit of Henry's stomach. He should have ascertained, through pleasant and not too prying comments and questions, her family situation. That was what one did, if one had any conversational skill.

He said, "You have my heartfelt sympathy, Miss Novak, in the great loss you have suffered."

She gave him a wistful smile that seemed designed to melt his heart. "Thank you. It was a long time ago, but I miss them every day. I know you understand."

He nodded. "But we must still take care for your reputation."

She laughed again and perched on the arm of the chair. "Nobody's worried about my virtue, promise. And I mean, that ship has already sailed."

Impudent woman. "I cannot imagine your brother would be pleased by my presence here."

"My brother's going to think this is amazing. And hilarious."

Henry stared at her. "But why would he be amused? A young woman's close association with gentlemen would lower her value as a future wife."

Her face screwed up into an expression of disgust, and she held up her hands, even though she held a mug in one of them. "Okay, none of that manosphere bullshit. Being with men doesn't *lower my value*. I'm a woman, not a purse on Poshmark!"

He frowned. "I was speaking of a universally held belief! I perceive that I have greatly offended you, but I have not the slightest conception of why." Nor did he know the meaning of *manosphere*, which might have been an astronomical term, or *Poshmark*.

Her expression softened. "It's okay. Things have changed a lot since your time."

She forgave quickly, even in the absence of an apology—and even though it had been quite clear that his words had been extremely distasteful to her. Perhaps he should leave it at that. But his ever-present compulsion to learn how the world worked won out over his sense of propriety, which seemed to be a foreign currency to her, anyway.

He considered sitting down, but was not sure of the etiquette, as she was not quite sitting down herself. "But Miss Novak, if anyone may . . . associate amorously, outside the bounds of marriage, are ladies not often left with the burden of raising children alone?"

"That happens sometimes," she admitted. "But weren't there some unmarried mothers in your time, too? Ones who should've been getting help from the children's father?"

"I am sure there has been no era in which all men fulfilled their moral duties."

"But right now, women can take medicine so they don't get pregnant." While he repeated this in his head to make sure he'd clearly heard such an astonishing claim, she added, "I take the pill now, even though I don't have a boyfriend, because otherwise I get the *worst* period cramps. I mean a solid week every month."

Was she talking about what he thought she was talking about? He could think of no other interpretation. His ears grew hot and he looked away. But along with his embarrassment, he felt something unexpected: a wrong and reckless pleasure in transgression.

"Do you always speak freely with men about such matters?" he managed to ask.

She laughed. "Not constantly, but sure, if it comes up."

Until he'd been married to Charlotte, his basic understanding of the courses of females had not included the knowledge that it caused considerable pain. There hadn't been much that he could do about her monthly distress, but he'd encouraged her to lie in bed reading novels as much as she liked during that time, and had instructed the kitchen to keep her favorite rum cake on hand.

"I'm sorry," Rose said sincerely. "I didn't mean to embarrass you. I think we're both doing the best we can here."

He supposed they were. "My curiosity has proven a distraction, as it often does. What I truly must know is this: How can I return, as soon as possible, to where I belong?"

She winced as if this was an impossible question, and Henry feared that it very well might be.

Then she said, "Let's go out on the roof."

"The roof?" he repeated, bewildered.

"That's where I like to sit when I'm trying to figure things out," she said, walking over to the door from which she'd first emerged. "It's the main reason I rented this place."

He gave a huff of surprise. "At Everly Park, there were windows one could climb out of to walk on the roof on either the West or East Court. But I have not done such a thing since I was a boy."

She cast him a mischievous look over her shoulder. "Then it's about time you did it again."

He did want to look more at this town of Chicago—dream, hallucination, or real. "Very well."

When he followed her into the next room and saw her large bed with several pillows, he felt another tiny jolt. He was hardly accustomed to entering ladies' bedchambers. Surely this bare-legged, whimsical Cyprian was attempting to seduce him? Maybe that was why she'd encouraged such salacious conversation?

But she walked right past the bed and the nightstand next to it, which held cards, curious objects, and the remains of a small pink candle. "This story is smaller than the one below it," she explained. "We can climb out here."

She set her mug of tea down long enough to open the window, then picked it up again. He stared, dumbfounded, at her plump, dimpled thighs as she straddled the sill and then hopped onto the roof on the other side.

Henry remembered to breathe again. It was the most ungainly, unladylike thing he'd ever witnessed. And the most seductive. What was it about this woman that had his body twitching ever so slightly to life?

It was nothing about her, personally, he decided. When was the last time he'd been alone in the company of a pretty woman? Certainly not since Charlotte had died. Well, yes, there had been the maids, but he was not a reprobate. And he'd spent a long evening with a clever lady at the Paris Observatory, who was said to be pretty, as well, and he'd felt nothing . . . but she had been a fellow scientist, so it didn't count.

No, he was only reacting to Rose's chaotic charms out of deprivation. A hungry man always declared the food was delicious.

"Come on!" Rose called to him, ducking and leaning in the window, showing off the globes of her breasts to great advantage. She seemed blithely unaware of the impression she was making, but any single man, deprived or not, would find that a delectable view.

He walked stiffly over to the window. As he swung his leg over the sill, he felt a glimmer of the joy and freedom he'd known when he was a boy. He hadn't known such feelings were still inside him anymore. Whether or not one could turn back time, perhaps one could coax out those past selves, those different boys and men one had been, and invite them to play.

The roof was flat. She settled herself, cross-legged, in the square of light from her window. He came over and sat next to her, not too close, in the darkness. Buildings surrounded them, three and four stories high, and he couldn't place the continuous rumble he could hear in the distance, like the sea.

"I always come out here when I can't sleep," she told him. "Look, the moon's going to set in an hour or so." She pointed down the street to where it hung low and large, partly blocked by the top of a single tree.

"Yes. But where are the stars?" He peered at the sky above them. It was not black or deep blue, but a murky violet-brown.

"The city lights are too bright," she explained.

He'd never considered that such a thing might be possible. "It is unsettling not to be able to see them."

"I suppose. But you know they're still there." She had a wistful look in her eyes. Was she thinking of a former suitor, perhaps?

He stared up at the starless sky again. "Have there been any scientific discoveries here about time? Experiments? Something that might have created an anomaly, to account for my presence here?"

"Not that I know of. But like I was saying before, I'm a witch, and—"

A blare of music from nowhere startled him. Rose dug out the little tablet—her *phone*, she'd been calling it. "Oh! It's Jason." She touched a button on the phone and held it up.

To Henry's utter astonishment, a man's face filled the screen. He had unruly black hair, threaded with silver, and slightly bleary dark eyes. A frame in the corner held Rose's own reflection.

"Hi Jason!" Rose said. "Sorry to bother you so late. Or early."

"Hey," the man said around a yawn. "What's up?"

Henry stared at Rose. "You *are* a witch," he realized aloud. He'd heard of them viewing others from a distance, by means of crystal balls.

"What?" She turned to him. "Oh, no, this is FaceTime. It's, uh, science."

"Who's with you?" Jason asked Rose.

Rose smirked, scooted closer to Henry, and angled the phone. He could see himself next to her in the corner frame. "This is Henry Leighton-Lyons, Duke of . . ." She cast him a questioning look.

"Beresford," Henry said—and Jason said it with him, his eyebrows raised.

"Uh, wow," Jason added. "Welcome." He grinned, as though Henry's presence were a delightful surprise, instead of a calamity that threw everything they knew about the workings of the natural world into question. What was more, the man had not even bothered to properly introduce himself.

"Mr. Yun, I believe," Henry said stiffly. "You are from the East, I take it?"

"The West, actually. California."

"He's American," Rose said quickly.

"Call me Jason," the man on the screen said. "Rose, thanks for being discreet in the text. How'd he get here?"

Henry bristled. He did not like being spoken about as though he were not present.

Rose exhaled, blowing out her cheeks. "I did a love spell."

In all the confusion before, Henry hadn't thought to ask her what the aim of her so-called spell had been.

"A love spell?" Henry repeated. "To summon *me*?"

"No! I mean, I saw the portrait of you earlier, and it crossed my mind, but I wasn't trying . . ." She shrugged.

Henry shook his head. "This cannot be why I have been wrenched out of time. For some foolish feminine fancy." There had to be another explanation.

Jason said, "Rose, just tell me what happened."

"Fine." She adjusted the phone again, taking Henry out of the frame, and seemed to be avoiding his gaze. "I got home from Emily and Griffin's wedding, and they seemed so happy, and I saw Aaron Coleman there. Who I'm still annoyed with, by the way."

Who was this Aaron Coleman, Henry wondered, and why had he troubled Rose?

"Since it was a Friday and a full moon in Libra, I thought I would do a spell to get an old-fashioned gentleman to fall in love with me. I didn't mean a literal old-fashioned gentleman, obviously!"

Could it be true? Henry frowned. "It was Friday and a full moon in my time. And in Libra, according to my watch . . . not that I give any credence to such twaddle."

Jason's eyes were bright with excitement. "This is fantastic. Can you go through everything you did?"

"I think so . . . Actually, hang on, I'll go get the stuff." She abruptly handed the phone to Henry, hopped to her feet, and scampered back toward the window. To Henry's dismay, he was left staring at this stranger.

Jason said, "This must be pretty strange for you."

"Strange? It is unimaginable. Abominable. I am in another time and place. Do you know how I might return to where I belong?"

"Uh . . . not exactly, but we can try to figure it out."

Below, a red light hanging over the intersection extinguished, and a green light shone in its place. One of those metal coaches, pulled by no horses, sped down the street. This was no dream or delusion. He had nothing in this world. He understood little of it. To be at the mercy of strangers, and common ones at that, was humiliating.

Rose climbed out to the roof again, straddling the windowsill with her bare legs, cradling some items with one arm against her chest. Henry looked away quickly.

Jason said, "Your Grace, would you be so good as to tell us exactly what happened before you crossed over?"

At least *someone* knew how to address him properly. And Jason's request was a sensible one. The first step in solving any conundrum was to make sure one had all the facts at hand.

"Very well," he said, as Rose again took her spot next to him . . . or was she sitting closer this time? She deposited a jumble of cards and trinkets in front of her.

He must not get distracted. "I was in the library of my home, Everly Park, talking to the artist. He'd finished the background of my portrait, but needed to add me. I laid my hand on the astrolabe, sitting on the—"

"Yes!" Jason said, in the tone a man used when the horse he had bet on won. "I knew it!"

"I beg your pardon," Henry said.

Rose said, "Wait, if Henry didn't finish posing for the painting, why do we have it? How did it get finished?"

That was a good question, Henry had to admit. "Perhaps it is because I will return directly."

Rose snapped her fingers. "Or maybe we *don't* still have it! But then . . . would I still remember seeing it?"

"You and I both still remember it," Jason pointed out. "Have you ever read about the Novikov self-consistency principle?"

"The what now?" Rose asked, but Henry perked up. This sounded like scientific theory, rather than occult nonsense.

Jason explained, "Basically, the theory is that if you change an event in the past, the universe rearranges events to make sure the present stays as much the same as possible."

"Oh, wow," Rose said.

Henry had hoped to return to his past and change it. There was no complete cure for Charlotte's weak heart, as far as he knew; he had never imagined being able to grow old with her. But if she was in the care of a more skilled doctor, and if Henry could better safeguard her against bumps and jolts, such as distressing stories in newspapers, overwrought plays at the theater, and marital quarrels, which had been rare but heated, her sensibilities might be less strained, and she might live just a few years longer.

But what Jason spoke of sounded like destiny. If Henry had found his way back to Charlotte, would his efforts have been in vain? Would she have died anyway, at the age of twenty-six? If not from heart failure, then from some other cause—consumption, or a spooked horse?

Even so, it would be worth it to relive those days with her, and to be a better man.

Jason shrugged. "Who knows, though. We're dealing with magic here, not physics."

Henry balked at this. "However remarkable my presence is, all scientific discoveries seem miraculous at first. There is a logical reason for me to be here."

Jason said, "Even in this century, all we have is theories. We haven't built a machine that can travel through time."

"Perhaps I would have," Henry said, "if I had been left alone to do my research."

"Sorry, but no," Jason said flatly. "Your knowledge was so far behind ours. Even if you worked your whole life, you couldn't have done it all on your own."

This opinion landed like one of Dunton's punches. There was no ill intent behind it, and yet it had the painful sound of truth.

Jason added, "So why don't you tell me everything you know about the astrolabe?"

Rose asked, "Is that the gold thing? Looks kind of steampunk?"

Jason nodded. "Where did it come from?"

"I don't believe it's any of your business, sir."

Jason made a steeple of his fingers. "Your Grace. I'm trying to get you home."

Well, there was that. "If you must know, it was a birthday gift from my wife, not long before she died." He still had the sentimental note that had accompanied it, which had included one of her favorite quotes.

Rose's mouth fell open, and she gazed at Henry as though seeing him for the first time. "Oh my Goddess, that's right," she murmured.

She knew? Henry's pulse pounded in the side of his neck.

"You asked if I was married," he said, setting the phone down in front of him. "Yet you know about Charlotte? Is this some kind of game?"

Rose blinked. "No, I didn't know you were ever married. That just reminded me of something . . ." Her brow knitted, and she shook her head. "It's nothing. I'm so sorry about your wife."

"Hey, guys?" Jason's voice came from the phone.

"Sorry, Jason," Rose said and picked it up again so they could see each other. There was nothing but innocence on Rose's face. Henry had been known to say awkward things sometimes, himself, and he found he was glad to set his suspicion aside.

"I'm sorry for your loss, Your Grace," Jason said correctly.

"She must've been so young," Rose said, pressing a hand to her chest. "How . . . ?"

"A weakness in her heart, they say," he said, his voice clipped. "Though no one warned us of it."

"That's so awful. I know sometimes there aren't any symptoms."

"But there were. She often had palpitations, and she fainted easily. Our family doctor told us they were merely signs of an excitable nature. I ought to have consulted a second physician. Instead, as I am predisposed to dullness, I supposed that marriage to me would have a salubrious effect."

"I'm sure she thought you were the opposite of dull," Rose said. That was charitable, for he'd given her no reason to say it. Well, other than appearing out of thin air. She was right in one aspect, though. Neither he nor Charlotte had been dull in the bedchamber.

He said, "We were married two years . . ." As reluctant as he'd been to speak of this, he also had every grieving man's urge to let everyone else know how cruelly life had treated him. The dangerous tightness in his throat, though, made him conclude abruptly, "She died in her sleep."

Rose reached over and put her hand over his. He startled. She was a sweet, kindhearted creature, he had to admit, and in the moment, when his world had tilted even further off its axis, her comfort steadied him. He grasped her fingers in his own.

Jason cleared his throat. "Your Grace, it's no consolation, but I doubt any doctor in your time would've been able to help."

"And it would be different in your era?"

"Yes. We have better tests, better medicine, and better surgical techniques. We even have machines that let doctors look inside the body at what the heart, or any organ, is doing, without even hurting the patient."

Could that possibly be true? Henry's gaze darted to Rose, who was nodding.

Jason said, "But back in your time, there wasn't nearly as much that even a good doctor could do."

Was this meant to also absolve Henry, as a husband, for not knowing anything was wrong? That crime could not be set aside so easily. He released Rose's hand, feeling that he should, although she hadn't pulled away.

Jason said, "The astrolabe must've meant a lot to you. My understanding is that it was made in Granada, Spain. Possibly in the tenth or eleventh century. Does that sound right to you?"

"Yes." Henry was so surprised that he set aside the awareness that the other man had, quite deftly, turned the conversation back to his own topic of interest. "That is to say, I was told it came from Spain, and there are inscriptions in Arabic, Hebrew, and Latin on the outer rim."

"Really?" Rose exclaimed. "That's so cool!"

"Well actually, southern Spain is warmer than England," Henry said politely. When she and Jason both smiled, Henry realized he'd been foolish, because they weren't in England. "At any rate, my astrolabe also bears the symbols of astrology, which are pure nonsense."

Rose peered at him. "Capricorn," she decided.

"I . . ." *Damnation.* How had she done that?

"It's a gift," she said with delight. She pointed at Jason. "Gemini?"

"That's hurtful," Jason said.

Henry folded his arms across his chest. "The fact that I was born on January third has no bearing whatsoever on my character."

"Which is exactly what a Capricorn would say."

Jason shook his head slightly. "Your Grace, the most interesting thing about your astrolabe is that according to a couple of early sources, it could be used for time travel."

"What?" Rose demanded. Henry just stared at Jason.

"I'm guessing you didn't know this," Jason said to him. "But is it possible that your wife knew?"

"I am sure she did not," he snapped. "This idea of her dabbling in the occult was nothing more than a product of vicious minds."

"Um, what?" Jason said, and Rose's features lit up with curiosity.

Henry reminded himself that they knew nothing of those absurd rumors. He said shortly, "It was a sentimental gift."

A faint shadow of doubt crossed his mind as he said it. Sometimes Charlotte's interest in magical tales had perhaps gone beyond the intellectual. Had he been traveling to arcane libraries, conferring with great minds, and poring over formulas for an answer that had been, quite literally, at his fingertips?

He shook his head. "I touched and held the astrolabe countless times. So did my wife. Nothing strange happened." He felt that familiar temper rising in him, as it always did when things were beyond his understanding.

Jason said, "It must work under unique circumstances."

Rose's face flushed pink. "It's me. I'm unique circumstances. I'll tell you what I did." She gathered up three of the cards in her little pile and held them up.

"First of all, these tarot cards were already on my altar. I didn't really think of them as part of the spell, but . . . maybe they were?" She laid them out. "Eight of Wands, Six of Cups, the Lovers." The last card depicted a man and a woman as naked as Adam and Eve. Henry had heard of tarot cards, but he had never seen them. He hadn't realized they were so scandalous.

Rose shook her head. "I draw three every morning to tell my fortune for the day, but I thought these were pretty random."

This was every bit as absurd as the ancient Roman practice of inspecting the livers of sacrificed sheep to divine the future, though Henry supposed it would be preferable from the standpoint of a sheep. And surely, Rose must be as guileless as a sheep, if she believed in such nonsense. He attempted to keep his thoughts to himself. It was an unfamiliar exercise, but he didn't wish to be called a *jagoff* again.

Rose said, "For the spell, I also used a picture of Venus." She set another card down next to the others. "I said an incantation and lit a candle. A pink one, obviously."

Jason asked, "Where did you get the incantation?"

"I always write my own. Although this one just popped in my head. It even rhymed." She gave a little laugh. "They're always stronger if you rhyme."

"This is nonsense," Henry couldn't help but say, shifting in his seat as though he could not contain his agitation. "I may not have discovered the secret of altering time, but my being here can have nothing to do with muttering words over a candle."

Rose's cheeks flushed. "I don't *mutter.*" Too late, Henry remembered why his criticism had touched such a nerve.

She was talking about a spell to make a perfect gentleman fall in love with her. A spell that had, in her perception, resulted in his dramatic appearance out of the very ether. She was in a humiliating situation, explaining this right in front of him. A true gentleman would've made every effort to ameliorate her chagrin, perhaps with a rueful joke at his own expense. He'd never been good at that kind of thing, but he could've at least refrained from mocking her.

Jason asked Rose, "Would you mind writing out what you said?"

She shook her head. "I can't remember exactly. I called on Hecate, too—the goddess of the crossroads? But I don't even know why."

"In the statuette at the museum, she's carrying keys," Jason said.

"That's right," Rose said approvingly. "She's pictured with other things, too. But the keys are because she can unlock the door between this world and the next."

"Or between this century and another one," Jason suggested.

Henry felt prickles on the back of his neck. This could *not* be an explanation of how he came to be here . . . but what other explanation was there?

Jason asked, "Your Grace, in the moment before you touched the astrolabe, do you remember what you were thinking or feeling?"

"This is preposterous. No, I don't recall."

And then Henry did recall. He'd been thinking of Charlotte, and missing her. Was that why Rose's love spell had plucked him out of that particular moment in time?

Impossible. His thoughts were not magical.

"All right," Jason said. "Rose, is that all you used for the spell?"

"No, hang on. I also used this moonstone necklace." The pendant had been face down before, but now she held it up, swinging back and forth on its chain like the pendulum of a clock.

Henry stared at the blue stone with its four-pointed star.

It couldn't be . . .

Rose looped the chain over her neck as she kept talking. "I don't know why I used it, because a moonstone is supposed to *reunite* lost lovers. I definitely don't want to reunite with any of my exes." She rolled her eyes. "But I was wearing it because of the full moon, so why not, you know?"

She shrugged. Belatedly, she looked from Henry to Jason—whose expression, Henry now noticed, was also intent. "What?" she demanded.

Henry said, "That moonstone was set in my astrolabe."

Jason nodded.

Rose shook her head. "It can't be the same one. I got it on Maxwell Street."

Jason said, "The astrolabe's been missing that stone for at least fifty years."

"Wow." Rose looked down at the pendant on her chest. "But the astrolabe's still in England, right?"

"No," Jason said. "It's in Chicago."

Six

W hat?" Rose and Henry said in unison, then exchanged a glance.

"Yeah, it's kind of a long story," Jason said. "We should talk in person." The last word was eclipsed by his yawn. Seeing him do it, Rose couldn't suppress a yawn of her own. She'd barely even gotten any sleep the night before because she'd been preoccupied with wedding details. All those worries seemed so trivial compared to the grumpy duke on her hands.

"Maybe we could get together for a late lunch tomorrow?" she suggested. "We could do the patio at Pilsen Yards." She and Henry could walk there. It was supposed to be nice out.

"Don't tell anyone else," Jason said. "It's important. I'll explain later."

"Okay. Wait. I *have* to tell Emily and Griffin the next time I see them."

"Uhh . . ." Jason pinched the bridge of his nose. "Yeah, all right. They might have good input."

"And I have to tell my brother." Jason seemed to consider his response, and she rushed to add, "I can't hide a new duke roommate from him! And he didn't tell anyone about Griffin."

"Her brother has a right to know," Henry said. Rose looked over at him with raised eyebrows. She hadn't expected his support on this. "To ask a lady to keep her association with a gentleman a secret from her family would be an unpardonable offense."

Rose jerked a thumb at Henry. "Exactly. Unpardonable."

Jason sighed. "Okay, but call him. Don't text. See you guys tomorrow." He hung up.

Rose looked at the time on her phone. It was past three, and Ryan got up early for work. "I guess I'll call him in a few hours. We should really go to bed." A quizzical line etched itself between Henry's brows, and she said, "I mean sleep! We should try to get a little sleep."

He nodded. "Perhaps when I awaken, I will be in my own bed again."

She cocked her head thoughtfully. "You *still* think you're dreaming? It would be such a long, complicated dream!"

"I could be in a coma."

"*How?*" she pressed him. "You were just standing in your library!"

"Perhaps I had a fit of apoplexy. Or perhaps the ceiling fell in on my head."

"Unlikely. Even if you did have a super old house, which I'm sure you did."

"Not that old, actually," Henry admitted. "It was finished in 1711. Nonetheless—"

"I wonder if your house is still standing?"

"Of course it is," he snapped. "Why would it not be?"

It could've fallen into ruins, or have been bulldozed, or both, but she doubted he wanted to hear about those possibilities. "What's your house called?" She couldn't help but add, "Privilege Place? Snooty McSnooterson Hall?"

"Everly Park."

"Oh . . . well, that's a beautiful name, actually," she admitted. "Let's see if I can find it." She picked up her phone.

"You mean, pictures of it?" he asked.

"Well, yeah. And information."

He moved closer to her to look over her shoulder.

"Here it is!" Rose said. The website landing page showed a photo of his ancestral home, seen from the park, with a stone bridge over the little river in the foreground.

"My God," he breathed. "Yes. That's it."

"Holy *shit*," Rose exclaimed loudly, only barely aware of his disapproving look. "Are you *kidding* me? This isn't a house. It's a castle!"

"No. But it was built on the grounds of a former castle." She swiped to a photo of a baker standing in front of what looked like a greenhouse, holding a loaf of French bread.

"What is this man doing on my property?" Henry demanded.

"They're advertising a food festival. It looks like they have a lot of events there." She flipped to another page. "Yeah, it belongs to England now. It's owned by the National Trust."

Henry snorted. "I should very much like to know who approved of such a thing."

"It's not the worst idea. Then a lot of people can enjoy it."

He looked thoroughly unconvinced, and she went back to the photos of the rooms. The next one showed a gilded suite with several paintings on the walls in elaborate frames. Watchful cherubs flanked the mirror over the fireplace.

"What the *hell*?" Rose said, completely astonished. "Did it look like this when you lived there?"

"No." When she looked over at him, he added, "It should have a Savonnerie carpet rather than a Persian, and it's missing the tapestry of the Battle of Ramillies."

She shook her head and flipped to an elaborate maze garden.

"Ha! It still looks neatly trimmed," he said.

"They probably replaced the shrubs."

"The configuration is the same. Even as a young lad, I knew the way out, but I still loved the detours."

The next picture was of a great hall. Rose had known he must've been rich, of course. But *nobody* should be this rich.

"How is this your *house*? You should be ashamed of yourself."

"*Ashamed?*" He got to his feet. "Most people would say I should be proud."

"I'll bet," she muttered, swiping to an image of the front of the great house of beige stone. Columns flanked the central entrance and the great stone towers.

He stood over her, staring down. "Where does the present Duke of Beresford live?"

Rose had actually done a quick search when she'd left the roof to gather her witchy things. "There isn't one. The dukedom died out or whatever."

"But this is appalling." He paced a few steps on the roof.

Rose flipped to the state dining room with its ruby red walls. "It's crazy for one person to live here. A hundred people could live here!"

"There's a large staff."

"Servants, right. How many?"

"Why does it matter?"

She dropped the phone to her side. "You don't even know!"

It made her think of when her father had been laid off. A sweet, gentle man, he'd always been willing to take extra shifts. He'd been proud of the work, saying how the tractors they built in the factory were used all over the world. The day he'd lost his job, he'd tried to smile and tell Rose and Ryan everything would be all right, but there had been a new thinness to his voice, as though he'd been punched in the throat. Rich people used workers like him and discarded them like used tissues, never thinking about what might happen to them or their families afterward.

She held up her hands, the phone in one of them. "I'm just saying that for a few people to be that rich, a lot of people have to be poor."

He snorted. "Would you haul me to a guillotine? We each travel in our orbit, the way the planets travel in their orbits above."

"That's a horrible analogy," she said.

"What of it?" He pointed down at the phone. "That is my house, and if your magic brought me away from it, then you had no business attempting it."

Rose felt a stab of hurt. He could be a little more sensitive after she'd had to admit in front of him that she'd been looking for a boyfriend.

"You know I didn't mean to bring *you*. Obviously, this was a mistake." He was a first-rate snob who thought he was divinely ordained to be superrich, and he didn't even want to be in the same *century* as her.

Besides, he didn't laugh at her jokes. He was clearly a monster.

Standing at a distance from her, Henry set his hands on his hips, looking out over the rooftops. "As far as living alone in that house . . . it was meant for a family, at least."

Regret washed over her. Her family's past problems weren't Henry's fault. And regardless of whatever he was complicit in as a member of the ruling class of England, and she didn't really know, he was grieving. Not to mention hopelessly lost.

A siren wailed on the street below, accompanied by flashing red lights.

Andy War-Howl burst through the windowsill, barking, his claws clattering as he landed on the roof. Out of Rose's reach, he launched himself toward the offending noise, toward the edge.

Rose felt as though her soul had left her body. With a wordless shriek, she ran two steps after him. She lunged for him and missed—

Then Henry was there, sliding to his knees, grabbing the dog firmly by the back haunch and hauling him backward. Ignoring the dog's surprised yelp, Henry grasped him by the collar as the siren faded into the distance.

Rose pressed her hands to her face. "Oh, shit."

Henry scooped Andy up in his arms without letting go of the collar. "Troublesome cur," he growled, breathing hard. Now that it was quiet again, the dog looked up at him with curious eyes. Henry stalked over to the open window and carried Andy inside.

Feeling shaky, Rose followed him. "He's got a crate over here . . ."

She pointed to the corner of the living room. Henry strode over to it, deposited the dog inside, locked the door, and rattled it to make sure it was secure.

"I didn't even think about leaving the window open," Rose said as Andy pawed at his blankets, unperturbed. Her throat tightened. It had been the craziest night of her life, and this scare on top of everything else was too much. "I'm such a flake!"

Henry came over and took gentle hold of her upper arms. The contact and his closeness distracted her, and she gazed up at him. She was used to him looking cold and stern, and she hadn't been prepared for the concern in his dark eyes.

"You have had a terrible shock," he said gravely. "You must sit down at once." He extended one arm to the armchair.

"Okay, good idea," she said. He was being very nice, but missing the point. Emily had trusted her with Andy. "I'm the worst dog sitter ever."

He took her by one arm. "Dogs are mischievous creatures. When I was a boy, we had a spaniel who was always finding trouble." He guided her to the chair. To her surprise, as soon as she sat down, Henry crouched next to the chair, holding her hand and regarding her closely.

"You are unwell. I must call for a doctor."

"What? No! I'm okay. I'm just freaked out."

His worrying over her made something inside her melt. She wasn't fragile. She was the one who took care of everyone else. But it was so nice, just this once, to have someone looking after her . . . even if he didn't think she was anything special, and even if she hardly knew him.

"I will not insist for now. But consider that you have had not one, but two great frights this evening." She appreciated him pointing that out. It made it sound like he didn't blame her *completely* for his being here. "We must avoid further assaults on your sensibilities."

She had to smile at that. "I agree. I hate assaults on my sensibilities."

He was still staring at her. "Still, you have gone pale. Is there something you could take to settle your nerves? Perhaps a glass of wine."

She gave a shaky half laugh. "You mean, if I promise not to throw it at you?"

His mouth curved up in the slightest of smiles. Wait. Was he laughing at her joke? Well, not *laughing*, and it hadn't been much of a joke, but still, he was visibly appreciative.

He looked irresistible with that smile and the warmth in his eyes.

"I will fetch you the wine," he declared.

He rose to his feet, and as she watched him go into the kitchen, she wondered if he'd ever fetched anyone a glass of wine in his life.

"The bottle's on the counter, and the glasses are over the sink," she called after him. Apparently, he did know what a sink was, because he opened the right cabinet door. "Do you want one, too?"

He looked over at her. "I suppose I don't care if I do."

When he returned to the living room, with his erect posture, his fancy if spattered clothes, and a glass of wine in each hand, Rose drank in the sight of him. It would've been wonderful to conjure up a man like him . . . if he'd actually been interested in her.

"Thank you," she said as he put them both on the table and took a seat on the couch across from her. She had to admit that a little bit of her missed him crouching at her side.

As she took a sip, he said, "Some color has returned to your cheeks."

They were probably getting even pinker now, the way he was staring at her again. "I'm fine. I'm just glad you were here to save Andy." She forced a smile. "Even though *you're* not glad you're here. If there's anything I can do to make you feel more comfortable, let me know."

He adjusted his scarf thing. "I daresay that had I known I would be dragged into another century, I would have packed some clothing."

"Oh, right!" she said, snapping her fingers. "I have some things you can wear. A while back my brother brought me some more clothes to give to Griffin, but then Griffin sold his armor and he didn't really need hand-me-downs . . . Anyway, I was going to give them to charity, but I kept forgetting."

He stared at her blankly.

"I'm sorry. I'm talking too fast," she guessed. "I'm saying I have some clothes for you that'll be much more comfortable."

She wished Emily and Griffin could come over to help him adjust to the twenty-first century. But of course, he didn't *want* to adjust. And she couldn't even blame him.

She added, "I'll do everything I can to help you get back to 1818."

Seven

Later that morning, Henry woke up and for a moment could not work out why he was in a room with purple, paperless walls. Then he noticed the warm weight on his feet. Andy War-Howl, snoring softly.

When Rose had offered him the bed, he'd pointed out that some dog hair had been shed upon it. She'd laughed and apologized without the slightest suggestion that she intended to do anything about it. It was the sort of hospitality one might expect in a rookery full of thieves.

Maybe he shouldn't have been surprised. Her words had suggested that she was poor . . . But how could that be? She was all soft curves, suggesting luxury and ease.

Her reaction to Everly Park had taken him aback. Most ladies were delighted to hear about one of the finest houses in England. If she disapproved of even that subject, she would never find him a charming companion.

Not that he wanted to charm her. True, he'd taken hold of her arms at one point, and had guided her to a seat, but that had been because she looked as though she might swoon, and because he knew how dangerous an excitable nature could be. It had nothing to do with his wanting to touch her or be closer to her. In exceptional circumstances, even a gentleman could set aside a modicum of reserve.

He plucked at the soft, stretchy shirt she'd given him. When she'd discussed dressing him in castoffs, he'd been appalled, but the prospect of wearing stained clothes was even more appalling. He'd always detested being dirty.

As it turned out, this shirt and the slick trousers she called "track pants" were exceptionally comfortable for sleeping. He had not held out high hopes for the bed, which had no posts, let alone a canopy or curtains, but the mattress didn't have a single lump.

From this bedroom, he heard the front door to the apartment bang open. Andy let out a volley of roaring barks and Henry jumped to his feet and strode out into the main room, expecting an intruder.

It was Rose, carrying filmy bags in one hand. "You're up!" she said, pushing the door shut behind her. "I called Ryan this morning. He was dying to meet you, and he's off today, so I invited him to lunch with us." She leaned down to pat Andy, offering Henry an unparalleled view of the creamy valley between her breasts. "You don't think Jason will mind if he's there, do you?"

"Indeed, I have no idea," Henry said stiffly, walking over to the couch to sit down. It had not occurred to her to ask whether *he* minded.

Bags in hand, she walked over and sat down next to him.

She did not have naked legs, as she'd had last night, but the sight of her was nonetheless astonishing. He'd never seen a woman in trousers before. This faded blue pair, regrettably, had a hole in one knee; she hadn't even made an attempt to patch it. She wore it with a flowing shirt and sandals that bared most of her feet. They seemed to be made of rope, fashioned in a wedge shape, and he could not help but notice they had the effect of thrusting her generous but-tocks up in the air and exaggerating the sway of her hips.

He asked her, "What is your brother's trade?"

She tilted her head in confusion for a moment, then said, "Oh! He moves furniture. Like when people are moving from one house to another?"

"A laborer, then."

"Yes, but listen, he's got some thoughts about the whole time travel thing. He's into physics."

"He is educated?"

"He almost graduated from college." She lifted her chin in defi-ance. "He got into some trouble and he was in jail for a little while, and he's turned his life around."

Henry found himself mildly alarmed. "Did he kill someone?"

"No!" She shook her head, seeming half-annoyed, half-amused. "Do you think there might've been a more polite way to ask that?"

"No doubt there was," he admitted. "I have never been good at those indirect ways of speaking that society so admires."

Her expression softened. "I'll keep that in mind." She was al-ways quick to forgive him, he could not help but notice. "He broke into someone's house to steal some money, but they'd stolen it from him first. Don't be a dick about it, okay?"

"A dick?"

"Don't be rude."

"Very well," Henry grumbled. He still feared that her brother might take sharp exception to his taking up residence in his sister's quarters, and the revelation of his criminal past was scarcely reas-suring.

Rose picked up one of the bags. "Anyway, I got you a few things. But we'll need to stop at the sneaker store after we meet Jason." Off his perplexed look, she added, "The shoe store."

Henry hardly knew how to react to generosity from a woman

with a hole in her trousers. "Thank you, but I already have a fine pair of shoes."

"They're nice, but they don't really go with modern clothes."

"I don't have modern clothes, either."

"You're wearing them." She indicated his ensemble with a wave of her hand.

He looked down. "But surely these are only for sleeping." Even in her presence, he felt rather undone. "I can hardly go out in public in these shapeless garments. Everyone would stare and jape."

"No, it's your old clothes that would bring on the japes. This outfit's fine for now. Although . . ." She scrunched up her face in amusement. "You probably don't want to keep going commando."

This was outrageous. He sat up even straighter. "I have made very few commands since I have arrived! Far fewer than a man of my position, in such a—position, might well have been expected to. And may I say, I am not certain that even *one* of them has been obeyed . . ."

He trailed off because she was laughing at him. Not smirking; not tittering. Leaning over with her hands on her thighs, *guffawing*, one might even say.

"Sorry, sorry," she said, waving her hands, and not sounding particularly sorry at all. "Here, hang on . . ."

She bent down to rummage in the other bag at her feet and pulled out a packet. On the front was an image of a man's naked torso, wearing some kind of tight breeches that only came down to the middle of his thighs. Above it read the message, 2 BOXER BRIEFS.

What was this, and what did she mean by waving that in front of his face?

"That is an indecent illustration," he said.

"It's just a photograph of what's inside. A photograph is like . . . a realistic illustration that you can make in a moment. Like that."

She snapped her fingers. While he puzzled over this astounding statement, she set the packet on the table.

"Where did you buy such garments?"

She shrugged. "Walgreens. Who knew, right? Anyway, I got a few packs for you."

His outrage flared—even as the idea of wearing so little, in her presence, caused a stirring in his loins. She meant well. She simply had no concept of what was respectable.

"You have my thanks," he said, "but I cannot wear these on the street."

She pressed her lips together, appearing on the verge of laughter again. "Yeah, you don't want to do that. They go *under* the track pants you're wearing."

"Why?"

"Because . . . okay, how do I explain a dick print?" There was that word again, *dick*, which apparently meant *rude*. "The outline of your, uh, manhood is showing." He stared at her, trying to make sense of this statement, which sounded vaguely flattering.

She motioned toward the juncture of her thighs, astonishing him even more. His whole body roused, as if she had issued an invitation. "Through your pants," she said.

Then, to his utter mortification, he understood. Yes, that was a rude print, indeed. And her lascivious gesture had no doubt made that certain part of his anatomy even more obvious.

Henry picked up the bag from the floor and set it on his lap. "This would not be a problem if I were wearing properly tailored trousers, and not these pantaloons of slippery silk."

"I was fresh out of tailored trousers. Look, why don't you go to the bathroom and try those on and wash up and everything? I got you some shaving stuff and socks and a few other things. Like this . . ." She reached into the bag on his lap, and he startled, acutely aware of her hand's proximity to his privates. Was there no end to her shocking behavior? "Do you know what this is?"

He glared at the item in its clear case. "Of course I know what a toothbrush is."

She put it back in the bag and held up her hands, palms outward. "You clearly don't need my help, so I'll leave you to it."

Perhaps he did need her help, for once in the bathroom, he could not find a jar of tooth powder among her purchases. It took him a minute to realize the tube labeled *toothpaste* served the same purpose, and he accidentally squeezed out a great deal of it. It tasted violently of mint, but once he was done brushing, he had to admit that it felt as though the inside of his mouth was sparkling clean. He had always been fastidious. The modern plumbing she'd introduced him to the night before, as well as the ability to wash up every place that needed washing with warm water, had earned his grudging admiration.

She had also purchased an instrument labeled a razor. After turning it back and forth to inspect it, he decided to put off shaving, though he preferred to have his valet do it daily.

The undergarments Rose had purchased for him had no laces, but the fabric stretched. He tried one on, and it hugged his body in a strange but not unpleasant way. Perhaps they would restrain any traitorous twitchings of his loins.

He'd never even been aroused by a lady with whom he was not well acquainted, and especially not one from the lower classes. He'd always supposed that he was too intelligent and high-minded to leer at buxom beauties the way other men did, like dogs slavering over pork chops on their masters' plates.

So how was he to account for the way this fey creature roused his body and his senses? Or for his own alarm when she'd been pale and overcome with nerves, after the dog had run out on the roof? He'd felt that he could not bear to see her unwell.

Her manners were coarse, she swore like a fishwife, she had no fortune or family of consequence, and by her own blithe admission, the flower of her maidenhood had been plucked long before. True, almost any man would've been roused by her careless manner of dress, her voluptuous charms, the peal of her laughter, her fine blue eyes, and her disarming honesty . . . but all of that was not the point. He was not almost any man.

Perhaps it was her free spirit, or her nurturing nature.

Or perhaps traveling through time had scrambled his faculties . . . which seemed altogether likely.

He emerged from the bathroom carrying himself stiffly. Well, one part of him was not stiff, at least, and he meant to keep it that way. He half feared she would be staring at that particular part of him. The fact that she'd been bold enough to mention it aloud before still shocked him . . . even if he was glad to understand it.

She was in the kitchen, and her gaze didn't drift downward as she asked, "Do you want some coffee? I made some. Or would you rather have more tea?"

"I will take some coffee. Thank you." He didn't drink it as a habit, but some academics swore it sharpened their wits, and he supposed he needed every possible advantage.

She poured him a mug and handed it to him. "We'll have a big lunch at the restaurant. I'll just cut up some fruit now, if that sounds good?"

"Yes," he said, sitting down at the nearby dining table. It was still strange to be in a household so humble it did not employ even one servant. "That would be most satisfactory."

She reached into a deep basket and pulled out a large pineapple.

Henry couldn't help getting back to his feet to gawk at it, his chair scraping on the floor. How on earth had a lady of such limited means gotten her hands on one? The thought crossed his mind that she might've stolen it.

She lay it on its side on a wooden board. Surely, she didn't mean to actually—

She raised a large knife.

"Stop!" he thundered.

She jumped and gave a little shriek, the large knife falling from her hand and clattering onto the counter.

"What the hell!" she demanded, whirling around. With a shocked laugh, she added, "You scared the shit out of me!"

"Forgive me, madam," he said, as though his civility might balance out her vulgarity. "But you cannot mean to *cut up* that pineapple and *eat* it?"

Merriment danced in her eyes. "What else would I do with it?"

"Why, set it in the middle of the table and admire it. It must've been rashly expensive."

She shrugged. "It was on sale at the Jewel."

"You exchanged a jewel for it?" he asked, to clarify.

"No. That's the name of a grocery store." She turned around and chopped off the grand leafy crown.

Henry startled as though he'd witnessed some lesser form of execution. "Now you've ruined it. Even I, a duke, would not cut up and eat a *pineapple*."

She shot him a perplexed look over her shoulder. "Why are you being so weird?" Then she turned back and sliced away a length of the spiny rind.

He expected the fruit to be brown. People often kept them and displayed them until the leaves shriveled and the fruit grew soft with rot. But no. Her knife revealed golden, juicy flesh.

"You don't have to eat it if you don't want to," she told him as she cut away more of the rind. "I've got grapes and strawberries."

An incredible scent filled the air; the scent of indulgence itself. Almost involuntarily, he drew nearer to watch her cut the fruit into chunks. Juice soaked the wooden board.

"It's not that I don't *want* to," he said. "What is it like?"

She looked up, startled and slightly breathless. "What?"

"The fruit . . ." His mouth was watering now. He was standing right over her, so near that the tropical fragrance of the fruit mingled with the warm scent of her skin, and his awareness of her tempting curves made him feel like he'd been sleepwalking for the past two years, and had just woken up again. He swallowed. "It looks so succulent."

She was perhaps affected by their nearness, too. Her bosom heaved with a deep breath. Or was it that she was still startled from him shouting at her? He had never wanted to upset her nerves.

Tilting her head, she asked, "Are you telling me you've *never tried* pineapple?"

"I don't know anyone who has. It costs as much as a good horse."

"Seriously? I buy a couple of them a month. They cost about as much as . . . I don't know, three or four apples?" Rose's eyes danced in delight. "I guess I do have some luxuries you don't, Fancy Man. Like running hot water, and pineapple." She picked up a chunk and held it out to him. "Here."

He was aware that ordinarily, he would've balked at taking a piece of fruit someone was handling. But an image flashed through his mind of not only eating the pineapple right from her hand, but then licking the juice from her fingers.

He took the chunk of pineapple from her, put it in his mouth, and bit down. Flavor exploded in his mouth. Tartness, sweetness, sunshine.

"My God," he marveled, once he'd swallowed. "It's extraordinary."

She gave him a teasing look. "Well, I'm glad you like *something* here. I'll fix you a bowl. Do you want strawberries, too, or—"

"No. Pineapple." He'd had strawberries a hundred times or more.

She filled a good-sized bowl to overflowing, grabbed him a fork, and handed it to him. Still a bit stunned by the largesse, he sat down

with it. She took a transparent box out of the cabinet that he had
already discovered kept a wide array of food chilled.

"How does that cabinet stay cold?"

"Uh, it's refrigeration. It uses electricity, and . . . honestly, I have
no idea."

She sliced a few strawberries and put them and the rest of the
pineapple into a bowl for herself, then sat down with him. After
he'd eaten a couple of bites in silence, he realized he might reasonably be expected to make at least a polite effort at conversation.

"I am accustomed to taking my meals alone," he said, by way of
explanation.

"Oh." She frowned doubtfully. "I guess you can take your bowl
to the guest room."

"I—no, I did not mean it was my preference." Although he supposed it had been, in the past couple of years. "I only mean that I
am out of practice with conversation."

"Oh!" She looked a bit relieved as she laughed. "Well, good news,
we're *all* out of practice now. We just stare at screens and type at each
other. It's horrible. You'll love it."

But as they ate their fruit and drank their coffee, Rose chatted
easily about the size of various cities in the United States, and the
state of modern London—they had built a large clock tower, which
Henry could not help but approve of—giving Henry the opportunity to learn while admiring her captivating countenance.

He told himself that it would be well to remember that, if what
she'd said was true, he'd been ill-used by her. She'd cast a spell, like
a mythical siren singing across the waves, and had wrecked the
steady ship of his life upon her shores.

But he did not believe in magic. Surely, there was some other
explanation.

Before they left the apartment, Rose persuaded him to leave his
walking stick at home, explaining that it would look strange with

his modern clothes. They went down the stairs and stepped out onto the street, greeted by sunshine and a cacophony of growls and whines and beeps.

"What is that smell?" he asked Rose.

She took a sniff. "Italian beef." She pointed to the shop across the street advertising sandwiches.

"No, the acrid smell."

"Uh, exhaust, maybe? From the car engines?"

"How do those engines work?"

She laughed. "I have no idea. Aren't there bad smells in London, in your time? And in the country?"

"Of course." London smelled much worse than this city, mainly of cesspools, and the pastures and stables in the country had the expected odors. "But they are stenches I can name."

Redbrick buildings a few stories high, some with bright signs and messages, lined both sides of the streets, along with those steel coaches—cars. The only things of beauty were the trees, growing in squares of earth along the paved pathway. He looked up at the foliage, and a movement in the blue sky caught his eye.

He stopped and touched Rose's arm. "What is that? Some sort of kite?" It was narrow, with wings, so it was not a hot air balloon.

She grinned. "That's an airplane. Like a ship that flies through the sky."

He peered at her. "What do you mean, a ship?"

"Uh, there are a couple hundred people on there, and it's flying to another city."

"That cannot be true," he muttered, and stared up at the plane again. "How does it stay up?" He waited for it to plummet from the sky at any moment.

"I have no idea," she admitted again. "But I've been on them a bunch of times." The mere thought of that made him feel dizzy, and he looked down at the sidewalk.

"Children still play Scotch-hoppers," he realized aloud, seeing the sequence of squares chalked there.

"We call it hopscotch," Rose said, and to his surprise, she hop-skipped the boxes. As a mother pushing a little girl in a sort of little cart passed, they both looked at Rose and smiled. Rose beamed back.

Henry felt a smile twitching at his own lips. Perhaps he shouldn't be surprised to learn that she was reckless enough to fly through the sky.

Several men and women stood in line in front of an establishment a few doors down. A few of the women wore scarves that covered their head and shoulders. They looked down at Henry's good shoes, exchanged a look, and giggled among themselves. Clearly, Rose had been correct about his inappropriate footwear.

A short woman of middle age opened the door of the establishment as they passed, flipping a sign on it to read **ABIERTO** and **OPEN**. Rose waved at her, and the woman's eyes widened.

"*Tu nuevo novio?*" she asked Rose as she waved customers inside.

Rose shook her head, smiling. "*Solo un amigo.*" Henry's curiosity must've shown on his face, because she told him, "She asked who you were, and I said you were a friend."

As he continued with Rose down the sidewalk, he asked, "Were you two speaking Italian?"

"Spanish. It's common here, especially in this neighborhood." She gestured with her thumb back at the restaurant. "Those tacos are halal. That's why they get a lot of Muslim customers."

Tacos? Halal? Were these English words?

"Do you speak Spanish fluently?" He had met ladies and gentlemen from France, an Italian, and a Bavarian, but never a Spaniard.

She shook her head. "I only know the basics. A lot of my neighbors spoke it when we lived in Cicero, and I studied it at college." She glanced up at him. "Did women go to universities, in your time?"

"Rarely. But do not suppose, Miss Novak, that I have never before met an educated female. I will have you know that I am acquainted with two different female scientists."

"It's two more than I would've expected," she admitted.

He paused to stare at a large mural, depicting a grinning embellished skull, with living eyes in the sockets, surrounded by flowers.

"Isn't that amazing?" Rose said.

"It's terrifying," he snapped. "Is this meant to be art?"

She glanced around them and then stepped closer. "That's rude. You're going to get your ass kicked."

He snorted. "I do not have an ass."

A mischievous smile curved her lips upward again. "Oh yes you do."

"I have four thoroughbred stallions in my stables, and I might be riding one across Everly Park right now, had it not been for your fecklessness."

He felt a twinge of regret when her smile extinguished. But he was a man of truth, and what had he said that was not true?

"I already told you it was an accident," she retorted.

"Yes, well—you are provoking me excessively with your nonsense."

She sighed and looked back at the wall. "Seriously, we're proud of our murals."

Henry gestured again toward the skull, wreathed in flowers. "But it is blasphemous." A mockery of those who had buried loved ones. "She is a dead woman, and yet she lives!"

Rose gave a little shudder, and Henry felt vindicated. "See?" he asked. "It sends a shiver down your spine, too."

"No, it doesn't," she protested. "I just had a weird feeling for a moment. But this celebrates *Día de los Muertos.* Day of the Dead. It's big in Mexico, and other places, too."

"I've never heard of it," Henry admitted.

"It's when you remember the people you love who have died.

You set out their favorite foods and drinks on altars, or by their graves. In this neighborhood, they have a parade, and some people paint their faces like that." She gestured at the woman on the wall.

"This is a painting of a live woman?" He considered it again. "I suppose that is a bit less gruesome. But remembering the dead is not festive."

She gave him a sympathetic smile. "I know what you mean. But maybe it's a way of remembering that the people we've lost are still really with us."

"They're not," he said shortly.

"Agree to disagree. Come on, we're late."

Eight

Rose beckoned him to keep walking, and he fell into step with her. He surprised her by asking, "Do you truly think you're a witch?"

"Oh, I don't know. Do you truly think you're a duke?" she teased.

"I am less convinced of it by the moment," he grumbled. "But if you were truly a witch, why would you live in such reduced circumstances?"

She whirled on him. "What do you mean, *reduced circumstances*?"

He gave her a look that said, *Come on*. "Miss Novak. You live in a few rooms, in an undistinguished neighborhood, you are a spinster, and you have holes in your clothing." He gestured at the knee of her jeans. "Is this the life of someone with great magical power? I mean no offense, of course."

"Mean no offense?" she echoed. "It *is* mean, and I *am* offended. Most people don't live in a freaking castle!"

"No, of course not, but—"

"I've worked really hard to get all I have!" She crossed her arms under her breasts—and caught him glancing at them, but only for a fleeting moment. When he'd first arrived, she didn't mind him checking her out. Now, it irritated her. "And now I have a decent job, and—"

"What do you mean, a job?"

"An occupation? Place of employment?"

"You have a place of employment?"

"Of course! How do you think I pay for things?"

"I assumed your brother . . ." He trailed off, and she shook her head. "What is your profession?"

"I work for the museum. You wouldn't understand. And I *like* my life. I've never done spells asking for extravagant things. Until I asked for an old-fashioned gentleman, which was obviously—" She cut herself off before she said, *A huge mistake.*

She gestured at the front of the restaurant, with its black painted bricks and its bright red door. "Anyway, we're here."

Henry looked as though he was trying to think of something to say, but couldn't find the words. Fine. He'd said enough.

Rose led Henry into the restaurant buzzing with customers sitting at tables. The air-conditioner chill and the smell of grilled burgers greeted her. Local artwork hung on the walls. Henry would probably hate that, too. She told the hostess they wanted to sit on the patio, and they went through the restaurant and the back door. Her brother, wearing a Rage Against the Machine T-shirt and jeans, was sitting alone at a table.

"Ryan!" she called with a wave as she and Henry walked over to him. The wooden pergola that covered the patio turned the sunshine into stripes. "This is Henry."

Ryan shoved his hair back from his forehead and stared up at Henry with raised eyebrows. His eyes, always swimming-pool blue, looked even bluer because they were slightly bloodshot. That worried her a little. She'd seen that before.

"Shit," he said.

It wasn't the most polite greeting, and Henry glowered at him.

Rose sat down and motioned for Henry to do the same. "Your eyes look red," she couldn't help but say to Ryan.

He gave a huff of irritation. "Have you seen the pollen count?"

Right. Seasonal allergies had always hit him hard. He took after their mom that way.

"I thought that was it," she said, not expecting him to believe the lie, but hoping he'd appreciate the effort. She knew it didn't help him when she feared the worst. At the same time, he had no idea how exhausting it had been to love him while worrying about his addictions.

"There's Jason," Rose said, spotting him walking in their direction. He wore a button-down white shirt and navy suit pants and had a suit jacket draped over his arm. She raised a hand in greeting, but he was staring down at his phone.

Turning back to Henry, she said, "Ryan saw your portrait, too."

"Yeah, before it got fucked up," Ryan said.

Judging from Henry's appalled expression, he was familiar with the f-word. "Watch your language around him," Rose told Ryan. As Jason reached their table, Ryan's words sunk in. "What do you mean, it got fucked up?"

"Take a look," Jason said. He turned his phone around to show them a photo.

It was the same painting Rose had stared at the night before, in its gilded frame, depicting a library, a golden astrolabe on the desk, and an open window to the countryside beyond. But instead of Henry, there was a gray shape delineated with a few sketchy brushstrokes.

"Oh my Goddess," she blurted out. "Who did that?"

Jason, who'd been staring at Henry, gave her a wry look. "Best guess is you."

"That's how it looked right before I was unexpectedly dragged here," Henry said.

"I figured." Jason held out a hand to Henry. "It's good to meet in person, Your Grace."

"I suppose," Henry said, looking cross, but shaking his hand. Jason pulled out a chair and sat down with them.

Still trying to puzzle things out, Rose said, "But we remember the finished painting."

"Everyone does," Ryan said. "It's already in the news. That it's been vandalized."

"Ohh, that's bad," Rose breathed.

As Jason set the phone face down, he glanced around them. The nearby tables were empty. "Could be worse, but yeah," he said in a low tone. "I spent the morning with the police and Aaron Coleman."

"Ugh," Rose said. "Is he going to be hanging around Chicago, then?"

"I'm even less happy about it than you are," Jason said.

Rose shook her head. "I don't understand why it's ruined. You were saying with that rule of consistency or whatever, everything else would stay the same."

Ryan shrugged. "Or maybe, like in Deutsch's theory, when you zapped this guy to the present"—he jerked his thumb at Henry—"you opened up a parallel universe. We could be in a dimension now where the painting was completed, but then uncompleted."

"A parallel universe?" Henry repeated, staring at Ryan. "Explain."

Ryan leaned forward. "Oh, dude, you've got to hear about this." He paused and squinted thoughtfully. "But first, you're going to need to know a few things about subatomic particles."

Jason raised a palm. "Hold off on that, okay?"

A smiling server came up to the table. "Hi, guys!" She passed out menus. "Can I get you started with some drinks?"

They all ordered. When she had retreated, Jason said, "Let me tell you what we know about the astrolabe. There's a letter from someone in the early 1700s in Zugarramurdi, Spain. He claims he used the astrolabe to travel about one hundred years forward in time to escape the Spanish Inquisition."

"Zugarramurdi," Ryan repeated. "Basque Country, right?"

"Yeah," Jason said, sounding mildly surprised. Rose wasn't. Ryan knew all kinds of things. "The letter writer refers to notes from his father, who said he'd also used it to time travel."

"Did it still have the moonstone in it then?" Rose asked.

"Yeah. But when the astrolabe got sold in 1840, the moonstone had already been removed, and there aren't any accounts of actual time travel with it after that."

"So my spell with the moonstone brought Henry here, just as he was touching the astrolabe," Rose said. "Moonstones *are* called the Traveler's Stone. Are you thinking the astrolabe might be a time travel device, if we put the moonstone back in it? And then maybe I could do a reversal spell?"

Jason said, "I think it's worth a try. This isn't the first time you've shown a lot of talent with stones."

He meant the malachite she'd blessed and given to Emily that had helped free Griffin from stone. All this time, and Rose still had trouble believing it. But now that this moonstone had made its way to her, and she'd used it for time travel . . .

"Maybe you're right," she said.

Frowning, Henry turned to Jason. "Do you have the notes from the father who used the astrolabe?"

"I wish. An art collector in the 1950s heard that your painting contained a secret message about it. I don't even know where he got that from. So I acquired the painting to get a better look at the astrolabe and to look for the message."

Rose perked up. "Did you find anything?"

"I thought there might be something in the details, or the back side of the canvas, or under infrared light, but no." He sighed, tapping something on his phone. "Nothing on the frame, either."

"Of course there is no secret message," Henry declared. "I met the painter. He is a common man."

"He's a famous artist," Rose said, with a note of reproach.

Henry waved this off. "Where is my astrolabe?"

Jason looked up from his phone with a grin. "Glad you asked." He turned the screen around to them again. "This guy's got it. Victor Reuter."

Rose looked at the photo of a handsome, mustached, gray-haired man in a tuxedo. Jason asked her, "Name ring a bell?"

It did sound familiar. Ryan was about to say something when it came to her. "Yes! He's donated a bunch of money to the museum."

"Right in one," Jason said.

"We moved him last year," Ryan said. Rose turned to him in surprise. Ryan added, "Into that mansion in Lincoln Park."

Jason gave a low whistle. "That could be good."

"That one you sent me a picture of?" Rose asked Ryan.

Her brother nodded, looked around them, and said in a lower voice, "I heard a rumor that he bribed two aldermen to get a billion-dollar parking garage contract."

"Corruption, here in Chicago? I'm shocked," Rose quipped. She loved her city, but bribes were a time-honored tradition.

Jason looked over at the server approaching with the drinks. "Figure out what you're going to order," he said.

Ryan and Rose chose quickly, but Henry gave a hassled sigh over what he called a *confounding bill of fare*, and Rose cringed as he demanded to know what black beans were. When the server informed him they were beans that were black, he gave a second hassled sigh and ordered the pork and black beans.

Once the server retreated, Jason informed Rose, "She'll get a big tip."

Rose told Henry, "If you don't like the beans, I'll trade you my French fries."

"Thank you, but I do not care for French cuisine."

Ryan was peering at Jason. "Does Reuter know this thing is magical?"

"He must know it's rumored to be. It's not the first time he's bought something we wanted."

Rose raised her eyebrows. "Why is that?"

Jason paused, looking as though he was deliberating. "One of the reasons my group exists is to keep things away from people like Reuter."

"How did he obtain it?" Henry asked.

"He bought it at auction from a private collector in Dubai. Unfortunately, I didn't see it was up for auction until after the sale."

Henry grunted. "I would offer him a fortune, could I but draw upon my bank."

"He doesn't need more money," Jason said.

"Then what does he want?" Rose asked.

Jason shrugged. "All these superrich guys either want to rule the world, or want to be immortal. In this case, it could be both. So we'd like to get it away from him before he finds a way to track down the moonstone, or finds a way to make the astrolabe work without it."

Henry gave a huff of frustration. "It is rightfully mine."

"It's somewhere in that house." Jason took a sip of his tea.

"You don't know that," Ryan said. "He must have other properties."

Jason nodded. "Sure. He's got a mansion in Zurich."

"Lake Zurich?" Rose asked, thinking of the northwestern suburb.

"Zurich, Switzerland," he clarified, as Ryan laughed at her.

"Shut up," Rose protested, but she laughed, too. "Lake Zurich's kind of fancy!"

Jason said, "Plus an estate in Florida, where he used to spend every winter. But ever since he bought the astrolabe, he's barely left the Chicago residence. So yeah, I don't know for sure, but in my experience, with objects like these, people's primitive instincts kick in. They don't want their prized possession out of their sight."

"It can't be easy to get in there," Ryan said.

"Usually, no. But he's hosting a charity gala at the mansion in a few weeks."

"Why would he do such a thing?" Henry asked.

"For good PR. Or so he can meet with someone without anyone noticing, because he'll talk to dozens of guests." His gaze slid to Rose. "There are still a few tickets available."

Ryan folded his arms across his chest. "The guy's trouble. My boss said he's got a lot of enemies."

"And I'm one of them," Jason said. Rose's head swiveled around to stare at him, waiting for an explanation.

Jason shifted in his seat. "I, uh, once bought something right out from under him."

Rose asked, "So Henry and I could try to find the astrolabe at the mansion and . . ." She shook her head. "Use it for a reversal spell? I don't even really know how." Henry nodded, agreeing with her skepticism.

"Even if it can be used, it would probably take a lot of tries," Jason agreed. He swept the café again with a glance. "I'm sure my colleagues would offer a generous reward to anyone who obtains it for us."

Henry sat straighter in his seat. "Mr. Yun," he said, even though Jason had definitely said to call him Jason. "Are you suggesting you'd like to hire us as common thieves?"

Jason looked to Ryan. "You know the house's floor plan."

Ryan seemed to be staring right through Jason. "Count me out. I'm not going to jail again."

Jason raised a finger as if to say, *Hold that thought,* and the server arrived at the table again with their food. "Oh, this looks great!"

Rose said too brightly. Jason seemed to be texting with someone. Once they were alone again, she asked in an undertone, "Why would your group hire us, anyway? Instead of, you know, professionals?"

Jason grimaced. "We don't have a contractor right now."

"What happened to the last one?"

He held up his hands. "He retired. And every time we bring someone new in, we run the risk of exposure."

Rose glanced at Henry. She really did want to help him get back, if she could. He was cautiously putting a forkful of black beans into his mouth, and he gave an unconscious shrug as if to say, *Not bad*.

She considered what Jason was saying. "No one would be surprised if the social media manager at the museum went to a museum benefit."

Jason scrunched up his face. "I think it would be better to go under assumed names. And maybe even change up your look."

"I can see that." If she was seen sneaking around, it could be awkward. She looked to Henry. "What are you thinking?"

"Under the circumstances, I cannot object to this bit of trickery. If we can find the astrolabe, we do not need to take it . . . but we can attempt to return me to my time." He cut a piece of his pork. "Or perhaps, since time travel appears to be possible . . . a few years before that?"

Her heart sank. Of course he wanted to be with his wife again.

"I have no idea how I would do that," she admitted. "That's a whole different thing from a reversal spell. I just feel in my gut that I can't put someone in any year they want to be."

Henry nodded soberly. "But you think you could undo what you did."

"Yeah. Reversal spells are common, so I feel like it's at least possible? Though it probably won't work, either."

"Almost certainly not," he said, which made her feel bad and took the pressure off her at the same time. He looked to Jason. "It is not against the law to skulk around a fine house, I presume? Guests do it at Everly Park all the time."

"No, that's fine."

Ryan asked, "What if he's got, like, a hidden GPS tracker on the astrolabe, or some kind of motion sensor, or something?"

Jason shook his head. "Trackers aren't small enough to hide. We don't even use them in the museum, because you risk damaging the piece."

"I wouldn't attach something electromagnetic to something magical," Rose mused aloud. "It seems like you might ruin its energy."

Ryan picked at the label of the bottle of his nonalcoholic beer. "He's going to have security cameras everywhere. And if you knock out the Wi-Fi, they'll know something's up."

"Not if you do it a few minutes here and there," Jason said. "I've got a portable jammer, and I can give you anti-recognition glasses that look like regular ones."

"Sick," Ryan said, sounding impressed in spite of himself. Rose felt as befuddled as Henry looked. Ryan explained, "They reflect infrared light so your face doesn't show up on CCTV footage."

"Wow," Rose said.

Ryan added to Jason, amused, "For a museum curator, you're a sketchy motherfucker."

Jason's mouth quirked upward, but Henry gasped.

Rose assured Henry, "He doesn't mean it literally. It's just an insult."

"An insult not to be borne!" He turned to Jason. "Does honor not require you to call him out?"

"Nah, I'm good," Jason said and checked his phone. "I've got a call with PR in twenty minutes."

Rose felt a pang of guilt that she'd put Jason into this predicament—not to mention what she'd done to Henry. "At least it's not a theft."

Jason nodded, still looking at his phone. "If you could tell me where in the house the astrolabe is, that would be a huge help. We can give you and Henry fifty grand apiece for that. And any close-up photos would be great."

Holy crap. That was a lot of money for something she'd been about to do anyway. Although scoping out a house for a possible theft was probably a crime, too, now that she thought about it.

Ryan sighed. "I bet I know where it is."

"How?" Rose demanded. "Reuter didn't even have the astrolabe when he moved in, right?" Ryan had said that was a year ago.

"No. But a guest bedroom had that raised paneling, whatever you call that?"

"Wainscoting?" Jason suggested.

"Yeah, I guess. One of those panels is on some kind of hinge? It swings right out and there's a storage space. I don't know if it was always like that, or what."

Rose gaped at her brother. "How did you find a secret compartment?"

"We banged a nightstand too hard against it, and it sounded weird. So I went back later to see why."

Henry was looking at Ryan with new respect. "It was uncommonly observant of you to notice such a thing." Jason nodded his agreement.

Ryan gave a dismissive snort. "I've pushed a lot of furniture against walls." He took a drink of coffee.

"As I said before, keen observation and investigation are two of the hallmarks of a scientific mind," Henry insisted. "Few would have noticed, and fewer still would've investigated, especially amid what was surely a long day of heavy labor."

Rose wanted to hug Henry. Ryan didn't get a lot of praise for his intellect these days, after getting a constant stream of it growing up. Ryan gave a dismissive shake of his head, but she knew how much he appreciated it.

Ryan said, "There are back stairs by the kitchen. That's how we took everything up. The guy's got all these vintage pinball machines and arcade games like Frogger and whatever that weigh a ton. But the bedroom I'm talking about was a guest bedroom near the top of the stairs."

"There could be many such secret compartments in the house," Henry said soberly. "I do not like our chances, but we may at least look."

Rose nodded. "We'll look in that guest bedroom first."

Ryan picked at a cuticle. "I still don't like it."

"It'll be fine," she assured him.

Jason said, "In the meantime, should we put Henry here up in a hotel room? I can arrange something."

Inwardly, Rose sighed. Of course, that made total sense. The duke would feel much more at home in a luxury hotel suite than in her guest room. His presence here clearly had more to do with the magical astrolabe and its missing moonstone than with her amateur love spell . . . even if part of her still kept thinking that maybe, despite his grumpiness at being in the twenty-first century, he might wind up liking her, after all.

Henry cleared his throat. "As I understand it, my being a guest in Rose's home will cause no harm to her reputation. If I am not importuning her too much, I am sure it will be more convenient to our shared endeavor if I remain there."

Rose's heart did a little leap. "I'm not importuned."

"If fortune favors us, I will not be there for long," Henry added, making her heart settle right back down again.

"It'll make things a lot easier," Jason agreed. "Your Grace, let me give you some walking-around money. It's the least my colleagues and I can do. Rose can hold on to it for you." He added to Rose, "Put your purse on your lap." It was such an odd order that she obeyed.

Jason glanced around again at the empty tables near them and then handed Rose what appeared to be a fat stack of hundred-dollar bills secured with a silver clip.

Ryan leaned back in his chair as if it were poison. "Okay, that looks like drug money," he muttered. Rose stuffed the cash in her purse, and before she zipped it up again, she peeled off a couple of bills and put them in her wallet.

Henry was averting his eyes, as if to avoid witnessing something indecent. "Never in my life have I been in need of financial assistance."

Ryan gave him a patient smile. "Bruh, you were born with financial assistance."

Henry repeated, "Bruh?"

After learning the term *jagoff*, he probably thought it was another insult. "It's short for brother," Rose said quickly.

Henry said to Ryan, "It is true that I have always enjoyed great privilege." He looked thoughtful. "It is possible that I have made justifications for it that do not withstand my own intellectual rigor."

Awww. Rose admitted, "I think it's human nature to take good luck for granted."

"I've got to go," Jason said abruptly, looking at his phone. He stood up, his chair scraping against the floor.

The meeting with the PR team. "Good luck," Rose told him, and he headed for the door.

Henry turned cautiously to Ryan. "I have two questions, if I may."

"Shoot," Ryan said around a mouthful of his sandwich.

Henry paused, and then asked, "Why was Mr. Yun not offended by the epithet you bestowed upon him?"

Ryan blinked. "The what now?"

Henry's face colored slightly. "The insult having to do with Mr. Yun's mother."

"Motherfucker?" Ryan gave a Robert De Niro–esque shrug, the corners of his mouth turning down. "It was just a joke. I mean, it's not polite."

"Politeness has never been one of his things," Rose said lightly.

"Be careful who you call that, though," Ryan advised Henry. Rose grinned. Henry would never, in a million years, say that word. "What was the other thing?"

"You were going to explain . . . particles?"

"Subatomic particles." Ryan sat up straighter and launched into an incomprehensible explanation as Rose finished her French fries. She couldn't tell how much of it Henry was following, but he seemed riveted. *Nerds*, she thought fondly.

When they reached a pause in the conversation, Rose said to Ryan, "We're going to buy Henry some gym shoes. You want to come with?"

Nine

N ah, I gotta get going," Ryan said, pushing his plate away and standing up.

Henry hoped they would have the opportunity to talk again, for Ryan clearly had a superior intellect. And he'd surprised Henry by calling him *brother*. Henry had never been the kind of man that others befriended easily . . . but perhaps his station had been a barrier, as well as his personality.

Ryan surprised Henry further by clapping him on the shoulder in a familiar manner. "I'll bring you a few books about multiverses. You've got to read about gravitational time dilation."

"That would be most kind." The opportunity to learn about futuristic scientific theories and discoveries was certainly one advantage of being hurled forward in time.

He couldn't deny to himself that Rose's company was another. She was impulsive, and occasionally maddening, but even in this strange new world, he found himself surprisingly at ease with her.

Ryan added, "Oh, and you should go to the Adler."

"We should!" Rose exclaimed, squeezing his other arm. "It's a planetarium."

This meant nothing to him. Ryan said, "It's like a science center about the universe."

"Ah. I would very much like to go," Henry said. Perhaps there would be other men of science there who could shed light on his predicament.

"Let's do it!" Rose said. "Shoes, and then planetarium."

After Ryan departed, Rose got the attention of the server and gave her two of the bills Jason had given them, asking for change. A short, awkward pause hung between him and Rose once they were alone again.

Then Rose asked, "If you don't mind my asking, what was your wife like?"

"Ah. Well . . ."

He wanted to give her an adequate answer, because Charlotte deserved that much. And because it might suggest to Rose that he was not as disagreeable as he seemed, having secured the love of an excellent wife. Perhaps, too, if Rose knew what he had lost, she would have a better understanding of why he was the way he was.

"Charlotte was the daughter of a gentleman, but not of the nobility. That caused some to cast aspersions, though not to my face."

"Oh, *really*?" Rose's face lit up. Given her egalitarian nature, he was not surprised this pleased her. In fact, he'd probably said that first in order to impress Rose.

"Yes. I met her at a country ball."

She leaned forward, apparently fascinated. "You didn't strike me as someone who'd like dancing."

"I did not say I *liked* it. But it would be absurd to not know how. It would be like not knowing how to ride a horse. Or to catch a fish, which I also do not like."

"Right." Rose had a soft look in her eyes. "But I bet you liked dancing with Charlotte."

"Well, yes. You will, perhaps, appreciate the nature of our first conversation. She said she'd heard I was a man of science, and talked about her collection of minerals." Which had not been easy to do during a Scotch reel, given the loud music and the skipping about.

"Seriously? This is a woman after my own heart." She was smiling, but he caught a hint of wistfulness in her tone.

In Henry's time, he had experienced a few uncomfortable social situations, but none of them had compared to being the apparent answer to a lady's love spell. He hardly knew how to behave. He could only console himself with the fact that she'd already declared it a mistake . . . which, somehow, did not feel like much of a consolation at all.

"Did your wife have a favorite stone?" Rose asked.

"Yes. A rose quartz, although they are hardly rare."

"It's my favorite, too! It's a love-stone. I mean, for all kinds of love," she hurried to add. "Including self-love."

Unlike Rose, Charlotte had not ascribed magical powers to minerals. He surely would've known if she had. Yet was it not strange that he should find himself in the close company of another female who was fascinated by stones?

Another female who fascinated *him*.

There was no need to deny it, at least to himself. Affections were fickle things. He'd often observed this in others. No doubt his shocking circumstances had confused his brain. The server returned and set a tray with banknotes and coins in front of Rose. If the woman was surprised that Rose was paying, and not Henry, she didn't show it.

Rose set a few banknotes on the table and put the rest, along with the coins, in her purse. "I love hearing people talk about things they're obsessed with. They get this energy in their voice and this light in their eyes, and it's adorable. Like when you and Ryan were talking about particles."

Was she saying that she'd found him attractive, just then? Henry felt a smile creep across his face.

"In my youth, I was somewhat given to impromptu lectures about topics such as asteroids and battles, much to my father's chagrin."

"I don't believe that," she said loyally—though why she should be loyal to him, he had no idea.

"It is quite true. Once after a particularly fine dinner party, with no less than the King of Prussia also in attendance, my father told me, 'Many people envy me my position. But when they learn how much you talk about the stars, and how little you manage to say in response to anything else, I believe they envy me a bit less.'"

Her mouth fell open in indignation. "That's a terrible thing to say to a child!"

"I was fifteen."

"Still a child," she said stoutly.

He would've called a fifteen-year-old a young man, but maybe there was some truth to this. By then, he had grown to nearly his full height, and his voice had deepened, but his moods had been fickle as ever—perhaps even more so—and he had not yet developed his confidence.

She asked more seriously, "Was your father always mean to you?"

"Not at all. He was kind enough." Henry had a great deal of sympathy for his father. Every man hoped for a certain kind of son, with an amiable manner and conventional interests, and Henry had never been that.

"And he only said that in jest," Henry added truthfully. It was a curious thing, how people could say countless things to you over the years, and yet one careless comment could become lodged in one's heart.

"Well, you can always be a nerd around me," she said. *Nerd* meant an artless enthusiast, he supposed. "Once I dated a guy for a year because every time I was about to break up with him, he'd talk about crypto and he'd look so cute and excited."

"Crypts? He was an archaeologist?"

"No, sorry. Cryptocurrency."

Henry looked down at the banknotes in front of her. "How can currency be cryptic?"

She laughed. "Well, *I* don't really understand cryptocurrency. But he finally broke up with me because I wouldn't invest in it."

"He sounds like a cad," Henry declared. "You must avoid men with strange currency."

"It might be a red flag," she said doubtfully. "That's what we call a warning signal about someone."

"Ah. Such as a reason to avoid them?"

"Exactly." She gave him a sheepish smile. "Unfortunately, when there's a red flag, I tend to run toward it like a bull. And I'm not even a Taurus!" She pushed her chair back and stood up.

"Astrology again," he said wryly, getting to his feet.

"I get to be a nerd about something, too," she said as she picked up her purse.

"Fair point." They walked toward the door. "If you are not a Taurus, then . . . ?"

She gave him a playful look over her shoulder. "Henry Leighton-Lyons. Are you asking me what my sign is?"

"It was you who originated the subject," he said in his own defense.

"I'm an Aquarius."

"And what is an Aquarius lady like?"

She grinned. "I guess you'll find out."

Out on the sidewalk, Henry walked a half step behind her, clasping his hands behind his back in his usual manner. They passed another mural, this one depicting a woman with monarch butterfly wings. Butterflies, he knew, were a symbol of rebirth. They went into the slumber of a chrysalis and emerged in a triumphant new form. Why did the idea tickle at his brain?

"So you're staying with me for a while," Rose said lightly. "In my reduced circumstances."

She was smiling, but he winced. Rose, he now suspected, was not poor, despite her trousers with a hole in them. She was just not rich, and he was used to everyone being rich.

"Miss Novak. I fear that I have been . . . a jagoff." Surprise lit her features, and then something that looked like actual delight. "I did not mean to insult your home. I would say more, but my father often told me to never spoil an apology with an excuse."

"That's good advice," Rose admitted. "Though it sounds impossible to follow."

Henry gave a rueful chuckle. "Isn't most good advice?"

"Well, you've got a right to make excuses. One minute, you're in your nice castle, and the next minute, you're in bizarro world. I think you're doing pretty well, under the circumstances." She gave him a sideways look. "And you didn't mind sitting down with a criminal, after all."

He'd all but forgotten that. "Your brother clearly has a lively intellect," he said, aware that his assessment was influenced by the fact that Ryan seemed to like him. "And he strikes me as a good man."

"He really is. But he had an expensive drug addiction." The sudden sadness in her eyes made Henry want to embrace her. At the same time, hearing her words, everything made sense.

"I understand perfectly," he said in a low voice.

She peered up at him. "You do?"

"I know of a man who has come under the thrall of opium." He was thinking of an astronomer who had once published a theory about an invisible sort of radiation emanating from the sun. "It has been my unhappy observation that a fine mind is no defense against the world's troubles, and there are cures that become their own disease."

An unwelcome bright ray of realization pierced his consciousness. He could've been speaking of himself.

His hands were still clasped behind his back, but Rose slowed down, reached over, and extricated one of them, taking it in her own. "What's the matter?"

He hadn't said anything. How was it that she could read his thoughts and feelings so well? He wasn't sure that they should be holding hands, but he didn't want to pull away.

"I realize now that my search to turn back time was a sort of addiction," he confessed. "Like opium or liquor, it dulled the pain." How had he not seen it before? Embarrassed by the sympathy in her eyes, he looked down at their joined hands. "This world of yours is filled with uncomfortable truths."

"That's always been my experience," she said gently, and gave his hand a squeeze. "But don't be too hard on yourself." She let go of him and tilted her head to the right.

She pointed up at the sign that read **SNEAKER STARS**. "Here's the shoe store."

When he walked in, he expected the smells of leather, wax, and polish. Instead, the odors were faint and alien, and a wall of shelves displayed perhaps forty shoes, many in brilliant colors. Two men in the corner of the shop were engaged in earnest conversation, and he supposed the one wearing blue trousers was the shopkeeper.

Rose grabbed a bright purple shoe. "What do you think? This would be so fun on you."

"I have seen more tasteful shoes on circus performers."

The shopkeeper walked over to them, asking, "Hey. What are you looking for today?"

With a mischievous sparkle in her eyes, Rose set the purple shoe back in place. "My friend here is from England, and he wants something really wild."

The man's face brightened. "All right, all right." He strode over and grabbed a pair in a shocking shade of green-yellow with confusing, crisscrossing orange stripes. "These just dropped. Straight fire."

"Good Lord," Henry said. "They look as though they glow in the dark."

"Yep. Shoelaces, toe box, and heel," the man said, pointing to each.

Henry gave Rose an admonishing look, and then explained, "The lady was teasing me. In truth, I would prefer something . . . unobtrusive."

"Ahh, a minimalist." The man walked over and grabbed an all-white shoe. "These are your grails."

"White is great for summer," Rose said, not teasing now.

Henry hoped to be gone before summer . . . didn't he? Henry scanned the wall again. There were no brown shoes, and the black ones were tall and reminded him of a horse hoof.

"Very well," he told the shopkeeper, wondering why this white shoe had a curved patch on the side and small holes punched into the top. "How soon can they be ready?"

Rose laughed and explained the store had the shoes already made in every size. After trying on one pair that was too large, and one that was too tight, he sank his feet into a perfect shoe.

It felt . . . soft. He tightened the laces and tied them, put on the other shoe, and stood up. It felt as though he was standing on pillows. Firm pillows, molded to the arch of his foot.

"Who made these shoes?" he demanded.

The man said, "Uh, they're Nikes?" His lips twitched. "Super niche, you probably never heard of them."

"No, I have not." Henry stood up and walked a few steps. "They are remarkable! I feel as though I am walking on clouds."

"We'll take them," Rose said to the shopkeeper. She scooped up Henry's dress shoes and tossed them into her voluminous purse. "He'll wear them now."

"Great." The man picked up the box and took it to a counter. Rose followed him.

Henry walked slowly over to join them, appreciating the comfort of each step. "The Nikes are masters of their craft."

Rose giggled as she pulled out a few of the banknotes Jason had given her. "I'm pretty sure you just like modern gym shoes."

After they left the store, Henry said, "I noticed that Mr. Yun's clothing was more similar to that of my time."

"Oh." Rose stopped on the sidewalk. "Well, yeah, he was wearing a suit, because he went into work."

"I would like such attire, as it is acceptable." If he'd been dressed like Mr. Yun, he would've felt a little more like himself.

Rose shrugged. "I mean, I could order some business wear for you, but it won't be that comfortable."

Henry looked down at his shapeless attire. "On the contrary. I should be much more comfortable."

As soon as the words were out of his mouth, they sounded absurd to him. How could he ever be comfortable in this world?

"Ready for the planetarium?" she asked brightly.

Suddenly, the idea of going to yet another unfamiliar place, and speaking to more foreign people, seemed like too much to manage. Even in his own time, he would have found it taxing to have lunch with two strangers such as Jason and Ryan. Well, Rose was a stranger, too, he reminded himself, even if she did not quite feel like one. But he had not even had time to consider the many startling things all three of them had said, and to ponder what it all meant for his current predicament.

"Might we go tomorrow?" he asked, after what he knew had been too long of a pause. "I do want to go, but today I would like some time to myself, to . . . to think."

Sympathy and understanding washed over her face. "Oh, I'll bet. You probably feel like your brain is full."

That elicited a startled chuckle from him. "Yes, precisely."

She gave him a winsome smile, clearly pleased that she'd gotten it right. "And with your big brain, that's saying something. This way." She indicated the direction with a tilt of her head.

As they walked, she said, "If you want to hole up in the guest room, I won't bother you. You can just make yourself at home." She winced. "I mean, *not* your home, obviously."

"I understood what you meant," Henry said. It came out too brusque, so he added, "Thank you."

Ten

On the following morning, Henry felt ready for the excursion to the planetarium. He had slept from seven p.m. the night before to seven a.m., which had shocked him. Ordinarily, he had a propensity for insomnia. Rose pointed out that he really hadn't gotten much sleep the night before that, and reminded him that the time travel had made him dizzy.

After they left the apartment building, she led him to the corner and pointed at a bench covered with a small roof. "Here's where we wait for the bus. Which is, like, a big car with lots of passengers."

As they waited, Rose asked him about his mother, who had died giving birth to him, and seemed glad to learn that his much older sisters were still alive and happily settled with children. She asked him about how his father died, and when she learned it had been after a long bout of consumption, she pointed out that expected deaths were still difficult.

He learned that her mother had died when Rose had been twenty, of cancer, but her father had been killed years before that, in a road accident. Henry expressed his condolences again. He did not say that he never would've guessed such a lively lady had such a tragic past.

"Thanks. Ryan and I miss them a lot," she said. "They really loved each other, too. They got engaged after seeing each other for three months!"

"Is that unusual?" Henry asked. "I courted Charlotte for two before proposing to her, and we were wed the month after that."

Her pretty mouth fell open. "That's so fast! And it's not much time to plan a wedding."

"There is not much to plan, is there? We obtained a special license from the archbishop in London, and set a date at the parish church. It should have been sooner, but one of my sisters and her husband insisted on attending, despite living far away."

She tilted her head. "How many people came to your wedding?"

Henry counted them on his fingers. "My other sister and her husband, a neighbor with whom I had attended Eton, Charlotte's brother and his wife, and her parents."

She looked astonished. "Why so small?"

The question struck him as silly. "Seven witnesses are surely enough. When the Duke of Devonshire married Lady Georgiana Spencer, there were only five."

"Huh." She shook her head. "Here and now, people usually have at least a few dozen people. Some of them have a hundred, two hundred guests." She grinned, evidently enjoying his expression of horror. "And they all go to a fancy party afterward."

"A breakfast, you mean," Henry prompted.

"Uh, it's usually in the afternoon, or the evening, like Emily and Griffin's."

"But at that hour, do not the newlyweds wish to be alone?" The words escaped his mouth before he realized how suggestive they were. "For private discourse," he clarified.

Her lips curved upward. Really, he had to stop staring at her lips. They were perfectly ordinary. On the full side, perhaps. And they looked very soft . . .

"Private discourse," she teased. "I never heard it called that."

He never had to worry about scandalizing Rose. She would outdo him at every turn . . . while making heat course through his veins like molten gold.

It was *her* fault he kept imagining her in his bed—or hers, given that he had no bed here. Her naughty words and immodest dress were to blame. Not to mention her frank and open manner, and the playful look she sometimes had in her blue eyes.

No, not her fault. Nobody compelled him to stare. And the rational part of his mind, which he had lately realized was not nearly so dominant as he had assumed, acknowledged that she was making no conscious effort to seduce him. Despite her love spell, when he'd said he wanted to go home, she'd accepted that.

He was the one who could not stop thinking about her spectacular breasts and what he might do to them . . . her mouth and how she might employ it on him.

"Anyway, I wish I could've known your wife," she said sincerely. "I know I would've liked her."

"Yes," he said absently. "Rose was truly exceptional."

A strange look came over Rose's face. "Charlotte," she said.

"What?"

She gave a little shake of her head. "Nothing. You said Rose instead of Charlotte."

How mortifying. Prickly heat rose on the back of his neck. "Ah," he said stiffly, while frantically searching for an excuse.

"Everybody does that sometimes," Rose said with a wave of her hand.

The so-called bus pulled up with a hiss and a cloud of noxious fumes. She had told him it would be large, but as they boarded the vehicle, its size still shocked him. Once they were on their way, he marveled at the driver's adroitness as she sped down a broad street, darting in and out between other rushing cars.

They disembarked on a street where buildings in the near distance stood taller than Henry could've ever imagined, some of them made of glass and steel, glinting in the sun. Henry paused for a moment, staring up at them.

He asked Rose, "Can we go in one of these buildings, and go to the top?"

She grinned. "Yes! But you should go to the tallest one." She pointed north. "See the black one, with the poles on top? That's the Sears Tower. Well, officially, Willis Tower. We need to buy tickets in advance, though."

"Have you been up there?"

"Yes, but it's been forever. I'd love to do it again." She was being very obliging, seeing to his clothing and footwear, and arranging tours of her city.

"The planetarium is about a mile in this direction," she said, pointing. "Unless you want to take another bus?"

Henry looked around them. The streets seemed to form vast plains of concrete. Several orange-and-white-striped barrels stood in a line on one side. He'd always taken great satisfaction in understanding how things worked, from refracting telescopes to naval battle strategy. Here, he understood nearly nothing.

"Let us walk," he said.

They passed on a bridge over long trains, then over a narrow river, and finally toward a tranquil turquoise sea that she identified as Michigan, one of the Great Lakes. Before too long, they reached a fair green park.

"That's the Field Museum," she told him, pointing to an enormous building on their right whose columns suggested a Greek temple.

"Is that where you are employed? And where my portrait hangs?"

"No, different museum. This one is for natural history. And there's the Shedd Aquarium." She pointed to a similar grand building to the other side of them. "They have giant tanks with octopuses—octopi—and sharks and sea otters and . . . let me think, what else?" She tapped her fingers on her lips as Henry stared at her, astounded. "Beluga whales, and penguins, and every kind of fish you can think of."

"But it is impossible to keep all of these in a building," he protested. "They all need different climates, different diets."

She shrugged. "They've got it figured out."

"Can one go inside the building and look at them?"

"Of course!" She beamed at him. "That's what these places are for. Oh! And you have to see the Museum of Science and Industry."

Henry found himself gaping at her again. "How many museums do you have?"

"Oh, lots of them. There's one not far from my apartment, for Mexican art. And there's a writers' museum, and not far from here, there's one for military history." Henry's curiosity was piqued anew, but she wrinkled her nose. "No, wait. They moved that one. But the Museum of Science and Industry is huge. You can walk through a submarine . . . that's like a battleship that travels underwater, that people lived in for weeks at a time."

Henry's boyhood fascination with battleships surfaced in his mind. "I should like to see it."

"It's pretty cool to tour. They used to have a giant heart that you could walk through, too." He must've looked mystified, because she explained, "A model of a human heart, like twenty feet tall. And when you were inside it, it sounded like it was beating."

Henry raised his eyebrows. "That would be a remarkable experience."

Rose sighed. "It was. But they destroyed it."

"Why would they do such a thing?"

She shook her head. "Maybe they thought it was old-fashioned? They broke it up in pieces and threw it in the garbage! I know this is crazy, but I felt sorry for it, you know?"

Henry gave her a sideways glance. "But it did not have emotions."

"I think like that sometimes," she said, waving her hand. "Once, when I was a kid, my mom started crying because the coffeemaker didn't work anymore. She was upset about other things. But I was little, so I started thinking, did the coffeemaker have a personality or something?" She smiled. "And hey, as an adult, I met a stone statue with a personality, so I wasn't *totally* wrong."

"The coffeemaker was just a coffeemaker, I presume," he said. Rose had a similar device in her kitchen.

"It was. But I didn't want my mom to cry, so I told her we'd get a new one, and the spirit of the old one would go into the new one, just like *my* spirit had gone into my new body."

That brought Henry's busy mind to a halt. "I beg your pardon?"

"Oh. I kind of believe in reincarnation. Do you know what that is?"

He considered this for a moment. "Like Pythagoreanism?"

"I've never heard of that."

"The great mathematician and philosopher Pythagoras believed that the soul was enshrined in one human body after another, until the soul was perfected. Do many people believe that now?"

"Not really. Not in this country, anyway. But I always did. As a little kid, I'd talk about how I used to be a grown-up pretty lady. I had memories of it . . . but they're gone." She had a faraway look in her eyes now. "It's like a dream, where you forget once you're wide awake."

"Perhaps you did dream it, and confused it for a memory."

She shook her head. "That's what my parents said, too. But I remember being five or so and lying in bed, and thinking about how I hardly took up any room. And I was thinking, How did I get so little when I used to be big?" She laughed.

A childish fancy, Henry thought, though he could not deny that it was an extraordinary one. "So you do not believe in Heaven?" He did not, though sometimes he'd hoped.

"Oh, I believe in a happy afterlife, too. I think that's what happens with most people."

"But they cannot both be true," Henry pointed out.

"Why not? Maybe we have a choice. Do you want to stay here, or would you like another round on Earth?" She smiled at him. "I think that would be lovely."

He scoffed. "You cannot believe in things simply because they are lovely."

"Oh, I *definitely* can," she assured him.

Henry supposed there was no arguing with that. "What else is at your science museum?"

"Oh, let's see . . ." She glanced upward, thinking. "They have a spaceship they flew to the moon."

He stopped walking. "Men *flew* to the *moon*?"

Perhaps he should not have been stunned. He had seen the improbable airplane in the sky, and he'd tried to unlock the secret to traveling through time. But flying all the way to the moon seemed nearly as astounding.

She laughed. "Oh yeah, a bunch of times. They'll have something about that at the Adler, too." She pointed ahead of them at the building with a domed roof at the tip of a peninsula that jutted out into the lake.

Her city had built great temples to learning. He needed to explore all of them. If he did not return to his own time first . . .

which, of course, he wanted to do as soon as possible. They walked on, Henry still reeling from the idea of a lunar excursion.

As they approached the planetarium, Henry remarked, "There are children everywhere."

"It's for adults, too," she assured him, though he had not expected it to be for children at all. She paid for tickets at the entrance.

"The solar system show is in fifteen minutes," she said, taking his hand. He liked that she did that so naturally, even if it was only because she wanted to drag him through a crowd.

He paused at the poster outside the auditorium, next to a boy and his mother, that read, **TAKE A QUICK FLIGHT AROUND THE EIGHT PLANETS OF THE SOLAR SYSTEM.** He looked to Rose, astounded. "But which is the eighth one? What comes after Uranus?"

The boy erupted into a fit of giggles for no reason Henry could tell.

"They really need to rename that planet," Rose murmured.

"The next one is Neptune," the boy told Henry. "And then there's Pluto, but it doesn't count."

"*I* think it does," Rose said, but Henry's attention was caught by the boy's mother staring at him. She quickly turned away when she met his eyes.

The woman thought he was thick-witted. Hot shame crept up the back of his neck.

"Let's go sit down," Rose suggested.

Once they had found seats in a back row, Henry looked up. The room seemed to have no ceiling—only a starry sky.

"But it's daytime," Henry muttered to Rose, trying to make sense of it.

"It's called a movie," she whispered back. "It's an illusion."

It was a wonderful one, Henry had to admit to himself, but as he searched for familiar constellations, he could not shake a feeling of gloom. A few more people drifted into the amphitheater, and he felt vaguely pleased that no one was sitting in front of them, or directly on the left or the right.

Rose leaned close to him and whispered, "What's wrong?" He caught a whiff of her rose-and-incense perfume.

Nothing, he almost said. But something about her presence—her caring voice, the lovely scent on her skin—compelled him to vent his spleen.

"I was a well-respected amateur astronomer in my time," he murmured to her. "I published papers in two respectable journals."

"I'm not surprised," she said sincerely. "You're very intelligent."

"Am I?" he demanded. "My whole life, the stars and the heavens have been my passion . . ." He waved an arm at the giant false sky above them. "And now, I am schooled by a child."

"But that's not your fault," Rose said. "So why should it bother you?"

A good question. He spoke slowly, trying to make sure he got it right. "I have always prided myself on knowing how the world works, and of being capable no matter the circumstances. But now I discover that I know nothing about how the world works, so how can I be competent in it?"

Rose slipped her hand in his, but didn't have the chance to answer. The semidarkness faded to black and a loud, disembodied female voice welcomed them to their excursion around the solar system.

When Henry stared at the dome ceiling above him, they seemed to be floating through the night sky. He could easily imagine leaving the Earth, as he'd left his own time, and losing himself in the celestial realm that he had studied for so long. The moon with its austere chalky light. In the distance, amber and purple clouds . . . gasses? Nebulae, close up?

Above them, the sun advanced, pulsing, and the voice spoke of solar flares. Henry listened attentively. The show included dozens of facts he'd never known, and he wished he'd brought a notebook. When the voice asserted that Jupiter had ninety-five moons, he shook his head in wonder. No one ever would've imagined that in his time.

Then a realization struck him.

He murmured to Rose, "When I go back to my time, I will know more than anyone."

She whispered back, "You don't worry that you'll somehow change history in a bad way?"

"Your friend Jason suggests it may not be a concern."

The lively show of stars and planets above them cast gold and purple light across her face, making her appear . . . well, other-worldly.

She leaned even closer to him. "It's good to know things." His gaze fell on her plump lips, so close to his own. "But it's not why you're valuable. I hardly know anything about science, and I'm still valuable."

She was correct about herself, but wrong about him. Fundamentally wrong. "Of course you are," he grumbled. "You have different gifts."

"Like magic," she said lightly.

"Well, I suppose." The idea of her magic was still difficult to accept, and he could be forgiven if he didn't think it was a benefit . . . even though, in moments like this one, when he was close to her and they were speaking to each other like people who had known each other for years, he wasn't sure what to think.

He went on to say, "But you are warm and generous, forgiving, hopeful in the face of misfortune, and you are always your genuine self." He knew he sounded cross, even though now they were making renewed effort to keep their voices down. It always irritated him to discuss the obvious. He added in a grumble, "You obviously need no other qualities to recommend you."

Tears welled up in her eyes. "I think that's the nicest thing anyone ever said to me."

He felt deeply uncomfortable. If she cried, he could take her into his arms, but he hadn't held a woman like that since Charlotte. He wanted to hold Rose. And he had no idea what to make of that.

She asked, "You don't think you have any of those qualities?"

"I cannot flatter myself," he said. "I have never had that amiable nature that pleases people so much. Having knowledge, being capable—these things made up for that."

She leaned so close he could see down her blouse. He tried not to look and failed.

"You're dependable and loyal," she said.

He let out a huff of derision. "That can be expected of any gentleman." She shook her head, about to say something, and he added, "What makes you say that, anyway?"

She gave him a disbelieving look. "You spent two years trying to get back to your wife."

And it finally worked.

The thought startled him. What in the world did that mean?

He wanted nothing more in that moment than to kiss Rose. It would not be a betrayal of Charlotte. Not at all.

Rose leaned closer again. Christ, she was exquisite, in the shifting light of the illusory cosmos. "And you're intense," she murmured.

"It is hardly desirable to be intense."

"Oh, it's desirable," she purred. The words seemed to escape her mouth before she'd considered them, her voice like honey and smoke.

"Rose," he whispered.

He thought fleetingly that she wouldn't hear him over the disembodied voice. It spoke of a cold, remote sphere that had been rejected from the confederacy of the planets. Rose lifted her face to him, her soft lips parted, a tentative invitation in her eyes.

The unreal stars above them slowed, or so it seemed. The moment hung suspended: the grains in an hourglass would've hovered in the air. Carefully, not wanting to jostle it, he raised one hand to cup her cheek. His heart knocked in his rib cage. And then he brushed her lips with his own.

He felt a delicate tremble in her body, and she put his hand on her shoulder as she kissed back. Her scent filled his senses.

His hand cupped Rose's jaw, his thumb stroking her cheek, as he deepened the kiss, delving into her mouth, reveling in its silky, willing warmth. The music around them swelled. The tiny, needy sound in the back of her throat heated his blood.

Applause. The show was over. With regret, Henry brought the kiss to an end. Rose gave him a conspiratorial smile, then bent down to find her large bag. Reality dawned on Henry along with the bright lights in the auditorium.

He'd been passionately kissing an unmarried lady. He and Charlotte had not kissed like that before they had been engaged. Rose had seemed to welcome it . . . but by her own admission, she possessed a carefree spirit, and did not always consider the consequences. He'd noticed that she often put what pleased others above what was good for her.

He'd made her no promises of affection; there was no arrangement between them. Had he just taken flagrant advantage of her blithe and generous nature? He hoped to return to his past, after all.

"Maybe we could see this show again later," she suggested, her eyes sparkling. "I don't think you learned much this time."

"I—no, thank you," Henry said. "I think we have enjoyed enough."

Her face fell.

"But this is a splendid institution," Henry added. "I am eager to see the other exhibits."

She forced a smile. "I'm glad you like it." He could actually *see* her muster up her good cheer, like hoisting a patched sail to manage a rude squall, and it made him feel that she was the finest woman he'd ever met.

Besides Charlotte, of course. But putting on a smile as she braved disappointment had been a talent of his beloved wife's, too.

Rose had said he hadn't learned much from the show. On the contrary: he'd learned a great deal. Despite his bad temper when she'd first met him, she had a high opinion of him. Higher than he had of himself, truth be told. She'd developed an affection for him . . . and what he felt for her had already swelled beyond affection.

But he didn't have the slightest clue of what to do about it.

Two hours later, as they stepped outside the planetarium, the daylight seemed obnoxious to Rose.

They'd wandered through exhibits about the planets, space travel, and the birth and death of stars. It had given her ample time to wonder just what the hell had happened in that auditorium.

She'd been lost in a delirium of passion, romantic images flitting through her mind. She'd felt as though she'd found exactly what she'd been missing. She had been certain that her spell had worked, after all.

And then Henry had immediately regretted kissing her. With just a few words, he'd made that clear.

"Thank you for bringing me here, Miss Novak," he said to her now, looking around at the lake and the skyline. He cleared his throat. "I fear I must apologize for my shocking behavior earlier."

"You mean . . . the kiss?" She wanted to curl up in a ball. Of course that was what he meant. She just didn't want him to apologize for it.

"Yes." He met her gaze, and she sensed that took some effort from him. "I do not know what came over me."

"Well, it was my doing, too," she said with a laugh, though it wasn't a joke, and she felt more like crying.

"No, in fact, I do know what came over me," Henry corrected himself, looking upon the vast lake. A breeze toyed with her hair. "You are a lovely woman with a sweet temper, and I utterly forgot myself and my present circumstances."

Oh.

Rose leaned her head a bit to intercept his gaze. "But that's what I think of you, too. I mean, you're not a lovely woman. You're a lovely man." That wasn't exactly the word she was going for, but *smoking hot* would require some explanation. "And you don't have a *sweet* temper, exactly . . ." He raised an ironic brow. "But you're honest and really smart and I like you a lot," she added in a rush. "So you don't need to *apologize.*"

He was looking at her lips again. "An amorous entanglement would be wrong," he said soberly. "If there is any way I can return to my time, I will."

She didn't ask the question her mind shouted: *But what if you change your mind?* Of course he wouldn't stay here on purpose. He was a duke who lived in a palace.

"Besides," he said, "I am certain I can never truly love any woman but my late wife."

Rose's spirits sagged. That was very romantic of him . . . unfortunately for her.

"Thank you for being honest with me," she said. If they weren't going to get involved, it was better to know sooner than later. "I suppose we can be friends, though?"

"I know you did not mean to bring me here, and you have done much to befriend me," Henry said. "I am honored if I am counted among your friends."

She managed a smile. "Okay, pal."

As they walked back to the train station, she looked at the sky-scrapers reflected in the aqua water. In her own time, in her own big city, there had to be someone who was right for her.

Fleetingly, she thought of Aaron Coleman. He would be in one of the hotels right around here. After he'd found out he'd be in town longer to investigate an apparent vandalism, had he thought of her? Had he already decided there was no point thinking of her, since she'd flat out told him that?

On the way home, Henry had questions about how the skyscrapers had been built, but she wasn't much help. Once they'd gotten home and she'd taken Andy War-Howl around the block, she found a Wikipedia page on the topic.

"Here, you can read at the table while I figure out something for dinner," she said, setting the laptop down. "Are turkey and cheese sandwiches okay?"

"Of course."

"Oh! But we should learn about Victor Reuter."

"Is there a way to do so?"

"Of course." She picked up her plate, got up, and circled the table to take the chair right next to him. "Look, we'll do Wikipedia." Henry's sharp gaze traveled from her fingers to the screen as she typed the name in the search bar. "That's him."

Henry raised his eyebrows. "First, can you show me again how you found that?"

"Sure." She scooted the chair closer to him and angled the laptop. "What's a topic you'd like to know more about?"

"Refrigerators," he said promptly.

It took a few minutes to show him how to search, and when she put her hand over his to place it on the trackpad, little fairy lights seemed to sparkle along her nerves at the touch, even though she let go of him again immediately. They pulled up a detailed page on refrigeration.

"*My God*," Henry said, as though he'd witnessed the explosion of a star. Well, his brain was probably exploding, right about now. "How long would it take to read this Wikipedia?"

"You can read it now if you want," she said, figuring he really was curious about refrigeration. He looked at her askance, and then she realized she'd misunderstood him. "Wait, you mean . . . how long to read *all of Wikipedia*?"

He nodded.

"Well, you can't. I mean, it's impossible. There's too much for one lifetime."

"I see." His elbow on the table, he pressed his knuckles to his lips thoughtfully, contemplating the screen. "What a remarkable resource."

Henry insisted on doing the search for Victor Reuter, which took hunting, pecking, a muttered *Damnation*, and the introduction of the backspace key. They read it together. She felt hyper-aware of his presence, so close to her they were practically touching. If she had been anyone else, would he have moved a little farther away?

"I only knew Reuter as someone who gives to charities," Rose said. "I didn't know about all the lawsuits."

"Yes. Organized crime, real estate fraud, breach of contract, and more real estate fraud." Henry pointed to the photo of him grinning, in a heavy parka, while on a trip to Antarctica. "And yet, for seventy-two years of age, he seems remarkably hale and spry."

"He does." He obviously stayed fit, and a superrich guy could probably afford to have excellent work done, if he wanted to. Rose wouldn't have judged him for that—his face was his business—but she definitely judged him for all these accounts of him screwing people over.

"Clearly, the charities are a feint," Henry said.

It was Rose's turn to be confused. "What's a feint?"

"If you are boxing, it is a motion that makes your opponent believe you will do one thing, and then you do another. Let me demonstrate." He got to his feet. "For instance, you lunge forward and pretend to be about to throw a punch"—he moved his fist a few inches forward—"but as he blocks it, you change your angle." He raised his elbow and mimed a hook.

"Got it." As Henry sat down again, she asked, "You go to boxing matches?"

He shrugged. "I have been to a few."

She wasn't surprised. He was interested in literally everything. Well, except her, as it turned out, but no point dwelling on that.

Henry frowned thoughtfully at the laptop. "Can you learn about anyone on here? Including people from my time?"

"If they were rich or famous."

His shoulders sagged a little. "Of course."

"Why? Who did you want to look up?"

"Uh . . . my butler, for one."

She hadn't expected that. "Why? Oh! Are you worried he wouldn't have a position?"

"Well, yes. If I disappeared unexpectedly, my sisters might have dismissed many of the staff. But also . . ." His face colored slightly. What was he embarrassed about? "The fact of the matter is, I intended to settle a goodly sum on my butler's daughter, so that she might make a fine marriage, and I was not able to do it."

"Oh, wow." Rose leaned back in her chair, impressed. "Did he know that?"

"Of course not," Henry said crossly. "I was dreading having to tell him, though I could figure out no way around it."

She laughed. "Why were you dreading *that*?"

"No doubt he would feel the need to express his appreciation," he grumbled. "It was going to be irretrievably awkward." Rose found that adorable. A lot of people would've basked in that kind of gratitude.

Henry pressed his knuckles to his lips again, deliberating. "Moreover, I worry that my sudden disappearance may have cast undue suspicions on him. Or anyone in the household, truly, but butlers are often suspected in such cases . . . and a valet tried to kill his master, not long ago."

Rose hadn't even thought about that. "They couldn't arrest him, though, could they? Without any evidence?"

"No, I should think not. But even suspicion could besmirch his reputation, and then who would hire him? How would he provide for his wife and family? And he has been with my family since I was a boy."

The stressed note in his voice touched Rose's heart. She'd gotten the wrong idea about him before, thinking he didn't care about anyone who worked for him.

"What was your butler's name?"

"John Brady."

Rose sighed. "That sounds like a common name. But we can try."

For the next half hour, with Henry watching intently over her shoulder, Rose tried and failed to find any record of Henry's butler.

"This is a fool's quest," Henry finally declared, pushing his chair away from the table. "There is nothing else for it. I *must* get back home."

Andy War-Howl had come to sit next to Rose's chair, giving her doleful looks. "I need to walk him," she said.

Henry nodded. "Can you first direct me back to Wikipedia?"

"Sure." She pulled it up. "But you can't believe everything you read online, okay?"

Henry frowned up at her. "Are you saying that people use this"—he gestured toward the laptop—"to circulate lies?"

"It's mostly for lies," she admitted.

"But why?"

"There's a lot of money in lying. Plus some people think it's funny."

"That's appalling." He drew back a little in his seat, as if the Internet might infect him.

Henry really was honest. More honest than she'd like, sometimes, but she still admired it.

He asked doubtfully, "I don't suppose you are acquainted with anyone who owns a substantial science library?"

"Uh . . . Chicago has libraries. You could take my card and check out books."

A faint line of puzzlement appeared between his brows. "You are a member of a library?"

"Yeah. The big one's not far from the museum."

"I have heard of such library clubs and societies, but they are far too dear for common folk."

Rose laughed. "Yes, it's very exclusive, but you can be my guest. In the meantime, I think Wikipedia is *mostly* accurate."

"Thank you. Might I trouble you for a pen and paper?"

"Sure. Hang on." She grabbed a notebook off the end table in the living room, found a pen in a kitchen drawer, and set them next to him. "Here you go."

He peered at them. "Might I also trouble you for some ink?"

"It's right in the pen. You don't have to dip."

"Ah. How convenient." He flipped it open—and then froze,

looking down at the words on the page. "What is this?" He flipped the page over.

"Oh, I forgot I wrote in there."

Henry's stare was dark and intense, as if he was trying to see right into her soul. *"Why did you write this?"*

Eleven

Henry's heart pounded, and his body felt unsteady, as though gravity itself had relinquished some of its grip. In the notebook was written, several times over, the lines from Shakespeare that Charlotte had been fond of:

> Doubt thou the stars are fire,
> Doubt that the sun doth move,
> Doubt truth to be a liar,
> But never doubt I love.

She'd written the words as part of a letter to him, soon after she'd accepted his proposal of marriage. In the note she'd given him along with the astrolabe, she'd written the lines out again. Given his obsession with the stars and the truth, it had naturally seemed appropriate to both of them.

Rose had been writing those words again and again in this notebook. And that wasn't even the most alarming part of it.

She'd written them in Charlotte's handwriting.

The rounded, easy-to-read letters. The long crosses of t's that sheltered letters that came after it. The pen was different, but the loops on the lowercase s's, the flourish on the lower loop of the f . . . it was all Charlotte's writing, exactly.

"It's a quote from Shakespeare," Rose said, sounding a bit uncertain. "I was memorizing it for my speech at Emily and Griffin's reception, so I wrote it out a bunch of times."

His breaths were coming faster. "Has your handwriting always looked like this?" he asked, straining to keep his voice calm.

"Like what?" She looked down at the page in the notebook. "Yeah. My teachers always thought I had good penmanship."

"Yes," he said. "You do."

"Hey, are you all right?" she asked, studying his face. "You look a little freaked out."

She'd used that expression once before. As far as he knew, the word *freak* referred to a sudden, inexplicable change of place. That, or a capricious prank. Both meanings seemed to apply. Something inside him had leaped with joy when he'd first laid eyes on those words in her hand . . . but that was all the more reason to fear that this prank might be monstrous.

"Yes," he said slowly. He placed both his palms on the table as if to steady himself. "I am freaked out."

She gave a sympathetic little sigh. "It's like we were saying before. You've had so much to take in. Do you want to take a walk to the dog park with me and Andy? Or have you walked enough for one day?" Andy put his paws up on her thigh, dismayed that the walk had been delayed this long, and she scratched the top of one of his ears.

"I would very much like to go," he said. Some fresh air would do him good.

It was a strange coincidence, the handwriting, and the quote. What else could it be?

Once outside, Rose led him in the opposite direction of the way they'd gone before. Two-story brick houses, rather than shops and restaurants, occupied these blocks, along with some trees; mulberry and ash, mostly, but here and there a dogwood or cherry tree showed off its elegant blossoms. More than one resident had planted bright tulips in the tiny strips of land in front of their houses, behind short wrought iron fences. An old man sitting on the front steps of his home called Andy War-Howl a *handsome pup*. The hound lifted his head a little higher and had more of a spring in his step upon hearing the compliment. When he craned his neck to sniff the base of a tree, Rose indulged him by stopping.

She told Henry, "You've actually handled all this pretty well, under the circumstances. I mean, can you imagine if I lived in your time?" She laughed, and he could tell she was hoping to lighten his spirits, too. "Although I do like the dresses."

"Yes, you might take pleasure in wearing a fine silk ball gown," Henry found himself saying. It wasn't the first time he'd imagined her wearing one that draped over her soft curves and set off her bosom with a rounded neckline. Her curly hair would be put up in a chignon, adorned with jeweled combs or a filigree headband.

"But everyone else would look better in them than I did," she said good-naturedly.

Was this false modesty on her part? He'd thought she was more honest than that. Since no subject was apparently taboo with her, he said, "You would look very well indeed, with your figure inclined to the luscious."

Rose's eyes sparkled and a fine blush rose on her cheeks—both reactions that gentlemen also greatly admired. "No one in your time would want a wife like me, though."

"Some gentlemen would hesitate to pursue you," he admitted. "Men who wanted a demure mother for their children."

"One who doesn't play with witchcraft or hang out on rooftops," she suggested.

They reached the park and she headed toward a fenced-in area where several dogs, large and small, not all of them breeds Henry recognized, cavorted with one another or sniffed around the perimeter.

They went through the gate, blocking the attempts of two dogs to escape. Once Rose had latched it behind them, she unclipped the leash from Andy's collar and he bounded across the field more quickly than Henry would've thought possible, having seen the dog laze about at the apartment.

Henry still regretted saying that Rose had small charms, and he didn't want her to get the wrong idea now. He said, "Were you to be introduced at a ball in Mayfair, you would've fixed a few gentlemen's attentions."

"Is that right?" she said, feigning coquettishness. "Would they all be worthy gentlemen?"

He snorted, momentarily jealous of these gentlemen who did not exist. "Hardly. Some would look at you like a horse to be tamed."

"Eww."

"Yes, I have seen it before. There are men who pursue a light-hearted girl for their wife, and then with admonishments and tones of contempt, day after day, they subdue her into an anxious and resentful matron. And then they complain to their fellows that she is no longer the lively girl they married, and they take a young mistress."

Rose wrinkled her nose. "Did all the men take mistresses? I mean, I know some people think that's fine, but it's not for me."

"Or for me," Henry said, as their hands accidentally grazed.

They watched Andy War-Howl bow to the ground, his rear end wiggling in the air, expressing his desire to play. A ginger-colored dog with a curly coat obliged, chasing him.

"There must've been some better men in your time, too," she said.

"Marginally better," Henry allowed. "Some would see courting a lady like you as an act of rebellion, a statement that he could not be forced to play by everyone's rules." There had been a little of that in Henry when he'd courted Charlotte. But before long, what he felt for Charlotte had nothing to do with anyone's censure or approval.

"I better stay here then, I guess," she said lightly. "I want to be liked for me."

They had been speaking hypothetically, but now, Henry couldn't help but wonder: What if Rose could come back with him in time?

He dismissed the thought immediately. True, he had developed a tendre for her, and despite his displeasing words on more than one occasion, he believed those feelings were returned. But they had only just met.

Besides, she had a full life here. A brother she loved dearly and who, if he wasn't mistaken, still relied heavily on her encouragement and support. She apparently did not mind having to work at the museum. In fact, he'd gathered that she quite enjoyed it.

"I bet a lot of ladies in your time want to marry you," Rose mused. "Being a duke and all."

"Yes. Whereas you have no use for titles. If you lived in my era, you would no doubt try to persuade me to turn Everly Park into a boardinghouse."

She laughed. "Affordable housing, yes. That's a great idea."

He'd never before met someone who was not only indifferent to his status and wealth, but actually disapproving of them. Without them, and without much knowledge of the world he found himself in, he did not have much to offer. He was tolerably good-looking, he supposed, but also a too-serious, often awkward man who preferred a lot of time for solitary study. Clearly, her spell should have brought her a charming doctor, professor, or solicitor—though there could be no shortage of these in her own city.

A strain of music had Rose reaching for her phone in her purse. Once she pulled it out, she exclaimed, "Oh! It's Emily." She put it to her ear. "Hi! How's everything?"

After a long pause, she cooed, "Ohh, that's amazing. I'm so happy for you guys. So listen—"

Apparently, Emily had interrupted her, because she fell silent. She frowned, and in a few moments, she said, "Yeah, hang on a sec." She held the phone away and whispered, "She read about the portrait in the news."

"Ah." How strange to think that the portrait he'd never posed for was public knowledge.

Rose brought the phone back to her face. "*Ugh*, I'm so sorry . . ." Another pause. "Okay, but listen—it didn't get vandalized. I did this spell and the duke in the painting time traveled to my apartment— No! Why would that be a joke?—Yeah, I'm with him right now."

There was a pause, in which Henry could faintly hear an excited, high-pitched voice emanating from the phone, though he could not make out the words. Then Rose said, "I'll call you later and tell you more, okay?"

Henry took a step away from her and pretended to be absorbed in the inspection of the flag flapping from a pole on one of the houses—white, with a bold blue *W*. He could well imagine what Rose might want to talk to her good friend about. This Emily and her husband from the Dark Ages would hear how Henry had declared that he and Rose could not consider a romantic entanglement— after he'd kissed her passionately. Henry ground his teeth. There was no explanation that put him in a good light.

"Don't be silly. I *love* having him stay with me," he heard Rose say. Pleased, he took an involuntary step closer. "He hasn't even barked that much." Ah. She was talking about the dog.

"Okay, see you! Love you!" Rose said. Putting her phone back in her purse, she bounced over to Henry. "They're coming over Tuesday night to pick up Andy and meet you. They would come sooner, but Griffin's got work."

Once again, she had not asked him whether he wanted to meet them. But the dog had to be returned, and since it was her apartment, he could hardly object to her receiving her friends.

"Very well," he said. Perhaps if he talked to them, they would have some clue to offer about time travel.

Andy and a new arrival to the park became acquainted in the usual canine fashion, by sniffing each other's posteriors, which Henry always found distasteful. After Andy and this dog had roughhoused for a while, Rose decided that they should be heading back home. As they walked back up the sidewalk, she discussed this Griffin again.

"I am so excited that you get to meet him. You guys are going to have so much in common! He's from the early 1400s, and he was an actual knight in shining armor."

"It sounds as though we will have little in common," Henry said.

"But you're both in the wrong era! Although, he loves this era. He's super friendly. He can talk to anybody." The exact opposite of Henry, then. "You're going to love him."

Henry felt quite sure that he was going to loathe the man, though it would be impolite to say so. The breeze picked up, and not far ahead of them, a cherry tree discarded a few of its petals.

Mostly to change the subject from the wonderful Griffin, he said, "It always seems a little melancholy to me when the trees lose their blossoms."

She gave him a disbelieving look. "Melancholy? It's celebratory! It's like nature's confetti."

She ran a couple of steps ahead of him and raised her arms—just as a stronger gust blew a veritable rain of cherry blossom petals down on her. Laughing at the magic of the timing, she twirled.

His breath caught. He'd never seen anyone lovelier. No, it wasn't only that . . . he'd never seen anyone more natural, more alive. It made him feel more alive, too: as if all the youthful dreams and impulses he'd discarded had come rushing back to him, more vital and vivid than ever.

He imagined advancing in a few strides and grabbing her around her waist. She would give a little gasp of surprise, perhaps. Maybe she would gaze up at him, joy shining in her eyes. Her lips, as pink and soft as the petals, would part. She would wrap her arms around his shoulders, and he would smell that rose-and-incense perfume of hers that stayed close to her skin. He'd bring his mouth down on hers in another kiss.

But none of that happened. She laughed and jogged a few steps back to his side. In his agitated state, her mere proximity was a torment to him.

Had he been wrong to draw back from an affair? Had he really needed to do it in such indelicate terms? He'd told Rose plainly that there could be no romance between them, so there was no way for either of them, by word or action, to revive the possibility again.

And any fool could've seen that she was not much troubled by the matter. She'd responded to his kiss in the planetarium, yes, but that had been an impulse of pleasure, like twirling amid the spring blossoms. She shared some predilections with Charlotte, and even wrote in the same hand, but she was herself, a wild and enchanting nymph, and he had no claim on her heart.

Twelve

When Rose came out of her bedroom on Monday morning, Henry was sitting in front of her computer at the kitchen table—where she'd last seen him the night before. Had he gotten any sleep?

"A white dress," he commented. "Many women wore those in my time."

She looked down at the midi dress she'd picked out for work. "I usually wear white or light blue on Mondays, in honor of the moon. And Selene, the moon goddess. I could wear gray, but I hate gray."

"You wear colors that correspond to the planets, which also correspond to both pagan deities and the days of the week," he said slowly.

"Exactly! Red or orange on Tuesday for Mars. Purple on Wednesday for Mercury. Bright blue or green on Thursday for Jupiter. Pink on Friday for Venus. Saturday is black for Saturn."

"That one makes sense," he said. "The Jews of old, and even the ancient Babylonians, called Saturn the black star, though I don't know why."

"I didn't know that!" It was fun being around someone who was into the planets, even if he didn't think they had spiritual meanings. "Well, the god Saturn is also known as Cronus."

"Yes. The god of time," Henry said. "But do you want to honor such a god? He swallowed his own children."

"Nobody's perfect," she joked, and felt gratified when he chuckled. "Time swallows us all up. But the children came back, and so do we."

As soon as the words were out of her mouth, she had an uncanny sensation, like a mental shiver. It was the same feeling she'd had the other day, when Henry had demanded to know where she'd learned to write like she did. He'd seemed genuinely shocked, and she didn't know why.

"Why do you do this?" he asked now. "Wear these colors?"

She didn't get the sense that Henry was challenging her. He sounded more like he wanted to understand, in the same way he liked to understand everything.

"Uh . . . it makes me feel in tune with the universe?" She went over to the counter to pour herself a coffee. "I know it's not logical."

"It isn't," he agreed, "but I very much like systems and routines."

"Especially ones involving planets," she suggested, and they exchanged a smile.

The day before, Rose had stopped into the Mexican bakery across the street to buy conchas—sugar-topped rolls. She grabbed one out of the white bag on the counter, set it on a plate, and brought it to the table with her mug. Andy War-Howl, whom she'd fed and taken for a quick walk when she'd first gotten up, stationed himself beneath her chair, obviously hoping for crumbs.

"Help yourself to breakfast," she told Henry. "There are conchas"—she waggled the one in her hand—"and coffee, and there's still cut-up pineapple in the fridge."

As Henry got a plate, he asked, "How is your, ah, work going?" She'd spent the evening before trying to come up with a spell to return him to his time.

"I still don't have an incantation I'm happy with." If they were going to sneak around Victor Reuter's mansion looking for the astrolabe, she should at least have a plan about what to do with it.

She sighed. "It's not usually this hard! But I don't usually try to do something nearly this *big*. And I'm not quite sure how I'm supposed to use the astrolabe, assuming we do get our hands on it." She took a sip of coffee. "I want to tell my boss I'm sick and stay home, but everybody's going to be upset about what happened to the painting. Do you still want to spend the day at the library while I'm at work?"

"Yes." He glanced down at his small, impossibly neat handwriting in the notebook she'd given him. "I am going to read about combustion engines, satellites, the theory of relativity, parallel timelines, and other ancient astrolabes in private collections, as well as wormholes, theories about decreasing entropy, and reversible dynamics within closed timeline curves."

"That does sound like enough for one day," Rose admitted. "And it's probably better than being stuck in my apartment."

"I like your apartment," he surprised her by saying.

"Really? I thought it would seem like a prison cell to you, compared to your estate," she admitted.

He shrugged. "Everly Park is grandeur and duty and dynasty, designed to awe the visitor. Your modest rooms are not meant to impress anyone."

Rose gave a rueful laugh. "That's true." She picked at the pink sugar–crusted top of her concha.

Henry frowned. "I mean that your apartment, with the cushions, and the candles and the curios . . ." He gestured to the large, colorful pillows on the sofa, and then the crystals, figurines, and candles on the wall shelves. "It is an expression of yourself, and that is why I like it."

Oh. That was sweeter than pink sugar.

But why was he saying things like that to her, when he didn't want to kiss her or get involved with her?

As smart as he was, he could be kind of clueless when it came to social things. Any person from a different century would be, now that she thought about it. He wasn't trying to flirt with her. He was just saying she had cute décor.

Andy looked up with hopeful brown eyes. She cut off another tiny piece of the sweet bread and tossed it to him. He caught it and wagged his tail hard. Somehow, it made Rose feel for the dog, that he was so happy with crumbs.

Once they were on the train, Rose looked up news stories about the painting, with Henry reading over her shoulder. The first one was in the *Chicago Tribune*, no less: A Vandalism Mystery at the Art Institute of Chicago.

"This is bad," she murmured to Henry. "It mentions Emily and Griffin's wedding. And the fact that Emily was arrested for the theft of the missing sculpture."

"Surely, it would be strange," Henry said, "for a lady to get married, attend her wedding banquet, and then somehow slip away unnoticed to meticulously deface a painting."

"True," Rose said. "And there's been a lot of vandalism as political protest. They're saying maybe a group will take credit for this one." Rose's mother would've said, *Don't hold your breath.*

Rose sent Emily a couple of quick texts.

> Are you coming into work today?
> Sorry your wedding got in the news. ☹

The Pink Line deposited them right in front of the Harold Washington Library Center. Henry looked up at the ten-story red brick building, crowned with a pediment of steel and glass, that occupied a whole city block. The watchful owls and fanciful flames on the roof, made to look like copper with a green patina, gave the library a dramatic flair.

"The library is in here?" he asked Rose.

She grinned, happy to show him something that she was sure he'd love. "This whole building is the library."

He whipped around to look at her, wide-eyed. "It cannot be."

"It is!" She checked the time. "It's eight twenty, and they don't open till nine, so you'll have to wait outside. I hope you don't get bored." He didn't have a phone to look at, after all.

He scoffed. "I am sure I don't mind sitting with my own thoughts for a mere forty minutes, particularly as I can watch the parade of modern humanity go by."

A man with inner resources, Rose thought. That was hot.

He asked, "To whom do I introduce myself, once I enter?"

"Oh. No one. I was kidding about it being exclusive. Anyone can go in here."

The corner of his lip curled with annoyance . . . and maybe a little amusement? She hoped so. "Miss Novak, I find your century and your city confounding enough without your whimsical jests."

"You're right. I'm sorry. Find a nice place to sit and pull anything you want off the shelves to read." His eyes widened again. "You can ask any of the people behind the desks what you're looking for, and they'll help you. Oh, and you have to go up to the top floor! It's so pretty. I'll meet you up there around six thirty, okay? Take any books you want up there, and I'll help you borrow them."

"Extraordinary," he murmured, looking up to the top of the building.

"Well. I should get going," Rose said.

His gaze returned to her. "You must not walk by yourself. I will accompany you and then return to the library."

Rose waved off the suggestion. "This isn't a dangerous area. The museum's like ten minutes from here."

He cast a skeptical look down the block. "Be cautious for those ten minutes."

Something inside her melted a little bit. She was used to walking by herself, occasionally at night, sometimes palming the mini pink-glittered canister of pepper spray on her key chain. But it was nice to have someone worry about her. Especially when that someone was Henry.

"I will." She had a wild urge to kiss him goodbye. She settled for squeezing his upper arm. "Have fun."

Ten minutes later, as she went up the front steps of the Art Institute of Chicago, she could hardly believe that only a weekend had passed since she'd attended the wedding there on Friday night. So much had happened. She went to her office on the second floor, responded to a few emails, and then attended the marketing department staff meeting in the conference room led by Lisa, her boss.

Lisa was a white woman in maybe her fifties, with long, dry-looking brown hair and a shiny face. Rose had held down several jobs from the time she'd turned sixteen, including nighttime cleaner at a restaurant, cashier at an occult bookstore—which had spurred her interest in magic—cocktail waitress at a bowling alley, intern at an ad agency, and part-time marketing associate for a historical mansion with an art collection, the Richard H. Driehaus Museum. Except for the ad agency guy, she'd been lucky enough to have decent bosses, and Lisa was her favorite so far.

"I'm sure you've all read the stories in the *Trib*, the *New York Times*, and elsewhere," Lisa told the staff.

Rose said, "I didn't see the *New York Times* one."

Jayla shook her head. "Yeah, me neither!" The Chicago State

University grad had been hired after her fall internship, and Rose had been relieved to hand off the email marketing to her. Today, Jayla was wearing her braids piled up on top of her head, and a small gold cross pendant glinted at her throat.

Lisa sighed. "'Latest Art Crime Raises Questions About Chicago Museum's Security.' They brought up the knight sculpture and raised the question of whether the same people might be involved with both."

They were, Rose thought. It was their curator and his shady friends, bringing hinky art into the museum in the first place.

She asked Lisa, "Is it still on display?" She was dying to see it. But if it was, it would become a new star attraction, and she could expect the museum to be tagged in a bunch of new videos and posts.

Lisa shook her head. "It's in Paintings Conservation, where they can take a closer look at it." Good—Rose could stop by, say hello to Daniela, and get a closer look herself. Lisa went on to say, "PR has drafted a statement. It mentions how we have fewer art crimes than several other prominent museums our size."

"Yeah, we just have the weird ones," said Holly, their blond senior designer, who always wore a white button-down shirt and jeans and who hated almost all fonts.

"I'll get the statement up on the press release page," Doug said. He was a heavyset man with glasses who had been in charge of the website for decades.

Rose nodded. "I can share it as a post."

Lisa shook her head. "Actually, we'd like to talk about this as little as possible. It's the second scandal in two years . . . It's embarrassing for the museum. We'd like to schedule extra content, especially short videos, to distract from it."

"I can do that." It wasn't the best week to take on more work, of course, what with the upcoming shenanigans at a rich guy's mansion, and the whole trying to reverse time travel thing, but that couldn't be helped.

After the meeting, she brainstormed ideas as she walked over to the conservators' offices. Although she always tried to highlight a variety of works from a range of eras and cultures, she got the most clicks on the famous paintings in the collection. But was there anything new she could say about the dour father and daughter of *American Gothic*, the late-night loiterers of *Nighthawks*, or the bustling citizens of *Paris Street; Rainy Day*?

She walked past Seurat's cordoned-off masterpiece, *A Sunday on La Grande Jatte*. Two kids were standing as close as the rope barrier would allow, staring at all the tiny dots that made up the painting. Was there something Rose could say about the similarity between pointillism and modern-day pixels? On her phone, she searched the name of the painting and the word *technology* . . . and found a fantastic idea for a short video. By that time, she'd reached Paintings Conservation, and she swiped her badge and went inside.

The lab had a wall of windows and track lights above. One conservator dabbed at the surface of a seascape with a long cotton swab; another mixed paint on a large palette with dozens of hues. Several paintings from various eras, with wildly varying subjects and styles, were propped up along the row of supply cabinets, forming an impromptu, eccentric exhibition. Rose only recognized one of the pieces: a Degas, showing ballet dancers on the stage.

She took a few steps closer to study that one. Many of Degas's paintings of dancers showed them backstage or in rehearsal, adjusting their costumes, rubbing their sore muscles, and just being generally awkward and real. These dancers, though, were smiling, light and lovely, with flowers in their hair.

When Rose had been in the fourth grade, she'd convinced her mom to enroll her in ballet lessons. The studio hadn't looked as glamorous as Rose had expected, sitting next to an Ace Hardware with a grain elevator looming behind it. She'd kept losing her balance whenever she had to be on one foot, and she'd overheard the teacher describing her to her teenage assistant as *the husky one*. *Husky* was a word for boys. It was as though, by being a little chubby, she'd become less of a girl.

Quitting the class hadn't been an option; her parents had already paid for it. She stuck it out, dancing with her class at the winter recital, and had never looked at the photos.

Henry's wife had probably been graceful and willowy, she thought. All the ladies of his time probably had, gliding around in their delicate gowns, like porcelain figurines of themselves.

"Rose!" Daniela's voice called out. Rose looked over to see her sitting in front of the now-obliterated portrait on a wooden easel, removed from its frame, along with the back of Daniela's dark-haired head. As Rose approached, she had to ask herself again if she'd seen the painting in a book somewhere. Even though Henry was now a gray blob, the backdrop still looked so familiar.

"Hey, Daniela," she said lightly as she reached her. "I guess it's going to be a bigger job than you thought." Her gaze fell on the museum label lying on a side cabinet. She read the first line and it was as though her vision tunneled . . . as though she could see nothing but that line, glowing with light.

HENRY LEIGHTON-LYONS, THE DUKE OF BERESFORD

(1782–1818), AMATEUR ASTRONOMER . . .

"Daniela?" she asked. Her voice shook a little. "This guy died young?"

Daniela blinked and looked over at the label. "Yeah, I guess so. That's sad, isn't it? I guess a lot of people died young in those days."

"But . . ." Rose felt like she was going crazy. "Didn't we talk about him living a long time? Right after the wedding ceremony?"

Daniela squinted as though trying to remember. "I don't think so?"

"Rose. I'm glad you're here."

Rose startled and whirled around at the sound of Aaron Coleman's voice.

"Hi." *Ugh.* She should've realized that he might be there. He wore a white button-down shirt, a navy striped tie, and navy pants, and he would've looked even more handsome if he hadn't looked so serious. She gestured at the canvas. "This is so weird, right?"

"It is," he said, unsmiling. "I'm talking to as many people in the wedding party as I can about this incident. Got a few minutes?" He was using his Special Agent Voice now, not his Sort-Of-Ex-Boyfriend Voice.

"Um, yeah," she said automatically. *Wait*—should she say no? Emily, following the lead of one of her coworkers, had flat out refused to talk to law enforcement about the missing sculpture. Rose had even said that was smart. But unlike Emily, Rose could hardly be a prime suspect. Over sixty people had attended Emily's wedding, for one thing.

"But I can't stay long," she backtracked. "I was going to ask Daniela how the restoration was going."

Daniela looked pained. "Like I told Aaron, I don't know if there's anything to restore." She pointed, her finger hovering above the canvas. "It looks to me like the brushstrokes of the library and window are on top of the gray. There are a couple of outline marks, here and here"—she pointed at faint lines Rose had missed. "Like they were going to put the duke in there later."

"Wow, that's crazy," Rose said. Her face warmed. She'd never been a great liar.

"It's got to be a forgery." Daniela pointed to the right border of the painting next. "Remember when I showed you the wear marks, because another painting was leaning up against it? They're gone. This is in pristine condition."

"We need the infrared images before anything else," Aaron said. He looked to Rose. "Let's take a walk."

She felt a bit shaky, and as she walked with Aaron back out into the hall, she reminded herself that she hadn't done anything wrong. "Where are we walking to?"

He lifted a shoulder in a shrug. "Let's go sit by the Chagall windows."

As they walked toward the staircase, he said, "On Friday night, after we talked, you said you had to ask your brother something. Then you walked back to join him and Daniela in front of that portrait. What did you have to ask him?"

His tone sounded casual—pleasant, even—but the question made her bristle. "I didn't have to ask him anything. I just said that to get away from you."

He said nothing, looking at her expectantly, as they went down the stairs and walked toward the cobalt windows.

She took a deep breath. "Look, I'm sorry I was so mad when I found out you weren't really dating me. But I wouldn't have gotten so angry if I hadn't liked you so much."

Aaron looked away as she took a seat on the bench, and then he sat down himself, leaving more space than necessary between them.

Rose added, "I know you were just doing your job."

"We do good work sometimes." He seemed to regain his bland professional demeanor. "At the beginning of the year, we recovered this collection of hundreds of stolen Native American artifacts, and we, uh, had a ceremony in Albuquerque to return them to the Hopi and Zuni tribes."

"That's amazing." She gave a wry smile. "Are you telling me that to make me feel worse?"

"No. I just never got to brag to you." He met her eyes. "I wish I'd met you a different way."

"So I take it I'm not a suspect this time?"

He sighed. "Everyone's a suspect. I do have to ask you some questions."

"Fine." She couldn't imagine any way that she might incriminate herself.

He held up his phone. "Okay if I record this?" She didn't love the idea, but nodded anyway.

He pulled up an app, hit the red button, and asked, "Do you know what happened to the portrait of the duke, painted by Walter Wilke?"

"Don't you usually work up to that question?" Rose adjusted the chrysocolla crystal she was wearing on a chain, recalling that she'd worn it on her and Aaron's first date. "No, I don't."

It wasn't completely a lie. She knew she'd dragged Henry into her timeline before he'd posed for the painting, but none of them understood the time glitch that had left the painting here at the museum, in its unfinished state, with everyone remembering the completed painting that no longer existed.

"Why were your brother and Daniela lingering by the painting on Friday night?"

She felt hot all over. Even though they'd just made nice, if Aaron accused her brother of doing anything wrong, even indirectly, he was going to regret it.

"Daniela was telling Ryan about the restoration work she was going to do."

"Why were they talking about that?"

Rose gave a little huff of impatience. "Just making conversation? Conservators always like talking about their work." It occurred to her for the first time that maybe Daniela had been a little bit interested in Ryan.

"You were also talking with your brother right after the ceremony ended."

"Creepy," Rose interjected. If he'd noticed that, he must've been staring at her.

Aaron ignored this. "Did either of you say anything about the portrait then?"

"No! We hadn't seen it yet."

"How long did you look at the painting with Ryan and Daniela?"

"I don't know. A few minutes?"

"Why so long?"

Well, she wasn't going to tell him that it was partly because she'd been riveted by the image of the duke. She touched the chrysocolla again. "It was a new acquisition, so I was thinking about what I would post about it." Plausible, if not exactly true.

"So you three discussed the portrait for a few minutes, and then you walked directly from there to the reception?"

Rose nodded.

"That's an affirmative," he muttered, for the sake of the recording, she supposed. "When you were walking to the reception, did you see anyone coming the other way?"

"No. But wouldn't you know if someone did? This museum has cameras everywhere, doesn't it?" They even had security cameras in the windowless photo rooms of the conservator labs now, she happened to know, though that hadn't been the case when Griffin had come to life.

He asked, "How well do you know Daniela?" He hadn't answered her question about the cameras, she noticed. Maybe there was something wrong with the footage. Or maybe they suspected it had been messed with, somehow.

Rose shrugged. "I haven't known her for that long. Emily got to know her when they were both working on a piece together—like a cabinet with painted panels? I went to lunch with them both a couple of times. And I saw Daniela a few times because of the wedding." She gave Aaron a skeptical look. "You can't honestly think she had anything to do with it."

"I don't think anything yet."

"But if Daniela's right and it's a different painting, how does that make sense? Someone stole the duke and hung this new forgery in its place? Why would anyone even do that? And how?"

"That's what I'm trying to find out. How well do you know Jason Yun?"

Maybe she should've expected that question. In addition to both the knight sculpture and the duke portrait, Jason had also acquired a haunted suit of armor. But that didn't seem to be haunted anymore, and Jason had managed to convince everyone that what had happened with the armor had been theatrics.

Besides, he'd acquired many things over the past few years. The ancient Egyptian mirror with the Isis handle, which Emily had restored. The contemporary sculpture of a cow that appeared to be made from butter, though it really wasn't. The dollhouse-like interior, a New York ballroom in the late Gilded Age, that was a new addition to the Thorne Miniature Rooms. None of those were magical. Were they?

"I barely know him," Rose said. It was true, even if the guy had convinced her to go creeping around a man's mansion soon. Jason struck her as hard to get to know, now that she thought about it.

"Did you talk to him at the reception?"

Rose thought about that for a moment. "No." She'd FaceTimed with him later that night, but she supposed she didn't need to volunteer that information.

"What time did you leave the reception?"

"A little after eleven. I'm watching Emily's dog, and I wanted to check on him."

"Did you go straight home?"

"Yeah."

"And what time did you get home?"

"I don't know exactly, but about eleven thirty?"

"Can anyone vouch for that?"

"Other than the dog?" she quipped, though it unsettled her to be asked about her alibi. "Actually, the lady who lives downstairs can probably vouch for me. You cannot believe how loud that dog barks when someone comes to the door. Oh!" She lifted a finger, realizing something. "There's a record of my ride, too. On the app."

"And you were home alone the rest of the night?"

Fresh heat rose to her cheeks. "That's none of your business."

"It literally is."

She could take the moral high ground. She leaned closer to the phone to make sure what she would say got picked up on the recording. "Well, I don't feel comfortable talking about my personal life with you, and that's your fault for fake-dating me and lying to me before."

"So you're in a relationship," Aaron said, unfazed.

"What did I just say?" And was this a Special Agent question or a Sort-Of-Ex-Boyfriend question? Either way, she didn't want Aaron sniffing around to see if she had some new art crime genius lover, so she added, "No, I'm not in a relationship. I'll say that much."

"Do you know what time your brother left the reception?"

"No. I left before him." She wanted to tell him that if he bothered Ryan, he'd be wasting both of their time, but she didn't want to sound like she was covering for anything.

Aaron scrutinized her face. Then he touched the button on his phone to stop recording.

"Any thoughts on why this museum is becoming the home of seemingly impossible art crimes?"

Rose glanced around them. No one was listening.

"I don't think it is," she said. "I know Griffin told you he used to be the stone sculpture. You're his friend. You still don't believe him?"

After a pause, Aaron said, "I believe he believes it."

"You mostly believe him," Rose guessed.

He gave a thoughtful tilt of his head. "More than I believe you."

"What?"

He sighed. "Rose, I'm pretty good at telling when someone's not being truthful. And you have an obvious tell."

What tell? Rose realized she was touching the crystal at her neck again. She jerked her hand away.

Did he really suspect her of something?

She said, "One minute you're telling me you still like me, and the next minute you're telling me I'm a liar."

"I didn't say lying. I can tell there's something you're not telling me. That doesn't mean I don't like you."

There was no way she was going to explain to Aaron that she'd accidentally made a duke from the early 1800s time travel to her apartment. If he didn't completely believe Griffin, he definitely wouldn't believe her.

And what if the U.S. government really did believe Henry was from the past? And Griffin, too, for that matter? She hadn't thought about that before. Would men show up and stuff them in vans and take them to some undisclosed location to study them? It wasn't hard to imagine.

"I don't know anything that'll help with your investigation," she said.

He stood up, so Rose did, too. He said, "Listen, after I get this case wrapped up, we should go out again."

Rose gaped at him. "Seriously?"

Aaron spread his hands. "You know I'm just doing my job here, right? Like I say, not while I'm still investigating."

He must not really suspect her, if he was bringing this up again. Or Ryan, Emily, or Griffin, either, for that matter.

Probably, she should say no. How would they ever overcome such a weird beginning?

But the few dates she'd been on with him, even if they'd been mostly fake, had been nice. Fancy restaurants, but not fancy enough to make her feel weird. Conversation had never hit an awkward lull.

She'd never had that electric feeling around Aaron that she had with Henry—as though the very air between them were charged. But what good had that feeling been? Either Henry hadn't felt it, or he hadn't cared. The truth was, now that Henry had backed away from her, it was pretty flattering to have a good-looking, intelligent man be genuinely interested in her. Persistent, even.

"Give it some thought?" Aaron suggested.

"I'll, uh, I'll unblock your number," she said with a fake laugh—feeling misgivings as soon as the words were out of her mouth.

With a sparkle in his eyes, he said, "You do that."

He told her he was meeting Jason at the café, and Rose wondered how that would go. Maybe Aaron was good at getting information out of people, given his job, but Jason seemed equally adept at not sharing. She wouldn't have been surprised to learn that Jason, unlike her, was an excellent liar.

As she walked back to her office, she checked her phone and found she had a text from Emily.

I'm here! Meet me at the doors at 1?

They usually went out to the food trucks that parked between the museum and Millennium Park. Rose's spirits lifted as she gave Emily's text a thumbs-up.

Back at her desk, she spent some time monitoring comments on a couple of museum accounts, then edited and uploaded a lecture to YouTube. The lectures didn't get a lot of views, but she was trying to do a better job with the keywords so that more people would stumble across them. A little before one, she left her desk, and she was halfway down the light-filled Modern Wing when she heard Emily's voice behind her, calling her name.

Rose turned around to see her best friend jogging up to her. Emily was wearing her glasses, like usual, though she'd worn her contacts on her wedding day. She was dressed simply in jeans and a black top, but her gold medieval-replica wedding band gleamed on her finger.

"Hey!" Rose said, giving her a hug. "You still have that bridal glow! How was your weekend?"

"I want to hear about *you*." Emily grabbed Rose's arm and urged her into a fast pace toward the doors. In an undertone, she demanded frantically, "How did you get a Regency duke out of a painting?"

"I didn't mean to!" she scream-whispered back. "I saw the painting after your ceremony, but . . ." She looked around them to make sure no one was listening to their conversation, but other than a cubist woman painted by Picasso, who looked too miserable to be curious, they were in the clear. "Your wedding was so beautiful, and I did this spell to meet an old-fashioned gentleman, and he showed up in my apartment!"

Emily's mouth dropped open. "So he . . . wanted to come into the future?"

"Actually, he wanted to go into the past. He hates it here."

After a moment of silence, Emily said, "He must think it's *kind* of cool."

"I really don't think he does," Rose said lightly as they reached the glass doors.

They stepped outside into a gorgeous late spring day. The sound of a street musician playing the guitar and singing a Bob Marley song mingled with the traffic, and across the street, beyond the trees of the park, skyscrapers rose into the blue sky.

As briefly as Rose could, while she and Emily waited in line to buy tacos, she explained the situation. "Henry and I met with Jason, and Jason says this astrolabe Henry had might have time travel powers."

"Astrolabe . . . that's like, something astronomers used to use?" Emily asked.

"Exactly. And the moonstone I was wearing at your wedding was originally part of Henry's astrolabe, which this rich guy in town owns now, and Henry and I are going to go to a gala at his mansion to try to find it and do a spell to get Henry back to his own time." Rose took a deep breath.

Emily blinked. "Okay, I *think* I followed all that." They reached the front of the line. Emily ordered taco baskets and drinks for both of them, then turned back to Rose. "This is crazy."

"I know." Rose shook her head.

"Who's this rich guy?"

Rose leaned even closer. "Victor Reuter. He's really bad news."

They took their food and drinks from the vendor. Emily paid and stuffed a five-dollar bill in the tip jar. As they went over to the short wall where they usually sat to eat, Rose listed off some of the allegations about Reuter.

Emily asked, "Are you sure you want to be sneaking around this guy's house?"

Rose got herself situated on the wall's edge. "Henry really wants to get back to his gigantic palace, and he wants to give a bunch of money to his butler's daughter so she can find a good husband . . ."

"That's nice," Emily said, hopping up to sit next to her.

"Yeah. So I have to help him."

Emily took a sip of her Diet Coke. "I just can't help thinking, since it was a love spell that got Henry here . . . maybe he's going to fall for you, but he's just freaked out right now. Which anyone would be."

"He told me straight-out he doesn't want to get involved, because he wants to get back." It was good for her to remind herself of this.

"When did he say that?"

Inwardly, Rose cringed. "After he kissed me at the planetarium."

Emily slammed her Diet Coke down. "What?"

Rose sighed. "We went to one of the shows there, and I don't know how it happened . . . We wound up kissing."

Her friend stared at her. "So was he a good kisser?"

Rose's heart sank. "It was the best kiss of my life."

"Rose." Emily grabbed her hand. "If the kiss was that good, and he was the answer to a love spell, you guys are meant to be together."

Rose felt a rush of wistful affection for her friend. "You're blissfully in love and you just had a fairy-tale wedding, so you want everyone else to be happy, too. I still want to hear about your mini-moon weekend."

"You will, but don't change the subject. If Henry doesn't want to get involved, why did he kiss you?"

"I think he just got swept up in the moment."

"If he wasn't into you, there wouldn't be moments to get swept up in," Emily insisted. Rose had to admit she could appreciate the logic. "You can't just give up on him!"

"What am I supposed to do? Try to seduce him? Usually, I just say yes when guys ask me out, and regret it later."

"Guess there's no need to change, then," Emily teased.

"But I'm never going to learn how to seduce anyone," Rose said despondently. "It's not like I'm a Leo. Or a Gemini."

"But you're a Scorpio rising."

"How did you know that?"

"You told me like three times," Emily said around a bite of chicken taco. "Didn't you say Scorpios are spicy?"

"Yeah, it's supposed to mean that I have a danger-loving, sexy side." Rose shook her head. "My inner Scorpio has yet to rise."

Emily asked her a few more questions about Henry, and Rose tried to convince her that she and Henry really were too different for romance to even be a possibility. When she was finished with her tacos, she checked the time and asked Emily, "Want to walk down to the lake and back?"

"Yeah," Emily said, hopping down from the wall.

Now was Rose's chance to change the subject. "Okay, I want details. I'm guessing you two were exhausted on Friday night, but—"

"I thought we'd be tired, too!" Emily said. "We didn't get to our hotel room until after midnight. But then I didn't even get my cor-set thing off."

Rose laughed. "*That's* spicy. And impressive."

Emily said, "Well, we did sleep in late the next day. And then Griffin convinced room service to bring us pancakes, even though technically they weren't serving them anymore, and . . . honestly, we didn't leave the hotel room until dinner."

"That sounds perfect," Rose said, even though it was bringing up bad thoughts like *That'll never be me* and *No one will ever love me for myself.* But she'd never had a lot of patience for self-pity, especially when it was her own. She knew she had a lot to be grateful for. She couldn't regret asking Emily about all this, because what kind of best friend would she be if she didn't?

They came to a stop at the corner, waiting for the signal to cross Lake Shore Drive. "We had dinner at their rooftop restaurant on both nights," Emily said, speaking a little louder to be heard over eight lanes of busy traffic. "It's so pretty! It overlooks the Riverwalk."

This reminded Rose of another rooftop dinner—with Aaron.

"Aaron talked to me at your wedding," she told Emily. "He said he really likes me."

"Is that right?"

As they crossed the busy street, Rose said, "You don't sound surprised."

Emily looked sheepish. "He told Griffin he was still thinking about you, and Griffin told him he should tell you."

Rose's mouth fell open. "Thanks for the heads-up."

"I didn't know for sure he was going to say anything!" Emily protested.

They reached the opposite curb. Now green parks lay on either side of them. "And I saw him again this morning. He was questioning me about the painting."

"Oh yeah. Well, I heard there wasn't a camera facing the painting straight on." Emily shook her head. "It makes no sense as a crime, anyway. If you were going to steal a painting and leave a really good forgery, why would you leave an unfinished one?"

They'd reached the sidewalk next to the lake, where people were jogging or out for walks with their dogs or their children. Rose even liked walking the block to the lake on her lunch break in the winter, when she had to wrap her scarf around her nose and mouth and the bitter wind made it feel as though Chicago really was the Windy City, although many American cities were actually windier. Sometimes in a cold winter, the lake would be covered in circular plates of ice, thicker on the edges, like big lily pads. In extreme cold, the whole top of the lake froze solid—and then, when it started to thaw, the surface ice would shatter into shards, a field of broken blue glass.

Not everyone could appreciate the lake in the wintertime, but anyone could appreciate it on a sunny day like this, when the teal water reflected the skyscrapers and the waves lapped the shore. One father and daughter were flying a kite that darted and weaved against the blue sky.

"I told Aaron I was sorry for holding a grudge," Rose said, "and he asked me if I'd go out with him once the case was over, and I said I'd think about it."

Emily turned to her in surprise. "Really?"

"I mean, it's not like he's going to solve the case anytime soon," Rose said, justifying herself. "Plus he isn't mad about having to live in the twenty-first century." It would be crazy not to give Aaron a chance.

"I wonder how many people he's talking to?" Emily asked. "He hasn't called me yet."

"He was going to lunch with Jason."

Emily gave a soft laugh. "I have a *lot* of questions for Jason."

"Right? But you know more about him than I do. He's your boss."

"My boss's boss, now," Emily reminded her. When Emily had first started working at the museum, in a temporary position, the museum had been between directors of conservation, so she'd reported directly to Jason. "He came to the wedding, but I hardly ever see him at work."

Emily checked her phone again. "We should head back. Laurie's mad because I'm not done with the stereomicroscope yet."

Rose was well aware of Emily's colleague's moods. As they turned and walked back the way they came, she said, "When I'm talking to Jason, I feel like he's this normal, trustworthy guy. It's only afterward that I think of all these questions I should've asked about his secret art brotherhood."

"I think he's like that with everyone," Emily said. "I know he's really good at schmoozing and getting people to donate money."

"Do you think he practices magic, too?" Rose asked.

"No." But Emily didn't sound completely sure.

"I can imagine him carrying a charm bag that bends people to his will."

"I can't help but trust him," Emily said. "He was always nice to me, and he did so much to help Griffin." She leaned over and bumped Rose's shoulder with hers. "Of course, he wasn't the only one."

"Maybe it's better we don't know. But I wonder. Why is this secret brotherhood tracking down magical things? And how did Jason get involved with them?"

Emily was nodding along. "And where do they get all their money?"

"I'd invite Jason over tomorrow night, too, but I just told Aaron I barely know him. I mean, he's probably not staking out my apartment, but still."

"Griffin will want plenty of time to talk to Henry, anyway," Emily said. "He's really excited. He's never met anyone else who's from a past century before! I mean, obviously." She gave Rose a hopeful look. "Maybe he'll even convince Henry it's not so bad here."

"That would be great," Rose admitted. After all, there was a strong possibility that they wouldn't be able to send Henry back, and she would've ruined his entire life.

But she needed to think positive thoughts. She'd try to figure it out.

In the meantime, maybe it would be easier for Henry if he and Griffin were friends. And there was a good chance they would be. Who didn't like Griffin?

Thirteen

Henry had camped out at a small table on the top floor of the library, just where Rose had recommended. Its potted trees and the glass-domed ceiling crisscrossed by girders, framing a still-blue sky, suggested a conservatory, but with its wide-open space and its marble-and-terrazzo floor, it would've made a handsome ballroom, for those who enjoyed that sort of thing. Piles of books surrounded him on the table and the empty chair next to him.

He checked his pocket watch: six thirty. She should be here any minute.

It was an unfathomable luxury to learn about scientific principles and even advancements he never could have dreamed of in his time. A luxury, too, to have several uninterrupted hours in which to read. He should not have been impatient to see Rose again.

But when she stepped off the little moving chamber—the elevator—he smiled and then felt suddenly awkward as she walked toward him. "Hi there!" she called out. When she drew up to his table and looked around at the books, she asked, "Do you want to take any of those home?"

"How many can I take?"

"Oh, as many as you want," she said with a wave of her hand. "I think fifty's the limit."

Fifty? Henry's spirits soared. He surveyed the volumes around him, then pulled the most interesting ones related to time travel to form a new stack.

Her eyes widened. "But you're going to have to carry them on the train."

"Naturally." He began a second stack of books on other topics. "I will have no trouble."

She pressed her lips together, then said, "I'll go get a cart."

Once she had procured one and Henry had loaded it up with his choices, they took the elevator to the ground floor. There, she purchased bags with handles, printed with the message **FRIENDS OF THE LIBRARY**, to make his spoils easy to carry. He took two overstuffed bags in each hand and was obliged to allow her to carry the fifth one.

When they went outside, the late-afternoon sun had turned the city to amber, glinting off the windows of the tall buildings. In the golden hour, Rose's sweet face was somehow one of the most real things he'd ever seen. He felt an ache like nostalgia for the very moment he inhabited.

"I'm afraid we're not going home for a few more hours," she said, a note of apology in her voice. "I have to go somewhere else for my job."

The fact that he had no inclination to grumble about this surprised him. Henry usually despised a change in plans, and he'd undergone a bigger one, surely, than any other man who had ever lived. But after a day of fascinating reading, interspersed with several long daydreams about Rose that were anything but scholarly, he could not even label being in Chicago, in the twenty-first century, as a complete misadventure.

There were worse things, truly, than having one's schedule demolished by Miss Rose Novak.

He said, "Well, then. Where are we going?"

"I don't know how to explain it. You'll just have to see it. But I hope you'll like it! It's kind of like art and science coming together."

They took a different train, which delivered them to the banks of a river, lined with more tall buildings. She led him down a broad, handsome flight of stone stairs. The books he carried *were* extremely heavy. But it had been a little while since he had exercised with dumbbells and Indian clubs, so he told himself it was just as well that the books would fortify his muscles as well as his mind.

People traversed the river in small white boats and kayaks. The now-setting sun made pink and orange streaks on the little waves, disturbed by wakes and oars. Across the river stood a huge building, twenty-some stories high, but much wider. Couples, families, and small groups of friends milled along the river or sat at outdoor tables, eating their dinners or sipping coffee or wine. Had he and Rose arrived earlier, perhaps they might have dined here, too.

Rose suddenly dashed forward, heedless as a child, and plunked her bag of books on a table that had been vacated by another couple moments before. Henry had to laugh as he joined her, gratefully setting his burdens down.

Triumphant and slightly out of breath, Rose said, "I always have good luck with getting a table. It's one of my things."

To Henry it seemed to be more a matter of shameless abandon than luck, but he meant it when he said, "Then I am lucky to be with you."

"I'll get us something for dinner," Rose said, pointing to people waiting at a nearby counter. He was not accustomed to dinners being so spontaneously declared and arranged, though he found he didn't truly mind.

As she got in line, he opened a book about multiverse theory. She soon returned with sandwiches and two bottles of water.

"Thank you," he said as she sat down. "So this outing is part of your duties? I daresay that thus far, it does not strike me as arduous labor."

"Right? We're here to see a show. It'll start in maybe a half hour."

Henry attempted and failed to guess at what that might mean. "Perhaps you might use this time to tell me what, precisely, you do for the museum."

She leaned forward eagerly. "I was just thinking about how to explain that to you. In your time, you had newspapers, right?"

"Indeed."

"And did they have advertisements in them?"

"Yes, for goldsmiths, and pianofortes, and seaside resorts, and all manner of things."

"Perfect. What I do is a little like news, but more like advertising. Here, I'll show you one of the ways I do it." She took out her phone, tapped on it a few times, and turned it to face him.

On the screen was a grid of rectangles, each with an image of a different object. A brightly colored basket, a painting of a contemplative saint, a golden mask, a stairway with illuminated words, a painting that appeared to have been produced by a drunk.

"Are these works in the museum?"

"Yes. I choose them, and I write about them. Here, I'll show you." She tapped on one, a bronze jar gone green with age, topped with a dragon figure. It filled more of the screen, with printed words beneath.

She handed the phone to him, and he read aloud. "'Was the fierce dragon on the top of this jar inspired by dinosaur bones?'" He lifted his head. "What, pray tell, is a dinosaur?"

"You don't . . . ? Oh. Dinosaurs were these giant reptiles, like as big as an elephant, or even as big as a whale, I guess. They don't exist anymore. They died out before the time of humans."

"What do you mean, before the time of humans?" he asked.

She raised her eyebrows. "Well . . ." He realized, to his chagrin, that she had been momentarily stunned by his ignorance. "Let's get back to that one. It's going to take a long time to explain."

"Asking you questions," Henry said, "is sometimes like peeling an orange to discover another orange."

"It kind of is."

"I gather these enormous reptiles did not die out because they were hunted. So why do they no longer roam the Earth?"

"Oh, you're going to like this," she said. "Because an asteroid hit the Earth."

"*What?*"

"Read the rest of it," Rose urged him. "That was only the first sentence!"

He directed his attention back to the phone. "'This vessel, found in Shizhaishan, China, was created between 300 to 200 B.C.E.'" He did not ask about how they knew the date, nor about the mysterious E after the abbreviation for *Before Christ*. "'The most remarkable thing about it was what it contained: both cowrie shells, used as currency by the Dian kingdom, and bronze coins, the currency of the Western Han dynasty that later conquered it. War and conflict are as old as time, but so are hopes that different cultures can mingle in harmony together.'"

Henry looked up at her. "You wrote this?"

She blushed. "Let me find you a better one. That was too sentimental." She grabbed the phone out of his hand.

"I disagree. I have learned not only about natural science, but also about ancient cultures, from one object. That is remarkable."

He'd made her forget her embarrassment. "Exactly!" She clicked back to the grid. "Every piece tells you so much about the world, and societies, and what they believe."

When he'd first met her, he had not credited her with intellectual gifts, but it seemed she loved learning almost as much as he did, except about art and magic instead of science.

"May anyone in Chicago see these?" he asked, gesturing toward the phone.

"People from all over the world can see them. There are . . ." She tapped a couple of times. "Over eight hundred thousand followers. Kind of like newspaper subscribers."

"Good Lord," Henry said seriously. "You have a very important position."

"Thank you." She practically twinkled at the compliment.

"How many objects are in the museum?" He wondered if she might run out of ones to discuss.

"In total? About three hundred thousand."

"Inconceivable," Henry muttered. "Is it difficult to choose which works to feature?"

"Sometimes. But I feature all the big exhibitions, and I do posts based on the seasons. Like this one was for the first day of spring."

When she turned the phone to face him again, he almost spit out his water. It was a detailed illustration of two women cavorting in a field without a stitch of clothing on, each holding one end of a garland of flowers.

"Isn't it fun?" she asked. "It's from around 1900, from France."

Henry snorted. "French. I might have guessed."

"I did have to delete a few comments on this one," she admitted. Henry was confused by more than one part of that sentence, and he must have looked it, because she pointed and said, "Look. People can comment on the post."

He did, indeed, see messages from other people.

☺ me & who??

Lovely! Very Belle Époque. Reminds me of Choubrac.

Must be nice to have time to frolic 😒 😂

I mean, this is just lesbians

Ladies. This is Chicago. You're going to get frostbite.

Is this in the vault? I don't remember seeing it with the French drawings.

ohmygod they were bloommates

While he was puzzling over a few of these, she said, "If someone says something offensive, I can just make their comment disappear."

"Does that happen often?"

She lifted a shoulder in a shrug. "Not really. But sometimes people criticize artists who are different from them. And I've had rude comments about me when I've interviewed people."

"Rude comments from strangers?" Henry asked. When she nodded, he felt his blood simmer. "What sort of comments?"

"Nothing serious. Just saying I'm fat, or they hate my voice, or whatever." She rolled her eyes and took a bite of her sandwich.

Nothing serious? Her composure was admirable, but this was not to be borne. "How might I pay each of them a visit?"

She made a confused noise and, after swallowing, said, "You mean . . . go where they live?"

"The ones in Chicago," Henry said. He supposed he could not pay a call to any of the vile fellows who lived farther away.

Her expression hovered between amusement and disbelief. "Henry, what are you going to do? Go punch them in the nose?"

"I merely intend to have a conversation." A conversation in which an abject apology might be extracted. Although if the apology were not forthcoming, then yes, a punch in the nose might be just the thing, assuming they were men. If some were women, then his most withering lecture would have to do.

"Well, you can't," she said. "I don't know where any of them live. Most of the mean ones don't even use their real names."

"Contemptible cowards!" Henry spat out.

"I agree," she said. "But people insult each other all the time on the Internet. And like I said, they lie, and the news is all bad . . . that's why I like sharing art. It's beautiful, and interesting, and you learn about different times and places . . ." She smiled. "I think it inspires people."

A loud fanfare made Henry look around them. "It's starting!" Rose exclaimed, grabbing her phone again and holding it up in front of her.

They had been sitting in a pool of light from a streetlamp, and with his attention fixed on Rose, he had not realized how dark it had become. Crowds surrounded them now, standing or sitting on the pavement. And then, on the face of the huge building across the river, synchronized to the music, a great burst of colored lights dissolved into sparkling waterfalls.

"But the fireworks will damage the building," he exclaimed, even as the crowd cheered and clapped. Were they all mad?

"They're just lights," she reassured him in a murmur.

Clusters of dots appeared, multiplied, in one color and then another. They danced in whirls over the surface of the building. Henry stared, transfixed. As dots settled into place, they began to form a picture. The bank of a river or lake, with tall trees and sailboats on the water. Two dogs chased each other, followed by a mother with a parasol, and a little girl. The park filled with more people, walking, lounging, enjoying the day.

Rose set her phone down. "Isn't it amazing?"

"I've never seen anything like it!"

"This is the first show of the year! It's called Art on the Mart. But this one is based on a very famous painting in the museum. It's called *A Sunday on La Grande Jatte*."

The spectacle must've lasted for fifteen minutes or so. For Henry, it was over far too quickly. When it rippled and disappeared in bright bursts of light, he and Rose got to their feet, applauding and cheering with the rest of the crowd.

"I see now what you meant," Henry said. "Art and science."

"And a little magic," Rose said, smiling up at him.

Henry thought, *I cannot leave.*

And then he remembered how he'd confused lights for fireworks, embarrassing himself, and how he could not trust his own instincts after being ripped away into another timeline, and how Rose had never invited him to stay indefinitely, and he told himself, *I must.*

Fourteen

On the following night, Henry was sitting on the sofa, reading about how stars were formed from vapor and cosmic dust and the force of gravity, when the sound of a door opening made him look up.

Rose had taken a quick bath before her friends arrived, and he now had a clear sight of her in the hallway, with nothing but a pale blue-green towel wrapped around her.

Her damp sandy curls stuck to her naked shoulders. Her whole body was flushed bright pink. He could imagine that if he laid his hands on her curvaceous thighs, which had made such an indelible impression on him on their first meeting, or her derriere, which he had not yet seen and could well imagine, they would be hot to the touch.

It only lasted a moment. She went straight to her bedroom and shut the door, not even knowing that he'd witnessed such an arresting vision.

He wished he and Rose could spend the evening alone. But perhaps it was just as well that her friends were coming over. How many nights could he bear being alone with her, without letting his feelings take over?

Rose emerged from the bedroom a few minutes later, fully clothed now in a red paisley dress.

"Red, in honor of Mars," he commented.

She beamed at him. "That's right! Both of my red things were in the washer this morning, so I wore that blue dress to work." She shuddered. "I felt off all day."

"You look very—presentable," he said, not wanting to overstep the bounds of politeness.

"You look very presentable yourself," she said wryly.

He was wearing one of the two suits Rose had ordered for him, with one of the white shirts that buttoned down the front. He had found the process of ascertaining his measurements and supplying them to her awkward in the extreme, but he'd been astounded by how quickly the clothing had arrived by post and how well it fit.

Andy War-Howl launched into a barrage of bellows and barks.

"That must be Emily and Griffin!" she said, smiling brightly, and she fairly bounced over to the door.

He groaned inwardly. Based on an earlier conversation with Rose, he'd already reached the conclusion that her friends would be useless when it came to time travel. So what was the purpose of his meeting them? His hunger no doubt increased his irritability. He had not eaten lunch, but Rose had told him that they would all order a dinner, which would be delivered to them.

As he reluctantly closed his book, she opened the front door. "Hi! Come on in!" He supposed he had no choice but to get to his feet and walk over to greet them.

Emily, brunette and bespectacled, was perhaps Rose's age. Her husband, Griffin, was a solidly built man with a mustache and beard and blond hair that reached past his shoulders. He looked as uncivilized as anyone might expect of a man from his era.

"Hi!" Emily said and then let out a soft *oof* as Andy barreled into her. She crouched down to scratch behind both his ears and talk to him in a high voice. "Hey, buddy! Oh, I know, I missed you so much! Did you miss me?"

The hound let out an alarming, baleful howl, as though his heart had been broken, even though he'd seemed cheerful enough minutes before.

"Ohh, my good boy," Emily crooned. Griffin hunkered down next to her. Andy jumped on him, rubbing his head into the man's torso with more pitiful whines.

Rose's brow knotted. No doubt, she was feeling guilty about the incident on the roof. Henry tried to think of some lighthearted jest to set her conscience at ease.

Griffin beat him to it, telling the dog, "I am glad to see you, too, sir, but I have no doubt that you have been much loved and cosseted here." He looked up at Rose with a huge smile. Rose returned it at once, her blue eyes sparkling.

Henry had been gratified, once or twice, to see Rose's eyes sparkle when she talked to him, but clearly, that had not been such a rare occurrence.

Emily and Griffin got to their feet, both casting curious glances in Henry's direction. Was he supposed to introduce himself? Or was Rose supposed to do it?

"Thank you for looking after him!" Griffin said to Rose. He spoke in a booming voice, much louder than was necessary in such modest quarters. Some might've called it boorish. Then he stepped forward and threw his arms around Rose.

"You're welcome," Rose said with a laugh, hugging him back in a way Henry found improper. Griffin's new bride was unperturbed; indeed, she was beaming at them as though this were perfectly normal.

Griffin released Rose and turned to Henry. "And you are the Duke of Beresford! I am Griffin de Beauford, son of William de

Beauford, at your service." He gave a slight bow. "Welcome to Chicago, Your Grace."

Maybe Henry should've felt relieved that Griffin had taken the lead with introductions, and had actually addressed him correctly. But the man's jolly tone was improper. Henry was not, after all, here on holiday.

"Thank you," Henry said stiffly, with a slight bow to both him and Emily. The latter made no move to curtsy, and no one introduced her, so Henry added, "This is Mrs. de Beauford, I presume."

"Actually, I'm still Emily Porter," she said cheerfully.

"I . . ." Henry stammered. Had he made a grave faux pas? But hadn't Rose said . . . ? "Forgive me, Miss Porter. I had been under the misapprehension that, well—"

"Oh, we're married!" Emily reassured him. "I just didn't take his name."

"Not everyone who gets married changes their name now," Rose added.

Henry stopped himself from asking how anyone could tell who belonged to whom. But perhaps he should not have been surprised. Rose had told him earlier that now, a man might marry another man, or a woman another woman. In his time, despite the existence of molly houses where gentlemen who were thus inclined could meet, and the occasional pair of confirmed bachelors or devoted lady friends who chose to live together, a bold statement of marriage would've been out of the question.

With a loud laugh, Griffin clapped his large hand on Henry's shoulder, startling him. "It will take you some time to learn the ways of women and men in this world!"

Henry's blood simmered. They were not friends, and Griffin was the son of an earl; Henry outranked him. Griffin had no business touching him in such a familiar manner. Moreover, Griffin was mocking Henry, pointing out his ignorance in front of Rose.

"Well, come on in and sit down!" Rose urged with a shooing motion. "I'll order dinner. Do you want pizza, Mexican, or Thai?"

"Oh!" Emily said as they moved to the living room. "We actually grabbed something right after work. I'm sorry. I didn't remember we were getting dinner." She looked apologetic as she and Griffin sat down. Andy War-Howl hopped into her lap, and Henry took a seat on the sofa opposite them.

Rose waved off the worry. "It's okay."

"You guys should go ahead and order something if you want," Emily urged Rose.

"No, that's fine. We can eat later," Rose said, though Henry and his growling stomach did not feel so indifferent. "What would you like to drink, though? Griffin, I got you that ale you like."

Griffin smiled broadly. "I cannot say no, then. That was very kind."

Emily asked for a Diet Coke, and Rose said she was having the same. Henry had tried the drink earlier. It tasted like a mixture of sugar, iron filings, and bad champagne.

"What would you like, Henry?" Rose asked.

He wanted a cup of tea, but that would mean that she would have to go to the inconvenience of making it. It was not as though she had a maid to help her entertain.

In order to make things simple for her, he said, "A glass of brandy, if you please."

Rose exchanged an amused glance with Emily before saying, "Sorry. Best I can do is Malört."

Why were Emily and Griffin chuckling? How was he to know that Rose would not have on hand what he believed to be the most common of spirits?

Rose added, "Seriously, I have wine, beer, coffee, or tea?"

"What is Malört?"

"It's a liquor made here in Chicago." She added to Emily, "I got it at a gag gift exchange at work a few years ago."

Griffin shook his head. "Your Grace, you will not enjoy Malört. I recommend the ale."

Henry was not inclined to take the recommendation of a warrior from the Dark Ages. He said to Rose, "I will have a Malört, thank you."

Rose shrugged, smiling. "I guess everyone should try it at least once. I'll be right back."

As she headed to the kitchen, Griffin leaned forward. "Your Grace, where is the ducal seat of Beresford? It was not a dukedom in my time."

Was that a veiled insult? Henry sat up a little straighter. "No, it is not the oldest dukedom, but it is no lesser in dignity for that. The title was conferred on my great-grandfather for his exemplary service in the War of the Spanish Succession."

Rose came back into the room with a bottle in one hand and a can in the other. "Henry's estate is incredible," she said, setting the drinks in front of Griffin and Emily. "And it's gigantic." She retreated to the kitchen again.

Griffin leaned forward and asked Henry, "Tell me, did they have hot showers in your time?"

"No," Henry said.

The other man grinned. "Are they not wonderful?"

If Griffin thought his rustic bonhomie was charming, he was mistaken . . . although Emily and Rose apparently felt otherwise. They were both grinning in the knight's direction. What a vulgar and vexing era this was. One's bathing, surely, was a private matter. Although Henry could imagine inviting Rose to shower with him, and lavishing the lather onto her beautiful breasts—

"He *loves* them," Rose called out from the kitchen.

Showers, she meant. "Yes," Henry said, striving mightily now not to think of her tempting bosom. "They are most pleasurable."

"You know so little about this modern era," Griffin said. "I remember what it is like to be so confused about so many things!"

Henry bristled. He hated almost nothing more than not knowing things, unless it was having others know of his ignorance.

"On the contrary," he said stiffly, as Rose, standing on a chair, banged around in the cabinet over the fridge. It seemed she was having trouble finding this Chicago liqueur. "I believe that I grasp most things with ease."

"No, no, you're like a newborn babe in the wilderness," Griffin insisted cheerfully. "You can hardly comprehend anything around you." He pressed his palm to his chest. "I will be your guide."

"Thank you, sir," he told Griffin coldly, "but in the event that I have needed some small piece of information, Rose has provided it."

Griffin shook his head. "She can't think of everything you need to know. A person of this time simply takes it all as a matter of course. For instance, do you know how to floss?" Emily laughed.

"Of course I do," Henry lied.

"Really?" Emily asked, looking intrigued. "You flossed in the Regency period? I had no idea! How often?"

"It varied," he said vaguely.

A loud clatter came from the kitchen, as though something metal had fallen to the floor. They all looked over, and Henry felt grateful for the interruption.

"Sorry!" Rose called over. "Found it!"

Griffin told Henry, "Well, I think you will find that this era is better than any that came before." He took a swig from his bottle, then glanced at his bride. "Though in truth, I would be filled with joy in any era, and under any circumstances, as long as I was at sweet Emily's side."

She beamed and leaned over to kiss him on the cheek. Henry found himself unduly annoyed.

Rose returned with more drinks and a bottle under her arm. "I thought you might want to see the label," she said to Henry, setting the bottle down in front of him. It appeared slightly dusty, with the words JEPPSON'S MALÖRT LIQUEUR under a red and blue shield. She poured a measure of the golden liquid. "But I don't think you're going to like it."

"We shall see." Perhaps his tastes were old-fashioned, rendering some food and drink strange to him, but that was not always the case. He'd rather liked the conchas, for instance.

"Well, you don't have to finish it." She set down a glass of water as well.

"Thank you," Henry said and lifted the glass of liqueur. It smelled . . . bad, actually, but Henry supposed he could not judge by that. Once, in France, he'd enjoyed a soft cheese that had smelled more or less like a horse's hoof. He took a sip.

His mouth was filled with the worst taste he'd ever experienced.

Or one of the worst. Once, after a dinner of slightly under-cooked sturgeon, he'd violently ejected the contents of his stomach. This tasted very similar. Only his awareness of all their gazes fixed on him kept him from spitting it out.

He swallowed hard. At least the foul drink was off his tongue, though who knew what it would do to his insides. He was aware that his face was screwed up in horror and disgust. The others laughed as he grabbed the water glass Rose had put in front of him and drained it. This didn't rinse away all the foul taste.

"So that's Malört," Rose said lightly.

Henry turned on her, astounded. "Why would you serve me such an abomination?"

"I did warn you, Your Grace, that you would not care for it," Griffin said, merriment dancing in his eyes.

"So did I!" Rose protested.

"It's kind of a rite of passage," Emily said. "Now you're a true Chicagoan."

"I am not a Chicagoan," Henry snapped.

After a moment of silence, Rose said, "Yeah, Henry really needs to get back to his own time."

That was, indeed, the best he could hope for. So why did her words also leave a bitter taste in his mouth?

Rose turned to him. "Do you want a glass of wine, after all? That'll help kill the taste."

"I—yes, thank you."

"He's had a lot of surprises," Rose told her friends as she stood up. "He was so freaked out when I cut up a pineapple the other day! Apparently, in his time they cost about the same as a car."

Emily and Griffin both laughed again as Rose made yet another trip to the kitchen. There was no malice in their laughter, but Henry could not help but wish she hadn't mentioned it. Tasting the pineapple with Rose had been a sweet experience in more ways than one, and he didn't like having it reduced to an amusing anecdote—one at his expense, at that.

Griffin said, "While you are here, Your Grace, you should avail yourself of the pleasures Chicago has to offer."

Only with effort did Henry keep himself from looking over at Rose. Yes, there were very particular pleasures he'd like to avail himself of, but he had no right to do it, not when he had no intention to stay.

Instead, he gestured at the vile bottle in front of him. "I am not impressed by Chicago's idea of pleasure."

Griffin laughed good-naturedly. "You have hardly seen any of it! You must come with us to a Chicago Cubs game."

"A what?" Henry asked. Rose returned with the wine, smiling.

"It is a sport."

"It's kind of like cricket," Emily interjected. "You have that, right?"

"We do." Henry took a cautious sip of his wine. To his relief, it tasted pleasant enough.

As Rose settled next to him again, he took a larger swig and tried to be discreet about swishing it in his mouth to rid it of the taste.

Griffin said, "It is played in an amphitheater large enough to hold forty thousand people."

Was he trying to trick him, so they could all laugh at him again? "I believe you exaggerate, sir."

"I do not," Griffin said. "There is no finer place to be in the merry month of May."

"I'm not into baseball," Rose said, "but you should go with them."

Why would he do that? He had no desire to make friends, and even less desire to be away from Rose.

"Thank you, but I have no interest in sport," he said. "I would sooner spend the time trying to go back in, well, time."

All three of them looked disappointed in his answer, but Emily said, "Is there any way we can help you?"

Rose scrunched up her face. "Actually, yeah. Maybe you guys could get tickets to the gala thing, too, and you could help search for the astrolabe? I know it's a lot to ask."

Emily exchanged a glance with Griffin and then said, "We talked about that. The tickets are sold out now, though."

Griffin looked thoughtful. "If you go back and pose for the painting, will the picture in the museum be restored?"

"I never thought about that!" Rose said. "That would confuse Aaron even more."

"And he would have no reason to trouble you," Henry said. Rose had told him about how the investigator, someone akin to a Bow Street Runner, had questioned her about the supposed vandalism. Although she maintained that neither Aaron nor anyone else suspected her of the supposed crime, it made Henry uneasy.

"Ah, but he would," Griffin said, smiling. "For if there is no investigation, he is free to court Rose, which he has told me he is very eager to do. And Rose, I understand that you have told him you would at least consider his suit."

Henry swiveled his attention to Rose. A pretty flush suffused her cheeks. For this damnable Aaron Coleman. Emily glanced up from her phone, a bemused smile playing at her lips.

Rose gave a self-conscious shake of her head. "Who knows? I guess part of me always knew he was doing his job, even if I did get embarrassed."

Griffin nodded. "And that was truly unfortunate. But as you know, I do believe him to be a good man. And I am hardly surprised that he has persisted in his affections."

"Right?" Emily chimed in. "Rose is the sweetest person I know, and she's beautiful, and literally magical. Of course Aaron's still crazy about her."

Henry's neck felt hot under his collar. He agreed with all of Emily's words, of course. Rose's qualities just didn't make a difference, when he couldn't stay here. But did they need to go on and on about a man of their time who could enjoy what Henry could not?

Griffin said, "Perhaps Aaron is the old-fashioned gentleman Rose attracted with her spell. After all, the mystery of the painting has kept him here in our city." He raised his bottle in Henry's direction. "Though your presence here is inconvenient to you, Your Grace, you may take comfort in the fact that it may bring two fine people together."

Inconvenient?

"I take comfort in nothing of the sort," Henry snapped. "Have you come over to cheep and jeer at my predicament?"

Emily rolled her eyes. "Nobody's cheeping. We came over to see if we could help you, you silly potato."

"Potato?" Henry echoed indignantly.

Griffin raised a finger. "I can explain. A potato is a vegetable. A root, in fact, which—"

"I know what a potato is, you lout," Henry snapped.

Griffin straightened up in his seat. Every trace of his good humor, which Henry had perceived as being a permanent stamp on his features, was now gone.

"It would be wise, sir," he said, "to blunt your sharp tongue, lest it endanger your teeth."

Was the man challenging him to a fistfight? Well, Henry had trained for just such a contingency.

Emily grabbed Griffin's hand and told him, "Henry's confused and upset." She looked at Henry. "They didn't have potatoes in England in Griffin's time. How was he supposed to know you had them?"

"I'm sorry," Rose said to Emily and Griffin.

"It's not *your* fault," Emily said. "We should go. You guys want to get some dinner!" She stood up and Griffin and her dog followed suit. The latter gave himself a good shake, making his dog tags jingle, as though shaking off the ill temper of the meeting. Henry got to his feet, too, but only because Rose did.

Emily said to Rose, "Thank you again for watching Andy. I appreciate it so much."

"Anytime, seriously," Rose said. "I'm going to miss him!" It was not hard for Henry to imagine that Rose had found the dog to be a much more agreeable houseguest than a misplaced duke.

That impression was only heightened when, after exchanging more goodbyes with her friends and closing the door, Rose whirled around to demand quietly of Henry, "What is your problem?"

"What problem do you refer to?" he rejoined. "That of being served a liqueur so nasty, they wouldn't serve it in Hell—"

"We warned you!" Rose walked past him to pick up cans, bottles, and glasses. "Plus, believe it or not, some newcomers to Chicago have a sense of humor about doing a shot of Malört!"

"I should've thought that was amusing?" he demanded. "And

should I have laughed to be told I am stupid as a newborn babe, by your very chivalrous friend?"

Rose looked over her shoulder on the way to the kitchen. "He said that because that's how he felt sometimes, when he first came to life here!" Henry followed her. As she put her burden down on the counter, she added, "How was he supposed to know you take yourself so seriously?" She pitched the empty beer bottle and Diet Coke cans in the blue bin under the sink. "You didn't have to insult him."

"His wife had just insulted me."

Rose picked up the bottle of Malört. "You mean when she called you a silly potato? That didn't mean anything!" she protested. "She calls her dog that all the time."

"That hardly makes it more flattering," he parried.

"Yes, it does! She loves that dog." Rose considered the bottle for a moment. Then she stood on a chair, opened the cupboard above the refrigerator, and put it away.

"Why are you keeping that!" he demanded, equal parts angry and mystified.

"I don't know, I might need it!" She hopped down off the chair. "Not all insults are insults."

"Yet Griffin de Beauford threatened me with violence, just because I called him a lout!"

"Because you meant it!" She shoved the chair sharply back into its place at the table.

"He threatened to knock my teeth in," Henry snapped.

"I know. That was totally out of line. But you hurt his feelings. He was just trying to help, and he thought you guys were going to be, you know, time travel bros!" She leaned back against the counter as though settling in for a long argument. "They're my best friends. You owe them an apology."

"I certainly do not," he said hotly. How had he become so aggravated?

Rose added, "And you owe *me* an apology, for putting me in an awkward position!"

He scoffed. "No one is in a more awkward position than I! Dragged to the—"

"Oh, here we go," Rose said, throwing up her hands. "Poor me, I'm in the wrong century."

Henry gaped, astonished. She was usually so kind and sympathetic about his predicament. "How dare you?"

"I'm sorry, but it sounds like you were miserable in your own century, too."

"I . . ." To his further vexation, her point was hard to refute. "It is more difficult to be here than you can imagine! And who is this Aaron Coleman, who courted you before?"

She shook her head. "He *pretended* to court me."

"Why would he do such a thing?"

"Because he was trying to figure out who stole a stone statue at the museum. Of course nobody did, because Griffin just came to life and ran off, but Aaron suspected Emily. He was, like . . . being a spy?"

Henry nodded slightly, to show that he understood, but he was aware that he was scowling.

Rose said, "And I liked him, and I got my feelings hurt when I found out he was just faking it, but he says he still likes me, and . . ." She shrugged.

"He sounds like a cad," Henry said flatly.

"So Griffin's a lout, and now Aaron's a cad." Rose puffed out her cheeks in a frustrated exhale. "What the hell is your problem?"

He clasped his hands behind his back and paced a few steps. "Do you think it can be pleasurable to me to hear your friends speak of a man who intends to renew his suit? Am I to listen to such conversation and smile, as though we were speaking of pleasant weather?"

"You're the one who said we couldn't get involved!" she said, holding a hand out to him.

It was true, but his frustration was boiling over. There was no doubt in Henry's mind now that had he met Rose in 1818, he would've courted her in earnest, with the aim of making her his bride as expeditiously as possible.

She went on to say, "I know you don't want to be here, and I know you don't want to be with me, so—"

"I do want to be with you!"

Fifteen

Rose's belly did a little flip at the agitation in his cultured baritone voice. If he'd been jealous of the talk with Aaron, that explained a lot. And she hadn't even tried to make him jealous, exactly. She'd just encouraged the talk about Aaron to let Henry know that if he didn't want her, well, someone else did.

But the way he was looking at her left no doubt in her mind that he absolutely, thoroughly wanted her.

Henry closed the space between them, cupped her cheek, and slanted his lips over hers. She took hold of his forearms, deepening the kiss.

Her backside was still leaning up against the kitchen counter. His hips pressed into hers, and through their clothes, the hard ridge of his arousal ground against her most sensitive place. As a reflex, she arched her back, the tight, tingling tips of her breasts pushing against his chest as she invaded his mouth. He buried his hands in her hair, messing it up. And she felt very ready to be messed up even more.

He pulled back abruptly, bracing one hand on the wall above her.

Ugh, what now?

"We must not do this," he said hoarsely. "I will be tempted to go further." He took a few steps away from her and put his hands on the back of his head.

"But I want to," she protested, closing the space between them. "Like, way further. All the way, actually."

He pinned her with an agonized gaze. "It would not be right. I am going back to my time, or so I hope."

Her spirits sank again. "I know. But . . . there's no reason why we can't do whatever we want to do in the meantime."

The frown line appeared between his brows. He retreated to the living room, sat down on the sofa, and looked up at her as though making an appeal.

"I understand that such brief assignations are no longer a matter of scandal, but when you did your spell, I believe you were hoping for a husband."

Rose came over and sank into the chair opposite him. "Um, not necessarily."

Lie. He was right. She'd just come from a wedding. Although she hadn't exactly admitted it to herself, she'd totally been hoping for a husband. And she hated not being honest about it now. One of the things she loved about being with him, after all, was that they seemed to be able to be honest with each other.

But she couldn't tell a man she'd known for less than a week that she was kind of hoping he'd fall in love with her.

She said, "I wouldn't mind, um, a brief assignation . . . We call them flings."

"Flings," he repeated. "Because you are flinging caution to the wind?"

"Um, maybe."

She wasn't going to beg this guy to have a fling with her, though. Maybe he was the best kisser she'd ever met, but still . . . she wasn't going to beg. Much. Or more than whatever was a normal-person amount.

Rose picked up her half-full glass of wine. She lifted it to her lips as Henry said, "Even if we were to have amorous congress, you would not be likely to enjoy it."

Rose sputtered and clapped her hand over her mouth to keep from spitting out her wine. She snatched a tissue from the box on the end table and blotted her mouth with it.

"Why would you say that?" she demanded. She would *love* it. She was sure of it.

Henry clasped his hands between his knees and looked down at them. In his dress shirt, with the sleeves rolled up, he looked ridiculously sexy.

"I have only bedded my wife. Through many months of experiment and observation—which is not to say that I was not utterly engrossed by every encounter—I learned how to kiss her, taste her, caress her, mount her, and serve her in the ways that brought her the greatest pleasure."

Rose pressed her fingertips to her lips. Hearing about this man's sex life with his now-dead wife was turning her on. And that was wrong. But she could just imagine Henry being utterly engrossed by an encounter. Not to mention him doing the caressing, and the mounting, and the serving.

He said crossly, "But I have no doubt that every woman is different."

Rose suspected he wasn't really upset about the fact that different women liked different things. Of course they did; they were human beings. He was irritated by the idea that she might not like it enough, and the fact that Henry really wanted to please her was incredibly sweet.

"I don't think we're all *completely* different, though," she said, scooching forward a little on her chair. "And we could learn about each other. I don't know everything you like, either."

He looked away and scoffed. "For me it would obviously be one of the greatest pleasures of my life."

Her heart skittered—even though he wasn't smiling, or even looking at her. "What makes you say that?"

"Because you are beautiful, and kind, and vivacious, and you excite my senses in a way that I never dreamed would be possible again."

Her breath felt a little shaky. "But Henry, it's the same way with me. I mean, I know we were just fighting, but . . . usually, being with you is wonderful."

She was already leaning forward and sitting on the edge of her seat. She slipped out of it and crawled over the short space to him, then sat back on her heels right next to the sofa, resting her folded arms on the cushion next to him. He stared down at her, his eyes even darker than usual, his lips parted.

She said, "Anyway, there's only one way to tell if we would enjoy it."

"Are you suggesting . . . an experiment?"

She nodded.

Then in one swoop, he was kneeling on the floor facing her, setting his hands on either side of her throat. *Appropriate*, she thought dizzily. *This man does have me in a choke hold.* But his hands were gentle as he drew her close and captured her mouth in his own. He stroked beneath the hinges of her jaw with the pads of his thumbs as his mouth urged hers open.

So good. Didn't he feel how right this was, too? This was no experiment. This was a demonstration of some inevitable law of the universe: magnetic pull, combustion. Every part of her, body and soul, wanted to yield itself to his fierce kiss, and to anything else he wanted. As one of his hands reached down to cup her breast, she blindly reached out and felt for the buttons of his shirt, undoing one of them.

He pulled away and released her. She opened her eyes. He was unfastening the rest of the buttons while staring at her, his breaths short and harsh. In only a few moments, he had it off and pulled off the ribbed undershirt. His pale torso, with minimal dark body hair, was muscled, with a firm belly. Rose had to sit back on her heels. Why did he look like that? He was a pampered, practically royal guy. She'd thought his main exercise was flipping book pages.

He yanked the hem of her dress to her waist. She unzipped the back zipper, and she heard a seam rip as he pulled it off over her head. She'd never had anyone literally tear her clothes off before.

She was wearing a pink bra with lace trim and matching bikini underwear. Nothing too racy, but Henry's wondering gaze took her in like he'd just discovered a new . . . well, heavenly body. It was impossible to feel shy when he was looking at her like that.

He gave a dazed shake of his head. "Forgive me," he said in a low voice. "This floor is too hard for someone so soft and lovely." That was such a sweet way to talk about her softness. She didn't know about that, but she had been thinking something along the lines that it was too unswept for a duke. He took her hand as he got to his feet and helped her up.

"Should we go to the bedroom?" she whispered.

"Yes, if you will have me."

She nodded, feeling the irrepressible smile on her face, and led him down the hall. Halfway there, he took her hand, pulled her to his side, and kissed her again.

He's not serious about you, she told herself firmly, even as her knees trembled. It wasn't the first time she'd told herself not to get too emotionally involved. But the way Henry was looking at her and speaking to her, and the way he kissed her so deeply, seemed really serious.

"It's, um, this way," she said with a soft laugh, when she could get a breath.

Once they were in the bedroom, Henry stopped her again by taking hold of her shoulders from behind. She felt his hands at the back hooks of her bra—he must've seen where it fastened. Maybe she should've let him do it, but she was too impatient. She unfastened the bra and took it off, turning to face him as she let it fall to the floor.

He gently cupped her breasts with his hands, replacing the support that had just given way with an intimate caress. She looked down as the pads of his thumbs traced the area just around the tight, aching tips, now a deeper shade of rose, without actually touching them. Her breasts rose and fell with a shaky breath as she put a hand on his strong shoulder for support.

He bent his head and pressed his open mouth reverently to the top of one of her breasts, and the slight scratchiness of his days' growth of beard abraded her tender flesh as he dragged his mouth to the other.

"Henry," she pleaded softly, touching his hair, and he dipped lower and flicked his tongue across one of her hard nipples. She drew in a sharp breath. He sucked it into his mouth, sending currents to her just-kissed lips and down between her legs. His teeth delicately scraped the oversensitive flesh. Any rougher would've been too much, but this . . . this was perfect. An involuntary shiver of pleasure went through her as he released the tingling tip, but stroked it with his thumb and, ever so lightly, stroked the underside of her breast with his fingertips. *Yes.* It seemed like that part of her body always wound up being neglected, but she always wanted to be touched there, just like that . . .

Rose moved to kiss him again, but he was bending his head to her other breast, cupping its fuller-than-usual weight to his mouth. A tiny sound escaped her lips as he nipped the peak lightly and then took it into his mouth and sucked. She arched her back without meaning to. *So good.* Why had she thought he would be reticent and awkward? Because he usually was. She'd very much expected to take the lead here, the cosmopolitan modern girl, seducing the nerdy scholar. Instead, she hadn't gotten a move in edgewise, and his caresses and his mouth had her shaking all over.

"I can barely stand up," she managed to say breathlessly.

He lifted his head. "Then lie down." He urged her over to the bed and kissed her once, and then twice, as she lay down on her back.

He moved to join her and she said, "Take off your trousers." In her dazed state, she was proud of herself for saying *trousers*, like he did, instead of *pants*.

"Yes, quite right," he said distractedly, unbuckling the belt in a rough, efficient way that sent a tingle through her nether regions and unzipping his fly, all while staring at her body. He shucked off his pants and the boxer briefs she'd gotten him and bent to yank off one sock, then the other.

The sight of Henry—the man who was more comfortable in suits than T-shirts—stark-naked, his hard, flushed cock jutting up against his belly, lust darkening his eyes, had to have been the sexiest thing she'd ever seen in her life. He knelt next to her on the bed, staring at her.

"What?" she asked.

"You are still rosy here." He brushed a fingertip over one of her erect nipples, making her squirm. "But less so than when I stopped to get undressed. Here as well." He touched her sensitized bottom lip. Impulsively, she sucked on his fingertip for a moment, and enjoyed the way his breath caught.

"Good observation," she murmured. "Are you going to do something about that?"

He cupped her cheek and brought down his mouth on hers, kissing her so deeply she writhed under him. She'd never felt like any of her exes spent a long enough time just kissing her, and it wasn't for her lack of mentioning it. Repeatedly, in fact. But Henry took his time, with kiss after long kiss, plunging into her mouth, as he stroked the undercurve of one of her breasts again, making every inch of her body feel alive. Then, as he kissed her, he pinched the hard nipple, making her moan right into his mouth. He lowered his head to tease that aching peak again, gently tugging it with his teeth, sending bright sparks of sensation along her nerves.

Finally, he raised his head and brushed the pad of his thumb across her lip. "There's that red."

She gave a breathless laugh. She was more than ready for him and reached down toward his cock, but he caught her hand and, with a slight shake of his head, pinned it on the bed next to her. He held it firmly there as he trailed rough, open-mouthed kisses down her quivering body and to the hollow inside her hip bone, just above the pink satin bikini underwear.

Oh, Goddess.

He released her hand to pull off her panties, and she eagerly raised her hips to make it easier. Then he knelt between her knees. He took hold of both of them and, with one definitive motion, spread her legs farther apart on the bed.

Fuck. This man did not mind taking charge. She was wide open to him, as exposed as she could possibly be. He could see how much he'd aroused her. But she didn't feel vulnerable. He'd entranced her, and she couldn't wait for whatever he did next.

"Beautiful," he murmured, and dragged his thumb straight up her soaked cleft, coming to rest with insistent pressure at precisely the right place. She couldn't help bucking her hips up to grind against him. With a knowing look, he pressed his other palm down flat on her belly, holding her in place.

The sweet, heavy ache between her legs was becoming sharp. "Henry," she begged.

He slipped one finger, then two, inside her, and she squeezed around him. The pad of this thumb circled her clit. *Yes.* Her head tilted back on the pillow. He was still holding her down, but as he expertly brought her desire higher and higher, she drew up her knees, and her toes curled on the comforter. She flung her forearm over her closed eyes. A high-pitched cry escaped her, then another.

"You're close," Henry said, his voice hoarse.

"Yes," she managed to say.

And then he *stopped*. His thumb moved away from where it should have been. His fingers, still inside her, were still.

Her eyes popped open. "Don't stop!"

"Just a moment," he murmured. She'd half expected him to be laughing at her, teasing her, but he was staring into her eyes, his expression rapt. "Stay with me, all right?" She couldn't help but trust him. She nodded. He lowered his head and deliberately kissed the inside of one of her thighs, then the other. His free fingers stroked lower, near her ass. Was this really the same man who'd fussed about what to do with a tea bag?

He kissed the springy curls on her mound, just a fraction of an inch from where she wanted his mouth or his touch. She thought she was going to scream. What the fuck was he *doing*?

Then he dragged his tongue across her needy clit, his fingers thrusting into her.

"Yes!" she cried out. He sucked there, ever so lightly, bringing her up to the edge again. She grasped his hair. She wanted to beg him not to stop again; it came out a scream as her orgasm crashed over her, a pleasure more intense than anything she'd ever experienced before. It went on and on, pulsing outward in waves, making her legs shake.

As the ripples of pleasure subsided, he stretched his body over hers, propping himself on his elbows. His hard length pressed against her. It had been years since he'd had sex. And here he had been ignoring his own wants while meticulously tending to hers. That was so wrong.

"Come on," she murmured, reaching down between them, and

when her hand encircled his girth, he made a choking sound. Hmm, it might be fun to . . . No, next time. She guided him to her entrance.

But he pulled back, frustrating her once again, searching her face for a moment. "You do not want to get with child," he murmured gravely.

Oh, that was sweet. "The pill, remember?"

Sheer relief washed over his face. "Yes."

Then he thrust home.

She heard herself cry out again, and at the same time, he made a kind of growl in the back of his throat. He filled her up completely. She loved having her hands on his strong shoulders. He pulled back.

"Is that good?"

"Yes!" she almost cut him off. "It's so good." She reached down and skimmed her palm over his bare ass. *Fuck me,* she wanted to say, but didn't, in case the vulgarity would take him out of the moment.

He obeyed the unspoken command anyway, with long, even strokes. She lifted her hips, matching his rhythm. There was none of the strangeness, the self-awareness that came with a first time. It felt so natural to be joined with him, as though they'd done it a hundred times before, although that didn't take away any of the excitement. She caressed his neck and shoulder, and although his eyes were closed, a line of concentration between his brows, he nuzzled into the touch like a cat. Sunk deep within her, he ground his hips against hers, sending bright sparks of pleasure through her that intensified with the next few strokes. She ran her hand down his back and could feel his body straining to maintain control.

"Let yourself go," she whispered to him. "Don't hold back."

He opened his eyes and stared at her as though she'd said something surprising. Was he surprised to see *her*? The thought filled her with dread. Had he been fantasizing about his late wife?

"Rose, my love," he said hoarsely, and the ardent look in his eyes chased away that thought and filled her heart with simple happiness. He bent to kiss the side of her neck as he drove into her faster, riding her with unleashed male power, their bodies moving together. Rose gripped his shoulders more tightly as her pleasure spiraled upward. As if aware of that, Henry slipped his hand between them, brushing her most sensitive place once more, pitching her over the edge into mindless bliss again. He plunged into her a few more times, savage and rough.

"Oh, God," he groaned as he shuddered and pumped himself into her. She hooked one leg around him, reveling in his satisfaction, as he bowed his head to her shoulder, breathing hard.

She wanted to say, *I love you*. But that was wrong. She hadn't known him nearly long enough to say that. That was probably just the dopamine or whatever chemical was currently surging through her veins after what had been, hands down, the best sex of her life. She kissed his cheek and stroked his hair wordlessly.

He kissed the side of her neck and she squirmed, every inch of her body still wildly sensitive. Then he lifted his head to search her expression.

"Are you well?" he murmured.

She gave a shocked laugh. "Am I *well*? Yeah, I'm really good, if you didn't notice."

"I did notice you were very good," he said, deliberately misunderstanding her and tracing a finger along her décolletage.

"I barely even did anything," she muttered. He'd taken charge and had seemed to know exactly what he wanted to do. Although she was fairly sure that if she'd insisted that he get on with it at that one point, or asked him to do something, not do something, or do something a little bit differently, he would've listened attentively and done it. And possibly have written down a few notes in a notebook later, in his impeccable handwriting. But she had no notes.

How was that even possible? "How did you know to tease me like that?"

He rolled over to his side and propped himself up on one elbow. She'd expected him to look smug about his own skills, and she would've even enjoyed seeing it, but his expression was still serious. "It is my theory that a slight delay, on the precipice of release, makes that release all the more powerful."

She had to laugh. "Okay, successful experiment. But I don't know if I want you to do that every time. You might kill me." Inwardly, she winced. That was the wrong phrase to use with someone whose wife had died in bed. "I mean, you'll drive me crazy."

Was that still a faux pas? There was going to be a next time, right? She felt that all-too-familiar postcoital rush of doubt. It had been a long time ago, but she'd known a guy to hit it and quit it before, ignoring her texts the next day and then actually blocking her number. It would be hard for Henry to ghost her while he was sleeping in her guest bedroom, but that didn't mean he couldn't have a change of heart.

"Not every time, then," Henry agreed, soothing her worry immediately. He took hold of one of her curls falling around her shoulders and gently pulled it straight, then released it to watch it bounce back again.

"You probably have other theories, anyway," she teased, and raised herself up to kiss him.

She realized, to her utter shock, that his eyes were wet. What? Why? Because he'd been lonely for a long time, she supposed. Her heart went out to him as she pressed her lips to his in a quick, sweet kiss.

"I do," he said. "Too many, perhaps, to test out in such a short time."

"Ah." Her heart broke a little, thinking about the short time. "We'll just have to do as much as we can."

After Rose excused herself and retreated to the bathroom, Henry lay back on the bed, his body utterly spent, his soul as alive as it had ever been.

His desire for Rose had grown into a torment, making him envious of happy newlyweds and the affections of friends, enraged by talk of another suitor, oversensitive in her presence to even the slightest of slights. And now that he'd given in to that irresistible magnetic attraction between them, he felt filled with light, like a newly forged star.

Emily had been right in saying that Rose was sweet, beautiful, and magical. In Rose's world, children's games were not just for children, falling spring petals were a sign of celebration, and old walls could be painted over with new dreams, as though nothing could be truly lost.

Knowing that their time together might well be a short season, too, he'd endeavored to bring her the greatest pleasure he could, given his own overwhelming need.

When he'd delayed her bliss in order to increase it, he'd more than half expected her to protest. If she had, he would've immediately capitulated. Nonetheless, he'd followed his instincts. Was it not fortunate that on his first time with her, he'd been able to please her so well? And that she had so pleased him? Was it not strange, truly, that their bodies and souls had joined so perfectly together?

Sixteen

On Thursday evening, Henry went with Rose to Jason Yun's home to discuss their plan for the gala at the Reuter mansion. Henry would've preferred to stay in.

The evening before that, he and Rose had enjoyed a second amorous encounter, and he was more than ready for a third. They'd spent a long while in bed while the rain pattered on the windows and little pink candles burned in their holders here and there in the bedroom, casting dark shadows and quivering golden light. He'd discovered that she loved long, slow, featherlight caresses up the sides of her body, the sides of her breasts, her satiny inner thighs. After sex, she'd gotten up and made him a cup of tea, bringing it back into the bedroom. Never in his life had he been served a cup of tea by a naked woman. And Henry could well imagine other ways he'd like to serve *her*.

He'd never imagined having such passion and pleasure again. But in his sober moments, while Rose was away at work, he reminded himself that a life couldn't be built on passion and pleasure. Getting their hands, literally, on the astrolabe was their only idea so far for returning him to where he belonged. And to do that, they needed Jason.

Rose said that ordinarily she would've taken the bus there, but she hired a car because Jason had given them all that money. Jason's home, which she called a *condo*, was in a neighborhood called River North.

They took the elevator to the fifteenth floor of the building, and once Jason welcomed them inside, Henry could not help but gape at the glittering view of the other tall buildings and the dark, vast lake beyond.

The condo itself, sparsely furnished, was not much larger than Rose's own apartment. This surprised Henry, because the man was wealthy. It was obvious to Henry not only from the way Jason handed over money, but also in the perfect tailoring and high quality of his clothes, his manner of carrying himself, and more than anything else, the way he'd exhibited no discomfort or shame whatsoever when making an outrageous request. Even from century to century, some things didn't change.

"I love your place," Rose told Jason as they sat down on his gray couches. "I thought a curator would have art, though."

"If I did, I'd want to change it too often," he said. He gave them what he called a Wi-Fi jammer: a black box a little bigger than a box of matches, with two prongs, presented in a steel case. Rose had already explained to Henry the concept of security cameras, and this device, it seemed, would prevent them from operating.

Turning the case over, Rose asked, "Why is the label in Russian?"

"It's from Russia," Jason said, and she looked a bit sheepish. He showed her where to switch it off and on again, then gave them pairs of anti-recognition glasses.

He said, "Ordinarily, I would keep your first names, so if you happen to see someone you know and they say your name, it doesn't look suspicious. But Henry, you don't know anyone in town, and

Reuter's probably seen that portrait in the news, so you're going to be Michael. And Rose, since you're connected to the museum, you're getting an alias, too."

He handed them each a stiff card with their images and false names that read *Illinois* and *Driver's License* at the top.

"Sarah Martin," Rose read aloud. "I don't think I can get my hair to look like that." In her photo, she had straight, smooth dark brown hair that didn't quite reach her shoulders.

"Hang on." He retreated to one of the bedrooms and emerged with a package that proved to be a wig.

"Wow. Okay." She peered at Jason. "So your group does this a lot? Disguises and false IDs?"

"I wouldn't say a lot."

She persisted. "Do you meet a lot of time travelers?"

"No," Jason said. "Here's what you can use to put gray streaks in Henry's hair, like on his driver's license." He handed her a plastic bottle. "Just apply it with a clean toothbrush."

Rose set the wig down in her lap. "What if we get caught handling the astrolabe? What do we say?"

"That you wanted a picture with it."

"Could we get arrested?"

"Just for touching it? Not likely. It would be impossible to prove attempted theft." Jason leaned back in his chair. "Reuter's doing this gala to look good and make people forget about the aldermen scandal . . . and probably, to have a clandestine meeting or two in plain sight."

"Calling the cops on his guests over nothing would be a bad look," Rose mused aloud.

"Yeah. Let me go over some more details."

Henry asked, "Mr. Yun, do you and your cohorts intend to steal the astrolabe later?"

"We don't have plans to do that. And speaking of plans, I've got something for you."

From a drawer in the coffee table, Jason pulled out a large piece of paper and unfolded it. "Here's a blueprint of the Reuter mansion that you can take home. I talked to Ryan again."

"You did?" Rose asked, clearly surprised.

Jason nodded. "Here's where he found the secret compartment." He pointed to a small red star on the wall of a second-floor room. "But don't bring this with you to the gala, obviously."

Henry tapped his fingers on the blueprint. "I will commit this to memory."

"Good. Your Grace, I'd like you to carry this messenger bag with you to the event." Henry had not noticed it next to the sofa before, but now he set it on the table. It was made of smooth black leather with a long shoulder strap and tiny letters on the side that read SMYTHSON.

"Isn't this your bag?" Rose asked.

"Yeah, I'd like it back, actually."

She looked dubious. "People don't usually bring big bags to galas, though."

"Yeah, but Michael is an excessive worrier, and he refuses to go anywhere without . . ." Jason opened the bag and took items out one by one. "A first aid kit, hand sanitizer, an extra pair of glasses, his phone, a power bank for his phone, his wallet and keys of course, medication in case he has a panic attack, Tylenol in case he gets a headache, and a cashmere cardigan in case his date gets chilly."

"All practical items, as far as I can tell," Henry said.

Jason told him, "And if someone says you can't bring the bag inside, you're going to get really haughty and arrogant and demand how they could dare treat you like this."

"He can do that," Rose said, at the same time Henry exclaimed,

"But it would not be arrogant to protest. Truly, it would be outrageous for them to confiscate my personal belongings!" Then he caught Rose and Jason exchanging an amused glance.

"Why does he need the bag?" Rose asked.

"Because you should have a plan for a quick change. That's what the cardigan's for, too. Now the good news is, you're going to be dressed up, and it's always easier to dress down . . ."

D amn it," Rose exclaimed an hour later, as they returned to her apartment.

"What is it?" Henry asked. He'd become accustomed to her cursing. And he could hardly judge, when she'd used even more shocking language in the bedroom, and he'd enjoyed it.

"I didn't ask him anything about his secret society!" She closed the door and locked it behind them. "I was going to ask him who they are, and how he got involved in it, and all these other things."

"Our task at hand is complex," Henry said, setting down the messenger bag Jason had given him. "It is hardly a wonder that you could think of nothing else."

"I guess." She sighed and walked toward the kitchen.

Henry followed her and saw she was pouring herself another glass of wine. She asked, "Do you want a glass, too?"

"Yes, thank you. Are you anxious about the gala?"

As she poured, she shrugged. "It's not like we're committing a crime. We're just going to use the astrolabe right where it is, if we can find it. And Jason has planned everything out pretty well." She brought his glass over to him. "But it makes me a little nervous."

Henry nodded. She probably wanted to talk about it more, and maybe he did, too. "Shall we go out onto the rooftop?"

She brightened. "Let's."

They climbed through her bedroom window, but before she sat

down, he said, "One moment." It was still damp from the last night's rain. He removed his jacket and spread it out. "There."

She touched a hand to her heart. "That is so sweet. But your butt's going to get wet. I'll go get a blanket for you." She made a move back to the window.

He took her arm gently. "No, do not trouble yourself. It will make my gallant gesture seem foolish. And you know that if there is one thing I cannot abide, it's seeming foolish."

She giggled. "Okay, but it wouldn't. That was *fairy*-tale romantic." She sat down, and he took his place next to her, noting that his arse would be only a little damp.

"We have to remember to use our fake names at that party," she said.

"Very well, my dear Sarah," he said, making her giggle again. He added, "As a duke, I never imagined the need to assume a false identity."

"I'll bet. When I was looking at that blueprint, with all those rooms, I remembered how Everly Park is so much bigger than that."

He stilled. "What do you mean, remembered?"

"From the website? Of course. I was looking at it again at work." She shook her head. "It just made me think again about how I took you from having everything, to having absolutely *nothing*."

"I would hardly say nothing," he said, thinking of the night before, and the night before that.

She gave him a wistful smile. "Still. I know you miss it. At work today I was thinking how I'm surprised that you're not still mad at me."

"My feelings, as I think you know, have quite changed."

"They might change back, if I can't figure out this spell, and you get stuck here." She set down her wineglass to push her hair away from her face, a motion that lifted her breasts enticingly beneath her purple blouse.

"I am confident you will," he said with a twinge of misgiving. "How did you learn how to do magic spells? Was your mother a witch?"

"Oh no. I worked at an occult bookstore and started reading about it . . . though I didn't like some of the books. And I did a lot of research online, and kept a whole journal full of notes about herbs and stones and rituals and things." She shrugged. "There's a lot of contradictory info out there. So I just try to listen to my instincts. And then I try different things and see what works."

"That is very similar to the scientific method. Observation, reason, and experiment."

"In my case, it's scouring the Internet, intuition, and experiment," Rose said, numbering them off with her fingers. Then she cast a worried look at him. "I really am sorry I can't just whisk you back to the year of your choice. My intuition tells me it's impossible. And I can't find any advice about how to do it."

He had been considering that. "I am not sure going that far back in time would've worked as I once hoped."

She lifted her eyebrows in surprise. "Why not?"

His unexpected affair with Rose had led him to this thinking. It was so marvelous, despite the future being so uncertain.

He stared out over the rooftops. "I would never have told her that she would die young, for that would've stripped her days of joy."

"Definitely." Rose nodded.

"For me to know, and not to tell her, would've been a terrible secret, and there were no secrets between us before. I would have been constantly anxious, always endeavoring to prolong her life . . . it would've changed the nature of our love. It might've ruined it."

Rose pressed her fingers to her lips. "Maybe it's just as well you didn't figure out how to turn back time. It would be terrible if you didn't even have all your good memories."

Henry's gaze slid to her. "Not to mention memories of a certain charming witch."

She leaned over and kissed him, and he felt a twinge of longing. If he had met her in 1818, things would have been very different.

"It is good of you to try to return me to the year from which I came," he said. "And to go on this mad escapade with me."

She smiled. "Hey, at least I get to go to a swanky party."

"I generally loathe such affairs. Will we be expected to dance?"

"Even if there's dancing, it'll be optional. Hardly any men will dance."

He cocked his head. "The ladies will dance with each other?"

"No, they'll just . . . You don't need a partner to dance, most of the time."

"Ah. Is it like ballet, then?"

She laughed. "Definitely not. People just get out there and do what they feel like doing."

How was that even dancing? "Show me," he demanded.

"Nooo." She set down her wineglass and hugged her knees. "I'm not even a good dancer. I just think it's fun at a party."

"But I want to know what modern dancing is like."

"You first. Show me how to do the . . . what was it? The reel."

He stood up. "You will not master it in one lesson, but I can give you an introduction." He held out his hand to her.

"Hold on." She tapped on her phone. "Let me see if I can find Scottish reel music." He watched her thumb move against the screen. "See if this sounds right."

The familiar strains of a reel reached his ear. "Yes, very good."

She jumped up and stood next to him. "Okay, show me."

His memory flashed back to his first meeting with the dancing tutor, long ago. "The main step is like this . . ."

"Oh, wow." She laughed as she tried to follow the footwork. "This is so dainty."

"Hardly. This is a vigorous country dance. And then you kick one side and the other, like this . . ."

"Look at you!" she squealed. "You're so good!" Henry had never considered his dancing to be anything more than passable, but he could not help but be very pleased by the compliment.

She tried in earnest to imitate his steps, then declared, "This is so hard." Giving up, she skipped and whirled around the roof with abandon, waving her arms in the air as if she didn't have a care in the world.

He laughed, took a few long steps toward her, and caught her up in his embrace. "I am afraid you are doing it wrong."

"Oh, I disagree," she purred, looking down at his arms around her. "I think I'm doing it right." The next moment, he was kissing her deeply.

When she pulled back and gazed up at him, her eyes were shining. "When I rented this apartment, I imagined spending time out here with someone special. But I never did, until you."

He felt again the longing for things that couldn't last. "Have we made a mistake?" he couldn't help but ask. "With every day, we make a goodbye more difficult."

"Did it really feel like a choice?" She stood on her tiptoes to kiss his cheek. "You of all people know that all we have is now."

"No, I will also have the memory of it." He took both her hands in his. "It is strange how in one's memories, certain nights may mean more than whole years of one's life."

She said, "As far as I'm concerned, my time with you happens outside of time. It's never not happening. Anytime I want, I can come right back here and be with you again."

"That is one theory of time I have not heard yet," Henry said and kissed her again. "But I will believe it, too."

Seventeen

After work the next day, Rose found a seat on the bus going south, settling the bags of groceries next to her that she'd kept in the fridge at work during the day. She worried a little about Henry, who'd spent the day at the Field Museum. They'd taken the bus there together, and she'd walked the rest of the way to work. She'd given him a printout of a street map, along with her spare key; he'd insisted he wouldn't mind the almost three-mile trek home, and that it would be perfectly fine if she visited her brother that evening.

A couple of years ago, after Ryan's short stint in jail, Thursday nights had become movie nights for them. It had been Rose's idea. Now that he was doing all right, she kept waiting for him to suggest cutting back to one night a month, or opt out of them completely. If he ever did, she'd understand. Most brothers probably didn't want to hang out with their sisters every week, after all.

But he'd never once canceled, which had made Rose feel guilty for texting from work that day to say,

> **Hey, I'm going to stop by tonight,
> but I'm not going to stay for a
> movie, okay?**

She didn't want to stay out too late and leave Henry by himself, and bringing him along would've been uncomfortable, since neither she nor Ryan had ever brought a friend or a date. Ryan didn't even know that Henry now fell in the latter category, and she didn't plan on telling him. After all, she had even posed it to Henry as a friends-with-benefits type of situation.

Ryan had answered that she didn't have to come over, but she told him she wanted to. Griffin might or might not have told Ryan about their disastrous evening; if Ryan brought it up, she wanted to defend Henry. Also, Ryan had sent her a text the day before saying that maybe she shouldn't go to the Reuter mansion, after all. She wanted to reassure him that it would be no big deal.

She got off the bus and walked the short distance to Ryan's place, less than a mile east of the White Sox's Rate Field. His apartment was the lower floor of a small two-story brick house, smushed between two boxlike brick apartment buildings.

The truth was, she also hadn't wanted to completely break the tradition. They sat on his not super comfortable futon couch, took turns choosing the movies, and ridiculed each other's choices—Rose's rom-coms and Ryan's action movies. Once in a blue moon, Ryan selected an arty film that managed to be both smug and depressing at the same time. They ate popcorn topped with nutritional yeast and garlic salt, the way their parents had always made it. Maybe it wasn't much. But the weekly get-togethers felt like a little pocket of safety and stability.

When Ryan came to the door, in a hoodie and sweatpants, he frowned at the grocery bags in her hands. "What have you got?"

"It's nothing!" she said as she came inside. "It's just a few things."

She took them to his kitchen, where two baseball caps, an un-opened roll of paper towels, and various cleaning supplies sat out on the kitchen counter. His apartment was never dirty, but it was cluttered, lacking anything in the way of storage furniture, baskets, or bins. She cleared a space, plopped the bags down, and started taking out produce.

He leaned against the doorframe and watched her with an an-noyed look. "Why are you shopping for me again?"

"Because you're busy!" She brandished the box of protein bars. "Look, Costco had the ones you like."

"And you're not busy," he deadpanned, as she put the bars in his cupboard. "You've got nothing special going on."

"I'm *not* doing this so I can check your kitchen," she said, guess-ing what he was thinking. She'd not-so-secretly done that a few times, early in his sobriety, and she wasn't sorry. "I haven't even thought about that for a long time."

"I know. I'm just saying you don't need to do this."

She opened the fridge door to put the away the cantaloupe and oranges. "Obviously, I do. Look at this." She gestured to the mea-ger contents of the fridge—hot dogs, a tub of margarine, and two different brands of giardiniera. "You're going to get scurvy."

"You have to let me take care of myself," he said with more em-phasis. "It seems like you don't think I can."

Oof. Did he think that? It wasn't true at all. She shut the fridge and turned around, meeting his serious gaze.

"I know you can. You're doing great."

He was and he wasn't. The truth was, she wanted to fix more than his grocery situation. She felt like he was gritting his teeth through life, like someone recovering from a serious injury, except it wasn't heal-ing, and she didn't know what to do about it. He needed a purpose in life, and she couldn't give him that. But she could give him a melon.

She added, "They had great deals on fruit."

To her relief, he chuckled. "I don't buy very much at a time. I shop about every other day because there's a really cute cashier." He pushed off from the doorframe he'd been leaning on and sat down at the card table that was his kitchen table.

Oh. He didn't usually talk to her about things like this. She leaned back against the counter. "Why don't you ask her out?"

"Nah, she's got a wedding ring. I just think she's cute."

Rose laughed, but felt a little disappointed. A relationship might've given him a great sense of purpose.

Ryan said, "So Henry's got a crush on you."

She tried to arrange her features into a semblance of surprise. "What? No! You saw how grouchy he is. We're just friends."

"That's what you said about that hiking vlogger guy."

"*Ugh*, I forgot about him. I went out of my way for him, too!"

"Literally," Ryan added. Rose had told him how the trek through the state park had felt more like a forced march. But when it came to dating, she'd often put up with too much.

Ryan picked at the label of the hot sauce sitting on the table. "Well, Henry's all right."

Apparently, he hadn't heard about the argument with Griffin. "He is. But he's not staying here. In our time, I mean."

Ryan squinted up at her. "Do you really think you can send him back?"

She shrugged. "I'm going to try."

"But what if you can't? What's he going to do then?"

A little bit of hope sparkled like stray glitter. She mentally brushed it off. Although, like glitter, it was hard to get rid of completely.

"We'll see what happens," she said.

There was no point worrying about the future. Her arrangement with Henry wouldn't last long. If she was smart, she'd focus on enjoying every bit of it.

And in the next couple of weeks, for the most part, Rose did. When she was at work, Henry read at the library or at home, and they made the most of their evenings. On most nights, they stayed in.

But one night, she took him to a board game café that served jibaritos, the sandwiches invented by a Chicagoan from Puerto Rico, which used mashed, fried plantains in place of bread. Rose had always loved them. Henry didn't care for them, but he enjoyed trying to teach her chess; she taught him Scrabble, which she'd played with her grandma.

The café owner, glancing around at the hundreds of contemporary board games on the shelves, declared that Henry and Rose were old-school.

"Oh, you have no idea," Rose told the man.

He said, "Well, it looks to me like you both won."

Rose's boss, Lisa, approved her request for a few days off, although it was short notice. This gave Rose more time to show Henry the things she thought he'd enjoy. When she took him to the top of the Willis Tower, he marveled at the view from one hundred and ten stories up. However, he balked at venturing out onto the glass observation deck.

"Come on," she coaxed. "Hundreds of people step out on there every day."

"Then it is only a matter of time before it gives way."

She shook her head and got in line for the Skydeck. When it was her turn, she walked out to the edge. A bird flew over the tops of the other buildings below her feet. She turned around to look at Henry and stretched out her arms.

"Look! I'm standing on air!"

He reached her in a few long strides, picked her up, and ignored her surprised squeak as he hauled her back to the solid floor.

"What are you doing?" she said, laughing as he set her down.

"Rescuing you, of course." He kissed her.

She took him to the Griffin Museum of Science and Industry, mentioning that the name had nothing to do with Emily's Griffin. Nobody called it that, anyway, she explained; the "Griffin" had been a somewhat recent addition, and Chicagoans were hostile to name changes. Henry said he heartily approved of this civic trait.

He spent two hours at the U-boat exhibit, enthralled by the explanations of both the naval strategy and the science of submarines. But he also liked Rose's favorite room, the Whispering Gallery.

Maybe because the museum was about to close, they had it to themselves. She showed him the brass footprints that indicated where he should stand at the end of the long, curved room, then took her place at the other far end, her back to him.

In a low voice, she asked, "Henry, are you enjoying the museum?"

"Good God," he murmured. "It is as though you are right next to me."

She felt the smile spread across her face. The effect of the curved walls on sound waves was pure science, but it felt like magic.

"Don't you know?" she teased. "I'm always with you."

A moment of silence. She scrunched up her face. That had sounded too serious.

"And yet you are too far away," he said, his voice dipping into that lower, huskier tone that sent delicious shivers up her spine.

"Is that right?" she asked, with a quick glance at the gallery entrance to make sure they were still alone. "What would you do if I were closer?"

"Hmm. I do like you being able to hear me without seeing me," he mused aloud. "Maybe I will blindfold you."

Rose pressed her fingers to her lips. The tingles in her body traveled lower. "You have to really trust someone to let them blind-fold you," she said.

"And do you trust me?"

"Absolutely."

Much later that night, after Henry had found many ways to tease and indulge her, he slept naked next to her in the lamplight. The scarf-turned-blindfold had been set aside, and Rose looked at him for a long time, memorizing his dark straight brows, the contour of his jaw, the texture of his skin. She could've asked to take a picture of him, but she knew no photo would capture him the way her memories could, the image filtered by the unnamed feelings in her heart.

Eighteen

O n the Saturday of the gala at the Reuter mansion, Rose
remembered Jason's quick-change talk and spent a few
hours buying extra clothing items. She didn't know why
she'd left it until the last minute.

Late in the afternoon, after carefully turning Henry's hair mostly
gray with theater stage paint and a toothbrush, she showed him what
she'd purchased.

"First of all, this is like a cotton beanie thing you can put on, like
this." She put the slouchy black hat on herself.

He smiled. "That'll hide my hair."

"Exactly. And you can wear this under your shirt and tie." She
dug into the bag and held up her thrift store find: the cream-colored
T-shirt with an illustration of people at Grant Park.

"Lollapalooza," he read aloud slowly. "What is that?"

"It's like an outdoor concert with a lot of performers."

He shrugged. "Well, that seems respectable, at least. You have
planned things out very well. Will you try the same spell you tried
before?"

He didn't sound skeptical, but Rose felt like some skepticism would've been called for.

"Yes. Hopefully, with the astrolabe, it'll work."

They got dressed in the bedroom, Rose changing into a black midi dress that she hoped would blend in. The full skirt hid the small Wi-Fi jammer in a thigh holster. She was pairing the dress with ballet flats, made for sneaking.

Then she went to the bathroom to put on the wig. She'd watched about twenty YouTube videos for tips on how to keep it secure, involving a headband called a wig gripper and an adhesive that seemed so powerful, she was hoping that it really did come off in water. She applied a bright red lipstick, which she never wore, put on the anti-recog glasses, and studied her reflection in the mirror.

The moonstone pendant would've looked perfect with it . . . but she'd pried the stone out of its setting, put it in an empty mint tin, and tucked it into her large black beaded purse. She'd put all her spell essentials in there, including the incantation she'd written on a page torn out of a journal. The purse's crossbody strap would leave her hands free as she skulked around a giant mansion.

She came out into the living room where Henry, wearing his black tuxedo, stood looking out the window, his hands clasped behind his back. He turned around and his intense gaze on her made her knees feel a bit watery.

"I prefer your curly hair," he commented.

"Well, you look great with glasses and gray hair. Which doesn't seem fair, to be honest. We should go . . . . Wait." She snapped her fingers. "I almost forgot the heliotrope."

"The flower?" he called after her, as she scampered back to the bedroom.

"No, but I'm using that, too," she called back. She plucked the polished, oil-slicked stone from her altar. Then she returned to the living room, holding it out in her palm for him to see. It was dark green with bright red spatters.

She said, "It's also called a bloodstone. Have you ever heard of a guy named Pliny the Elder?"

Henry's brows raised, and he said with a touch of hauteur, "One of the first true scientists, in ancient Rome. Who has not heard of him?"

"Pretty much everybody," Rose said. "Anyway, he said that if you combine a bloodstone with the heliotrope flower, it'll make you invisible."

"That is impossible," Henry said promptly.

"*There are more things in heaven and earth, Horatio, than are dreamt of in your philosophy*," Rose teased. He got a strange look on his face, and she realized she should explain that he wouldn't *really* be invisible. As far as she knew.

"I think it means people won't notice you. Anyway, I rubbed it with heliotrope essential oil and I did a spell, so hopefully, it'll keep us out of trouble." She slipped the little stone into the satin bag so it wouldn't get oil on her phone, and put it in her purse.

Henry pursed his lips dubiously. "Perhaps we can also rely on good judgment to stay out of trouble."

"If I had good judgment, I'd stay home," Rose said. "Don't forget your bag!"

She'd booked a driver to take them to a popular theater a few blocks away from the mansion. Since she was using her own name on the app, she didn't want to go straight to the party. She'd even managed to buy a couple of tickets to the stand-up comedian's show there, in case she needed a cover story later. Once they were in front of the theater, they put on the anti-recognition eyeglasses.

They walked a few blocks to Armitage Avenue, where several cars waited to turn right onto Burling Street in Lincoln Park. Finally, they got close enough to see their destination.

Bright lights illuminated the three-story limestone with wrought iron balconies, and fairy lights twinkled from the trees. Two women got out of a Mercedes. The passenger, wearing a sleek white halter jumpsuit, waited while the driver, in a tuxedo, gave her keys to the valet. An elderly couple, a man and a woman, made their careful way up the front steps to the door, where two large men in uniforms stood . . . Security guards.

Rose's stomach plummeted, even though in some part of her dreamy brain, she'd known that there would be tight security. This was no joke: she really *shouldn't* be doing this.

Henry regarded her seriously. "Are you unwell?"

She looked up at the mansion. "What if someone catches us removing that panel, and we get arrested for property destruction or something? I could lose my job."

"The panel your brother spoke of is designed to swing open," Henry pointed out logically.

"Right."

And there was a worse option. What if her spell actually worked?

Rose took a deep breath and let it out. She couldn't think like that. All along, she'd been promising to do her best to get him home. She and Henry had just been having a fling. A beautiful, soul-altering fling.

Henry offered his arm to her, she took it, and they proceeded up the front walkway.

"This place is *huge*," she said. "Maybe not to you, but to normal people."

"It is very fine. French Baroque, I believe. When was it built, anyway? In the 1700s?"

"2010, according to Zillow." The builder must've purchased and torn down a few of the narrow three-story houses of brick or limestone, which all looked to be well over a hundred years old, that lined the rest of the street.

"Ah. Revival," Henry muttered. As they reached the door, Rose let go of his arm to pull up the tickets on her phone. Henry reluctantly opened and handed over the messenger bag so the woman could poke around in it with a flashlight and a stick, then watched with interest as a woman wearing a name tag welcomed them and scanned the QR code on Rose's phone.

He and Rose stepped into a foyer with a polished marble floor, crowded with people, some glittering, who chatted, laughed, and greeted one another with hugs. House music surrounded them, making Rose feel as though she'd stepped into a lavish music video. To the right was the enormous dining room, empty except for a few staff members placing silverware next to the plates with gloved hands. Chandeliers sparkled above them, and flowers spilled out of their vases on the white-clothed tables.

Henry peered around them. "Do you see our host?"

"No."

One group of thirtysomethings sat posing for a group picture on the winding staircase, which had an ornate railing of dark bronze with gilded accents. Halfway up, the steps were cordoned off by a heavy velvet rope. Good thing they were planning to use the back way.

Even more people thronged in the wood-paneled room ahead, clearly the location for the cocktail hour before the dinner. A white-jacketed server with a silver tray crossed the arched open doorway.

"I love the back terrace," she murmured. The floor-to-ceiling windows on either side of the back doors offered a view of it, along with the fountains and gardens beyond. Some guests mingled out there, drinks in hand, near the fire pit. A hired dancer in a circusy sequined leotard swirled ribbons as she spun and gyrated. Henry seemed to be watching her, and Rose couldn't really blame him.

"Those are some handsome statues," he said of the marble figures of Roman generals.

Rose shrugged. "I like the Venus in your secret garden better."

Henry gave her a strange look. Maybe he was wondering why she was thinking about the gardens of Everly Park at a time like this.

"But I don't see any doors to the kitchen," she added.

"Pocket doors. They slide open," he said. He inclined his head, and Rose followed his gaze toward the framed panels next to the bar. Two men in tuxedos stood at either side.

Henry murmured, "We must create a diversion to tempt those footmen from their posts."

"They're definitely security guards, but yeah," Rose agreed. "Should we split up?"

"By no means. If we are caught in the wrong place, we must pretend we have stolen away to enjoy a passionate embrace."

Even though a little thrill went through Rose at the thought, she said, "Isn't that kind of a common ploy, though?"

"That I do not know, but it is a common thing to do. Drunken louts love nothing more than a conquest in another man's grand house, which they may boast of later to their fellows at the club."

Hearing Henry say *at the club* made Rose smile, even though she was pretty sure he was talking about a very different kind of club. "But if we're together, who's going to create the diversion?"

"A third party, of course."

Before she could ask whether they were calling Jason, Ryan, or Emily and Griffin, a server appeared at Henry's elbow with a tray full of hors d'oeuvres: cucumber slices topped with something else, a dollop of pale cream, and, to Rose's delight, tiny flower petals.

The server said, "Ahi tuna with wasabi aioli?"

Disappointed, Rose shook her head, but Henry said, "Thank you," and accepted one. As the server retreated, he bit into it—and then his eyes widened. He gave a cough and spit it out into his hand.

Rose clapped her hand over her mouth in shock, and she darted a quick look around to see if anyone had seen him. No one was looking their way.

"What are you *doing*?" she demanded in an undertone. She hadn't known him to be so crass.

"The fish is nearly raw!" he hissed back in outrage. "Everyone will be ill!" He looked down at his cupped hand, appalled.

Rose laughed. She grabbed a tissue out of her purse and scooped up the half-eaten appetizer. Glancing around, she didn't see a trash can, so she tossed the trash in her purse for the time being. Then she surreptitiously took out a packet of hand wipes and cleaned off his hand.

He frowned. "You should not have to clean up such a disgusting mess."

Smiling, she waved off his concern. "I know you can't stand to be dirty. Anyway, I don't blame you. Rare tuna gives me the ick, too."

"Are you saying they serve it that way on *purpose*?"

"Yeah, people like it, and it's too fresh to make them sick." She shrugged. "I'd rather have a hot dog any day."

He recoiled. "You eat dogs?"

"No! I'll explain later. How are you going to create a diversion?"

"With the appearance of a very famous guest. I know how people behave when a distinguished person arrives at a ball." He looked slightly smug. "In fact, I have often *been* that distinguished person."

Rose squinted at him. "Okay, but who?"

"No one. It's going to be a ruse." While she tried to understand that, he scanned the room again. "Still no sign of our host?"

Rose peered around, too, and then spotted Reuter. "He's outside," she murmured, pointing at the glass doors that led to the back terrace. She was breathing a little too quickly, from nervousness. At least the billionaire or billionaire-adjacent guy was engrossed in conversation with another man.

"Perfect. Follow my lead." Henry strode back the way they'd come, and she hurried to keep up with him. He came to a sudden stop in the middle of the crowded foyer.

"Oh my Goddess!" he said in a baritone voice, loud enough to carry over the music and the crowd. He pointed out the front window. "She's here!"

As the chatter and laughter abruptly stopped, two things flashed through Rose's mind.

First, it was *hilarious* to hear Henry say, *Oh my Goddess!*

Second, nobody would *ever* believe this.

But as dozens of guests swiveled their heads in Henry's direction, she realized she might be wrong about that second thing. In any case, there was no way to walk it back. She had to help sell it.

She clutched Henry's arm and practically screamed, "That's her car! Ahhh!" She bounced up and down, staring out the window. "I can't believe she came!"

It was working. At least a couple dozen guests rushed back into the foyer. A woman came up to Rose, demanding, "Who is it?"

Henry interjected, nonsensically, "Yes, it's her!"

The woman's friend declared, "I'm livestreaming this!" She took out her phone and advanced toward the door.

More guests flooded the front hall. Rose heard one of them say the name of a very famous pop star, while another mentioned a media mogul with Chicago roots. The guests pushed past her and Henry toward the window.

Henry grabbed Rose's hand and pulled her back into the rapidly emptying paneled room. The two guards didn't seem to take notice of them as they abandoned their post. Whether they intended to keep an eye on the crowd or nab an autograph, they both drifted toward the foyer.

Yes!

Rose knew they only had a couple of moments, but it was all they needed. Henry took her hand in a firm grip and speed-walked toward the pocket doors. He slid one open, and after they darted through, he closed it silently behind them.

"Can I help you?" a male voice challenged them.

Rose jumped like a startled cat.

She looked up to see not Reuter, thank Goddess, but a man wearing a black apron over a white chef's coat and black pants. As he approached them, a dozen cooks in the cavernous white kitchen looked up from their bowls, pans, and trays.

Oh no. Of course the kitchen would be busy. Why hadn't they planned what to say?

"Mr. Reuter wishes me to inform you that his guest of honor is here," Henry said, with a snap of authority in his voice that sent a spiral of excitement through Rose's belly. He swept the kitchen and the staff with a haughty glance. "She will be taken on a tour of the house."

"Okay," the man said, wiping his hands on his apron. "Uh, who is it, again?"

"The one you were briefed about," Henry said without missing a beat. For once, his talent for grouchiness was really coming in handy. He turned to Rose. "Let us make sure they are ready on the back terrace."

Back terrace? *Oh.* There was another door on the other side of the kitchen. No one had to know they were going to sneak up the stairs.

Henry marched to the other end of the kitchen and she followed him, probably not quite matching his dignified bearing, though she tried.

Once Henry had shut the door behind them, Rose whispered, "You're brilliant." She remembered what Henry had said about boxing. "Was that a feint? Did we just do a feint?"

His dark eyes kindled with warmth. "I believe we did."

Her heart hammered in her chest as they trotted up the stairs. At the top, she whispered, "Hang on." She hiked up her dress to reach the signal jammer strapped to her thigh, feeling suddenly like a Bond girl. She clicked it and then straightened.

"Make a left, and then it's the first on the right," Henry muttered. They peeked into the guest bedroom, with gray walls and a grayish-plum comforter on the bed.

"That's it," Rose whispered. "It's behind the nightstand."

They went inside and Henry closed the door behind them. In tandem, they moved to the nightstand, lifted it, and moved it back, because it would make more noise to push it across the floor. Rose couldn't help but notice that they worked together very well. But that was probably just a coincidence, right?

Henry crouched in front of the painted wooden panel that looked like all the others surrounding the bottom half of the walls in the room. As Rose bent over him, he dragged his fingers along the wainscoting.

"Yes," he murmured and swung the panel open.

It revealed an empty compartment. Henry felt around it, knocking on a couple of the sides, then swung the panel shut.

"Shit," Rose whispered. Henry straightened and beckoned for her to help him move the nightstand back.

"Perhaps there is more than one secret compartment in this room," he said in a low tone. "Let us check."

He took one side of the room and she took the other. Several minutes later, they met in the middle, straightened, and looked at each other.

Henry went to the door and peered out, up and down the hallway. She was now feeling less like a character in a Bond movie and more like one from *Scooby-Doo*. Henry gestured for her to join him back in the hall, and once she did, she shut off the signal jammer.

She whispered, "It could be anywhere," adding mentally, *We'll never find it.* And she wasn't even sure she wanted to.

But then she got an idea. "Remember what Jason said about people keeping their prized possessions close?"

"His bedroom," Henry said. "According to the blueprint, it's on this floor, on the westernmost side."

As they headed that way, Rose peeked into the rooms that they passed: a personal arcade filled with vintage video games and pinball machines, just as Ryan had said; a bathroom with a marble floor and a chandelier; and another bedroom.

They went up the second flight of stairs, Rose looking wildly around them for any security guards. She activated the jammer again, and Henry opened the door.

"Boom," Rose whispered.

Four huge columns surrounded the bed. On one side hung a round gilded mirror, maybe six feet in diameter, and on the other, a painting of a ship in another ornate, gleaming frame. A sofa and two chairs in a separate sitting area overlooked the garden.

"Panels," Henry whispered, pointing to the lower third of the walls. "Let's look."

But this search for extra secret compartments was just as pointless as the first, leaving Rose feeling stupid and sweaty, one of her least favorite combinations.

"I hate this game," she said.

Henry appeared undeterred. "Try the closet," he said, pointing.

It was a room, really. As Henry upturned the mattress to look beneath and examined whether the mirror or the painting concealed a safe, Rose opened drawer after drawer of neatly folded T-shirts, boxer shorts, socks, and sweaters.

"Oh, astrolabe, where are you?" she singsonged under her breath.

Her phone in her crossbody purse vibrated. She wanted to ignore it, but what if it was Jason with important information? She un-zipped the purse—then paused.

It wasn't her phone. It was the moonstone in its little satin bag. And it wasn't *actually* vibrating. It was just sending out some kind of energy she could feel. She wanted to find the astrolabe as soon as possible and try to use it . . .

Or maybe *take* it. After all, what were the odds that she'd get the spell to return Henry right on the first try?

Besides, it's ours, a voice in her head insisted.

Footsteps sounded on the stairs.

Nineteen

enry hauled Rose over to the bed, wrapped his arms around her, and pulled her down on it with him. She gasped, but gave him a quick nod. He stretched his body over hers, propping himself up on his elbows, as the sound of the footsteps advanced. Beneath him, Rose arched her back, wrenched herself out of the top of the stretchy dress, and shoved it down to her waist.

An undergarment of burgundy satin and lace covered only half of her lush breasts. He caught a fleeting glimpse before she rose up and crushed her mouth to his.

Yes. As he kissed her, he blindly cupped one of her breasts and stroked his thumb across the soft flesh. He released her mouth to kiss the side of her neck, focusing on the sensitive place just behind the hinge of her jaw. She made a soft, delicious sound, writhing beneath him.

He was forgetting himself, his body roused and ready for duty. This was for show and nothing more. He lifted his head and both he and Rose listened.

"I think they're gone," he whispered to her. Her skin felt hot to the touch and her face was flushed.

"Did anyone see us?" she whispered back, a bit breathlessly.

"I do not know."

He stood and walked to the door, which stood ajar. He listened, but heard nothing.

It is time to abandon this mad quest, he thought as he walked over to her. "I am afraid there is no way to know where my astrolabe is."

"Oh! I was about to tell you. I think my moonstone is trying to tell me." She pulled the luminous blue stone out of her purse and held it up in her palm. Its star-shaped sheen on the surface appeared clearer and sharper than ever.

She asked, "Where is the astrolabe?"

Nothing happened, but her eyes fluttered shut. *This is nonsense,* Henry thought. But he thought of Rose teasing him with the Shakespeare quote earlier: *There are more things in heaven and earth, Horatio . . .* Charlotte had teased him in the exact same way, more than once, because his middle name was Horatio. Henry hadn't told Rose his middle name, and he knew perfectly well it had not appeared on the church record. Nor had it been in the title of his portrait, he'd noticed.

She opened her eyes again. "The pinball machines," she breathed.

"What?"

She peered out the door, looking left and right, and then gestured with her hand. "Follow me."

Having no better plan, he did. She hurried back to the room filled with peculiar booths and tables, all with flashing lights and garish illustrations. The various cabinets had mysterious names: **PAC-MAN. DONKEY KONG. GALAGA.** Henry supposed there was no time to explain their use.

She held the stone up in her hand, as though it were a lamp in the dark, and then strode directly over to one of the tables as though drawn by a magnet. He followed her.

"Ha!" she said. "It's *in* this pinball machine."

The letters at the top of the thing read: **BEAT THE CLOCK**. If his astrolabe truly could be used as a time travel device, hiding it in this machine suggested a droll sense of humor.

Rose looked wildly around, then picked up a stool next to a nearby table and raised it over her head, clearly meaning to smash the machine open.

"Wait!" He held up a hand.

She set the stool down again. Henry crouched down and ran his fingers along one side of the machine, then the other. As Rose bent down next to him, he said, "Here. A secret door."

"He must've gutted this machine," she murmured.

He swung it open. A round gold edge gleamed in the shadowy compartment.

Yes!

Henry grasped the astrolabe—

A blaring noise. They both nearly jumped out of their skin.

"*Shit!*" she hissed. "It's alarmed!"

Henry couldn't let go of the astrolabe. He just couldn't.

He said to Rose, "It's a good thing we practiced climbing out windows."

She gave him a little nod and a knowing smirk. And his skeptical soul sent up a wordless, fleeting prayer that he hadn't led her into disaster.

He shoved the astrolabe into the messenger bag as they both rushed to the window. He flung it open and kicked at the screen in front of it. A whole panel fell away. They would surely be seen by someone outside, and they might be caught, but what other choice did they have?

Rose straddled the window. At least they were only on the second floor. Heavy footsteps thundered up the main staircase.

"I'll land in the shrubs," she said, and before he could consider whether there were a better strategy, she maneuvered so that she was dangling from the sill by both hands, then let herself drop to the ground with a yelp and a crunch.

With the messenger bag tucked under his arm, and two large men entering the room, Henry climbed through the window and, in a split second, made sure he spotted her scrambling away before he flung himself down.

It felt like two dozen men poking him with sticks at once, but he didn't feel as though he'd broken anything. Rose grabbed his hand to help him stumble to his feet.

Several loud pops—*gunfire!*

No, fireworks. Peach and gold sparkling lights blossomed over the back terrace.

"Fuck," Rose said and sprinted in the other direction, along the side of the mansion, in the shadows. Henry took off after her, securing the now-heavy bag against his side and dearly hoping she had an idea of where to go. They reached the evergreens and the fence at the border of the property and she veered left.

She was heading toward Halsted, the busy street behind the mansion they'd walked along before. That was wise. She looked back at him and he made a shooing motion to urge her to keep going.

Then a barrage of deep throaty barks made Henry look back. A sleek, muscled dog rushed toward them, its white teeth flashing in the dark, and two guards were not far behind. Henry would have to knock the dog in the head with the astrolabe so it wouldn't bite Rose—

"Who wants a treat?" she squealed in a high-pitched voice and threw something at the dog, hitting his nose. The dog paused to look down.

The half-raw fish in the napkin. As the dog gulped it down, Rose threw herself at the chain link fence at the back of the property and climbed over it, Henry right behind her, as the approaching guards foolishly yelled for them to stop.

They reached the busy street. "This way!" Rose gasped, pointing to a restaurant with a sign that read **THE WIENER STAND**.

Perhaps a dozen people milled about outside, and others sat at a few outdoor tables, eating. The smell of fried food filled Henry's nostrils. They darted into the small building.

At least fifty people stood shoulder to shoulder, carrying out shouted conversations and laughing, and a woman behind the counter seemed to be berating a customer.

Rose grabbed Henry's hand and pulled him through the crowd, crouching down as she did so, and he followed suit. Once they reached the far wall, Henry did not have to be told to squat down where they couldn't be seen from the door.

"Take off your jacket and shirt," she hissed at him, grabbing the fake eyeglasses off his face and then whipping off her own. Somehow, Henry hadn't expected to actually *use* the quick-change techniques. They were for desperate circumstances . . . but these were very desperate circumstances.

The couple closest to Henry and Rose had their backs to them. They were holding up their phones, an action Henry understood now, recording the server who was yelling at yet another customer. Rose tugged at the wig. She winced, and Henry recalled her saying the glue was only supposed to come off with water. But she was glistening with sweat, and she had it off in a moment. She stuffed the items they'd removed into the messenger bag, then gave Henry the stretchy hat she'd purchased for him and pulled on her chunky gray cardigan.

"Let's stand up now," Henry murmured as she fastened the clasps on the messenger bag. She handed it to him as they rose to their feet.

"Oh, fuck," Rose whispered, turning her face back to the wall. Henry spotted the guards pushing through the crowd.

"Hey, assholes, wait your turn," a big guy told them. At the same time, Henry thought he heard the cook demand of a person in front, "Cheddar or American?"

Rose tapped the arm of a woman next to her and said, "Oh my God, why are those workers being so *mean*?" She was still out of breath.

The woman and her husband turned to Rose and Henry, smiles on their faces. The woman said, "That's what this place is famous for."

"Famous for being rude to their customers?" Henry couldn't help but ask.

The man laughed good-naturedly. "First time in Chicago?"

"Yes!" Rose said, as they moved closer to the front. "We're from Des Moines, and he's originally from London."

Belatedly, Henry realized what she was doing: making the four of them look like a group of friends. It was brilliant. Would this and the quick change be enough? How well had the men seen their faces? His heart hadn't stopped pounding in his chest.

"Hey! Little dicks in the suits!" A shrill voice from the counter made them all look up. The woman was shouting at the guards. "You don't come in here and push people! Get the fuck out of my store!"

The taller guy said, "Um, we're looking for—"

"Um, um, we're looking for," the woman mocked him, imitating his deep voice. "We don't tolerate rudeness!" That generated a wave of laughter in the crowd, several of whom were holding up phones now.

The woman turned to the next man in line, who had shoulder-length hair and thick brows. "What the fuck do you want, Caveman?"

The customer beamed as though he'd been paid a compliment. "Char Polish and large cheese fries." The guards had stepped back. Henry felt a chill as the taller one met his gaze, but didn't pause there as he scanned the room.

A man behind the counter banged something, metal against metal. He yelled at the guards, "We said get the fuck out of here!" He jabbed his finger at the door. "Have a good night, sirs!"

One of the guards muttered something in disgust to the other. Henry guessed it was along the lines of *We're wasting our time* or *They're not here, anyway.* They made their way toward the door.

The couple Rose had chatted with stepped up to the counter to order. Rose pressed up against Henry.

"I think we're safe for now," he murmured, wrapping his free arm around her and squeezing her tight.

When she pulled back from him and nodded, she looked more exhilarated than terrified. "Let's get some hot dogs. I'm starving."

Henry nodded. "Whatever those are, I am hungry, too."

"The guards might still be outside, though," she murmured.

"They don't recognize us," he reassured her.

When they reached the counter, the woman smiled at Rose. "What do you want, sugar tits?"

"Two char dogs, two regular fries, please," Rose said loudly over the din.

"Dragged through the garden?"

"Yes, ma'am."

Henry turned to Rose and asked, "Drag them through the garden?"

"All the toppings," she explained.

The cook laughed at Henry's confusion. "This bitch is from England and doesn't understand English."

Henry had never in his life been referred to as a dog, never mind a *female* dog. Astoundingly, the insult didn't give him a moment's distress. Clearly, the staff members doled out insults to entertain the crowd, and by chasing away the guards, they had earned Henry's gratitude.

The woman looked Rose up and down. "Baby, you don't want a strawberry shake? I know desserts hate to see you coming."

Rose laughed and rolled her eyes. "Not this time!"

She paid and stuffed a twenty-dollar bill into the tip jar. Once they had their baskets in hand, they moved toward the door, but the woman shouting again made them turn.

"Are you on drugs?" she demanded of the customer.

"What?" the man protested. "I just want ketchup on my hot dog." Several people in the crowd booed loudly.

"Did he want walnut ketchup, or oyster ketchup?" Henry asked as they went outside.

She raised her eyebrows. "Tomato ketchup."

"I have never heard of it."

They made their way to an empty table. "Well, you can try it. But *not* on a hot dog. This is Chicago."

As they sat down, Henry attempted to discreetly search the area for their pursuers, and realized Rose was doing the same.

"I don't see them," she murmured, and Henry shook his head to indicate that he didn't, either. He tucked the messenger bag firmly between his feet, looping the strap around one ankle in an abundance of caution.

Rose whispered, "That was *insane!*"

Henry's guilt unfolded like a dark bloom. Although he'd never considered himself an especially good man, he'd at least been raised to believe his word was a sacred bond. He'd tacitly promised Rose that he wouldn't steal the astrolabe. While he could not bring himself to accept that what he'd done was truly a crime—it was *his*, after all—Rose had made it clear that she had no intention of taking part in such a thing. He had forced her into it, anyway.

He cleared his throat. "My dearest Rose, I must—"

"I've never run that fast in my adult *life*," she said. "I think it was the adrenaline." She picked up her hot dog and took a big bite.

He said heavily, "You are not usually chased like a doomed fox."

"We were *clever* foxes. I mean you're a genius, obviously, but I never thought I'd be good at the sneaking around, and the danger—" She gasped, her eyes widening. "Scorpio rising!"

Henry had no idea what she meant. "Even so, I am certain you were very surprised by what happened this evening."

"You mean, finding our astrolabe using the moonstone?" That hadn't been what he'd meant at all, but his mind snagged on the way she said *our*. "I *am* surprised! For years, I would do these little spells, and when they worked, I wasn't sure if they were coincidence. I wasn't even sure I helped break Griffin's curse. But now I know I can do things with crystals. Big things." She paused for a breath, then peered at him. "Hey, what's wrong?"

Henry looked around them, but even the people at the other table, loudly joking among themselves, were not within earshot. Traffic whined from the street, punctuated with frequent honks.

He said, "Rose, by stealing the astrolabe, I went expressly against your wishes. I put your safety, your freedom, and your good name in grave danger. Once I had it in my grasp, and the alarm was sounded . . ." He shook his head at himself. "Never in my life have I done such a rash thing."

She gave him an impish smile. "Oh, I wanted to take it, too."

"What?"

She spread her hands. "Even before we went into the arcade room, I was thinking about it. And when the alarm went off, I knew we didn't have a choice. Not if we were going to try to get you back." She took another bite of her hot dog, as though she had no cares in the world.

"We were both of one mind," Henry said, his guilt diminished, if not dismissed.

"Eat," she urged. "You must be starving, too." He was. The hot dog was some kind of mild sausage on a roll. "But take those peppers off. You're not going to like them."

Henry removed the narrow peppers and then took a bite. The sweet flavor of the unnaturally green relish, the sharp mustard, the fresh tomato, the onion, and a pickled cucumber spear all blended with the slightly charred meat.

"It's very good," he said once he'd swallowed.

She smiled. "I'm glad you like it. I'll call us a car in a few minutes. Let's not talk about it while we're in the car, okay?"

Henry nodded. "That is wise."

Rose used a napkin to wipe off the faint black smudges under her eyes. The paint she'd applied to her eyelashes had smeared in her exertions. She then attempted to smooth out her chaotic curls.

"I've never felt more beautiful," she quipped.

But Henry found the disarray of her curls suggestive of a very different activity, as was the fresh bloom of her cheeks, which anyone would've admired.

"You always look like a goddess," he said. Her smile faded, and she looked uncertain.

It reminded him of an earlier conversation. "Do you remember what you said at the party, about liking the Venus statue?"

"Yes?"

"How did you know about that statue? It wasn't in the pictures we looked at."

"No, I remember seeing it." She shook her head. "It must have been on the website."

Henry was positive it had not been. And it was not the first thing she'd known of his life that she had no reason to know. When he'd first told her and Jason that the astrolabe had been a gift from his wife, Rose had behaved for all the world like she *remembered* that. The fact that Rose had quoted the same Shakespeare as Charlotte could, of course, be counted a coincidence, but could her handwriting? Too many strange things were adding up. And Rose believed she'd lived past lives. She said she didn't remember anything . . . but with the right questions, or in the right situation, might those memories come back to her?

He couldn't speak to her of the highly unscientific theory. The past few weeks with her had been some of the happiest of his life. He cared for her deeply, for the person she was, here and now.

But why had the moonstone found its way to Rose? Why had her love spell summoned *him*?

Was Rose the reincarnation of Charlotte?

Twenty

As soon as Rose shut her apartment door behind her and Henry and locked it, she sagged against it in relief. "I still can't believe we did this."

They'd taken an Uber home. During the ride, Henry had been silent, and Rose had chatted to the driver in a general way about the comedy show they'd supposedly been to. If the anti-recog glasses had worked, and their faces hadn't been visible on Reuter's security camera footage, they wouldn't even be suspects in the theft. Hopefully, the bloodstone with the heliotrope oil would keep them from being recognized, too. Still, she figured the alibi couldn't hurt.

Henry retreated to the bathroom and emerged a minute later with damp hair, having washed out the gray streaks. "I'm going to wash up, too," she told him. "I smell like hot dogs and fear."

When she emerged, deodorant-ed and more comfily dressed in a T-shirt and sweatpants, Henry was sitting on the sofa, the messenger bag on the coffee table.

He looked up at her. "I was waiting so we could take a look at it together."

"Amazing," she said, touched by his restraint. She came over, clicked on the lamp, and sat down next to him. Then he pulled out the astrolabe, set it on the table, and set the bag aside.

"Wow," Rose breathed. "It's gorgeous." It was about the size of a dinner plate, with two open circles, both with symbols and lines, attached in the middle to the base. It awed her to think that such an elegant device had been crafted so many centuries ago.

"It's much shinier than when I saw it last," Henry said.

"It's been restored. Like Emily does at the museum." She grazed a tentative fingertip along the rim. "What do all these things mean?"

"These lines here on the bottom plate show the sun's height. See, the horizon line is here." More energy came into his voice. He was always in a good mood when he got to explain something, she'd noticed. It was too bad that he had been stuck in a time and place where there were so many things he couldn't explain.

He pointed to the curved line. "At the top we have noon, and at the bottom, midnight."

"Okay, wow." Rose leaned closer to him, and he put his arm around her. That always felt so good. "What's the layer on top of it, with all these fancy curved shapes?"

"The tips of the shapes are the stars and constellations." He turned the plate a bit. "And this top plate shows the path of the sun."

"The moonstone goes here, right?" She pointed to what looked like an empty setting in the outer rim, at the bottom.

"Precisely. It's not part of the mechanisms representing time and space."

She unzipped her purse and took it out. "I'm going to get some superglue." She set it on the table and got to her feet, then paused. Henry was staring at the stone intently.

"What's wrong?" she asked.

He gave a quick shake of his head. "I am sure it is but a trick of the light. I thought that it seemed to glow, from within."

She looked down, then took in a quick breath. "No, you're right.

That star glow is brighter." She bent down to touch it. "And it's vibrating again."

Henry picked it up and held it in his palm. "I can't feel it."

"No, it's like . . . I don't know, spiritual."

She went to the kitchen and dug around in the junk drawer overflowing with takeout menus, aluminum foil, a plastic bag of High John the Conqueror root she'd forgotten about, and two measuring tapes. Finally, she found a tube of superglue.

She returned to the living room. As she carefully squeezed a couple of drops of clear liquid into the empty setting on the astrolabe, she winced. "I'm sure Emily wouldn't approve of my restoration methods." She screwed the cap back on the tube again and put the moonstone in its place. "Yep, it fits perfectly . . . I'm just going to press on it for a minute, and then it should hold."

"Perhaps you may attempt the spell in the morning," Henry said.

"We should do it tonight," she realized aloud. The exhilarated triumph of the evening drained out of her. "If we somehow did get arrested for stealing this, we'd miss our chance."

Henry's expression sobered. "It seems likely we will not face arrest. And surely you are exhausted—"

"No, listen. It's still Saturday, and it's almost midnight, so it's great timing for a spell reversal." The fact that it had been the full moon before troubled her, but she put it out of her mind. That had been a love spell. This was different.

His dark eyes bored into hers. "Is timing so important in magic?"

"I wish it wasn't." She wasn't going to cry while he was still here. "But in magic, timing is everything."

He took her hand and kissed it. In a low voice, he said, "In love, too, I suppose."

Her heart ached. "That's right."

She went to the hook by the front door to grab her purse, which still held what she needed for the spell. Then she returned and picked up the astrolabe, keeping it flat because the superglue would still be drying.

"Come on. Let's go to my altar."

She'd never invited anyone to join her at her little altar before. For her, it was almost more intimate than the things she and Henry had already done. He followed her into the bedroom and knelt down next to her.

After she set the astrolabe on the altar, she pulled things out of her purse, first returning her Hecate statue to its usual place. Then she put all three tarot cards back on the altar, but upside down. Instead of a pink candle, for love, she put a black candle, for undoing, in its holder, ready to be lit.

She asked Henry, "Can you, like, set the astrolabe to Gemini? Since the moon is in Gemini tonight?"

Henry frowned. "Yes, I can." He leaned forward and moved the middle plate.

As she took her matches out of the wooden box, she almost lost her resolve. But she had to do what was best for Henry. And as much as she would've liked to believe that staying here, with her, would be best for him, she knew that wasn't true.

She took out the page with the incantation and unfolded it, feeling horribly self-conscious. It wasn't like she really knew what she was doing.

"Let's both hold on to the astrolabe, okay?" she suggested, resting her free hand on one edge. He took hold of the other side of the rim. "I'll let go before I say the last words, but you hang on. I think if it works . . . you'll go back, and I'll stay here."

"Where will the astrolabe be?"

"I *think* it'll go with you?"

Henry took her hand that lay on the instrument and lifted it to his lips. Rose's heart skipped a beat. Then he gazed up at her.

"I do not know if this will work, but whether it does or not, I want you to know how much I . . ." He paused, as though looking for the right words.

Rose's throat tightened. "You're welcome. I really do want you to be happy."

He ducked his head, frowning.

"All right, here we go," she breathed, and began reading the new incantation.

She'd tried out several drafts, increasingly complex, involving myths associated with time and esoteric references. In the end, she'd chosen a more straightforward approach. Each of the five lines corresponded to one of the elements—earth, air, fire, water, and spirit—beginning with fire, for Hecate.

> O Hecate, torchbearer and the keeper of the keys,
> guide Henry on the tides of time to his own century
> and to the one place on this earth that he loves most dearly.
> Reverse what I have done so breezily and carelessly,
> and make things right for him, body and soul. So mote it be.

Nothing happened.

Rose opened her mouth to say, *Well, I tried.*

Then her vision went black and the floor fell away from under her feet.

She'd forgotten to let go of the astrolabe!

She couldn't see or hear. As far as she could tell, she wasn't breathing. Was Henry with her? She thought she felt his presence. They were floating outside time and space. The astrolabe was the only thing she could feel, and if she let go of it now, she felt like she might be lost forever.

Then a solid floor was under her bottom and legs where she sat, with the reassuring grip of gravity. Were they in Everly Park? Had she done it?

The air felt cold and damp. The darkness lifted—but only barely. In the dim light of a crescent moon, she could make out that they sat on an open stretch of land. She met Henry's astonished gaze.

"Rose. Why are you here?" His voice was hoarse.

"I didn't let go in time!" In fact, she was still gripping the astrolabe, and so was Henry.

His brow was knitted. "I should've made certain that you did. We must get you home safely."

Rose got to her feet. "Where *are* we?" Then a wave of dizziness and nausea hit her, and she swayed.

He stood up slowly, asking, "Are you unwell?"

"I feel a little messed up," she said.

"Yes, I feel it, too, just as before. And my head is once again starting to ache."

"Ugh, mine, too. Right behind my eyes." She pinched the bridge of her nose. "Are we near your house?" Everly Park was probably on a huge tract of land.

"No," he said, squishing her hopes as he scanned their surroundings. He had the calm, alert manner she'd seen in him at the mansion. This must be how he reacted in a crisis: by becoming very focused and trying to think his way out of it. Well, he hadn't been calm when he'd first appeared in her apartment, but those had been extreme circumstances.

Thick grasses, up to her knee, rustled in the breeze. Around them lay . . . nothing. The silence of this place freaked her out. There were crickets and tiny rustlings in the grass, but no hum of traffic, no drone of a distant airplane. Hundreds of silent stars glittered, and a cloudy purple streak arched down to the horizon. In another situation, the sky would've delighted her. But here and now, it filled her with dread.

"I believe we may be on the moors," Henry said. "If so, we are hundreds of miles away from Oxfordshire."

"Shit." Rose covered her mouth with her hands. "I'm so sorry! Do you think there's a way to get to . . . well, anywhere?"

"Yes, of course. You have brought us to another century. Traveling over part of England is nothing in comparison. First we must get you to Everly Park, safe and sound."

"But what if I can't get back to my time?" Panic tightened her throat. What if she couldn't see Ryan again?

He gently took hold of her upper arm and looked into her eyes. "You are obviously adept at time travel. Past success is the best indicator of future success."

She rubbed her forearms. It was *freezing* out here . . . though maybe that wasn't the only reason she was shivering.

"I will build a fire to keep you warm," Henry said. "As the dawn breaks, we will get our bearings . . ." An acrid stench made him trail off. "What is that?"

"Skunk." Rose switched on her phone's flashlight and searched the thick cover of wild grasses and brush around them. "I don't see it!"

To her own ears, her voice held a note of panic. She was scared, and not particularly about the prospect of getting sprayed. What if she was stuck here?

Henry asked, "A skunk? The black animal with the white stripe?"

"Yes." Weird question, she thought.

"And you are certain that this foul odor has been made by a skunk?"

"Of course. I've smelled it a hundred times." Hadn't he, since he lived in the country? Rose pressed her hand to her chest. She was hyperventilating.

Henry clasped his hands behind his back, looking around him. "In that case, we are not on the moors. I have read of your skunks, but we do not have them in England."

"No way." When Henry had said they were on the moors, she'd just automatically believed him. "Then where—"

"Chicago must've been small in 1818. You will recall that I'd never heard of it." He paced a few steps. "Is it possible that your part of Chicago did not exist at all?"

"Oh, *shit*. Are you thinking we're in the same spot?" She vaguely recalled the dioramas at the Chicago History Museum. "There was an army post by the river, and a guy named DuSable built a cabin there . . . but I don't know if there was *anything* out here. Maybe Native American settlements?" There was a land acknowledgment on the Art Institute of Chicago website, and she tried to remember what it had said.

Henry looked thoughtful. "Would the native peoples here be friendly to us, in 1818?"

Rose scoffed. "I doubt it. I think the army fought them off their land." She felt a crushing sense of failure. "Henry, I'm so sorry! I got your hopes up, and—"

"My hopes are not down," he said firmly. "One rarely succeeds the first time in any endeavor. We must simply . . . attempt to get back to your time, and reassess."

She gave a shaky laugh. "I don't know about *simply*." She still felt dizzy. Maybe from the hyperventilating. Or maybe from the hurtling through time itself.

Henry knelt down on the ground in front of the astrolabe and patted the place on the other side. She leaned the phone, with its flashlight still on, against some brush, and then knelt down. Her knee landed on a sticker bush, and she grunted and shifted her position. But as she stared down at the astrolabe, despair washed over her.

"I can't do it. I don't have my little Hecate statue or my candles or *anything*."

"But we have the astrolabe, and the moonstone in it." He grabbed her hand. "My dear Rose. You are a powerful witch. Do you need images of your goddesses for them to be present?"

His question distracted her from her fears. "Not really. They help me to feel connected to them. But—"

"Can you not envision the candle you would burn, in your mind's eye?"

"Uh . . . that could work." The candles themselves weren't magical until she used them. They were a symbol that strengthened her intentions. "But I don't think I can imagine it and do the incantation at the same time. It's too much to keep in my head."

"Then I will imagine it for you." He still had hold of her hand, and his dark gaze held hers with steady devotion.

Henry was, in general, not great at eye contact. To have him gaze adoringly right into her eyes was an honor. And it made her selfishly glad that she had failed to get him to Everly Park, because it meant they were still together.

Henry asked, "Should it be another black candle?"

Rose nodded. "I would do a pink candle, too."

Had she told him that a pink candle signified, among other things, romantic love? Would he understand that her desire to bring him back to her apartment might help the spell work?

"A black candle and a pink one," Henry said. "They are both lit now."

"But I don't have an incantation written for this."

"Take your time. These candles will never burn out." He cast a wry look at the prairie around them. "At any rate, I have nothing else to do."

Then the ground fell away and her vision went black.

She hadn't done anything yet! Were they going back? She continued squeezing Henry's hand. Even lost in some in-between, she could feel him with her, and it made all the difference.

A solid surface arranged itself below her—or at least, it felt like that. She opened her eyes. They were in her neighborhood, but outside . . .

No, they weren't. They were sitting in the middle of a vacant lot. Several of the buildings were different; shorter. Wooden signs read **BILLIARDS** and **CIGARS**. A group of white teenage boys sat on a stoop across from them, smoking cigarettes. They wore white T-shirts, their hair was slicked back, and two of them wore cardigans. What in the world . . . ?

One of them, wearing horn-rimmed glasses, looked right at them and yelled, "*Sakra!* Where'd you come from!" *Sakra* . . . She hadn't heard that word for a while, and only from her late Grandma Novak. He was cursing in Czech.

"Shit!" Rose said to Henry, for maybe the dozenth time that night, gripping the astrolabe like it was a life preserver. "This isn't—"

Then they were floating in nothingness again.

Rose prayed. *Hecate, goddess of the crossroads, please take us home . . .* For some reason, she felt the need to clarify. *Take us to my apartment.*

The sofa seemed to arrange itself underneath her. The floor was under her feet, and the ordinary air trickled into her lungs. She couldn't seem to get a full breath. She opened her eyes, and both she and Henry pulled their hands away from the astrolabe like it was a hot cookie sheet.

Henry cleared his throat. "Are we remaining here?" he asked politely.

"I hope so," Rose breathed, and they both waited a few long moments.

"Did that just happen?" she demanded. "We were *here*, in 1818?"

"And in another time, I believe," Henry said.

"I think it was around the 1950s. My great-grandma had lived there then. And my grandma, when she was still a kid. But I didn't mean to go there! I mean then!" The room was spinning. Was she not fully settled yet in this tiny pocket in space-time?

Henry covered their joined hands with his free one. His hands felt so dry and warm. He turned his intense gaze on her. "My love, you are very pale."

"I . . ." Oh, Goddess, was it happening again? Everything in her peripheral vision was dissolving into sparks.

Twenty-One

Rose's eyes slid closed and, to Henry's horror, her body went limp on the couch, her head and torso pitching forward. He rushed to take hold of her before she fell forward and cracked her head on the astrolabe lying on the coffee table in front of them. Her bare arms were chilly to the touch. Terror branched through him like lightning.

She's dead! It's my fault! A crime, an escape, a journey to another century and back—it had all been too much.

But her chest moved against his—she was breathing. He rushed to adjust her, cradling her in his left arm, against his shoulder, so he could set two fingers against the artery at the side of her neck. Her pulse beat slower than he would've liked, but it was steady.

His own heart was slamming in his chest. She'd fainted. That was all. He took a steadying breath, then lay her down on her back on the sofa, elevating her legs by tucking the two large throw pillows beneath them. A doctor had told him, regarding Charlotte, that this would aid in her recovery by speeding the blood flow back to her brain.

It was not unusual for a lady to faint. He still felt a bit seasick, or timesick, himself. He took her hand, still cool and clammy, in both of his and chafed it.

"Rose. Wake up, my love."

She didn't stir. He didn't want to call her name any more loudly. A lady who has passed out from shock should not endure a second shock of being shouted at. Did she have smelling salts anywhere? He got up, went over to her purse, and rummaged through it, looking for a vinaigrette. Like many ladies, Charlotte had always carried one in her reticule: a hinged gold and enamel box shaped like a heart. He found no such thing there, or in the medicine cabinet in the bathroom. It was too bad, because the strong smell was the surest way he knew to reverse a swoon . . .

Ha! He had a flash of inspiration. After checking again on Rose, he went to the kitchen and pulled down the bottle of Malört. It did not smell nearly as bad as it tasted, but it did have a strong, atrocious odor. He brought it to the living room and held his breath himself as he screwed off the cap.

"Rose," he urged, sitting down on the coffee table and taking her hand again. He held the open bottle as closely as he could to her nose.

She scrunched up her face and made a sound like *unngh* as she jerked her head to one side. Her eyelids fluttered open as Henry, feeling very pleased with his resourcefulness, set the devil's drink aside.

Rose looked around her. "I fell asleep," she said, and then, "Did we go to another time?"

"No. You swooned." Henry squeezed her hand.

Her eyes fixed on the bottle. "Did you make me drink that?"

"Good God, no. I used it in place of smelling salts. A noxious smell makes you pull away, which wakes you up." He screwed the cap back on the bottle and set it aside.

"I told you we might need it," Rose teased.

He smiled and stroked a damp curl away from her face. "How are you feeling?"

"Uh . . . embarrassed, I guess," she said on a laugh, moving to get up.

"Careful, my love," he murmured as he helped her to a sitting position. "Let me get some water."

He returned the accursed bottle to the kitchen, then filled a glass from the tap and came back to set it in front of her.

"Thank you." She took a sip. He must've been staring at her, his concern plain on his face, because she waved a hand and said, "I'm fine. You don't have to worry about me."

"Do you know if you have any problems with your heart?"

"What?" She looked up, and then understanding filled her eyes. "No, I don't. My heart is fine." She gave a soft, rueful laugh. "Other than . . . never mind."

"Never mind what? Do you ever suffer from palpitations?" He shouldn't get agitated. It would only make her more agitated, and that was the last thing she needed.

"No, never." She leaned over and kissed him on the cheek. "You fuss too much over me."

"I believe I fuss the proper amount."

"You are the sweetest man. You know that?" He had only been described that way by one other person.

She took another drink of water. "I think I was just really freaked out about being in a totally different century, you know?"

"Yes. It is a most disconcerting experience."

She set her glass down on the coffee table. "At least I knew what was happening. When you first came here, you had no idea. I didn't understand how . . . discombobulating that must have been. I teased you too much at first." Her lovely face filled with distress. "I'm really sorry."

"Do not trouble yourself," he said emphatically. "You have been very kind to me, even when I have not always been civil to you, or your friends. I am well aware that I was not the man you hoped for when you did your innocent love spell."

"You are, though," she said in a small voice. "You're exactly the man I was hoping for."

His throat felt tight and sore. "Meeting you brought me joy, when I thought joy had gone forever from my life."

She looked at him sadly. "You still want to go home, though."

His spirits plummeted. "I cannot remain in this strange modern world," he said with profound regret.

"I know. You're a duke, with a giant estate."

"Yes, I have no name here, no property. And here, because I know less than everyone else, I am useless to everyone."

"Not to me," Rose whispered. She tapped the astrolabe. "I think that's why I couldn't let go."

If they had found themselves in Everly Park, in his time, what would that have been like for her? Might it have seemed familiar? He cared about Rose herself, but was he insane to think there was the small possibility that in another, distant life, she'd been Charlotte?

"I wonder if you could come to my time," he said without thinking.

Her eyes widened. "You mean, to live? I couldn't leave my brother."

"No, no, not to live," he said quickly. It had been a ridiculous suggestion. His whole theory of reincarnation was ridiculous, in fact. "Of course you cannot leave your brother, or your friends, or your work . . . I only meant to visit," he concluded, to save his pride. "And you would hate it there regardless, I'm afraid. You'd chafe under the expectations of proper ladies like a . . . a butterfly in a jar."

"I'm sure you're right." She looked at the astrolabe on the table. "And I don't think I could just visit now and then. That thing glitches! I could get stranded in some random century."

"It is dangerous," he agreed. "Moreover, it may be unhealthy. You must let go."

"Aren't *you* scared to try it again?"

He sighed. "Yes, but I am stranded already. It is worth the risk, I think."

She nodded sadly.

He had to accept the fact that he and Rose must part. He'd spent two years wishing he could be with Charlotte again; he could not add another impossible yearning. There would be nothing left of him.

Twenty-Two

R ose woke up in her bedroom with Henry sleeping next to her, an arm flung over her midsection. Once again, it had been daybreak by the time they'd gone to bed. She was wearing her oversize *Not My First Rodeo* cowgirl T-shirt she'd been wearing on the first night she'd met him, with no pants, and Henry hadn't raised an eyebrow at that. How things had changed.

She sighed, picked up her phone, and saw she had several texts. She opened the one from Emily first.

I was just watching WGN, Cubs
are going to be good this year

Had she texted Rose by mistake? Emily loved the Cubs, but she knew Rose didn't follow any sports. If she had, she probably would've been a White Sox fan like Ryan . . .

"Oh no," she said aloud. Emily was texting in code.

Next to her, Henry stirred. "What is the matter?"

"Our stealing the astrolabe is on the local news." Of course it was. Because what they'd done last night hadn't just been shenanigans. It had been a major crime.

Henry frowned and sat up in bed next to her. "Have you been identified?"

Rose's heart was pounding. "Hang on." She pulled up the first news story about it she found.

Henry, looking over her shoulder, read the headline aloud. "'Mystery Couple Steals Artifact at Charity Gala.'"

"Whoa," Rose breathed. That would've sounded kind of badass . . . if she hadn't been terrified of going to jail forever. "Wait, there's a video." Her heart pounded as she clicked.

The security footage had captured Henry skulking down the hallway with balls of light covering their eyes and noses. As they moved closer to the camera, the light expanded to cover their entire face.

"Those glasses worked," Henry said, marveling.

"Thank Goddess," Rose breathed. "There are descriptions of us . . . which don't match us at all." They'd be looking for a man with salt-and-pepper hair, and a woman with the kind of straight brown hair you might see on ten different women if you walked down a city block. No one had recognized them at the Weiner Stand or after, apparently.

"They even say I'm two inches shorter than I am," she added. And she usually wore wedges, not flats.

Henry absentmindedly put his arm around her and stroked her arm as he read the news story. "Reuter has put out a five-hundred-thousand-dollar reward."

"I'm kind of surprised it's not more," Rose admitted. And right now it was sitting on her coffee table. She should probably move it.

"He didn't pay much more than that at auction," Henry pointed out. "Perhaps he didn't want to flag the attention of others, like Mr. Yun."

"You know, I still have a lot of questions for that guy."

The late-morning sunlight was flooding through the blinds, making it feel like an ordinary, safe Sunday, and Henry dropped a kiss on her shoulder. Somehow, she hadn't expected him to be so snuggly. Although if he wasn't careful, snuggly would tip over into sexy right quick.

"Did he send you any messages?" Henry asked. "I expect he will want to discuss the past evening's events."

"Good point. Let's see." She flipped back to her texts and opened the one from Jason.

11 at Lou Mitchell's?

"Who is Mr. Mitchell?" Henry asked.

"I don't know," she mused. "We're going to brunch."

"What is brunch?"

"Sort of a mix between breakfast and lunch?"

He snorted. "Brunch is a coward, then. It should be one meal or the other."

She giggled. "No, brunch is my favorite. You *cannot* hate on brunch."

"I certainly can. Because it still gives me no time beforehand with the most notorious lady thief in Chicago."

She turned and peered at him. "You're *enjoying* this!"

"Enjoying being in bed with the beautiful woman I adore?" His voice took on a husky note as he said, "I think you already know that."

Feeling as though she was glowing from within, she leaned her forehead against his. "What I mean is, you're enjoying getting away with a crime."

He seemed to consider this. "Perhaps I am pleased with such a successful adventure. Besides, it is my astrolabe."

A half hour later, she and Henry were both dressed. Rose, after some thought, removed a frozen pizza from its box in the freezer and put the astrolabe in its place. "Hopefully, I won't freeze the magic off of it or anything," she said to Henry, who was watching her from the doorway.

"I'm not an expert, but I doubt that very much," he said, crossing his arms. He was wearing navy pants and a sky blue button-down shirt with his sleeves rolled up to below the elbow. Rose had suggested to him before that it was fine for men to roll up their sleeves, and she'd been too honest not to add that she loved the look of his forearms.

They took the bus to the West Loop and walked to the over-one-hundred-year-old diner. The name **LOU MITCHELL'S** was spelled out in neon red cursive, and the bold claim **SERVING THE WORLD'S FINEST COFFEE** was also in neon below it. The smells of bacon and freshly fried donut holes were thick in the air as they went inside. A couple dozen people waited for tables. Henry froze beside her. Then she saw why.

Standing with Jason, who was nearly unrecognizable in a T-shirt and cargo shorts, were Emily and Griffin, who were no doubt the last people Henry wanted to see. Ryan was with them. He had that wide-eyed look he got when he was feeling especially on edge, and he carried a filthy white tote bag from a blood bank over his shoulder. She knew that look all too well, and it worried her.

"How are you?" Emily and Jason asked Rose as they approached.

Before Rose could answer, Ryan growled, "I thought you weren't going to do that!"

Oh, geez. She hadn't considered that he might be mad at her for stealing it. But as worried as he'd been about her before, she probably should've anticipated this.

"We should probably keep our voices down," she told him, but when she took a quick look around them, no one in the crowd was paying attention.

"I picked this place because it's loud," Jason said. "It's hard for anyone to overhear."

"Milk Duds?" a woman's voice interjected. They turned to see a smiling white-haired woman with a basket of small yellow boxes, the size one might hand out to trick-or-treaters at Halloween.

"Here you go, ladies," she said, handing Emily and Rose boxes before moving on.

Griffin looked bewildered, and Emily explained, "They give them to women and children. I don't know why."

"This is how the patriarchy hurts men," Ryan joked.

Jason smiled. "Rose, why don't you tell us what happened last night."

She took in a deep breath. "We weren't planning to . . . you know. But an alarm went off as soon as he got hold of it—*we* got hold of it."

Griffin looked grave. "My lady Rose, if it was none of your doing, you may say so. I know you have sometimes defended those who have not respected you as you deserve." He didn't even look at Henry.

"I beg your pardon," Henry said icily, not sounding remotely as though he was begging. "But no man respects, admires, and cherishes Miss Novak more than I, or wishes more fervently for the health and happiness she deserves."

Everyone stared at Henry in surprise. Emily's eyes sparkled and she fought a smile as she caught Rose's gaze.

Griffin was unmoved. "Easy words from a man who will be gone as soon as he is able."

Rose winced. "He never asked to be here. That's kind of the problem," she said, reminding herself as much as Griffin. She looked around at the rest of them. "I wanted to do it, too. And Henry was amazing. He's like the British James Bond!"

Ryan tilted his head in disbelief. "James Bond, famously, is British." She recalled that they'd watched a James Bond movie the month before, though in her defense, she'd fallen asleep.

"The British James Bourne, then," she said impatiently.

"*Jason* Bourne," Jason corrected her.

"Yun, party of six," the hostess called out, and a server approached and led them to a table in the sunny front corner of the restaurant. Emily hung back with Griffin for a few moments, talking to him about something. Once they'd all been seated and had ordered their drinks, Rose told them about the fake arrival of a famous person that had allowed them to slip into the kitchen and up the stairs.

Griffin said to Henry, "That was a clever diversion. Like Hannibal with his cattle."

Rose immediately thought of a certain fictional cannibal, but Henry said, "Yes. I was thinking of the Second Punic War."

At least Griffin and Henry were bonding over something, even if it was battle strategy. As the server returned with tea for Griffin, coffee for everyone else, and a complimentary donut hole, each with an orange slice, for men and women alike, she and Henry told everyone else the rest of the story. They all seemed impressed by the way the moonstone had led Rose to the astrolabe.

Jason asked, "When are you going to try to use it to send Henry back? Is there a certain day or moon phase you think would work best?"

"Oh, yeah." Rose ducked her head. "We, uh, tried it last night."

He nodded. "So it didn't work the first time. Well—"

"It worked," Henry said. The others turned to stare at him.

"But not perfectly," Rose added.

She described their experience on the Chicago-less Illinois plain, and then how it had seemed to go on the fritz, depositing them briefly in the middle of the twentieth century. "Jesus Christ," Ryan muttered at one point.

"I didn't even do anything to get back," Rose emphasized. "It was more like the spell didn't last for long."

"I'm just glad you got back okay!" Emily said to Rose. She looked around the table. "This is crazy!"

"Yeah, it is," Jason said, his eyes bright.

Ryan shook his head. "If you were on a plain and didn't see anyone, you don't know exactly what year it was. For all you know, you could've been several hundred years earlier."

"I mean . . . yeah, I guess so." She didn't know why she hadn't thought of that. Great. Now she was even more nervous about using the astrolabe.

Griffin asked, "May anyone use the astrolabe, or just Rose? Or perhaps it is anyone who has a magical way with stones?"

"Good question," Jason said. "Rose, can you write down exactly what you did to make it work?"

"Sure. I'll email you."

"Uh, can you write it out by hand, and give it to me tomorrow?"

"I guess."

"Let us hear more about the time travel," Griffin said impatiently. "I had thought that nothing would ever surprise me again, but I confess that I am astonished."

Emily frowned and asked him, "Do you want to go back to your time?"

Rose feared that if he said yes, Emily would seriously consider it. "But I can't even control the astrolabe yet," she interjected. "Plus you wouldn't be able to get decent glasses! And you would *die* without coffee."

"Or from the plague," Ryan added, with a worried look at Rose.

"By no means would I go back," Griffin said firmly, holding up a hand. "It has been so long that I would be a stranger in my own life. Nor would I wish to return to war and bloodshed, for I was already sick to death of them many centuries ago." He took Emily's hand. "I am more content than I have ever been in this good life I have built with my sweet bride."

Rose sighed inwardly. It had not been hundreds of years since Henry had been a duke. It had been a few weeks. If he returned to his own century, he'd fall right back into his old life.

Jason asked, "Why did the astrolabe travel back with you? When Henry came here, the astrolabe stayed in the nineteenth century."

"Before, my fingers just rested on it," Henry said. "This time, we were both holding on to it."

"I was going to let go, but I forgot," Rose added.

Jason nodded. "And the astrolabe took you back to the same geographical location, which is the way it worked in the historical documents we have. But you were able to move Henry through both time *and* space before."

"Maybe that was because Rose had the moonstone," Emily guessed. "It was meant to be with the astrolabe."

"That might make sense," Jason agreed.

Ryan, whose arms were folded across his chest, gave a short laugh. "Nothing about this makes sense."

Emily glanced at Rose, then pushed her chair away from the table. "I'm going to run to the ladies. I'll be right back."

"I'll go, too," Rose said, being fluent in girl code.

Once the door to the restroom had closed behind them, Emily demanded, "What happened with you and Henry?"

Rose had expected this exact question after Henry's talk about admiring and cherishing. "Like I said, I know he was the worst when you guys came over. But—"

"He was jealous," Emily guessed. "Wasn't he? About Aaron maybe dating you."

Rose felt a bit of relief that her best friend understood things so well. "Actually, yeah. We had this big fight right after you guys left."

"So he doesn't hate us?"

"No. I think he feels stupid. And then he told me, you know . . . that he liked me."

Emily fixed her with a stare. "And then what happened?"

Rose laughed. "Exactly what you think happened."

"Ahhh!" Emily grabbed her arm. "So now I'm not the only woman who's had sex with a man from another era."

The woman with spiky gray hair walking into the restroom raised her eyebrows at this, then passed them to go to a stall.

Emily demanded in a lower tone, "Was he all awkward and polite?"

"No. He's very . . ." Rose searched for the right word. *"Thorough."*

"Oh my God." Emily shook her head. "Does he really have to leave?"

Rose felt sad all over again every time she thought about that. "He doesn't know what to do with himself here. And he's not making a big deal out of it, but he's a freaking duke who lives in a palace. I wouldn't give that up, either," she said honestly.

Emily hesitated before saying, "You're not thinking of going there, are you?"

"Well, I wasn't invited." The toilet flushed and the spiky-haired woman went over to the sink to wash her hands. Rose wrapped her arms around herself. "He says I would hate it. And I could never leave Ryan. He's the only family I have left."

Emily frowned thoughtfully. "Couldn't you go back and forth, though?"

The idea filled Rose with dread. "Just doing it once freaked me out. And did I tell you I passed out afterward?"

"Oh, geez." Emily's eyes filled with worry. "Are you okay now?"

"I'm fine. But who knows what time travel does to your body, you know? Henry felt sick and dizzy, too."

"I should've thought of that." Emily shook her head. "Well, you're not going back with him next time, right? Just sending him back?"

"Yeah." Rose didn't want to talk about that anymore. "We should head back. Everyone's probably being super awkward."

As they moved through the restaurant, it took Rose a moment to realize that the male laughter she heard across the crowded dining room was coming from *their* table. What the heck?

Emily said, "What's so funny?" as she and Rose walked up. In their absence, the food had been brought out, and Rose's stomach growled at the sight of her pecan Belgian waffle.

Griffin smiled. "His Grace was telling Ryan and Jason about trying Malört."

Huh. So Henry was able to laugh at himself, after all. Rose exchanged an amused look with Emily as they took their seats.

"So Rose," Jason said. "You've got it hidden in your apartment?"

"Yeah. But I don't know how to get him home from there."

Griffin asked, "What if you tried it near the painting?"

Emily looked dubious. "But honey, he didn't come *out* of the painting."

Jason said, "Like I said, our documents talk about going back in time, not going anywhere in space, and that's how it worked the other night, too. I'm guessing you both have to go to his house in England."

Ryan asked, "How are they supposed to travel overseas with a high-profile stolen artifact?"

"Hey, guys," a familiar voice said. Rose looked up to see Aaron approaching the table.

Oh no. Had he heard Ryan? Her brother was looking up at the FBI agent and smiling, but she could tell he was scared.

She forced herself to smile, too. "Aaron, hi!"

Twenty-Three

So this was Aaron Coleman, Henry thought, gripping his fork. A chorus of overly cheery greetings came from around the table, and Aaron slapped Griffin on the shoulder, asking how married life was treating him. Henry recalled that Aaron was somehow in the business of investigating stolen valuables, as if Henry needed another reason to loathe him.

Aaron froze as his gaze fell on Henry. The man had no doubt studied his portrait, and judging from the photograph Rose had shown him, it had been a very close likeness.

Aaron took a step toward him. "I don't think we've met. Aaron Coleman."

Before Henry could reply, Rose blurted out, "This is my friend Horatio!"

What?

Rose was wise not to introduce him as Henry, given the way Aaron was staring at him. But why had she chosen his middle name, which he had never told her? When she'd quoted Shakespeare at him before, it had not been a coincidence, he was sure.

"Horatio?" Aaron said. "There's a name you don't hear often." His tone was magnanimous, but the way he was staring closely at Henry was unnerving.

If there was one thing Henry knew how to do, it was to put someone in their place. "*I* have heard it often," he said coldly, "because it was my father's name, and his father's before that."

"Right," Aaron said with an apologetic smile. "What part of England are you from, Horatio?"

Henry reminded himself not to say Oxfordshire. "Birmingham."

"Ah. Aston Villa fan, then?"

"No," Henry said flatly, having no idea what the man had just asked.

Jason cut in with, "Aaron, any updates on the painting?"

"Yeah, I just came from the labs," Aaron said. "I can tell you, because we're releasing the info to the press. Like Daniela said, there's nothing underneath that gray area in the middle. And it only contains pigments that existed in the early nineteenth century, including lead white paint."

"Isn't that banned?" Emily asked.

"In most countries." Aaron's gaze flicked to Henry as he talked.

Jason leaned forward eagerly. "Yeah, this is my theory. The artist painted more than one version, and this one's incomplete." He added to the group, "It's like how we've got one version of Van Gogh's *Bedroom*, and the other two are in the Van Gogh Museum and the Musée d'Orsay."

"I thought of that, obviously," Aaron said. "We took a sample of the lead white to carbon-date it."

"I didn't authorize that."

"We didn't need your permission."

Jason held up his hands. "I just don't want to compromise the integrity of the painting. If it's an alternate version, it's of real significance. It gives us a new perspective on the artist's process—"

"We know what we're doing. It's not damaged," Aaron said. He glanced at Henry again. "And that's not even the weirdest thing. Did you hear about the theft at Victor Reuter's mansion?"

Henry arranged his features into what he hoped was a mildly curious expression. The back of his neck felt hot.

But Jason's impression of mild curiosity was flawless. "Yeah. An ancient sundial, right?"

"An astrolabe," Aaron said. "One that looks exactly like the one that's in the painting."

Jason gave a bewildered huff. "That's crazy. Hey, you want to join us? We can squeeze you in here." He looked around as if for spare chairs.

"No, thanks. I was just heading out." He cast another glance toward Rose. "So Rose, just curious, how did you and Henry meet?"

"Oh, we go way back," Rose said, as an alarm sounded in Henry's mind . . . and then he realized why.

"My name," he said with all the hauteur he possessed, which was considerable, "as we just established, is *Horatio.*"

Rose's mouth dropped open. "Didn't he say Horatio?" She toyed nervously with the crystal at her throat. Henry could hardly wonder at her slip. No doubt she'd been mentally concocting a story about their acquaintance.

"It's so loud in here!" Emily exclaimed.

"Sorry, I misspoke," Aaron said.

"Yeah, we're, like, very old friends," Rose told him. "But I hadn't seen him in ages."

"Nice." Aaron looked to Henry. "Well, enjoy your visit to Chicago." To Jason, he added, "We need to talk more. Call you tonight?"

"Sure thing," Jason said, raising a hand in farewell.

From where they all sat, they watched him out of their peripheral vision as he headed toward the door. "Eat and chat," Jason prompted them while looking down, digging his fork into his omelet.

"Is he following one of us?" Ryan asked in an undertone, as Aaron Coleman, now far away from them, exited the restaurant without looking back.

Jason flattened his lips into a thin line. "It's possible he happened to come here, if he came from the museum. But I don't like it."

"Next time, let's meet by our house," Emily suggested.

"I was just thinking it had been too long since I'd been to *Schaumburg*," Ryan said, putting a dry emphasis on the last word.

"Shut up," Emily said good-naturedly. "The suburbs are nice."

"Have you ever been to the Woodfield Mall?" Griffin asked Ryan earnestly. "There are over two hundred stores under one roof! And many places to eat and drink."

"That is remarkable," Henry said. Then he noticed that everyone else was smirking at one another.

Griffin nodded. "And there are large lots of pavement, so when the stores are closed, I used to practice driving a car with my father-in-law." He tilted his chin up proudly as he added, "Yesterday I passed my driver's license test."

Emily squeezed his arm and beamed.

"Oh, wow!" Rose exclaimed, looking surprised, as her brother said, "Dude, nice! I bet you crushed it!"

To Henry, *crushed it* did not sound like a favorable circumstance, when it came to those metal carriages, but he gathered that Griffin had become adroit in driving them. It had not even occurred to Henry that he himself might be capable of doing such a thing. But if this medieval knight could do it, certainly Henry would be able to.

"Congrats," Jason said, raising his coffee cup to Griffin.

Henry found himself deeply curious about what Griffin's car

looked like. He was equally curious about this mall, which he imagined as a sort of Pall Mall that stretched for a few miles. What might
so many different shops sell, and why did they share a common
roof?

"I would very much like to go to Woodfield, if we meet again,"
he told Griffin. "It sounds as though we would not encounter Mr.
Coleman there."

Griffin frowned. "I count Aaron as my good friend, and do not
like concealing anything from him. I have told him plainly about
my curse and how I came to life again, and he has come to believe me."

"He *almost* believes you," Rose said.

Ryan said sharply, "Well, you can't talk to him about this."

"No, I understand," Griffin said heavily. "He has his duty, and
I would not for the wide world cause trouble for Rose."

"I think it actually helps that he knows her," Emily said in an
undertone. "He's not going to think of her putting on a disguise
and pulling off a heist. I'm kind of shocked, myself."

Jason said, "And fortunately, because they arrested the wrong
person before"—he pointed his fork at Emily in a way that would've
been insufferably rude in Henry's time—"and it cost them a ton of
money and humiliated them, they're not arresting anyone without
very concrete evidence."

Ryan said, "Okay, I know how you get the astrolabe to England."
All heads turned toward him.

"You're going to take a good-sized clock." He held his hands
about a foot apart. "With a thick case. Open it up, take the mechanisms, all the guts, out of it, and put the astrolabe in there. Then seal
it up again." He sandwiched his hands together. "And you bring it in
your carry-on. Even in the X-ray, it's going to look like clockwork."

"You're right," Jason said. "I have the dimensions from the past auction listing, so I can find the right clock. It would just have to look like it hadn't been tampered with."

Emily smiled. "If only we knew someone who was really good at that kind of thing."

Henry felt a keen sense of obligation to these people, still practically strangers, conspiring to get him back to his own time . . . and he still owed two of them an apology. He would've preferred to make it with only Rose there to hear it, but the time seemed right.

"Miss Porter, I should say that I have been uncivil in the past."

"Forget it," Emily said quickly, shaking her head.

"I have not forgotten it," he said. "Nor have I forgotten my words to you, Mr. Beauford, for which I am most heartily sorry."

Griffin grinned. He was not, it seemed, a man to hold a grudge. "No one understands better than I how perplexing this all must be."

No doubt that was true. Henry said to Emily, "Rose has told me of your remarkable skill in restoring objects. I will be most grateful for your assistance and expertise." Could he really say goodbye to Rose, though? For good? The thought made him feel stretched thin, pulled between one century and another. He added, "Indeed, there is no rush."

"There definitely isn't. I can't even work the thing yet," Rose reminded them. "We went back in time for five minutes. And what if it glitches like before and leaves Henry in a totally different era? Or in that nothing-place?" She looked to Jason. "There wasn't any hint in the painting?"

He shook his head. "I inspected the original, and I couldn't find anything. But now that we know we've got the right astrolabe, we're doing some more research. Maybe we'll uncover something."

Rose sat up straighter in her chair. "When you say *we*, like, how many people are you talking about?"

"A couple other people are researching," Jason said, which, Henry noted, answered a slightly different question than Rose had meant to ask. "Is there anything you can do to, uh, have a revelation?" He grimaced at his own question. "I don't know how you do what you do."

"The problem is, I kind of don't know, either," Rose admitted. "But I'll do a spell asking for inspiration."

Jason nodded. "Hey, what time is it?"

Henry took his watch out of his pocket and clicked the case open. "Twelve forty-three," he said, in unison with Ryan, who had picked up his phone.

"Nice watch," Jason said to Henry. "Can I see that for a second?"

Henry turned it to him for a better view.

"He means, can he *hold* it for a minute," Rose explained.

"Oh." An impertinent request, but no one else appeared to think so. "Very well, I suppose," he grumbled and handed the watch over to him.

Jason turned it in his hand and gave a low whistle. "Beautiful."

"It is exceptionally well-made," Henry said. "The watchmaker is a man called Breguet. He was—"

"He made the most famous watch in the world," Jason said. "*La Grande Complication*, number 160 for Queen Marie Antoinette."

"No, that watch was never finished," Henry said, surprised that Jason had heard of it. "Because the queen—well." It would be bad manners to speak of a lady's beheading at the breakfast table.

Jason grinned. "It was. Breguet died in 1823, but his son finished the work." He closed the case of the watch as carefully as though it were made of spun sugar. "Be careful with that, Your Grace. You're walking around with a million dollars in your pocket, easy." Rose's eyes widened. As Henry put his watch back into his pocket, he supposed that a million dollars must be a lot.

"I've got to get going," Jason said, leaving money on the table.

"Wait," Rose said to him. "What I was going to ask before is, how many people are in your group, total?"

"Not enough," Jason said dryly.

Emily nodded and reached for her purse. "We should get going, too."

Ryan said, "I just have one other question." He turned to Rose. *"Horatio?"*

"It was the first thing I thought of!" she protested.

Henry thought, *Because you're Charlotte.*

He asked, "Rose, do you remember my middle name?"

"It's Leighton. No, that's part of your last name," she corrected herself. "You never told me. What is it?"

"Is it weirder than Horatio?" Ryan asked.

Henry smiled. "I will decline to say."

He would tell Rose later. Believing so many things could be coincidences, at this point, seemed more fanciful than the theory that Rose was his beloved late wife incarnated. *This* was why her spell had been able to draw him across time and space.

Rose left the balance of what was owed for the breakfast, explaining that it was also Jason's money. As they got to their feet, Ryan said, "Hey, Henry, I got you some books." He handed Henry the canvas bag he'd been carrying. "A few on quantum physics, one on the many-worlds interpretation, one on cosmology and particle physics . . . You don't have to read them, but, you know."

Henry dug into the bag. "Thank you. These are different from the ones I got from the library. I wished I'd gotten more about quantum physics in particular." Hopefully, this meant that Ryan didn't completely blame him for getting Rose involved in a crime. "I will return them soon."

"Whenever."

As they moved toward the door, Griffin said to Henry in a low voice, "May I have a word?"

"Of course," Henry said, and they fell a few steps back from the others.

"I understand that you have a strong attachment to our dear Rose. If you sold that watch, you would have enough to begin a new life here. That's what I did with my armor."

Henry wasn't surprised at the suggestion. "I mean no offense to say that you and I are very different men."

Griffin's eyebrows raised. "I take no offense whatsoever. Nonetheless, like you, I once had a rank and station."

"It is not just that," Henry said, though he would've been lying if he'd said being the Duke of Beresford had no pull over him. "I have many reasons not to stay here." He did not care to belabor the fact, for instance, that if he had no hope of contributing to humanity's store of knowledge, and was less capable than any man he met, he had no purpose.

Then he noticed Griffin's gaze was fixed ahead of them. At the front door of the restaurant, Rose had turned back, and she had a stricken expression on her face.

There was nothing else for it. She'd have to come back to his time with him. His happiness would be far greater than ever before, and he would be the kind of husband he wished he'd been. The somber grandeur of Everly Park would become a sparkling paradise.

Her memories of their previous life were still inside her, somehow. Here and there, they showed up, like tendrils of ivy poking out between the stones of a wall. How could he make her remember?

After they got back to her apartment and Rose had shut the door behind them, Henry pulled Rose to him for a kiss. He had her full attention immediately: she wrapped her arms around his neck and allowed him to part her lips and taste her with a languorous stroke of his tongue. He cupped a gentle hand around the nape of her neck, savoring her kiss and her tiny sigh when he released her.

"Shall we go into your bedroom?" he murmured. She nodded. Over the past couple of weeks, there had been a high-spirited quality to their lovemaking, a defiant exuberance, but there was nothing playful about her manner now. The idea of parting from her was nearly unbearable to him, and he knew it weighed heavily on her, too. It gave her a solemn look, despite her yellow dress. Once they were in the bedroom, he tugged at it and she pulled it off easily over her head.

Not wanting a stitch of clothing between them, he undressed with brisk efficiency as she did the same. Then he pulled her close, reveling in the feel of her warm, satin-soft naked body next to his. He cupped the back of her head and kissed her again, in a way that would not let her doubt his passion and adoration. She was running her hands over his upper arms and shoulders and down his chest. She had no idea how much he loved her touch. How it made him feel strong and healed and whole.

He'd believed that love was forever lost to him. Then she'd plucked him out of time and space and set his soul alight. Now he needed to help her understand the most astonishing thing he'd ever learned, in all his studies of natural wonders: that nothing had been lost, after all.

She gently pushed him on the bed and, kneeling next to him, kissed him again, her sandy-brown curls falling on his naked chest and shoulders. When he attempted to roll her on her back in order to do the many things to her that he had in mind, she resisted, reaching down to curve her hand over his cock. It jerked under her touch and he took in a quick breath.

"This doesn't have to be all about me, you know," she murmured as she circled her fingers around it and stroked it, immobilizing him. Then she smiled. "Which I never expected to say in bed."

Maybe it should've troubled him: the fact that she'd been with other men. But even if she had once been Charlotte, she was thoroughly and completely Rose, a woman who hadn't known him until recently and had owed him no loyalty. And at any rate, she compared him favorably to the others—whoever they had been—and that was not especially his business, as long as he was the last.

All thought flew out of his head as she slipped a leg over him and straddled him, her slick heat flush against his cock. She rubbed herself up and down it, and he let out an involuntary groan. Was she going to mount him from on top? He had hardly expected it, and his body was more than willing, but he could not let this time go too quickly.

"Come up here," he said patting the mattress right next to his head. "Kneel over me."

Her eyes widened. "Okay, but I've never done that."

"Are you sure?" He wanted to tell her that she had.

She shot him a wry look. "I think I'd remember."

That gave him an ache of longing in his chest. "Well, you'll remember this," he said and patted the bed again.

"Why do I get the feeling that you're right about that?" she teased as she did what she was told, moving up and gingerly setting one knee on each side of his head, treating him to a superb view of her creamy thighs and rosy, glistening sex. His neglected cock was hard and aching, but it could wait. In the bedroom, as in his studies, patience and focus were his virtues. He set about making her feel more at ease, reaching up with both hands to gently stroke the sides of her breasts.

"Were you aware, Miss Novak," he said, kissing one of her satiny thighs, "that every inch and every angle of you is lovely?"

She gave a breathless giggle. "I wasn't, actually."

He kissed her other thigh, very high up, inducing a delicious squirm. Encouraged by that, he nibbled on her thigh, fully aware that his unshaven jaw was brushing against her folds. The scent of her lush arousal was enough to drive him half mad.

"It's true," he murmured. "I'm astonished that you've never noticed." He pinched her nipples hard, making her squeak.

He paused. "Too rough?" So far she'd responded just as he'd expected at every turn, but he was still watchful for variances.

"No."

He reached down between her legs and dragged the pad of his thumb across her most sensitive place, eliciting a needy sound from her that he loved. Two of his fingers delved into her, and she sighed with pleasure. She reached behind her to caress the side of his torso as his fingers worked her, and he reveled in her gasps and rising cries.

Then he transferred his hands to her hips and attempted to pull her to him. "Come down here to me."

She resisted, half joking, "I'm worried I'm going to smother you to death."

Who would've guessed that his modern libertine could be so timid? Amused, he said, "If one could choose a way to go . . ."

She laughed. "You're not making me feel better!"

"How can I, if I can't reach you?" he asked reasonably. "Just a little lower, please."

She obeyed, neatly positioning herself just an inch from his mouth.

He lashed his tongue across her sensitive bud. She reflexively jerked, and he held her hips more firmly and did it again.

"Goodness gracious," Rose breathed.

Rose did not say *goodness gracious*. He'd not heard anyone say it in this era, in fact.

But Charlotte did. He'd heard her whisper it and moan it countless times. His heart slammed in his chest. Maybe, with just the right nudge, Rose would remember.

He stroked his fingers inside her again and murmured, "Charlotte."

Twenty-Four

R ose stilled. Had he just . . . ?

He had. He'd called her Charlotte.

He didn't mean to, a treacherous voice in her head said.
It was a slip, from a man who'd been married to a beloved wife for
two years and had grieved her for longer than that. *Just go with it.*

But she was sick of being the one who put up with everything.
She moved from the position of kneeling over him and sat on the
bed next to him, her back against the headboard, hugging her knees.
As she closed her eyes, gathering herself together, she felt Henry
move beside her.

"My love, what is it?" He set a gentle hand on her knee. "Talk to
me. What is the matter?"

The sincerity in his low voice reassured her. Anyone could make
a mistake, and it had been an unguarded moment. It was painful,
yes, but he would apologize again and again—and for a duke who
had originally seemed like the definition of haughty, Henry was
surprisingly good at apologies. They could get over this.

She opened her eyes and looked down at him. "You called me Charlotte."

"Yes." He was searching her expression. "You do not know why."

"*What?*" Adrenaline jittered through her nerves. He'd done it on *purpose?* "No, I don't know why!" Was this some kind of sick game? She wasn't playing.

"I thought perhaps that you remembered," he said, getting up to his knees.

"Remembered what?" He was scaring her now.

He pried one of her hands away from where it was tightly wrapped in her other hand and cradled it in both of his own.

"You've told me that you lived past lives. This will sound strange to say, but I believe that you were Charlotte."

A spark of hope ignited in her . . .

And then her brain kicked in. No. This was awful.

He was saying, in all sincerity, "Please hear me out. There have been too many coincidences. Your choice of the Shakespeare quote for a speech, for one."

"It's Shakespeare. It's not exactly obscure!" She'd taken a Shakespeare class in college, and she'd seen the quote on a wedding website.

He shook his head. "Your handwriting itself. I thought I was looking at something written in her hand." She vaguely remembered him asking about why she wrote the way she did. "And do you not think it strange that you bought the moonstone that fits into the astrolabe in a—a bazaar? What are the chances of that?"

"The same chances as any of the other thousands of people who shop on Maxwell Street." This wasn't quite honest, maybe. The pendant had *called* to her. It had been well out of her budget, but she'd felt she had to have it.

"Listen to me." He leaned closer, blocking out her view of anything but him. Instinctively, Rose shrank away, her back against the headboard. "When I first said the astrolabe was a gift from my late wife, you behaved as though you remembered that. Why?"

Because for a moment, she'd felt a spark of recollection, like a long-forgotten scent bringing back a buried memory.

But that feeling had made no sense. She didn't recall any such thing. And Henry, who she'd thought might be falling in love with her, was only using her as a substitute for his dead wife. Why didn't anyone love her for *her*? For who she was?

She felt a sob working its way up her throat. "I don't know why I said that. I misspoke."

"My middle name is Horatio."

"What?"

"Your brother suggested it's a highly unusual name in this era. But that is the name you gave to Aaron Coleman!"

"That is a very weird coincidence," she admitted shakily. Even in her pain, she tried to empathize with Henry. "And I know it's been so traumatic for you to get dragged to another century. Maybe you weren't ready for a relationship, even a fun one—"

"Not a fun one!" he exclaimed.

"What?" She blinked at him.

He shook his head. "It is more than that, and you know it. Listen— the Venus statue in the garden. You mentioned it at the party. You never saw a picture of that statue. You remembered it!"

"I must've seen it somewhere!" She could picture it clearly in her mind's eye, with the dark green yew trees behind it.

He lowered his head and pressed his lips to her hand. Rose sat stiffly, fighting the urge to pull her hand away.

"Please, close your eyes," he urged. "Try to remember. You and I, walking in the gardens at Everly Park . . ."

The sob escaped now. Automatically, as if her body made the decision for her, she moved to the edge of the bed and stood up.

Was she finally learning her lesson? That love was for other people, and not for her? Blindly, she grabbed her robe off the hook on the back of the door and shoved her arms into it, covering up. It was still damp from her last shower. Sure. Because why should she have any comfort at all?

Henry crawled to the end of the bed, closer to her. "Please, open your mind to this possibility. Is it so much more extraordinary than other things we know to be true?"

"I thought you liked *me!*"

"I do!" He gazed up at her earnestly. "I understand that you are Rose. That your life here, your family, your friends, the places you've lived, the places you've worked . . . all have made you the wonderful woman you are, and there's never been anyone like you." These were romantic words, but he immediately ruined them with, "But you were Charlotte before that."

"No, I wasn't! Why would you call me her name in the middle of . . ." She gestured wildly toward the bed. She still couldn't believe that he'd done that on *purpose*.

"I thought you would remember this past life. Because you said, *Goodness gracious*, and those are not your words. That is something Charlotte would say."

She cringed, body and soul. That had been something she'd said in a vulnerable moment, and for Henry to repeat it back to her, as evidence that she wasn't really *her*, was too much.

"You haven't known me long enough to know all my words," she shot back.

A nagging voice inside of her pointed out, though, that he was right. She'd never said that in her life before. Her mother hadn't gone around saying it, either. She didn't know where it had come from. But as angry and hurt as she was, she pushed the thought away. People said all kinds of weird things in bed, didn't they?

Henry got to his feet. "I have presented several facts. You must at least consider my theory!" His flare of anger scared her. He actually might be out of his mind.

She said, "You need to leave."

Immediately, he softened. "Don't be like this."

Where would he go? Jason had said he could get him a hotel room. Her phone was still in her purse, hanging next to the front door, and she banged the door open and stalked over to retrieve it.

"Rose." He'd followed her out to the living room, stark naked, a beseeching look in his eyes. "Please. We don't have to speak of it anymore."

That wouldn't change what happened. In the middle of making love to her, he'd let her know that she was a substitute for someone else.

Her throat was so tight that it burned as she dug the phone out of her purse. "You can't stay here. I'm sorry. I don't feel comfortable with it anymore."

Henry turned away, his hands clasped on the top of his head in frustration or defeat. She wished he wasn't so beautiful. And that he didn't have the best round ass. And that he hadn't completely ruined a love affair that was already going to be bittersweet.

With shaking fingers, Rose pulled up Jason's number.

Jason answered after half a ring. "Rose, what's up?"

"Henry can't stay with me anymore. He needs a hotel room."

After a fraction of a moment, Jason asked, "Are you all right?"

That was sweet of him. But she wasn't going to talk about this with Jason, of all people. "I'm fine. I just need some space."

"Sure." His matter-of-fact tone reassured her. "He's agreeing to leave?"

"Hang on." Rose took the phone away from her ear and looked up at Henry, who turned, fixing her with another agonized stare.

Her heart wrenched for him. But it was just too weird. She couldn't
share her home with someone who thought she was his dead wife . . .
especially someone who she, unfortunately, was in love with.

She asked him, "You'll go to a hotel, right?"

His jaw flexed. "Of course I will not stay a moment longer where
I am not wanted."

She returned the phone to her ear and said quietly, "He'll go."

"Give me, uh . . . twenty minutes. I'll pick him up."

"Thank you so much. I'm sorry—"

"No, no, it's fine. Uh . . . Are you still going to help him get back
to his time?"

He was probably asking because he still wanted to know how the
astrolabe worked, and she still didn't know exactly why. But she
thought he actually felt for Henry, too.

"Yeah," she said.

After she hung up, she said woodenly, "Go get dressed and get
your things. Jason will come get you."

He threw up his arms in frustration. "If you would just consider
what I'm saying!"

"Don't you dare yell at me!" He hadn't *quite* been yelling, but
still.

His jaw flexed. "I would think that you, of all people, would be
willing to entertain the impossible—"

"Go get dressed!"

He stomped to the bedroom, and she felt a pang of sympathy for
him again. He was half out of his mind from grief and the disorien-
tation of being in the twenty-first century. But knowing that didn't
make it any easier on her bruised heart. She wanted him to leave so
she could cry and eat ice cream and maybe call her best friend for
support. Call her old-fashioned.

She walked back to the bedroom, where he was jerking up his
pants. "I told Jason I would still get you home if I could."

He picked up his shirt from the floor. "I am sure you're more eager than ever to be rid of me."

"I'm the one who wanted you here! You never wanted to be here!"

He walked over to her, his shirt unbuttoned. "Will you at least try to remember?" He touched her cheek, and she pulled away. "Please, Rose."

"No."

Twenty-Five

After Henry climbed into the passenger seat of Jason's car and wished him a stiff good evening, and Jason ordered him to put on his seat belt and was obliged to demonstrate the operation of the buckle, it occurred to Henry that the man might have a very dark view of what had transpired.

As Jason drove away, Henry said, "I hope it goes without saying that I in no way threatened Miss Novak, let alone injured her—well, other than inadvertently injuring her feelings, which—"

"That's none of my business," Jason said.

He was quite right. Henry should not be disclosing Rose's private matters to her business associates. Once upon a time, he'd had a strict sense of decorum. Now, at every turn, he was conducting himself miserably.

Jason added, "But if I thought you'd hurt Rose, I wouldn't be taking you to a hotel."

Henry didn't know what the other option would've been, but took glum solace in the fact that Jason did seem to have some concern for Rose personally, and was not only using her for his own mysterious ends.

They continued in silence for a few minutes, broken only by Jason muttering a curse under his breath when another car darted in front of them. Henry couldn't help but notice that they passed by one hotel, and then another. After the third one, Henry could no longer contain himself.

"Moreover, I would never even inflict my presence upon Miss Novak against her will, so you need not put distance between us. Any hotel will do."

"It's not that," Jason said. "I have points at this other place. Plus it's a better hotel. Griffin and Emily stayed there after the wedding."

"Ah. Well, thank you."

"Listen, about meals—"

"Rose gave me the money," Henry said shortly. "I will return the loan when I can." How humiliating to have to speak of such things.

"I'm sure we'll work something out."

Jason wanted to buy the astrolabe, no doubt. With Rose rushing him out the door, Henry hadn't considered the fact that it was still in her apartment. But Jason went on to explain how he could order food and have it brought to his room. Henry, receiving this lesson soon after being taught to use a seat belt, gave a huff of frustration.

Jason eyed him askance. "Are you mad at me for explaining things?"

"By no means," Henry grumbled. "It is only that I assume ordering dinner at a hotel is a fairly straightforward process for most."

After a few moments, Jason asked, "Did you study anything else, in your time, besides science and mathematics?"

Henry bristled. "I studied Greek, Latin, moral philosophy, logic, history, and everything else you might expect. As I was saying at breakfast, studying the Punic Wars inspired me to create a diversion at the mansion."

Jason abruptly steered the car into the next lane. Henry couldn't help but be impressed at how deftly he maneuvered the vehicle. "But I guess as a scientist, studying most of those things was a waste of time."

Henry scoffed. "The aim of a classical education is produce a fine mind. To enable one to think for oneself, to critique, and to reason. With a proper education, one learns how to learn."

"Weren't you already intelligent, though?" Jason asked.

"In my time, that would've been a rude question."

"Still is."

"I see." Henry looked out the window at the passing buildings and pedestrians. "As it happens, my intelligence was much remarked upon, well before I began my formal education."

"So you have high intelligence and a good education that you could apply to any subject," Jason said. "And you're starting to apply it to learning about things like quantum physics and multiverses. I'm sure you'll understand all the basic things like ordering dinner pretty soon."

Henry grunted. "That is well argued, I admit."

Hours later, after his dinner, Henry hung the **DO NOT DISTURB** sign he'd seen dangling from other guests' doors. What a convenient idea. What a shame that one could not display it wherever one went, when one wanted to be left to one's own thoughts.

He stood at the window of his hotel suite, looking at the windows of the opposite building. Some had their curtains open, and he could see people eating dinners, hunching over phones, or watching television; so many lives, stacked neatly in columns and rows, all where they belonged.

Although he'd told Jason he was an intelligent man, he was an idiot. At least about what truly mattered.

He'd been sure, in an intimate, unguarded moment, that Rose half remembered that she had been Charlotte. Passion had impaired his judgment. Just a nudge, he'd thought, would bring it all back. He'd never been more wrong.

He should've kept his tongue and bided his time. The memories of a past life might've eventually returned to her. And if they had not, he could have dismissed the idea of her reincarnation, counting evidence as happenstance.

His feelings for Rose had in no way depended on this theory being true. He should've told her sooner about all the reasons that he loved her. Yes, *loved* her, even if he could not work out what the next logical step would be.

Would there even be any point in telling her now?

As always, his timing had been terrible.

Twenty-Six

The next night, after work, Emily went with Rose to her apartment to commiserate and to pick up the astrolabe from Rose, so she could hide it in a clock once Jason found the right one.

"I just don't see how a love spell could've gone this wrong," Rose said, digging her spoon into the bowl of ice cream she'd picked up from Rainbow Cone. For a proper heartbreak like this, she figured she deserved the best.

"I'm so sorry," Emily said, curled up at the end of her sofa with her own bowl. "I know it's no consolation, but it's incredible that you could do that spell in the first place."

"Is it possible to become a more powerful witch and a worse one at the same time?" Rose wondered aloud.

"If you're getting more powerful, it might take some practice to get things under control."

Rose nodded. "Well, I get another try with the astrolabe, since I'm going to try to send him back. It's going to be so awkward traveling with him to England."

Emily gave her a sympathetic smile. "Henry just wasn't ready for another relationship. You're an amazing person, and I bet the next guy will like you for *you*."

Rose sighed. "I mean, Henry kind of said that he did. He said that all of my life experiences had made me the person I was, and that there had never been anyone like me before."

"Oh," Emily said, uncertain now. "That kind of does sound like he's into you, and not just missing his wife?"

"As long as he has this idea that I used to be Charlotte, how can he know for sure how he feels about me?"

"I see what you mean," Emily admitted.

Rose took another big bite of the ice cream. "It's just so stupid. Can you imagine me having a past life as a duchess?"

"Um . . ." Emily squinted at her. "Are you looking for an honest answer here?"

"I guess."

"Then yeah, I can imagine it. When I first met you, you were wearing one of your maxi dresses—the white one with the empire waist? I thought you looked old-fashioned."

Rose hadn't expected that. "Well, *I* can't imagine it. A lot of people who think they have past lives imagine they were royalty or whatever, but I never have. I couldn't have been that kind of person who has everything she wants, and who has people taking care of her. I'm the one who takes care of everyone else!"

"You do," Emily said. "And you're good at it. You take care of your brother, you've taken care of me and Griffin before . . . but it's okay if sometimes, other people take care of *you*."

After Emily left, Rose tried to cheer herself by watching episodes of an old TV show about two brothers who were demon hunters, but even that didn't make her feel better. She took a bath with a lavender bath bomb and tried to go to sleep, with no luck. Finally, she got up and checked the time on her phone. 1:07 a.m. *Ugh*. Before long, she'd have to go to work.

She had three new texts. The first one she opened was from Aaron.

Hey, just thinking about you.
Hope you're having a good week.

She wondered what he had thought of meeting Henry, aka Horatio, the other day. Well, she was going to avoid Aaron as long as he was still investigating the mystery of the painting. Maybe someday she would go out with him . . . but she wasn't sure she wanted to.

The next one was from Ryan.

Jason said you and Henry had a
fight. Everything ok?

Why did Jason keep talking to Ryan? She texted back, explaining Henry's delusion, but leaving out any details about her romantic involvement with the lost-in-time duke. It was over now, anyway.

And finally, she had texts from Jason. He'd linked the address of a hotel, adding, **Henry's in room 4343, under my name. Let me know if you need anything.**

Jason wanted her to get a better handle on using the astrolabe to time travel, but he didn't know how to help. Rose didn't know, either. Her nerves felt like old, thin rubber bands, the kind with no stretch left in them.

Maybe she should do a spell for divine intuition. She'd told Jason she'd do one, in order to ask for guidance about working the astrolabe.

She sighed, got out of bed, and lit the white pillar candle on her altar, the one that represented the element of fire. A little dish of rock salt represented the earth, and she lit a stick of incense, because the smoke represented air. She chose one infused with frankincense resin, her favorite for clearing away negativity. For the element of water, she took the little alabaster goblet to the bathroom sink and refilled it. She'd always done a little meditation while she did this— *I fill my own cup*, meaning that she had the power to make herself happy—but she couldn't bring herself to do that tonight.

She got up and went to the kitchen, taking the astrolabe out of its pizza box. It looked more magical than ever, sparkling with its thin layer of frost, and even though she'd handled it before, she had the ridiculous fear that just by touching it, she'd be whisked off to some other era. Maybe back to the time when Illinois had been underwater, and she'd drown amid all those weird creatures that had been discovered in fossils. With a shudder, she took it back to her room and set it on the bed next to her altar.

Then she knelt down in front of the altar, took a deep breath, and let it out. Instead of trying to think of an incantation, she recalled other names for Hecate and asked from the heart. *Hecate, Mother of Witches, Keeper of the Keys, She Who Lights the Path in Darkest Night, give me the key to using the astrolabe correctly. Give me the power to return Henry safely to his time.*

She had an intrusive thought. *You'll have to hold on to the astrolabe and go with him.*

That didn't make sense. Why had Henry come to her before, when he'd only been touching it?

Because you both wanted to be together.

Rose waited for her inner voice, or whatever it was, to elaborate, but it didn't.

It didn't make sense. *She* had wanted that, but Henry most definitely hadn't. He'd wanted to be with Charlotte.

"Fuck," she breathed aloud.

Was there a possibility, even a remote one, that what Henry was saying was *true*?

She'd been gutted when he'd called her by his dead wife's name. But if she took her feelings out of it, she could recognize that there were a lot of coincidences.

"I would remember," she murmured.

No, she wasn't going to gaslight herself. She had to hold firm. Men were always expecting her to accommodate them too much. She'd been willing to try to accommodate, and it had always ended in her feeling like garbage.

There had been the anime guy, and the guy she'd always driven out to Park Ridge to see because he didn't drive, although, well, trains and buses did exist, and there had been Jake the Snake. She'd taken care of his python for a whole month while he was supposedly in Bucharest, even though she'd been terrified it would get out of its cage and hug her to death in her sleep, and it had turned out he'd never left town. And then, of course, there was Aaron, who was like, *Sorry I lied to you while investigating you for a crime.*

But *Sorry I think you're actually my dead wife* topped them all, didn't it? Even if Henry was different. Even if she thought she felt a connection with him that she'd never felt with anyone else.

She'd always had strong intuition. That was a big part of being a witch. If she had been a little psychic with Henry, it wasn't surprising.

She looked at the Venus art card, sighed, and closed her eyes. *Bring Henry some peace of mind. And me, too. Even if we don't wind up together.*

At work hours later, after her staff meeting, Rose printed out a photo of the original painting of Henry, on the good color printer. Jason had read that the Wilke painting contained clues on how to use the astrolabe; he hadn't been able to find any, but who knew? Maybe something would jump out at her.

Were any of the book titles legible? Not in this photo, anyway . . . but maybe she could make them out in the original painting? She folded the photo, stuck it in her purse, and took another trip to the paintings conservation lab.

She half expected the painting wouldn't be at Daniela's station; they might be photographing it or doing some kind of test. But there it was on its easel, even though she didn't see Daniela anywhere. She raised a hand in greeting to one of the other conservators, who smiled back. The conservators had seen her in the lab several times, taking pictures and shooting videos.

Even though she'd seen the altered painting before, the ghostly absence of Henry made her heart ache. If she succeeded, he'd be gone from Chicago, and their brief, beautiful affair had already fogged over with hurt and regret.

Keeping a respectful couple of feet away from the painting, she peered at it. Maybe there was some writing elsewhere? On the vases?

Her brain registered the image of the woman carrying torches . . . and on the vase next to it, the woman getting out of the sea.

A smile spread across her face. They were part of the key. Jason hadn't made the connection, but then again, Jason wasn't thinking about spells all the time.

A moon globe stood next to them . . . of course. Was there anything else? Her gaze drifted across a fancy inkwell, an even fancier box with a lid, playing cards on the bottom shelf . . .

The eight of clubs was turned face up.

"Ha!" She hadn't meant to say that aloud.

Daniela's boss, a willowy woman in her sixties, came over. "Hey,

Rose. We're supposed to restrict the lab to conservators. For now, anyway."

"No worries! I was just looking for Daniela," Rose said hastily. "I'm just leaving."

She had to talk to Henry about this. It was good to have an excuse to call him. She still felt crushed . . . but she was constantly worrying about him, anyway. Not wanting to call him in her quiet office with her coworkers listening, she went to the café.

The phone rang five times before someone picked up. She heard Henry say *good morning*, but his voice sounded muffled.

"Henry, it's me," she said loudly. "Can you hear me?"

Some shuffling noises, and then his gruff baritone voice came through loud and clear. "Yes, I am here. Good morning, Miss Novak."

He'd been talking into the wrong end of the receiver, she guessed. Any other time, the thought would've made her smile.

"How are you?" she asked.

"I am . . ." He seemed to be considering the question. "I am very ill, indeed."

"Oh no." Rose pressed her hand to her heart. He'd been healthy when he left, other than his maybe-delusion about her past life. "How are you sick? Do you need a doctor?"

"On the contrary. I mean to say that I . . . am not doing well."

"Gotcha," she said gently, sad but relieved. "Yeah, me neither. I'm at work, so I can't talk too long. But can I come over to your hotel room after work tonight?"

"By all means." His voice grew husky on the last word.

Oof. She hadn't been trying to lead him on. "I want to see if Jason can come, too, and maybe Emily. I want to talk to you all about the ast—" She caught herself just in time. For all she knew, Aaron Coleman was sitting right behind her, taking notes. What else began with *ast*?

"About the Astroglide," she said firmly. Yes, it was a brand of lube, but she couldn't think of anything else. The man at the next table shot her a strange look.

What? she thought. *People are allowed to plan sex parties on their work breaks. And you're not invited.*

"Ah. Of course," Henry said stiffly. "Please come by at any time."

He seemed to understand what she was really saying. Given the tension between them, Rose felt grateful that Henry didn't know what Astroglide was . . . although, as curious as he was, he was likely to look it up as soon as they got off the phone. Well, no, he couldn't, because he didn't have her computer.

Was he bored? He'd taken some of his library books with him. Would he read them even when he was feeling depressed? Maybe he'd find a sitcom to binge-watch or something.

She told him, "It'll probably be around six or six thirty." There was a little ache in her throat.

"Rose, there is something I must ask you."

"What?" She felt like her whole body was listening.

After a long pause, he asked, "Would you like me to order dinner?"

"Oh." She gave an awkward laugh. "Sure, why not?"

"What would you like?" Henry asked.

"I don't know. No sushi, ha-ha!"

He didn't laugh. He probably didn't remember what that was, anyway. None of their time together was going to matter, in the end, and she felt close to crying. That made her feel pathetic . . . which made her feel even closer to crying.

"Whatever," she said. "You know what I like. I should get back to work." That was true, actually.

"I will not detain you." He hung up.

He was mad at her. Or maybe not. He wasn't used to phones.

Maybe he just didn't know how to say goodbye.

She sure didn't.

She sighed and thought of his question again. *What would you like?*

Oh, Henry. If I only knew.

Twenty-Seven

enry, in his suit jacket, was inspecting his reflection in the hotel bathroom mirror and practicing in his mind the words he wanted to say to Rose. A knock came at his door, and he rushed over to open it.

When he saw Emily Porter, he was sure his disappointment showed on his face. He'd forgotten the cardinal rule of entertaining: the person you felt the least comfortable talking to always arrived first.

"Hey, Henry." She gave him a tight-lipped smile.

"Good evening, Miss Porter."

"Rose went to pick up Ryan, so she told me to tell you she's on her way."

Rose would've told her all about what had happened. And knowing Rose's frank nature and her sister-like friendship with Emily, the fact that it had happened during an extremely intimate moment would not have been left out of the conversation. Emily might be imagining him in that situation right now, which was mortifying. She also probably thought he was either stupid or mad. He slightly preferred the latter, although she might think he was both.

"Can I come in?" Emily prompted him.

"Ah. By all means." He opened the door and stood aside. It still struck him as scandalous to allow a woman, alone, into such a private space, but no one else thought anything of it.

She closed the door behind her. "Oh! You got room service!" she said, looking over to the table and the ironing board, where over a dozen covered silver dishes waited. "A *lot* of room service."

"Rose said to order dinner."

"Thank goodness. I'm starving." She headed over to the table and lifted a silver lid. "Wow, lobster!"

Henry strode over to the table. "We will wait for Rose. And the others."

"No, yeah, of course," Emily said, setting the lid back down and holding up her hands.

Rose had said, *You know what I like*, but taking up the menu, he hadn't felt sure of that at all, and had been in an agony of indecision. In the end, he ordered most of the main courses, a few first courses, several desserts, and two bottles of wine: their most expensive white, and their most expensive red.

"Isn't the view amazing?" Emily asked, moving to the window. "This is where Griffin and I stayed after our wedding."

"I never conveyed my felicitations," Henry said, without looking at her or the view. "Allow me to do so now." He suspected his voice sounded cold, but he should still get credit for congratulating someone on their happiness when he himself had been rejected.

"Thank you." After a short silence, she said, "You know, Rose really cares about you."

His head shot up. "She threw me out. As you well know." Perhaps Emily also knew that he had stood naked in Rose's living room, tears in his eyes, pleading with her to understand. Had any man been so humiliated?

Emily sighed. More quietly, she said, "Rose is always helping everyone else, and sometimes she winds up feeling used. I think she's scared that nobody loves her just for being herself. You know?"

A knock on the door made him jump. Having no response to Emily, Henry stalked over and opened it. Rose, carrying a large quilted bag, stood there with her brother. Henry's mouth went dry.

"Hey bruh," Ryan said, though with less friendliness than last time, Henry noticed. "Nice room." He crossed the room to look at the view, too, and Henry imagined throwing both him and Emily out. Rose lingered by the doorway after Henry shut it behind her, looking at Henry with a wan smile.

"I am very glad to see you," he told her. She looked lovely as always, although more pale than usual. Or was that because . . . ?

"Why are you wearing black?" he demanded. "It's not Saturday."

She sighed. "I don't know."

Another knock sounded at the door, and Henry opened it to Jason. After everyone had said hello and Jason had left his suit jacket in the closet, Henry invited them all to eat dinner. Jason carried the duffel bag in his hand over and set it down next to a chair.

Ryan lifted one silver lid, and then another. "Ooh, cheesecake," Rose said, eyeing the dessert.

"I got that for you," Henry said quickly, since she seemed to want it.

"Sheesh, Henry," Ryan said as he continued to uncover dishes. "Think there'll be enough for all of us?" Jason, looking mildly exasperated, took the silver lids from Ryan and stacked them in the corner.

Once they were settled on chairs and with full plates, Jason said, "Rose, what did you find?"

"Well . . . maybe it's not a big deal. But I figured out the keys to using the astrolabe in the painting."

Jason set down his fork. "Go on."

"In the background, there's a vase with Hecate on it, and a vase with Venus."

"Those are goddesses?" Henry asked.

"What did you think they were?" Rose asked.

"Ancient Greek . . . ladies, I suppose," he said, trying to recall them. Charlotte had purchased the vases, and he knew that classical artifacts were a fashionable addition to a gentleman's study, but he'd never had any real interest in them.

Emily was already pulling up the image of the painting on her phone. "How do you know they're Hecate and Venus?"

"Hecate's carrying torches, just like she did when she led Persephone out of the underworld, obviously," Rose said. "And Venus is rising up out of the sea. So I was calling on the right goddesses every time."

"Are you sure?" Jason asked, as Emily did another furious search on her phone.

"Of course I'm sure."

Emily held up her screen toward Jason. "Look at this one in the Hermitage. It's pretty similar."

"Okay, yeah." He turned back to Rose. "This is really good to know."

"That's not all! There's the moon globe on the shelf . . . I think it's going to work better during the full moon. I even worried about that the last time. Moon phases are so important! And there's a deck of cards on the bottom shelf."

"I do not gamble," Henry interjected, because he thought it a low habit. "My wife Charlotte played a solitary card game."

As soon as he said her name, he regretted it. But he had to be free to speak of her. He met Rose's gaze—and saw that faraway look in her eyes, like that of a person who is trying to identify a voice from another room.

You remember, he wanted to say.

But what if he was wrong? The idea startled him. He'd felt so certain. But she felt certain, too.

He was not always right. In this new world, he was often wrong. And many things, it turned out, were shrouded in magic and mystery. Maybe, for once in his life, he could live without knowing.

"Uh, what's the significance of the cards?" Jason asked, looking from one of them to the other.

"Oh! It was eight of clubs!" She looked around them for their reactions. Getting only blank looks, she said, "Clubs in a regular deck are wands in a tarot deck! I used the eight of wands the first time!"

"So maybe that's another key element of the spell," Jason said, nodding. He'd pulled a small notebook out and was making notes now. "This is great."

"There were two other cards," Henry said. The Lovers. And one that he couldn't recall now . . . what was it she'd said? It represented memories. Home. "Are they not important, too?"

"I think they were just random," she mumbled, deepening Henry's stoic misery.

"Charlotte gave you the astrolabe," Ryan said to Henry. "But she couldn't have put clues in the painting. She was already . . ." He gave an apologetic shrug.

"She did tell me that corner of the study would be the place for a portrait," Henry recalled aloud. "But as I have said before, she never told me the astrolabe was magical."

"What would you have said if she had?" Rose asked.

He gazed into her blue eyes, regret filling his heart. "I would not have believed her. I did not know then that truth is not the same as logic, and some truths are very hard to accept."

"If Charlotte did leave clues," Ryan said after a moment, "does that mean anyone can use the astrolabe?"

Rose shook her head. "I think you have to be able to work with the moonstone. Like, magically."

"I am certain she is right," Henry said quietly. "She can feel its power—its vibrations. It *glows* around her."

Frowning, Emily asked her, "But you can just send him back, right? Without going yourself? Because you passed out last time."

"I think I can send him back on his own," Rose said.

"It's not the way it worked before," Jason pointed out.

"True." Rose frowned. "If I have to go with him, and then use the astrolabe to come back by myself, I will."

Henry felt a stab of alarm. He had never expected her to do that. He supposed that it would be the same as last time, except that at the key moment, she would let go of the astrolabe, as she'd planned to do before.

Perhaps this was all madness, and he should stay in Chicago. But Rose no longer wanted him there.

Ryan crossed his muscled forearms over his chest. "That's way too dangerous. What about winding up in the 1950s for a few seconds?"

"I think it was glitching because I had the timing wrong. We should've gone on the full moon."

Jason set his plate on the TV cabinet and leaned forward, his elbows on his knees. "Well, if you go briefly into the past, and then bring the astrolabe back here again, I can give you two million dollars for it. I would split it between you two, but I don't know why Henry would need it."

Henry no longer cared about giving up the astrolabe. He'd already lost Rose, it seemed. But it would be some comfort, at least, to know she was taken care of.

Before he could express his agreement, Rose told Jason, "I would just feel bad. It's his astrolabe. Maybe there's a way I can use it to come back without taking it with me—"

"Bullshit!" Ryan exploded, jumping to his feet.

Both women startled, and Henry found himself standing before he even had time to think. Ryan's anger was like a palpable flash of heat, and Henry's defensive instincts spiked in response. Jason and Rose had stood, too, but Emily froze in her chair.

"You always do this!" Ryan said to Rose. "You'll do anything for anyone else, and fuck whatever *you* want!" He looked scary. But he was angry because he loved his sister, and Rose didn't look scared at all. "You committed a *crime* to get that thing. And you're endangering your life by traveling through *time*. Two million dollars, Rose! And now you're like, maybe he can keep it? Are you fucking *kidding* me!"

"Ryan," Henry interjected in a loud, even tone. Ryan turned his wild-eyed gaze on him. "I agree with you completely. If Rose cannot send me back alone, she should feel no obligation to escort me to the past." Although what he would do in this new world, stripped of every familiar trapping of his existence, if he did not have her, either, he had no idea.

"I disagree," she said, more sharply than he expected. "I dragged you out here. I've got to make it right." It occurred to Henry that she might feel some relief in dumping him back into his own time.

She looked from Henry to Ryan and back again. "I'm the one who gets to decide."

"You need not make your decision yet," he said heavily. "And if you do go into the past and back to the present again, you must at least take the astrolabe with you and collect your reward."

Rose pressed her fingers to her lips. Then she said to Ryan, "Okay. If that happens, you and I can split the money."

Henry saw Jason take a breath to say something, but Ryan spoke first.

"I'm not taking a fucking penny! Think about what *you want*." Ryan punctuated the last two words with a hand gesture, his fingers and thumb pressed together. His gaze flicked toward Henry. "And can we be real? Maybe it's not the money!"

Panic flitted across Rose's face. "Ryan, don't—"

"I've been your problem long enough, don't you think?"

Henry tried to make sense of this. He'd never been good at hearing what wasn't said.

"You're never my problem!" Rose protested. Her eyes misted over. "I couldn't do without you."

"Okay, okay," Ryan mumbled, catching her in an awkward bear hug. "I'm just saying, think about what makes *you* happy, all right?"

Rose pulled back and looked around at the rest of them. "Sorry. This is a lot to deal with."

"No, I get it," Jason said. "I have two brothers and a sister. I don't know what I'd do without them, either." It sounded like sympathy, but Henry knew he wanted to preclude any scenario in which Rose remained in the past with Henry. He need not have bothered, Henry thought. Henry would have given anything for that scenario, if Rose could love him, and if she could be parted from her brother, but the first was now impossible, and the second had always been.

Everything Jason did, he did to get his hands on the astrolabe, and to learn how to use it. That was why they were all here. Henry would not have even been brought to this century, had it not been for Jason purchasing Henry's portrait. And Jason's secret society coveted all kinds of magical items. In the case of Griffin, that had led to a miracle and lasting happiness. But who knew what kinds of havoc they'd left in their wake?

Jason crossed the room. "We're dealing with priceless objects and journeys that should be impossible. It's no surprise that those are going to be volatile issues." Rose and Emily both visibly relaxed at his easy tone, and he poured himself a glass of wine. "But it does sound like we've got a good plan for getting Henry home, thanks to Ryan's clock idea and Emily's skills, not to mention Rose having actual superpowers."

He took a sip of the wine. "Mmm." He held the glass up toward Henry. "Great choice."

Henry warmed to the praise—to his own annoyance. With seemingly offhand compliments, four in a row, Jason created a mood of camaraderie between people who had not set out to help him, and normalcy in a situation that was in no way normal. Rose sat down and picked up her plate, and Henry supposed he might as well do the same.

Jason sat down, took another sip of the wine, and set it aside. He unzipped the duffel bag at his feet, saying, "Emily, I found a clock that I think will work." He pulled out a box from which he slid a wall clock with a walnut case. "There's a seam right here . . ." He traced it with a finger, then handed it to her. "Think you can open it up, gut it, and put it back together again?"

Emily inspected it. "Oh, yeah. It won't be hard. I could do the whole job tomorrow if I called in sick. No, the next day—I need to get some stuff from work."

"The dimensions are close, but there's going to be a gap inside," Jason said.

"No problem. I'll use adhesive putty strips for padding, and Rose and Henry will be able to pop it right out again. It's going to smell like varnish, so you can say it's a freshly refinished heirloom." Henry could not help but be impressed by her assured manner.

Rose looked to Jason. "Are you funding the trip to England?"

"Not personally, but yes."

"Even if you don't wind up with the astrolabe?"

Jason sighed and shoved his hand through his hair. "It's safest with us. It's the kind of thing that winds up in the wrong hands. But . . . you've already done a great thing by getting it away from

Victor Reuter, believe me." Henry could sense what it cost the man to say that, given how badly he wanted the device.

"The next full moon is in five days," Rose said. "I guess we could make it."

Henry thought for a moment that he'd misheard, or she'd misspoken, but the others were nodding.

"Excuse me," he said. "We cannot reach Everly Park in five days or less."

"You definitely can, with plenty of time to spare," Emily said cheerfully. He suspected she now wanted him on his way as quickly as possible so her best friend could put this muddled chapter behind her and perhaps marry Aaron Coleman. The thought galled him. She added, "Griffin and I have been planning our trip. It's an overnight flight to Heathrow."

Jason nodded. "And a few hours from there to Everly Park."

"Flight," Henry repeated, ignoring the rest.

Rose said, "You remember how we talked about airplanes? In the sky?" She was sincere, but the others smirked at one another in a maddening way.

"Of course I remember," he said testily, though he'd momentarily forgotten, and he felt foolish about it. "But I cannot travel in one of those. We must go by ship."

"No," she said, without even doing him the courtesy of considering it. "I can't be away from my job for that long. Especially with short notice."

"It is a tin *can*, hurtling at an unnatural speed through the *sky*."

Rose told the others, "He didn't even like Skydeck."

"Henry." Ryan was looking at him seriously. "Read about aerodynamics, okay?"

"You traveled the same distance before in one second," Jason said. "And you jumped ahead well over a century at the same time."

"Very well," he grumbled, feeling outnumbered. Rose seemed

to have no concern that they might plummet to their deaths. Then again, as much as he loved Rose, he could not credit her with a good deal of sense.

"Do you have the astrolabe here?" Emily asked. "I can take it home with me."

"Yes!" Rose held up the quilted bag. "It's still cold. I've been keeping it in the freezer."

Emily's face turned ashen. "The *freezer*?" Jason, looking dismayed, rubbed his mouth with his hand. Ryan chuckled.

"It's in a pizza box," Rose protested. "I thought it was a good hiding place."

Emily grabbed her hair in handfuls. "But it's forming ice crystals, which could damage . . ." She waved her hands in the air, shaking it off. "Never mind. Here, give it to me."

She took the bag from Rose and set it on the hotel bed, unzipped it, opened the pizza box, and lifted the astrolabe out with much more care than Henry or Rose had handled it. Jason got up and walked over to it, staring, as if he'd been pulled by a magnet.

"Amazing," he murmured.

"Yeah, there's condensation," Emily said grimly. She turned to Rose. "I should have thought of this, but what did you use to put the moonstone back in place?"

"Superglue."

"Okay, that's not bad," Emily said. Rose looked relieved.

Emily set it on the bed, marched to the bathroom, and returned with Henry's last clean towel. As she wrapped the astrolabe in it, she told Jason, "I'll take care of it. It should be fine."

"Thanks, Emily."

She put the bundle in Rose's bag and zipped it up. "I need to get home. I told Griffin I'd read his essay for his UIC application."

It was none of Henry's business, but his curiosity perked up. "What is that?"

Emily said, "University of Illinois Chicago? He's been going to community college, which is . . . well, never mind, but he wants to transfer to a university next spring semester."

"What is he studying?" Henry couldn't help but ask.

"Secondary education and history. He wants to be a history teacher." She gave a rueful smile. "He's been a little grouchy about the essay. I think he's nervous." Henry found himself unreasonably comforted to hear that even the gregarious knight could be out of sorts.

"He won't have any trouble getting in," Ryan said. "His GPA is fine."

"Um, thanks to *you*," Emily said.

Rose told Henry, "Ryan helped Griffin study for his math class."

They were all smiling. Griffin had good friends, which Henry did not, in this time or in his own. The fact that it was his own fault hardly tempered his envy. Moreover, Griffin was pursuing a serious education, despite having been a great deal behind Henry in terms of modern knowledge. The man had not even known what a potato was.

"We should be going, too," Rose said. Emily told Rose she would give her the clock with the astrolabe in it in two days' time, and as Jason put on his jacket, he talked about sending Rose travel itineraries.

Henry scarcely followed what they were saying. His heart had started pounding in his ears. Rose couldn't leave before he had the chance to speak to her in private . . . even though he feared saying the wrong thing.

As all his guests headed to the door, Henry said, "Rose. May I have a private word?"

Rose looked to her brother, who said, "I'll wait in the lobby."

Henry strode over to the window, not wanting his words to be heard from the hallway. He clasped his hands behind his back.

After Rose had locked the door behind their guests, she came over to him.

"Henry—"

"Please allow me to reiterate what I said the other night: that I am very sorry to have caused you such great distress," he said.

Although he was too agitated to meet her gaze, he heard her sigh. "I know you weren't trying to upset me. But it was horrible for me."

"It was for me, too, being turned out of your house late in the evening," Henry could not help saying. Yes, he intended to apologize, but surely she could see how uncivil that had been? Never in his life had he been treated in such a way.

"I had every right to do that!" She walked over to stand near him, though not too close. "I know it sucked for both of us, but I was so hurt. I still am! And like Ryan said, my feelings matter, too!"

"On that point, we agree." He finally met her gaze. Her eyes were watery. "Truly, I am more sorry than I can say. I reproach myself without ceasing for ever speaking of it at all."

"But you still think I'm Charlotte," she said.

"I have never thought you were Charlotte."

She threw her arms in the air. "What are you saying? You *called* me—"

"I thought you *used* to be!" He took a step toward her. "No, I never should have said that! I thought those memories might be locked away in your mind, and if I said the name, you would remember . . . but I am a fool."

It was probably the first time he'd ever referred to himself that way, but when he saw a glimmer of hope in her eyes, he continued down that path. "And if you say this is not one of your past lives, I would be even more of a fool not to believe you. It would not be the first time I misjudged reality."

"I appreciate that," she said softly. "I mean, it's not impossible . . . I just don't think it's true."

Henry dared to take her hand. She didn't pull away.

"It has been only two days, and I have missed you with every fiber of my being," he said. "While I remain in this era, might we not resume that close confidence that was such a pleasure to us both?"

A furrow appeared between her brows. "By close confidence, do you mean being friends, or . . ."

"Yes, friends, if I may not have more." He was grateful for that at least, but his heart ached.

She squeezed his hand and let go of it. "We're going to say good-bye soon, and you were right about getting involved . . . It just makes it harder."

He nodded. "It will be far more bitter than sweet, and yet . . . I cannot regret our tender relations and all that has passed between us. For me, it held enough for a whole other lifetime."

"I don't regret it, either."

She wrapped her arms around him in a tight hug. He held her, memorizing every curve and the scent of her hair. She kissed his cheek and then pulled back, giving him a sad smile.

"Let's get you home."

Twenty-Eight

On the following Saturday, Rose was waiting with Henry at the train station platform, ready to get on the train that would take them to the airport. It was the first really hot day, and she was wearing a straw hat with her black dress. Henry, in a button-down shirt and pants, was pretending not to sweat.

Each of them had a carry-on suitcase. Henry's was new, made of aluminum. In it, she'd packed the clothes he'd been wearing when he'd first arrived in her apartment. She'd taken them to a dry cleaner, who had gotten out the wine stains. That should've made her happy, but she'd teared up as she'd carefully folded the clothes with tissue paper to avoid wrinkles. Along with his clothes, carefully packed in a box, was the wall clock with the astrolabe now sealed inside. It had only left room for one change of clothes, but if all went as planned, he wouldn't be returning.

"Do you have your passport?" Rose asked Henry.

"Yes." He patted Jason's messenger bag over his shoulder. She supposed she'd be able to return it to him soon. In a lower voice, he added, "Or rather, I have the passport for Horatio Jones."

It was fake, and supplied by Jason, of course. "I think Horatio is better for a middle name," Rose said. "I mean, what's the nickname for Horatio?"

"Harry or Rory," Henry said promptly.

"Oh. That's not so bad. You look more like a Henry, though."

All day she'd been making idle conversation, doing anything to break the terrible tension of traveling with Henry and pretending they were just friends, while constantly having the urge to either kiss him or cry. Hopefully, she was also distracting him from their upcoming flight.

"I wonder what Horatio means," she added.

Henry gave her a tight smile. "It means Man of Time."

"Wow. I guess it does fit you."

A large man with a very precisely groomed dark mustache and beard approached them. Rose's first thought was that he was going to ask them for money, although in his clean T-shirt and jeans, he didn't look broke. He just had a purposeful look about him.

"You're friends of Jason Yun's." It wasn't a question.

Oh, shit. How did he know that? Rose felt the blood slamming hard in the artery at her neck. Was he law enforcement?

"I beg your pardon," Henry said testily. "I don't believe we are acquainted." The couple who had been standing next to them on the platform walked away, and she couldn't blame them. But Henry showed no signs of recognizing a threat, which scared her even more.

The big guy glared at him. "I *said*, you're friends with Jason Yun."

Victor Reuter. This guy had to work for him. Reuter could've easily suspected that Jason was behind the theft. Maybe he'd even figured out that Henry and Rose were the thieves. Rose wanted to grab Henry's arm and warn him, but how could she?

Henry scoffed. "I have never heard of the man, not that the company I keep is any of your concern." He sounded every bit the snobby duke. Rose desperately wished her pepper spray was still in her purse, but she'd left it at home because she couldn't take it on a plane. They were alone on the platform now. Could she do something magical to defend them?

"You're lying," the man said flatly. His gaze slid to Rose. "It would be for the best if you two would come with me and answer a few questions."

The warning bells for the approaching train started ringing.

Henry's eyes half closed as if the man were being tiresome. "By no means. I am a busy man. Good day, sir."

The man lurched toward Henry.

In the next moment, Henry punched the man first, across the jaw, hard enough to make a solid cracking sound. The man staggered back.

Rose gasped. What. Was. Happening?

The train was rushing up to the station. She gave a little scream as the stranger swung his fist with all his might at Henry's face.

Henry dodged it, evading the man's other fist as well, with shocking fluidity, as Rose realized in a rush, *Henry's suitcase is metal, idiot!* She picked it up as Henry landed another solid punch, this time to the man's nose, and her straw hat fell off her head as she bashed him in the side of the head with the case. The guy's balance had already been off, and he toppled to the ground.

"Another round, motherfucker?" Henry asked.

An incredulous laugh escaped Rose. But Henry was seriously pushing his luck, and the man was already scrambling to his feet—

Thank Goddess. The train doors were open!

She yelled at Henry, "Come on!"

Still clutching his carry-on in both hands, she lurched on board, Henry right behind her. A chime on the train sounded, followed by a cool recorded voice that said, "Caution. The doors are about to close."

Standing in the aisle, she whirled around to face Henry. "What the hell was that!"

The train lurched forward and Henry caught hold of her with one arm, grabbing a pole with the other for support. He'd grabbed her pink suitcase, she realized, and with one foot, he kept it from rolling away.

"Let's find a seat," he suggested.

Rose looked around. Several passengers were staring at them, wide-eyed. They must've seen the fight.

A guy in a ball cap held up his hands. "If you want to sit here, I'll move."

"No, no. We're actually really nice," Rose said to the passengers, smiling to put them at ease. "We'll, uh, just sit up there." She pointed to the next car.

Once they sat down, Henry said, "You must inform Jason of this incident at once. Emily, Griffin, and your brother, too."

"Ugh, you're right."

Rose took a couple of minutes to send them a group text, describing the whole incident the best she could. She avoided using Victor Reuter's name, referring to him as *our friend who had the party*. Jason had said before that he and Victor Reuter had a history. He might've already been on high alert.

When she looked up at Henry again, she said, "I didn't know you knew how to fight!"

"I didn't know you did," he countered. "I told you I'd studied boxing."

"But as a *spectator*, right?"

"No. I took lessons from an American prizefighter. I was not good at it at first, to be honest." He pursed his lips thoughtfully. "But I did not lean in to the man's left fist. Dunton would've been proud."

"You're an *astronomer*. A *duke* astronomer. Why would you do that?"

It had been too long since she'd seen Henry smile, and this was a different smile. It was *smug*. And Goddess, it made him look sexier than ever.

"A gentleman," he said, "should strive to be capable and competent in every circumstance."

Twenty-Nine

Rose had always liked the moment when an airplane touched
down: the bounce of the wheels on the tarmac, the rising
roar of the engine, and the feeling that a new little seg-
ment of life had begun. But as this plane landed at Heathrow Airport in London, she looked out at the cement-gray late-afternoon
sky and the tarmac with a feeling of dread. Henry's white-knuckled
grip on his armrest relaxed. He unbuckled and threw off his seat
belt.

"Wait," Rose said as he stood up in the aisle.

"Sir, please sit down and remain seated until the pilot turns off
the seat belt sign," a flight attendant scolded him.

He sat back down again as they taxied to the gate. "The sooner
I am out of this prison, the better."

"I know," she said sympathetically.

He'd seemed close to having a panic attack when the plane had
taken off, which one wouldn't necessarily expect from a guy who'd
just casually crushed a big attacker on the street. While they had

waited at the gate at O'Hare, Jason had called them. He'd apologized to Henry for not telling him to be cautious. As far as Jason had been able to tell, Henry and Rose had still not been identified as the thieves. Jason hadn't thought anyone would be targeted other than himself, but he guessed that Henry and Rose had been sought out as close friends who might have information.

Jason's group had already taken care of it. Among Reuter's enemies were members of a Russian mob who had used stolen art and artifacts for drug trafficking collateral before. Jason's group had planted a credible rumor, with a tip to the media, that Reuter and his men were behind the theft. He expected them to be on the defensive before long.

Rose said to Henry now, as they waited to deplane, "At least we got to fly first-class." She'd never gotten to do that before.

"Splendid accommodations, indeed," he groused, and plucked at the blanket on his lap. "A blanket the thickness of paper, and mortal terror."

On the flight there, Rose had told Henry more stories about growing up in Peoria and Cicero. She'd told him a lot about her college years already, but not about the various jobs she'd worked in the past, which Henry had seemed to find fascinating. Henry had told Rose about hunting with his father, which he'd hated, and about how he'd helped to discover an asteroid, in the time he'd studied at the Paris Observatory. It was as though they were giving each other as many parts of themselves as they could.

Once they were walking off the plane, Henry asked, "Is someone going to grope me again and search my bag as though I am a common thief?"

She leaned closer to murmur, "You are a thief."

"Hardly a common one."

"That's for sure. But no, nobody pats us down on this side." When they'd gone through security at O'Hare, a TSA employee had opened up the suitcase and looked at the clock, but nothing had come of it, and she hadn't really even been nervous.

In the airport bathroom, Rose changed from her black dress to the yellow one she'd packed. It was Sunday now, after all. She then lingered in the terminal, waiting for Henry, who was changing into his 1818 clothes. When he walked back to her, he got a couple of curious and amused looks, but for the most part, people were staring at their phones or rushing to their gates.

Rose sighed as he walked back to her. He was every inch the perfect gentleman she'd asked for. Maybe, when she'd done the spell, she should've specified "forever."

They found the driver they'd hired in advance, a man with black curly hair and glasses who was taking them to Everly Park. He greeted them without smiling and made no attempt at conversation as he led them to his small, bright green car. Maybe British people didn't smile as much, Rose guessed. Or maybe his last customers had been jagoffs. Despite the cramped back seat, she fell asleep on the hour-long trip.

"We're almost there," the driver barked, and Henry stirred next to her. He'd gotten a nap, too.

Rose opened her eyes to the rolling green landscape. "Wow. It's pretty out here!"

"I have always thought so," Henry said, clearly pleased, and then pointed. "Look! There it is!"

Rose gasped. Most tourist attractions, in her experience, looked slightly less magical in person, but the massive palace looked like something out of a fairy tale.

"I still can't believe this is your *house*!" she exclaimed. "I mean, the house where, uh, you used to work!"

"You used to be on staff here?" the driver asked.

Henry gave a melancholy smile. "In a manner of speaking, yes."

The man's black brows drew together as he looked at them in the mirror above the windshield. "You know it's closed."

"Yes," Rose said. "I'm just taking pictures of the grounds."

"Too bad it's about to rain."

"It'll look more English that way," Rose said, and was gratified when she got a smile out of him.

Henry leaned forward and pointed. "Leave us on the west side, if you please."

"The knot garden? It's locked, mate."

"I'm going to take a picture of the gate," Rose said, improvising. It actually would make a nice photo, if the original wrought iron gate was still there.

When he pulled up, she smiled and tugged Henry's sleeve. "Look, it's still the same!" She loved the ornate scroll pattern of the iron-work, mounted between two columns of golden-beige stone.

Henry turned to stare at her, wide-eyed, as though she'd said something insane. Right. An ordinary American tourist wouldn't know that a gate hadn't changed in over a hundred years. Still, it wasn't *that* big of a deal; this random driver didn't care about them. He unloaded their luggage out of the trunk, just two carry-ons with wheels, and Rose thanked him before he drove away.

She could feel her face flush, the way it did when she was emotional. Before long, if all went according to plan, she'd have to say goodbye to Henry.

"He was right. It's started to rain," Henry said.

Rose lifted her face, appreciating the sensation of the fine drops on her hot cheeks. "It's barely more than a mist."

Henry pulled her close. "Nonetheless, I'm afraid you'll catch a chill," he murmured.

He felt strong and warm, and his arms around her made her feel safe. She hugged him back, burying her face against his chest. She could feel his heart beating. When she looked up, he was staring at his big mansion.

"What is it?" she whispered.

"My love," he said, his voice hoarse and tight. "I thought when we came here, and I set eyes on Everly Park again, I would be strengthened in my resolve to return to my time."

She looked up at him. His dark hair was damp enough to be plastered to his forehead. "Aren't you? This place is beautiful."

"I know that it is," he agreed, "and yet when I look upon it, it feels as though I am returning to a prison. A lifelong sentence, after a glorious reprieve."

Her throat felt tight and sore. "What are you saying?"

He cupped her face in his hands and looked down at her with an anguished stare. "I am saying that meeting you, loving you . . . has brought me joy, when I thought joy had gone forever from my life."

So that's what it feels like, she thought, *when your heart skips a beat.*

"Love," she echoed. "You don't mean—"

"Yes, I love you!" he said fiercely. "Can you doubt it? For your kindness, and your beauty, and your . . . extremely confusing magic. I love you for the way you see the beauty in the world and show it to others. And for your impractical nature, and your cursing—and in fact, for your utter lack of propriety—because they are all part of the free-spirited woman I adore."

Rose gave a strained laugh that threatened to turn into a sob, and she covered her mouth with her hand. He saw her. He loved her for her.

A tear leaked out of one of her eyes. Henry kissed it away.

"I love you, too, Henry," she confessed, her voice wavering. "You don't even realize how wonderful you are, and it doesn't have anything to do with being a duke or a gazillionaire, or even super smart, though obviously, you are, and I had no idea how hot that would be." She shook her head. "I know I've caused you a lot of trouble, but when I did a spell to find an old-fashioned gentleman . . . I think it worked out perfectly."

Henry pulled her into a deep kiss. And even as he filled her senses, she realized that she was going to ask him the question she'd been dying to ask him.

She hadn't dared to before. But even in the shadow of Everly Park, she knew their love was enough. She was enough.

She broke away and looked up at him seriously. "Henry, will you come live with me in Chicago?"

He gaped at her. "Are you certain?"

"Yes!"

He lowered his head and kissed her hand. *Oh no.* He was being gallant before he turned her down.

Then he raised his gaze to meet hers. "My love, there is nothing that would please me more."

He said yes!

She threw her arms around him, squeezing him hard. "Yay!"

He laughed. "We have come all the way to England to take a walk in the rain for nothing."

"I think it's perfect," she declared. "Why don't we at least take a walk on the grounds, one last time?"

"Excellent idea. But first . . ." He stooped and plucked a few white starflowers growing near the gate. He put them in her hand and wrapped her fingers around them.

"These are just like the flowers on the Six of Cups card," she mused, looking up at him. "The one I used in the first spell? The boy is giving the girl star-shaped flowers." It was the card about happy memories and coming home. She shook her head. "I can't believe I didn't think of that before. After all the times . . ."

Her world swerved and wobbled on its axis. She swayed and grabbed a bar of the iron gate for support, closing her eyes.

She had not been saying normal things. Saying the gate was still there. Saying they should take one more walk on the grounds . . .

Henry's strong arm wrapped around her shoulders, steadying her. His other hand wrapped around her hand that held the flowers, which had gone ice cold. When she met his gaze again, his eyes were glossy with tears, filled with fear and hope.

"After all the times . . . ?" he prompted.

"After all the times," she whispered, "that you plucked these and put them in my hand."

Thirty

Henry could hardly breathe.

She was remembering. But was it just for a moment? Would those recollections fade into the mist again?

He had truly given up on this mad theory of reincarnation. Rose differed from Charlotte in so many ways, and he loved her. When she'd asked him to live with her in Chicago, he'd been overcome with happiness.

"We went on walks after dinner," she said, and looked down at the starflowers in her hand. Her whole body was shaking. "Kennicott thought these were too plain." Kennicott had been the head gardener and landscape designer, and Henry knew he had never mentioned him. "But you liked them because they looked like stars, and they glowed at night in the moonlight—" Her voice squeaked tight.

"Yes!" Henry raised her free hand, pressed it fervently to his lips, and cradled it with both hands against his chest.

"And I had him plant those roses, the Early Cinnamons . . . oh, Goddess, they smell just like my favorite perfume now!"

"Yes. I noticed. Like roses and incense." Henry laughed, but it was edged with a sob.

"On our first anniversary, we were in the secret garden, right over there . . ." She inclined her head in that direction. There had been a tall hedge on one border of the knot garden, and between it and the stone wall was the pocket-sized secret garden with the arbor of white roses, a place only they and the gardeners knew. "You *gave* me that Venus statue! It was a surprise! Right over there!"

"Yes!" He drew nearer and held her face between his palms. He was definitely weeping now. He didn't care. He kissed her cheek, her brow.

"And the way you kissed me . . ."

He pulled her in and crushed his mouth to hers. She wrapped her arms around his neck, and he pressed himself against her—he couldn't get close enough. There was nothing except her, and him, together, the way they always would be.

She pulled back to say, "I think I missed you the whole time!" Her voice trembled. Maybe everyone felt that way, when they finally met their soulmate. But for her, for them, it was doubly true.

Ungraciously, he rubbed his nose with his shirtsleeve. Then he searched her face. "What else do you remember?"

"So many things." She looked around them in wonder. "Being here made me remember . . . But how did I forget?"

"You forgot because you are Rose now," he said gently. "I know it was long ago for you, and a whole other life."

"Hold on," Rose said and dug in her purse. She pulled out her phone and tapped on the screen. "It's nine twenty-nine. The moon is rising."

Henry looked toward the east. "I don't see it yet, but the trees would block it."

"I want to see it," she said.

"I would have no objection to watching the moon rise with you, but it is rather damp," Henry said. It had begun to rain in earnest. "We cannot have you catching a chill."

"No! Everly Park. I want to go back."

Not long ago, Henry's heart would've soared at such a declaration. Now, it felt wrong.

"Your life in Chicago—"

"Not to live there! Just for an hour or two." She clutched his arm. "I want to see everything exactly the way it was, so all the memories come back to me."

Henry would've felt the same way, in her extraordinary circumstances. And she'd seemed very certain about the full moon timing.

Still, he shook his head. "It is very dangerous, my love, and I do not want it to make you ill."

"I don't care if I faint afterward. I know I can do this!"

He sighed. "I, too, would like to pay a brief visit to the past, if only to leave a note explaining that I have left. A note in my own hand would go a very long way to allaying any suspicions of foul play."

"I need to find a dry place, for the candles," Rose said.

"And for you as well. The folly near the Great Court," he suggested, pointing. It was only a short distance away. The round stone structure with pillars was meant to resemble a classical temple, though with its small size, no more than two people could occupy it at once.

"Perfect!"

As they hurried toward it, Henry reflected that this was the greatest night of his life. He had not been religious since he had been a boy, but now he offered up a silent prayer of gratitude to the universe itself.

It was dry inside the folly, but the light from Rose's phone illuminated large cracks in the stone floor that had been smoothly paved in his time. They knelt and Rose took out the astrolabe and the other accoutrements for her spell from the suitcases, with all the ceremony of a child taking out her toys to play. She set up and lit the pink and black candles. The moonstone in the astrolabe glowed with heavenly fire.

They held hands and both gripped an edge of the astrolabe. Rose spoke the words of the incantation from memory. But no—there was a new phrase, about lovers and coming home.

The nothingness that followed, the whirling abeyance, was slightly less alarming than before.

Then birdsong reached his ears. He opened his eyes and looked out the open doorway at the grounds and house, now in daylight.

"I know we did it," Rose murmured, "because I feel like I'm going to faint again." She was holding her head in her hands.

Henry, dizzy himself, quickly extinguished the small candles she might need again later. The stone floor no longer had cracks. He moved over to sit in front of her, laying a hand on her shoulder.

"How can I help?" he murmured, already wondering if this had been a mistake.

"Just give me a minute." She took a couple of deep breaths and let them out, then nodded and looked up at him. "I'm fine. The world's stopped spinning."

"Well, I hope not," he said with a small smile, reassured by the color in her cheeks. He packed the astrolabe and her other items carefully away, and with their suitcases, they stepped outside. It was cool and cloudy, as it had been when he left, but it had not been raining.

Pointing across the Great Court, he told Rose, "That is my boxing instructor with his luggage, and the carriage that will take him to London."

Rose let out a squeal. "It's 1818!" She broke into a trot, her long-handled suitcase bumping behind her.

"Wait!" Henry took long strides to catch up and took her by the arm. "You nearly fainted. You should not be cavorting like a spring lamb."

As they reached the courtyard, Quentin Dunton was striding toward them and squinting. He called out, "Is that you, Leighton-Lyons? I forgot to give you my card with my new address."

"Yes, yes, very good," Henry replied as they reached him. "Rose, this is Mr. Quentin Dunton, the famed prizefighter from Boston. Dunton, this is Miss Rose Novak, from Chicago. But never mind that. There is no Chicago."

Dunton blinked as though wondering if one of his blows had landed too hard and addled Henry's brains. At least Rose's dress—like many of her dresses, actually—would not cause too much confusion. Its tailoring was foreign, but it reached her ankles.

Dunton said to her, "Very nice to meet you, ma'am."

Rose beamed. "It's nice to meet you, too!"

Henry considered how the man's instruction had proved invaluable. Here was an opportunity to pay him more handsomely than previously arranged.

"Dunton, may I trouble you to come back into the house for a short while? There is something else I meant to give to you, too." Some heirloom or other, he supposed.

"No trouble at all," Dunton said.

Rose practically skipped rather than walked, telling Dunton, "You did a great job of teaching Henry how to fight! He beat up a big tough guy."

Dunton's eyebrows shot up. "Here on the grounds?"

Henry realized that to any sensible person, and Dunton was certainly one, it would appear that in the past hour, Henry had given a man on his property a sound thrashing, gone for a refreshing swim in his pond with his clothes on, discovered a wild-haired buxom female in the possession of strange luggage doing the same, and had persuaded her to come with him to his house.

"You know how these matters are," Henry said vaguely. Then they were all distracted by the clatter of a second carriage drawing up to the first.

Henry sighed. "Damnation. Who is this?" He wanted to take care of his business and reminisce with Rose, not deal with uninvited guests.

Then a bald man with spectacles burst out of the carriage in a rush and dashed toward the entrance, making Henry's spirits soar again.

"My solicitor!" He strode toward him, waving. "Kirchhoff!"

"What's a solicitor?" Rose asked, trailing after him.

"Lawyer," Dunton translated.

Upon seeing Henry advance on him, Kirchhoff paled. "Your Grace, I must express my most abject apologies for my tardy arrival. In my own meager defense, I—"

"Not at all," Henry said quickly. It occurred to him that Kirchhoff had never once been late before. He clapped the man on the shoulder, giving him a start. "I daresay you are perfectly on time. But do you have your notary seal?"

"I—yes, always, Your Grace," Kirchhoff said, brandishing his attaché case.

"Excellent!"

When they stepped into the foyer, Rose gasped and clutched her heart. "Look at it! I remember so much." She stared up at the pictures on the walls. "I remember everything!" Belatedly, she noticed Dunton and Kirchhoff were both staring at her, and she breathlessly added, "I used to live here."

Dunton raised an eyebrow. "You were a maid?"

Rose laughed and dashed down the hallway with abandon. In her yellow dress she was like a beam of pure sunlight, heedless of the disapproving portraits of his illustrious forebears, bringing joy to this grand, grieving house once again.

Then his butler, Brady, turned the corner, and she ran smack into him.

"Goodness gracious! Sorry!" she exclaimed. Although Henry no longer had any wish for Rose to be anything but modern, he could not help but be charmed by another one of her lapses into old-fashioned speech. Walter Wilke emerged around the corner, looking like a perplexed bear.

Brady glanced from Rose to Henry and inclined his head. "Your Grace, Mr. Wilke was just looking for you."

Wilke exclaimed, "I turned around, and it was as if you'd vanished into thin air! Begging your pardon, Your Grace."

Henry gave him a chiding look. "You may not be a man of science, as I am, Wilke, but I am sure you are aware that men do not vanish. All of you, come into my drawing room at once."

It was only steps away, as his rooms were at the heart of the great house. The room's red Persian carpet, olive-green walls, and ornamental gilding struck him as foolishly opulent now.

"Sit down, sit down," he urged them, gesturing to the elegant chairs and settees. Rose, who'd flitted over to the window, looked over at him. "Not you—you do as you like," he told her with a wave of his hand. "Kirchhoff, at the table. I have a number of items to attend to."

With alacrity, his solicitor sat down and drew paper, ink, a pen, and a notary seal from his attaché case.

Brady asked, "Shall I ring for tea, sir?"

"No, sit down," Henry said. Brady raised his eyebrows, but obeyed.

Henry walked over to the table. "First things first. I am going to write a letter, which you all may witness, and Kirchhoff will notarize." He took a leaf of paper, dipped a pen in the ink, and they all stared at him as he bent over, scrawled out a few lines, and signed it with a flourish. Then he straightened again. "It says, *To whom it may*

concern, I, Henry Horatio Leighton-Lyons have on this day of May first, 1818,
fallen in love with an American lady. My title and estate may be transferred at
once, with the small amendments I make today, for I am leaving England
forever."

"What!" Kirchhoff demanded, as Rose drifted over to a seat, a
delighted smile on her face.

Brady leaned forward in his chair. "Your Grace, are you quite
well?"

"Never better." Henry looked fondly at the older man. "I will
miss you, Brady." Then he turned to Kirchhoff. "From my estate,
Brady's only daughter, Mary Brady, is to be bequeathed five thousand a year."

Brady looked as though he might pass out. Henry hoped not; he
had neither smelling salts nor Malört handy.

"I do not hear your pen scratching, Kirchhoff," Henry said to
his solicitor.

"Five *hundred*, surely," Kirchhoff said in a weak voice.

"I am certain I did not stutter. Five thousand a year for Mary
Brady, and . . . well, let's say, a ten thousand lump sum for Brady
himself, toward his retirement." Kirchoff was scribbling furiously now.

Brady rose to his feet. "Your Grace, I can hardly find the words to—"

"Not at all. Please sit," Henry said quickly, finding the gratitude
embarrassing. "Five thousand pounds for Mr. Quentin Dunton, for
his excellent instruction." Dunton's eyebrows raised and he flashed
a smile. "A thousand pounds for Wilke, I suppose, since he happens
to be here," Henry added.

"Thank you, Your Grace," Wilke said. "I am very sorry I will
not be able to finish the portrait."

Henry regretted that, too. But the artist could hardly finish the
painting before the full moon set. And if he and Rose stayed in
the past until the next full moon, he felt sure that she would grow

anxious about being away from her brother, her friends, and her work—even though in their year, no time would pass at all.

"Never mind that," he told the artist. "I believe the painting already captured my essence very well."

"But Your Grace, you are not even *there*."

"Indeed." Henry's gaze drifted to Rose. "In my heart, I was always and only with my beloved." Rose pressed a hand to her chest, her eyes sparkling.

Dunton folded his arms across his chest with the air of a man who was enjoying a show. "You met her a while back, then."

"Yes. Although since it is 1818, I suppose that in another sense, I have not yet had the pleasure of—"

"Oh!" Rose said, jumping out of her chair. "I just remembered! I think I can help." She went over to Wilke, pulling a piece of paper out of her purse, and held it up. It was a color photo of the finished painting. "Can you copy this, maybe?"

Wilke's jaw dropped. "Where did you get that?"

Rose threw her hands in the air. "It's too hard to explain."

The artist took the paper from her and stared at it. "Yes, I can recreate this. But what kind of sorcery—"

"Very good," Henry said crisply. "When the painting is finished, please give it to the World Astronomical Society."

He added to Kirchhoff, "See that they get their portion, as enumerated in my will."

Rose was raising her hand in the air. "What about the rest of the servants?"

"Ah yes. A hundred pounds apiece for them, along with letters of recommendation from me. Brady can tell you what to write for each of them," he added with a wave of his hand. Henry's solicitor had often written letters on his behalf. "Oh, and a thousand for you as well, Kirchhoff—do make a note of that."

The solicitor did, but he looked pained. "Your Grace, with these amendments, and the money settled on your sisters, not to mention your excellent society, the next Duke of Beresford . . . that is to say, your cousin . . . may struggle to manage Everly Park."

"He'll figure it out. He's a clever fellow," Henry said, leaning over and taking the pen from Kirchhoff. Then he paused. "No. I have only met him twice, and he is a dullard, and very disagreeable besides." He shrugged. "Perhaps it may pass into the National Trust." He and Rose exchanged a knowing glance.

He was aware of Brady and Dunton conducting a quiet, pleased conversation as he dipped the pen in ink, then signed and dated the bottom of his paper with the amendments. "Notarize that, Kirchhoff, if you please."

His solicitor took the paper and inserted it into the notary seal stamper. Looking warily up at Henry, he pressed the lever to emboss the paper with the seal.

Henry clapped his hands. "I believe that is all. Rose and I will leave today for America." He looked around at their astonished faces. "Yes, well. Do enjoy the rest of your lives."

After they filed out, Rose came and threw her arms around him. "That was amazing. You made a real difference for a lot of people."

"You liked that, did you?" he murmured, looking down at her. Christ, she felt good, pressed up next to him, reminding every inch of his body that he was alive. "Shall we tour the rest of the house?"

She quirked her mouth to the side, a mischievous twinkle in her eyes. "I thought I would want to, but now I just want to see the bedroom."

He hauled her up more tightly against him, locking her hips to his, as if she didn't already know the effect she had on him. "I must warn you, a tour of the bedroom will take a while."

"Really?" Her eyes widened in feigned astonishment. "Why is that?"

"Well, as you may recall, in addition to a four-poster bed, there is a large gilded mirror, and a very propitiously angled French chaise longue—"

"I vaguely remember those," she said, urging him toward the bedroom door, "but I do want to see them one more time."

Perhaps two hours later, Henry got up from the bed and looked down at Rose. She lay with her eyes closed on top of his tangled sheets, her arms flung above her head, her wild curls spilling out around her, the sunlight through the leaded glass windows casting little rainbows on her creamy naked body.

His sleeping duchess. It was a picture so unreal and lovely that no artist, not even Walter Wilke, could have captured it.

He moved quietly to his mahogany dresser, took a small lacquered box out of the top drawer, and put it in his messenger bag—Jason's bag, actually, but the man might not want it back, as it had gotten soaked and was streaked with mud. The box contained his wedding ring and Charlotte's, along with a rose quartz and diamond pendant he'd given her on their first anniversary, designed especially for her. When he proposed to Rose in the future, he would want a new ring in some twenty-first-century style. He'd make discreet inquiries beforehand, to learn what was appropriate. But she might like to have these as well.

Then he returned to the bed, leaned over, and kissed her on the cheek. "Wake up, my love," he murmured, when she stirred.

"Mmmm." She stretched and sat up.

"I have a question for you, but I do not know if you will remember." He sat down on the edge of the bed. "When you gave me the astrolabe, in another life . . . did you know it could be used for time travel?"

"I overheard a rumor at the auction house, but I didn't know if it was true. I knew you'd think it was silly if I told you." She smiled softly. "But I thought you might figure it out, with enough time."

Once they were dressed, they left the house and, pulling their suitcases behind them, walked to the secret garden with the Venus. They wouldn't be disturbed there as they made the return trip. He cast a backward glance at Everly Park and felt no desire to ever return. He continued forward with her, away from certainty, superiority, and everything else that, in the end, had never served him well.

He still had no idea who he would be or what he would do in her time. The one thing he knew for sure was that she was his miracle, now more than ever. He would never let her forget it.

Epilogue

I now pronounce you husband and wife for life."

Rose felt as though she was glowing from within as the wedding officiant—a seventy-something woman in long white robes—pronounced those words. In the next moment, Henry pulled her close and kissed her as though they were the only two people on the outdoor terrace of the Adler Planetarium, even as they were surrounded by cheers and applause. She melted in his arms. As many kisses as they'd shared, in this life and the one before, this would be one she would always remember.

Their guests' reactions gave way to scattered laughter. She pulled away from Henry, smiling. His dark gaze was filled with happiness.

The terrace offered a stunning view of the Chicago skyline reflected in the lake. The September sun was just setting, painting the sky, the water, and the windows of the skyscrapers peach, gold, and pink.

Rose's bridal gown, with its empire waist and dreamy layers of tulle, was the palest shade of pink, too, in honor of Venus, the goddess of love. Of course, it was a Friday.

She took his hand, and Emily, Rose's maid of honor—"matron of honor" sounded too, well, matronly, Rose had decided, even if her best friend was three months pregnant—stepped forward to return her bridal bouquet.

"You are the world's most beautiful bride," Emily said.

Henry, looking positively ducal in his tuxedo, said, "She certainly is."

As the string quartet played, Rose and Henry walked down the aisle between guests, most of whom had stood up out of their white folding chairs. Emily and Henry's best man Ryan followed behind them. It wasn't a large wedding, and they didn't have anyone else in the wedding party. Henry didn't know that many people yet, though he'd probably make friends at Northwestern. In the coming spring semester, he'd start there as an undergraduate, majoring in physics. He had hopes of eventually pursuing his PhD, and perhaps working at the particle physics and acceleration laboratory in the western suburbs, but as he said, there was no telling what would happen.

Rose and Henry filed into the glass solarium, decorated for the reception, and took their places inside the door to greet their guests. Emily hugged them both, and Ryan stepped up. Rose reached out to hug him, too, but he stopped her and said in an undertone, "I need to talk to you about something later."

"What?" she whispered back. Heedless of the guests queued up behind him, she demanded, "Tell me now!"

Ryan hugged her and said in her ear, "Jason's asked me to join his group."

Rose's mouth fell open. "What did you tell him?"

"Yes."

She knew Jason had asked Ryan for advice on a couple of things over the summer, and Ryan had been frustratingly vague about what those things were, but still, she hadn't expected this. This was big.

She whispered, "Is it going to be legal?" Creating false identities for people was a crime, after all, and for Jason's group, it seemed to be a routine procedure. Bankrolling thieves was, strictly speaking, also a crime. It was a good thing, from her perspective, that Victor Reuter was currently living in Switzerland rather than Lincoln Park, thanks to his worsening legal issues and his falling-out with mobsters, but Jason's shady brotherhood had arranged the latter. Goddess only knew what else the group did.

Ryan said, "I told him my part would have to be legal." As she pulled back to look at him, he added, "I'm really excited about it."

She could see that in his eyes. And she'd wanted so badly for him to have something that would challenge his mind and give him a sense of purpose. Even though this new development made her a little nervous, she simply said, "I love you. And they're lucky to get you."

"I love you, too."

Griffin was next and hugged the daylights out of her, then did the same to Henry. The two men had gone horseback riding a few times at a stable near Griffin and Emily's house. Even in her past life, Rose had never been a horsewoman; she was glad that Henry and Griffin could do that together.

After greeting a few more guests, Rose found herself receiving a hug from Jason. She said to him in an undertone, "You better not get him in trouble."

"I don't think I will," Jason said, which wasn't the most reassuring answer. "You know, we still haven't found anyone else who can use that astrolabe. I wonder if you'd reconsider a few more adventures in time travel—"

"*No.* It makes me feel sick. There was only one person I'd do that for."

As Jason had promised, his group had paid a cool two million for the device. Henry and Rose were house-hunting for a place more convenient to the campus in Evanston, although Henry had said he was in no hurry.

When Aaron Coleman came through the line, Rose said, "I'm glad you could make it."

"Sure," he said. "Thanks for inviting me."

She hadn't actually planned to, and he knew it. He'd been at Griffin's birthday dinner the month before, along with Daniela, Ryan, and Jason. When everyone had started talking about the wedding, she'd felt bad and had somehow blurted out that he was welcome to come. Which had been the rudest way imaginable to invite someone to a wedding, especially because Henry had remained silent. She'd been a little surprised when Aaron showed up.

Aaron glanced at Henry, who had gotten caught up in conversation with Rose's coworker Jayla. Then he asked in an undertone, "So now that the investigation's closed, do you want to tell me how you really met this guy?"

The original portrait had appeared in the painting conservation lab on a Sunday night, just before midnight. Security cameras had been locked right on it, but the only explanation was that the feed had been tampered with, because in one moment, the unfinished painting had been there, and in the next, it had been replaced. There was no evidence whatsoever of anyone going in or out of the lab. A month's worth of tests and study had confirmed that the painting was the original.

Daniela might have been a prime suspect for the bizarre and elaborate prank, but she had been out of town that weekend, and she'd cheerfully shared her meticulous notes on the painting. In the end, the FBI Art Crimes team had better things to do than investigate an incident that resulted in no missing artwork, no person of interest, no clear motive, and no clues.

Unless one considered the existence of a man who looked exactly like the duke in the painting, now walking around Chicago, a clue, and Aaron probably did.

"Like I said," Rose told Aaron now. "Henry and I go way back."

He tilted his head. "Well, you know what I'm going to say. He's a lucky man."

Rose's heart went out to him. "You'll find your soulmate, too," she said, hoping it didn't sound condescending.

"I don't think those exist for everyone. But thanks."

When they'd finished greeting the guests, Rose took Henry's arm and they walked toward their table.

Henry murmured, "How can we be so fortunate?"

"Maybe we aren't," she said.

He stopped and turned to her in surprise. "What do you mean?"

"Maybe soulmates always find each other again . . . in this world, or in some forever after."

Henry looked up at the night sky through the glass ceiling of the solarium. "Or in another world, out there in the stars."

Rose pulled him closer. "I can tell you this much: I am *never* letting you go."

Henry kissed her again. "And that is why I will always look forward to the future."

ACKNOWLEDGMENTS

I am so grateful to so many people for helping me tell Rose and Henry's story. Here are some of them!

My blog readers, the readers in my Brynsiders private Facebook group, the members of Chicago-North Romance Writers, bookstore owners, librarians, and fans of *Her Knight at the Museum* have all been so supportive and encouraging.

Thank you to Enrique Silva, who kindly took the time to talk to me about growing up in Cicero, IL; to the guy in the kitchen at the Arlington Heights Memorial Library, who I wound up talking to at length about his work in quantum physics; and to the Arlington Heights Memorial Library for being my writing home away from home.

I am so lucky to be represented by the wonderful Julie Gwinn at Seymour Agency and so fortunate to have Berkley as my publisher. Sarah Blumenstock, my talented and dedicated editor, respected my vision and helped me so much in shaping up the story. I am also so appreciative of my copy editor, Marianne Aguiar, for her meticulous work. It was truly a pleasure to work with them, Liz Sellers, and the whole Berkley team, who never cease to impress me.

I want to thank Bingley, our exceptionally loud beagle, for inspiring the character of Andy War-Howl in this book and *Her Knight at the Museum*. I also want to thank Pippin, our small senior mutt, who often sits on his cushion in my office while I write.

Thank you to my family, my friends, and my husband for helping me and believing in me. I love you so much!

Author photo copyright © Maia Rosenfeld Photography LLC

Bryn Donovan is the author of several romance novels. She's also written nonfiction books for writers and the story treatments for two Hallmark Channel movies. Her work has appeared in *McSweeney's*, *Writer's Digest*, and many literary journals. A former executive editor in publishing, she earned her MFA in creative writing from the University of Arizona. She's a voracious reader, a rescue dog lover, and a hopeless romantic who lives in the Chicago area and blogs about writing and positivity.

VISIT BRYN DONOVAN ONLINE

BrynDonovan.com

BrynDonovanAuthor

BrynDonovan

@bryndonovan.bsky.social

AuthorBrynDonovan

@BrynDonovanWriter

Ready to find
your next great read?

Let us help.

Visit prh.com/nextread

Penguin
Random
House